THE

Fey

QUARTET

EMILY
LARKIN

www.emilylarkin.com

The Fey Quartet / Emily Larkin. – 1st ed.

ISBN 978-0-9951358-5-7

Cover Design: The Killion Group, Inc

A Baleful Godmother

Collection

Contents

Maythorn's
WISH

A Baleful Godmother

Novella

ONCE UPON A TIME

In the northern reaches of England lay a long and gentle valley, with villages and meadows and wooded hills. Dapple Vale was the valley's name, and the woods were known as Glade Forest, for many sunlit glades lay within their cool, green reaches. Glade Forest was surrounded by royal forest on all sides, but neither it nor Dapple Vale were on any map, and the Norman king and his foresters and tax collectors and huntsmen knew nothing of their existence.

Within the green, leafy expanse of Glade Forest lay the border with the Faerie realm, where the Fey dwelled. The boundary was invisible to the human eye; nothing marked it but a tingle, a lifting of hair on the back of one's neck. Wise men turned back when they felt the tingle, and unwise men continued and were never seen again.

Despite its proximity to Faerie—or perhaps because of it—the sun shone more often in Dapple Vale than elsewhere in England and the winters were less harsh. The Great Plague bypassed Dapple Vale, and the Great Famine, too. Crops flourished, animals were fat and sleek, and the vale's folk were hale and long-lived.

One road led to the vale, but few travelers discovered it. No Romans found Dapple Vale, nor Vikings, and England's latest invaders, the Normans, hadn't found it either. Even folk born and bred in the vale had been known to leave and never find their way back, so well hidden was Glade Forest. Shrewd inhabitants took a pebble worn smooth by the clear, sweet waters of the River Dapple with them if they ventured from the vale, to be certain of returning.

Over the centuries, some Christian values crept into the vale, where they mingled with older beliefs, but no friars found their way in to build chapels, and the folk of Dapple Vale still held to most of the old customs. They prayed to many gods, and celebrated the solstices, summer and winter, and the equinoxes and cross-quarter days, and it wasn't a deity's wrath they feared most, but that of the Fey.

The folk of Dapple Vale didn't take their good fortune for granted. They had heard of plagues and famines, heard of marauding soldiers and starving serfs and murderous outlaws. Each was careful to respect the forest that sheltered them, and most careful of all was the Lord Warder of Dapple Vale, who went by the name Dappleward. Dappleward and his sons and his liegemen, the Ironfists, knew the location of rings of standing stones where the Fey had danced in olden times. They knew where to find the great stone barrow that held the grave of a banished Faerie prince, and they knew of the dark and narrow crevice wherein lay a hoard of abandoned Faerie gold. They knew these places, and guarded them carefully.

From time to time, trouble and sickness visited Dapple Vale, but it was never more than its folk could bear. While England suffered beneath the Norman yoke, Dapple Vale quietly prospered. The folk harvested their crops and tended to their animals. They hunted in the woods, and gathered berries and herbs and mushrooms. They wandered close to the border of Faerie—but took care never to cross it. For the Fey were dangerous—tricksy and fickle and cruel—and the folk of Dapple Vale knew better than to attract their attention.

4

All tales must have a beginning, and our tale begins in Dapple Bend, in the crook of Dapple Vale, where there lived a miller's son, a tall and handsome young man, with glossy black hair and a bold heart. The miller's son wanted to see something of the world before settling down to life as Dapple Bend's miller, so he ventured forth from the vale and in his travels he found himself a scholar's daughter who was as lovely as a maiden could possibly be. Her hair was the color of spun gold, her lips were as soft and pink as rose petals, and her eyes were the rich blue of cornflowers. The miller's son brought his young bride back to Dapple Bend, and then set himself to the work of grinding corn and barley.

It was commonly acknowledged that Mistress Miller was the most beautiful girl in Dapple Vale, but not for her golden hair or rosy lips or blue eyes; it was her smile that made her beautiful, for she had a smile that lit her face and gladdened the hearts of all who saw it. The miller's wife was barely fifteen, but she could read and write and sing as sweetly as a skylark, and for all her beauty and her accomplishments, she was a modest, kind-hearted girl and was loved by all who knew her.

After a year had gone full circle, the miller's young bride presented him with a daughter. The miller craved a son, but he swallowed his disappointment and told himself that his next child would be a boy. Although he was less cheerful than he'd been before and he drank more often at Dapple Bend's alehouse, few people noticed. As for Mistress Miller, motherhood suited her; there was joy in her eyes, joy in her step, and when she sang lullabies to her daughter, everyone in Dapple Bend stopped to listen.

Two years passed, and again Mistress Miller presented her husband with a daughter. This time, the miller dealt less well with his disappointment. He spent many evenings in the village alehouse, and when he came home he snarled at his beautiful young wife and took to hitting her. Mistress Miller's smile lost its joy. She tried not to cringe from her husband, and learned to hide her bruises from the villagers.

The miller's wife delighted in her second daughter, but she prayed for a son. Two years passed—and she gave birth to another daughter.

The miller took himself off to the deepest ale barrel he could find and when he returned to the millhouse that evening, to his wife and three young daughters, bitterness consumed him. He was bold and handsome—the boldest, handsomest man in Dapple Bend, perhaps all Dapple Vale—and yet his wife had given him only daughters. In a drunken rage he beat his wife with a stool, and when his eldest daughter, not yet four, tried to stop him, he beat her, too, and then he staggered outside and fell in the millpond and drowned.

Widow Miller healed, but she was no longer the most beautiful woman in Dapple Vale. Her nose sat crookedly on her face, and a blow from the stool had blinded one eye and staved in her cheekbone. A full dozen teeth had she lost. Her right hip was broken, leaving her with a shuffling limp. One wrist was crushed, and her hand withered, the fingers curling in on themselves.

The miller's eldest daughter healed, too, but her knee had been cruelly shattered. Even with the best bone-setting, her leg was weak. She would always need a crutch to walk. She would never run again, never dance.

The miller had made no provision for his young family, but Dapple Bend drew close around his widow. The empty cottage by Bluebell Brook was rethatched, and fresh rushes laid on the floor, and the widow and her daughters had a home. As for food, the cartwright offered Widow Miller a fine nanny goat in exchange for teaching his son to read and write, and the baker's daughters wished to learn the trick of writing, and the stonemason's twins, too; so in time Dapple Bend came to have the most literate population in the vale, in perhaps all of England, and two of the sheep that grazed on the village common and half a dozen goats and a noisy flock of hens and a beehive belonged to the widow.

The seasons passed, year followed year, and Widow Miller's

daughters grew to be the most beautiful young women in Dapple Vale.

Thus begins our story . . .

$\mathcal{C}$ HAPTER 1

$\mathcal{M}$ aythorn, the Widow Miller, shuffled through the forest. Her basket bumped against her hip with each limping step. A stream chuckled and burbled close by. *You will find fresh mint along my banks,* the water seemed to murmur. *And sweet thyme.*

The stream hadn't taken exactly this course the last time she'd been so deep in the woods, and it wouldn't the next time, but Widow Miller had roamed the forest for too many years to be disturbed by signs that the border with Faerie lay near. And she knew that the chuckling water spoke truly: she would find fresh herbs along its banks.

She turned her steps towards the stream, peering into the shadows with her one good eye, and on the grassy banks, she spied a patch of thyme.

The widow knelt painfully, awkwardly. "Thank you," she told the stream, and "Thank you," she told the thyme, and carefully she plucked a dozen stems and laid them in the basket and heaved herself to her feet.

A song thrush poured its heart out on a nearby branch. The widow listened for a moment. When she looked back at the stream, it had gathered itself into a pond.

The widow didn't draw her shawl around herself and

8

hobble home as fast as her crippled leg could carry her. She smiled a faint, ironic smile and set off around the pond. These woods were safer than any woods in England. Trees and mossy stones and sunlit glades might rearrange themselves between one blink of an eye and the next, but no outlaws roamed here, nor king's men, nor bloodthirsty beasts.

A patch of tender-leaved mint caught her eye, and alongside it, comfrey. By the time she'd worked her way around the pond, the widow's basket was full. "Thank you," she told the pond, and sunlight flickered across the water, as if the pond smiled at her.

The widow caught a glimpse of her reflection—the ruined face, the withered left hand hanging at her side—and turned away. Behind her there was a moment of silence and stillness, and then a low, musical burbling. She glanced back. The stream had returned, but now it flowed in the opposite direction.

Widow Miller turned her steps homeward. The stream lay along her path for the first half mile, chuckling and murmuring. "Thank you for your company," she told it when they parted ways, because it was always best to be polite, even to streams, when one was near the border with Faerie.

Without the stream alongside her, other noises filled her ears. She heard leaves rustling in the breeze, the twitter of birdsong, twigs snapping beneath her feet . . . and a sound like a lost kitten wailing, faint and high-pitched.

The widow cocked her head and listened.

The crying came again.

"I don't like that sound," the widow told the trees, and she clutched the basket more tightly with her good hand and shuffled in the direction of the noise.

Within a dozen steps, she came to another stream. This one was dark and swift and hissed as it flowed, as if whispering fierce secrets.

The crying sound came again, louder, closer, and it seemed as if both she and the stream were headed for it. Widow Miller eyed the dark water warily, and pushed through a

9

grove of prickly yews. The ground was rough and rocky, the trees gnarled, the forest dark with shadows. *I don't like this,* the widow thought, and she hesitated and considered turning back. Through the trees she glimpsed a deep, black pond, and bobbing on the deep, black pond was a basket like the one she carried, and in the basket was a baby.

The widow uttered a cry of horror, and she cast aside her herbs and hurried forward, lurching and hobbling. Boulders tripped her and branches clawed at her clothes, but the widow fought her way to the pond. She flung aside her shawl and plunged in. Two steps, and the bottom fell away beneath her feet. Dark, icy water engulfed her, filling eyes and nose and mouth.

As a bride, the widow had swum naked in moonlit river pools, but she no longer had two strong arms and two strong legs and a strong, young husband beside her. Panic spiked in her chest. She clawed frantically at the water. Her head burst free, and she gulped for air and turned desperately towards the safety of the bank.

The high, thin wail sounded again.

Widow Miller found the bottom of the pool with one foot, and wrestled with her panic. Her lungs heaved and her heart hammered and she felt the prickling of Faerie over her scalp. She was near the border of the forbidden realm. Dangerously near. Too near. Common sense urged her to turn back, but the widow had been a mother three times, and motherhood was in her blood. When the wailing came again, high and thin and desperate, she thrust away from the bank and swam towards the basket bobbing in the middle of the pool.

Widow Miller was crippled and lopsided, and the pool was wide—and growing wider with every heartbeat—but she kicked and swam with all her might, hauling herself through the water. The basket bobbed out of reach, and the kitten-like wail came again—and then the widow's groping hand found the woven rim and she gripped it tightly and pulled the basket towards her. "I have you," she choked out. "You're safe." But the pool grew choppy, as if a strong wind blew. Waves slapped the widow's face. Water filled her nose and mouth. She couldn't see the bank, could barely breathe. Her clothes dragged her down, her left hand was useless, her weak leg a dragging weight. She gripped the basket and thought, *We're both going to drown,* and then she thought of her daughters—solemn Ivy, bold Hazel, shy Larkspur—and she gritted her few teeth and kicked her good leg with all the strength she had.

Widow Miller fought her way back across the pond. The bank drew painfully nearer, and her feet eventually found purchase. She dragged herself clumsily ashore and knelt, gasping and shivering, clutching the basket. When she'd caught her breath, she lifted her head and gazed at the crying baby she'd rescued.

She saw a pale, heart-shaped face and a wailing pink mouth with tiny teeth as white and sharp as a fox cub's.

Fear prickled up the back of her neck. This was no human child.

Cautiously, Widow Miller stroked the baby's pale cheek. "You're safe," she whispered.

The wailing died to a whimper. The baby blinked and gazed up at her.

Every hair on Widow Miller's scalp stood on end. She had never seen such dark and terrible eyes. They were fully black, black to the outermost edges, as black as the deepest, darkest night, full of wisdom and cruelty.

Inhuman eyes. Faerie eyes.

Widow Miller suppressed a shiver. *A babe,* she told herself. *'Tis but a babe.*

She took up her shawl and gently tucked it around the infant in the basket, and then she stroked the pale, tender cheek again. "I shall take you home with me, and tomorrow we shall find your mother." And somehow, she found the strength to stand.

CHAPTER 2

Widow Miller's cottage lay a quarter of a mile beyond Dapple Bend village, on the far side of the village common, in a meadow where wildflowers bloomed and a little brook meandered.

The widow paused at the forest edge and gazed across the common. There was the meadow, and there her tiny cottage. She sighed with relief and weariness. "Home," she told the babe.

The Faerie baby uttered no sound. It was fast asleep, black lashes laid upon its milk-white cheeks.

Widow Miller tucked her shawl more warmly around the infant, and peered across the village common. She saw no people abroad. Cautiously, she hobbled out from between the trees. Dusk tinted the sky pink.

The widow was halfway across the common when a man stepped from the forest, leading a donkey laden with firewood. The man was giant-like in his proportions, as broad-shouldered as an ox. His flaxen hair glinted in the low sun. Renfred Blacksmith.

Widow Miller halted, and wished she could hurry back to the forest, but it was too late for that, for Ren was already lifting one hand in greeting and calling a cheerful "Good day."

The widow hastily covered the babe's face with her shawl. "Keep sleeping," she whispered, and she sent up a silent prayer: *Please, gods, let the babe not wake.*

Ren's smile of greeting faded. He released the donkey's rope. His stride lengthened until he was running. "By all the gods! What happened?"

One arm was about her, steadying her, and the widow was suddenly aware of just how much her legs were shaking. "What happened?" the blacksmith asked again.

Widow Miller leaned into him for a moment, taking comfort in his warmth and solidness. Ren Blacksmith, the kindest, brawniest man in all Dapple Vale. "I fell in a stream," she said, and blushed for her lie, and for her love of the blacksmith.

"I'll carry you home," Ren said.

"Oh, no!" the widow said, drawing away from him. She clutched the basket to her chest and made another silent prayer: *Keep sleeping, little one.* "It's only a few steps."

"It's halfway across the common, and you're done in. Come, let me carry you." Ren's donkey ambled up and gazed at Widow Miller with dark, patient eyes.

The widow shrank back and shook her head. "Oh, no," she said again.

"If you won't let me carry you, then Githa shall," Ren said, and he cast the bundled firewood from the donkey's back.

"Oh, but—"

Ren took the basket from her and placed it on the ground. He lifted Widow Miller as if she weighed no more than thistledown and settled her on Githa's back.

"My basket," the widow said, a note of alarm in her voice.

"I'll carry it."

And so, Widow Miller crossed the village common on the blacksmith's donkey, with the blacksmith striding alongside, carrying her basket. Her chest was tight with anxiety. If Ren knew what was in the basket he carried, he'd want to help, and she could *not* allow that. The Fey were dangerous, deathly dangerous, and Ren's wife was in her grave and he had a young son.

Don't wake, little one, she prayed silently. *Please don't wake.*

Widow Miller's cottage was small, but the thatching was plump on the roof and a cheerful plume of smoke rose from the little chimney. Two large red-brown hounds lay one on either side of the doorstep.

Both hounds lifted their heads. One sat up and gave a single loud bark; the other surged to his feet and bounded towards them, tail wagging.

The cottage door swung open. The widow's middle daughter burst from it and ran across the meadow to greet them. "Ren, what's happened?"

"Your mother's had a soaking." Ren handed her the basket. "Take this, Hazel. I'll carry her in."

"Oh, no," Widow Miller protested, but Ren gathered her in his arms and lifted her from the donkey.

"Mother!" the widow's youngest daughter cried, spilling from the cottage and hurrying towards them, her pale hair bright in the low sunlight. "Are you all right?"

"She's wet through," Ren told her. "And exhausted." He carried the widow as easily as if she were a child, and she felt ashamed of her feeble, crippled body and ashamed of her hopeless, hidden love for him.

They crossed the meadow, the blacksmith and the widow and her anxious daughters. One red-brown hound bounded around them like a puppy, rearing up on his hind legs to sniff the basket; the other stood at the doorstep, tail wagging, uttering yipping, anxious barks, not moving from her guard post.

"Keep that basket from Bartlemay!" the widow said.

A shadow filled the doorway and her eldest daughter stood there, leaning on her crutch. "Ren? What's wrong?"

"Your mother fell in the water."

14

The widow's eldest daughter stepped aside, and Ren Blacksmith ducked his head and entered the cottage and set Widow Miller carefully on her feet. Exhaustion almost made her legs crumple. He steadied her. "Larkspur, give her your arm."

The widow's youngest daughter hastened to do so, and the middle daughter placed the basket on the trestle table and drew up a stool for her mother.

Widow Miller gratefully sat.

"Thank you, Ren," the eldest daughter said. "You may be certain we'll look after her."

The blacksmith nodded, and gazed down at the widow. "Is there anything I can do for you? Anything you need?"

Widow Miller glanced fearfully at the basket on the table. "No, thank you, Ren."

"I'll stop by tomorrow to see how you do."

"There's no need—"

"I'll stop by tomorrow," Ren Blacksmith said. "You rest now." He dipped his head to the widow's three daughters. "Good day, Ivy. Hazel. Larkspur. Remember, if you need help, I'm only five minutes away." His great bulk blocked the doorway, and then he was gone.

Widow Miller sat shivering under the stares of her daughters.

"She needs to get dry!" The youngest daughter reached for the shawl covering the basket. "We can use this—"

"Careful!" the widow cried.

Her daughters all froze, startled.

"Careful," the widow said again, in a more moderate tone.

The youngest daughter cautiously drew the shawl aside. The sisters crowded close. They peered into the basket, and then their shocked gazes swung to their mother.

"What . . . ?" the middle daughter said, and "No questions now," the eldest daughter declared firmly.

CHAPTER 3

The widow's daughters fussed around her and soon she was dressed in warm, dry clothes and seated on a stool beside the fire, sipping meat broth, a blanket around her shoulders and the two large red-brown hounds at her feet. "Mother," Hazel said urgently. "What happened?" But Ivy shook her head and said, "Let her drink."

The widow drank her broth, and Hazel fidgeted and paced, and no one looked directly at the basket on the trestle table. Finally, the widow lowered her mug. Hazel stopped pacing. All three daughters looked at her.

"Mother," Ivy said quietly. "Mother . . . what happened in the forest today?"

Widow Miller sighed, and glanced at the basket on the table and the sleeping infant, and sighed again and told her tale. When she had finished, none of her daughters spoke.

"I'll take it back tomorrow and try to find its mother," the widow said.

"You won't cross the border!" Larkspur cried, at the same moment that Hazel said resolutely, "I shall go with you."

"I won't cross the border, my love—and you will not come with me, Hazel."

"But, Mother—"

16

"No, Hazel."

"Take Ren, then! He'd go with you—"

"No," Widow Miller said firmly. "Ren must not know about this. Would you have him risk his life? Think of his son!"

There was a moment of silence.

"No one goes but me," the widow said, and this time, Hazel raised no protest.

"According to the tales, Faerie women bear only one child," Ivy said quietly. "Its mother must be frantic."

They all looked at the babe.

"What if you can't find its mother?" Larkspur asked.

"Then I shall go to the Lord Warder."

As if their gazes had disturbed it, the sleeping infant woke. The widow recoiled slightly from the impact of those ink-black eyes, and the babe blinked once, twice, and opened its mouth and wailed.

Larkspur flinched, and Hazel clapped her hands over her ears, and the larger of the two red-brown hounds, Bartlemay, fled through the door, his tail between his legs.

"It needs dry clothes and food," Ivy said, reaching for her crutch and struggling to her feet. "Just as you did, Mother."

But changing the Faerie infant's clothing proved no easy task. It flailed its fists and kicked its feet and was as loud and fierce as a baby could possibly be. The second red-brown hound slunk from the cottage, her ears back.

Larkspur fetched a length of cloth. "We can wrap it in this." And then she peered down at the screaming child and said hesitantly, "Its teeth are very sharp."

"No sharper than Bartlemay's and Bess's were, when they were pups," Hazel said, and she set about the task of changing the baby's clothing.

The baby bit her three times, drawing blood, but Hazel didn't balk. She stripped off the tiny clothes—made of cloth as soft and fine as gossamer—and briskly dried each flailing limb. "It's a girl, Mother," she said, and "Stop that!" as the babe bit her for a fourth time.

Once the infant was warm and dry, its wailing didn't cease. "She's hungry," Ivy said. "Here. Goat's milk. I've warmed it." But the baby spat out the goat's milk, and screamed still more loudly.

"I'll sweeten it with honey," Larkspur said, but the baby spat that out, too.

The widow's daughters looked at each other helplessly. "Maybe meat broth?" Ivy said.

The Faerie infant drank the broth, but once fed, she screwed up her face and wailed again. "Larkspur, you hold her," Hazel said grimly. "Before I throw her out into the meadow."

Larkspur glanced at the baby's sharp teeth, and gulped a breath, and nervously took the child from her sister.

"Walk with her," Ivy said, leaning on her crutch. "Rock her."

Larkspur walked up and down the tiny room, gingerly rocking the Faerie child. After a few moments, she began to sing. Her voice was sweet and low and gentle. The wailing died to a whimper, and the whimper to a few hiccuping sobs, and then the baby fell quiet.

Larkspur stopped singing. "She's asleep," she whispered, but at that moment the baby's black eyes snapped open, and she drew a breath and opened her sharp-toothed mouth—

"Don't stop singing!" Hazel said, and then she said, equally firmly, "To bed with you, Mother," and she helped the widow into the next room, with its straw-filled pallets on the floor. "Sleep," she said. "We'll look after the babe."

The widow's three daughters cared for the Faerie baby all that long night. Twice, Widow Miller woke. Through the open doorway she saw flickering rushlight and the shadows of her daughters as they walked to and fro. She heard voices singing—once Larkspur, once Hazel—and the sound of someone putting more wood on the fire. The rich, meaty smell of broth mingled with the scent of woodsmoke. She huddled on her straw pallet, under coarse woolen blankets, and thought about the Faerie babe, and about her crippled body and Ivy's lame leg. Tales of the Fey drifted through her mind, tales of munificent gifts and cruel punishments.

The third time the widow woke, it was dawn. She struggled awkwardly from her bed—her hip was always stiffest in the morning—and hobbled to the doorway. Two of her daughters were in the next room, Larkspur stirring a pot on the fire, and Ivy at the trestle table, the babe in her arms, singing softly. The widow gazed at her eldest daughter, at her ruined leg stretched stiffly out and the crutch propped alongside her.

It was beyond human powers to mend Ivy's leg, but the Fey could heal it if they chose to. If someone dared to ask them.

Widow Miller kneaded her hip, trying to ease the ache. She imagined being able to walk freely again, to have the use of both hands, both eyes, imagined seeing Ivy run and dance again.

Dare she ask for those things?

Hazel came in through the door with an armful of firewood and both hounds at her heels, and said, "Mother, you're awake," and Bartlemay bounded forward and tried to lick the widow's face, and the Faerie babe woke and opened her mouth in a wail.

Widow Miller prepared carefully for her excursion into the woods. Her daughters helped her to dress in her best clothes, and to comb out her long, graying hair and plait it in a coronet around her head. The widow was outwardly calm, but her stomach churned with a mixture of terror and hope. Hazel fed the babe one last time, wrapped her warmly in a shawl, and tucked her back into her little basket. Then she said, firmly, "I'm coming with you, Mother."

The widow looked at her middle daughter, at the bright brown eyes and stubborn jaw. "No."

Hazel's jaw became even more stubborn. "If you think I'm going to let you go alone, then—"

"Hazel . . ." The widow touched her daughter's cheek lightly, silencing her. "If anything should happen to me in the woods today . . . you must look after your sisters."

Hazel opened her mouth to protest, and then closed it again. After a moment, she nodded.

Larkspur burst into the cottage, a pail of fresh water slopping in her hand. "Ren's coming," she said breathlessly. "With Gavain."

"Take the baby!" Hazel said, thrusting her towards the bedchamber, and Ivy said, "Sing to her."

Larkspur disappeared into the bedchamber with the Faerie babe.

Outside, Bess barked. Not a loud, warning bark, but a friendly, yipping one.

Widow Miller smoothed her kirtle nervously, and limped to the door.

Ren Blacksmith was coming across the meadow, his six-year-old son riding on his shoulders. Bartlemay pranced around them, wagging his tail joyfully, and at the doorstep, Bess waved her tail, too.

The widow stepped outside. "I give you good day, Ren Blacksmith. Good day, young Gavain."

"Good day." Ren swung his son down from his shoulders. "How are you?"

"As well as I ever was. Thank you for your kindness yesterday."

Widow Miller knew the sunshine was cruel to her ruined face, knew it showed her crooked nose and caved-in cheek, so she looked away from the blacksmith's clear gaze and smiled down at his son. "How are you, Gavain?"

Gavain grinned at her, his mouth as gap-toothed as her own, and held out a handful of wildflowers. "I picked these for you."

The widow exclaimed over the flowers and felt tears prick her eyes, for the motherless little boy was as dear to her as her own daughters. When she looked back at the blacksmith, he was patting Bess. "Thank you," she said again.

Ren Blacksmith nodded. He took his son's hand. "If you need anything, you know where to find us."

"Thank you," Widow Miller said a third time, and she stood on the doorstep clutching Gavain's flowers and watched father and son walk back across the meadow.

When they reached the village common, she inhaled a sharp breath and turned indoors.

Widow Miller wrapped a shawl around her shoulders and took leave of her three beloved daughters, wondering if she would ever see them again. She embraced them each, resolutely picked up the Faerie basket, and hobbled to the door.

"I'll carry it for you, Mother," Hazel said, taking the basket from her. "As far as the forest."

The widow looked at the determined set of her daughter's jaw, and decided not to argue.

Together, they crossed the meadow, Hazel shortening her stride to match her mother's. At the forest edge, they halted. "Mother . . . from what I've heard, the Fey dislike being indebted to humans. And this babe's mother will be very much in your debt. You have saved her child. Her only child—if the tales speak truly."

"I know," the widow said. "I intend to ask for a wish." She glanced back at the little cottage and the two figures standing in the doorway, one leaning on a crutch.

"Be careful, Mother. The Fey are said to despise meekness. If you behave too humbly . . ."

"I shall be as bold as you, boldest of my daughters." Widow Miller laid a kiss upon her middle daughter's smooth, young cheek. "Look after your sisters if I fail to return." And then she inhaled a deep breath, took the Faerie basket, and entered the cool green shadows of Glade Forest.

CHAPTER 4

$\mathcal{T}$he sun was high in the sky by the time Widow Miller reached the cheerful, chuckling stream where she'd gathered herbs yesterday. She searched for the second stream—dark and hissing—and the black pool where she'd rescued the babe, but found no sign of them. Finally, she spied her basket of herbs upturned alongside a mossy log.

"Hello?" She cautiously approached the basket. "Can anyone hear me?"

Leaves rustled in the breeze and a bird sang somewhere behind her, but other than those sounds, Glade Forest was silent.

I need to find the border, Widow Miller thought, but her feet stayed where they were, unwilling to move. Finding the border with Faerie seemed as sensible as standing underneath a wasps' nest and beating it with a stick. "But first I'll see to these herbs," she told the sleeping baby. "After all the effort of picking them, it's a terrible waste to just let them lie here and rot. See? They're only a little shriveled." She gathered the herbs as briskly as a one-handed woman could and set the basket beside the mossy log and clambered awkwardly to her feet. "Now, let's find your mother."

She picked up the baby's basket and took a deep breath—and for a moment her courage failed her. Her heart beat loudly in her ears and her feet were planted to the ground as firmly as tree roots. And then she thought of having two strong legs and two good hands and two clear-seeing eyes, and she thought of Ivy's crutch, and she took a second deep breath and hobbled between the tree trunks.

But the Faerie border was elusive. Widow Miller walked in great limping circles, ever wider, searching for the tingle on the back of her neck. "Hello?" she called. "Hello?" An hour passed, and then a second hour. The widow's legs ached, her arm trembled from the weight of the Faerie basket, and her voice grew raspy and weak. She began to despair of ever finding the border. *I could leave the basket here,* she thought. *Leave it and go home. Let the forest take care of the babe.* And then she imagined herself walking freely, imagined Ivy walking freely, and gathered her strength and hobbled further.

"Hello?" She entered a small glade with a patch of jaunty yellow primroses, a glade she was certain she had passed through three times already . . . and a tingling sensation crawled across the nape of her neck.

Widow Miller halted. She'd found the border. And then she thought, *No, it found me.* She stood, swaying in her tiredness, feeling the prickling tingle climb up her neck and crawl across her scalp, listening to the fearful thump of her heart. "Courage," she whispered to herself, and she tightened her grip on the basket, and called as loudly as she could: "Hello! Is anyone here? I seek this child's mother."

The Faerie babe woke suddenly and blinked her black eyes and opened her sharp-toothed mouth and added her thin, piercing cry to the widow's call.

"Hello!" Widow Miller called again. "I seek this child's—"

A gust of wind bellowed through the forest, so strong it snatched the widow's words from her mouth and knocked her backwards a lurching step. Trees groaned and swayed, branches whipped, and the air was thick with whirling leaves—and then the wind was gone as abruptly as it had come. The widow's ears rang as if there had been a clap of thunder.

Airborne leaves drifted to the ground. The Faerie babe fell silent. No birds sang, no insects hummed, no branches rustled. Widow Miller had the fancy that the whole forest held its breath. Her skin prickled with an awareness that someone—some*thing*—was watching her.

Widow Miller swallowed nervously. "I seek this babe's mother." She tried to speak loudly, but her voice was thin and fearful.

Another gust of wind lifted the leaves from the ground, making them swirl wildly—and when they settled, a woman stood beside the jaunty primroses.

The widow's heart stopped beating in an instant of sheer terror.

The Faerie woman had a cold, cruel, inhuman beauty. Her skin was paler than moonlight, her eyes deeply black. She wore a gown of blood-red velvet. Pearls glowed in her ebony hair. Her beauty was so terrible, so perfect, that the widow's eyes hurt to look at her.

"Give me my child," the Faerie said, in a voice as sharp and dangerous as a knife blade.

Widow Miller swallowed, and clutched the basket more tightly. "How do I know you're her mother?"

Scorn flickered across the Faerie's face. "Humans. Such blunt senses."

"How do I know you're her mother?" the widow repeated, her heart thumping loudly in her chest. "Someone tried to drown her. I won't give her to anyone but her mother."

"Her blood is my blood. If you had keener eyes, you would see it." The Faerie lifted one hand, and for an instant the widow saw the sap running in the trees, saw each unfurled leaf inside each burgeoning bud on each strong, outreaching branch, saw the kinship between woman and babe—and then her vision dulled once more.

Widow Miller blinked, and clutched the basket even more tightly. *Courage,* she told herself. "I saved your child's life at risk of my own. For that, you owe me."

The Faerie stiffened. Her cheekbones became sharper, crueler.

"My daughters cared for your child all night. For that, you owe them."

The Faerie's black eyes narrowed. The silence surrounding them took on a brittle edge.

Inwardly, Widow Miller cringed. Outwardly, she stood calm and proud. "If you bestow wishes on me and my daughters, it will wipe the debt between us."

"Wishes?" The Faerie's voice was soft and dangerous.

Stand your ground, Widow Miller told herself. *The Fey respect courage.* "Yes," she said firmly.

The Faerie released a hissing, snake-like breath. "Very well. Name your wishes and I shall bestow them."

"For myself . . ." Now that the moment had come, Widow Miller was trembling. "For myself . . . I wish to be fifteen years younger than I am now, and I wish to be healed of my injuries."

"Done," the Faerie said, waving a negligent hand.

Hope clenched painfully in the widow's chest. She was unable to inhale, unable to exhale. *Am I healed?* But even as she formed the thought, her field of vision widened and for the first time in twenty years she saw with both eyes.

The widow looked down and watched her left hand uncurl itself, watched the withered claws become strong, healthy fingers. Wonderingly, she touched her nose; it was straight and unbroken. She ran her tongue along her teeth and found them there. *All* of them. The constant, nagging ache from her right hip was gone.

She was Maythorn again.

Joy brought tears to her eyes. *Don't cry,* she told herself desperately. *Don't cry. The Fey despise weakness.* She gulped back the tears and cleared her throat. "Thank you."

The Faerie ignored the words. "Your daughters' wishes. What do you choose for them?"

"Ah . . ." Widow Miller tried to collect her scattered

thoughts. She knew what Ivy would choose, but not Hazel and Larkspur. "May they choose for themselves?"

The Faerie's pale lips pursed in displeasure, then she gave a haughty shrug and tossed her pearled head, as if she didn't care who made the choices. "They may. Upon their next birthdays. Now give me back my child."

Widow Miller hugged the basket to her chest. "Their next birthdays? Can't it be now?"

"No."

"But Ivy needs her wish today!"

"I have demands on my time you couldn't begin to understand, human."

"Just Ivy's wish, then," Widow Miller said desperately.

The Faerie grew still. A dangerous glitter entered her black eyes. "No."

Fear lifted the hair on Widow Miller's scalp. Her lungs contracted. She was terrified that the Faerie was going to strike her dead.

The forest seemed to hold its breath again—a moment of utter silence, utter stillness—and then a breeze fingered its way between the trees, stirring leaves and making the primroses nod on their stalks. The Faerie's eyes lost their glitter, and Widow Miller found she could breathe again. "Very well," she said evenly, as if she weren't in fear of her life. "My daughters shall choose their wishes on their next birthdays."

The Faerie inclined her head.

"How will they find you?"

"I shall find them." The Faerie held out her hands imperiously. "Give me my child."

Widow Miller handed over the basket. Emotions flickered across the Faerie's face, tenderness, relief—and a dark flash of scorn.

Is the scorn for me? But even as Widow Miller asked herself that question, she knew it was. And she knew why: she hadn't bargained hard enough.

"You still owe me," she said.

The Faerie glanced at her. Her face was cruel, beautiful, and utterly expressionless—but beneath the impassive stare was an odd sense of expectancy.

Yes, Widow Miller thought. *She knows she owes me. But why?*

In a flash, she understood. "I have returned your daughter to you. Your only child. Your bloodline will continue. For that, you owe me."

The Faerie tilted her head in a regal nod. "Choose your wish."

Widow Miller's mind went blank. *Think!* she told herself. *Quickly!* But she had what she wanted, for herself and her daughters.

"There's a man you love." For the first time, the Faerie smiled, a thin, disdainful, mocking smile. Her teeth were as sharp and white as a cat's. "I can make him love you."

For an instant Widow Miller saw Ren Blacksmith in her mind's eye—the flaxen hair, the strong, gentle hands, the smiling gray-green eyes—and her heart clenched painfully. To have Ren love her . . .

"He will worship you until he dies."

Worship? The widow took a step backwards, shaking her head. "No."

"No? Are you certain?" The Faerie's voice was sibilant and seductive. "It is easily done."

"I'm certain," Widow Miller said firmly. "Love should be given freely, or not at all."

The Faerie shrugged. There was scorn in her black eyes and amusement on her face.

Widow Miller looked away from that cold, cruel, inhuman face, and gazed at the baby.

"Through your daughter, your bloodline lives," she said slowly. "I gave you that." She glanced up, suddenly knowing what to ask for. "*I* gave you that. So what I ask for in return is this: as long as your daughter's line survives, my daughters' lines shall receive Faerie wishes."

The amusement vanished from the Faerie's face. "You ask too much, human."

"No," Widow Miller said. "I ask just enough. Fey have but one child. Your bloodline continues because of me."

The Faerie gazed at her for a long moment, her eyes dark and narrow, sucking up the light, reflecting nothing.

Widow Miller met those black eyes and listened to the *thump* of her heart and the sigh of the breeze in the trees and the chirrup of birdsong.

"Females only," the Faerie said abruptly. "As long as my daughter's female line survives, the females in your daughters' lines shall each receive a wish. On their birthdays. At the same ages their mothers were when they received their wishes."

The widow considered this carefully. Larkspur's offspring would be twenty-one when granted wishes, Hazel's twenty-three, Ivy's twenty-five. Women, not flighty young girls. Old enough to make sensible choices.

"Agreed," she said.

The Faerie gave a dismissive nod and turned away.

"Be careful."

The Faerie glanced over her shoulder, aloof and startled.

"Someone tried to drown your daughter. Guard her carefully, lest they try to harm her again."

The Faerie turned to face her fully. Beneath the coldness, Widow Miller saw surprise. "You care about my daughter? You feel affection for her?"

"Of course I do. She's but a babe."

A contemptuous smile curled the Faerie's lips. "Humans. So soft-hearted." Her laugh rang beneath the trees, bell-like and mocking, and then, in a brief gust of wind, she was gone. The echo of Faerie laughter hung in the air, but other than that, the little glade was empty.

Widow Miller touched her nose, her cheekbones, her jaw. "I'm whole again," she whispered, and then, more loudly: "I'm whole again!" She spun around and started back the way she'd come, her steps coming faster and faster until she was running, as lightly and fleetly and joyfully as a young deer.

The basket of wilting herbs was where she'd left it, beside the mossy log. The widow picked it up, breathless and laughing. "I'm no longer Widow Miller," she told the basket. "Look at me! I'm Maythorn again!"

*C*HAPTER 5

*B*ess and Bartlemay set up a great barking when she reached the cottage. "It's me, sillies," Maythorn said, and to her daughters, wide-eyed and anxious, clustered in the doorway: "It's me!"

Dogs and daughters were equally confused. They all crowded into the little cottage, and Maythorn told her tale. "And each of you shall choose a wish, too. On your birthdays." She hugged Ivy to her, laughing and crying at the same time. "Ivy, my precious Ivy. I wanted you to have your wish today, I wanted you to walk again."

"It's all right, Mother," Ivy said, and her grave green eyes looked merry. "I haven't long to wait. It's only six weeks."

"You look so different," Larkspur said wonderingly. "Your face! And your hair is the color of sunshine."

"How old are you?" Hazel wanted to know.

"Twenty-six."

"Well, I can't call you Mother," Hazel said forthrightly. "You're only a few years older than me!" And then: "What are we going to tell everyone?"

The four women looked at each other. "I'm your cousin," Maythorn said. "Come unexpectedly from York."

"What do we call you?" Ivy asked.

"Maythorn."

Hazel frowned. "But—"

"We shall say I was named for my aunt, whom I greatly resemble."

Hazel's frown didn't ease. "Whom you *exactly* resemble! Won't people remember?"

"It's been a long time." Maythorn touched her nose, her cheekbone. Twenty-one years broken, and now they were whole again. "I don't look much like the crippled Widow Miller, do I?"

Ivy shook her head. "You look nothing like her. It's . . . I'd swear the shape of your face has changed."

"But where shall *you* be, Mother?" Larkspur asked. "How do we explain your absence?"

"I am gone to visit my brother in York. A sudden journey."

"From which you will never return." The merriness was gone from Ivy's eyes; they were grave again.

"Can we not tell the truth?" Larkspur asked, hesitantly. "I don't like to lie."

"None of us do," Hazel said, her voice blunt and matter-of-fact. "But I think Maythorn's right. The truth is best avoided. Who knows what the consequences would be? Folk may turn from her or wish her ill."

"Wish her ill?" Larkspur cried, wide-eyed. "Why?"

"Because they're jealous of her good fortune."

"Mother's been crippled half a lifetime! How is that good fortune?"

"It's not," Ivy said. "But jealousy isn't a rational emotion."

"Or the Lord Warder may be angry at her and cast her from the vale," Hazel continued inexorably.

"Dappleward wouldn't do that, would he?" Larkspur said, her eyes growing even wider with alarm. "Mother *had* to find the border. How else was she to give the babe back?"

Ivy looked thoughtful. "It's true he may be angry. Not about the baby, but about the Faerie wishes."

"Or people may try to do what Mother has done, hunt out the Fey and strike a bargain for their heart's desire."

"Only a fool would try that!" Larkspur protested. "It's too dangerous!"

"The vale has its fools," Ivy said.

"Fools aplenty!" Hazel said. "And they will look at Widow Miller and want what she has—"

"Girls," Maythorn said firmly. "Enough."

Her daughters fell silent.

"You have made your point, Hazel." Maythorn sighed, her joy dwindling. "I'm sorry, my loves, but I must ask you to lie for me."

Ivy took her hand. "The lie will harm no one, Mother . . . Maythorn. I shall be glad to call you cousin."

"And I," Larkspur said sturdily.

"When shall you show yourself?" Hazel asked. "Not today! Ren saw you this morning."

"Tomorrow. Late tomorrow," Maythorn said. "That gives Widow Miller time to be gone from the vale."

"Gavain's coming for his lesson tomorrow afternoon," Ivy said. "Should we beg off?"

They all looked at each other.

"*We* could teach Gavain his letters," Larkspur said tentatively.

"Of course we could!" Hazel said.

"What think you, Mother?" Ivy asked. "'Tis your decision."

Maythorn thought of young Gavain, with his gap-toothed smile and his bright eyes and his eagerness to learn. "I should like to continue his lessons."

"Then Gavain shall be the first to meet you. Perfect!" Hazel laughed and clapped her hands. "Don't look so solemn, everyone. Today is a day for rejoicing!"

Maythorn stayed at home the rest of that day, and there was pleasure in everything she did, for she had two nimble-fingered hands to prepare the evening meal with, and two clear-seeing eyes to gaze at her beloved daughters with, and when she rose from her bed the next morning, her hip didn't ache and her strides were brisk and merry. But as the sun climbed in the sky, so too did Maythorn's nervousness, and by the time the sun was directly overhead, she was fidgeting. She set herself to altering her best kirtle, taking in the seams, adjusting the neckline, changing it from widow's garb to young woman's. Once that was done, she fell to turning her thimble over and over between her fingers.

Ivy eyed her thoughtfully, and said, "Are you all right?"

Maythorn laid down the thimble and gave a rueful smile. "I confess, I'm a little nervous. I don't know where my courage has gone! I must have used it all up yesterday."

She went to the door and looked out, walked the width of the little room and back, and peeped out the door again. Would Ren accompany his son today?

Part of her hoped that he would; part of her hoped that he wouldn't.

The afternoon ripened. Maythorn made a start at altering her second-best kirtle. The hum of bees in the wildflowers drifted in through the open door. The next time she peeped out, she saw Gavain coming across the meadow, riding on his father's shoulders. Her nervousness trebled. It was suddenly difficult to breathe.

Hazel entered the cottage with a skip in her step and closed the door. "Ren's here with Gavain," she announced.

"I know." Maythorn bundled her sewing away. Her heartbeat was fast and fluttery, her throat dry, her palms damp. She went to the tiny, unglazed window under the eaves and stood on tiptoe and peered out. Ren Blacksmith. The kindest man in the vale.

Outside, Bess barked a friendly welcome. Bartlemay bounded towards man and child, his tail wagging furiously.

Maythorn watched Ren pat the great, red-brown hound, watched them walk together along the path, Bartlemay frisking like a puppy. Ren swung his son down from his shoulders. A knock sounded on the door. "Widow Miller?"

Maythorn glanced at her daughters, ranged about the wooden table. Hazel's face was alight with glee—she was enjoying this—but Larkspur looked anxious.

"Hazel, get the door, please," Ivy said calmly.

Hazel trod across the rush-strewn floor, her steps almost dancing, and flung the door open. "Ren Blacksmith," she cried gaily. "And young Gavain. Come in, both of you. Mother's gone to York to visit her brother, but my sisters and I shall teach Gavain his letters."

Maythorn pressed herself back into the shadowy corner of the small room, feeling as flustered and shy as a young girl.

"York?" Ren ducked through the door and entered the cottage. When he straightened, the top of his head came to within an inch of the ceiling. "Is she up to such a journey?"

"Oh, yes!"

Ren frowned. "I hope there's no trouble in the family?"

"None at all," Hazel said. "The fact is, our cousin has come to visit, and Mother got the urge to visit back." She hauled Maythorn forward from the corner. "Meet my cousin, Maythorn."

"Pleasure to meet you," Ren said politely, and then he blinked and became very still.

"She was named after Mother," Hazel said cheerfully. "And it's said she looks just like Mother used to. But you wouldn't know how Mother used to look! You grew up in Dapple Weir—"

"I met her once."

"Did you? Well, then maybe you can remember."

Ren made no reply. He stared at Maythorn as if she were an apparition that had taken shape from the shadows. Maythorn found she couldn't look away, couldn't move. A buzzing sound grew in her ears. *Breathe,* she told herself. But how could she breathe when Ren was looking at her so intently?

"Sit here, beside me, young Gavain," Larkspur said, patting a stool.

The little boy scrambled up on the stool. "There's going to be a bonfire tomorrow night!"

"So there is," Larkspur said. "And we shall all dance around it."

"Father says I can stay up as late as I like!" Gavain's face shone with excitement.

Ren still hadn't moved. He seemed to have taken root to the floor.

"Ren?" Hazel said, a note of laughter in her voice. "Are you feeling quite well?"

Ren shook his head, shook himself. "Forgive me. I . . . uh . . . the resemblance is remarkable."

Maythorn swallowed and found her voice. "So I've been told." She felt heat rise in her cheeks, and knew she was blushing. She bobbed a quick curtsy. "It's a pleasure to meet you, Ren Blacksmith."

"Away with you," Hazel said, shooing Ren out the door. "We'll bring Gavain home before dark."

Maythorn inhaled an unsteady breath. The intensity of Ren's gaze had left her feeling light-headed.

Hazel closed the door and came to stand alongside her. She was grinning. She murmured in Maythorn's ear, "So . . . Ren Blacksmith, hmm?"

Maythorn's cheeks grew even hotter.

"A fine-looking man," Hazel said, her voice teasing. "And in need of a wife . . ."

"Hush," Maythorn whispered. The lightheadedness was fading. She took a deep, steadying breath, composed her face, and went to sit at the trestle table. "Hello, Gavain. May I help with your lesson?"

Gavain gave her a sunny smile. "Of course."

Maythorn had to stop herself reaching out to stroke his soft, dark hair. To him, she was a stranger.

Six-year-old Gavain was a quick learner. By the end of the lesson, he knew how to spell *bonfire* and *dance* and *spring* and had inscribed a full sentence on the wax tablet: *On the last day of spring we dance round the bonfire.* Maythorn stood on the doorstep and watched him walk home, hand in hand with Larkspur. She loved all the children in the village, but Gavain was her favorite. He had his mother's dark coloring and slender build, and his father's kind heart. "I wish . . ." she whispered.

She wished Ren would love her. She wished she could be his wife. Wished she could be Gavain's mother.

Hazel came to stand alongside her. "I never knew you felt that way about Ren."

Maythorn debated her answers. Evasion? A tart response? An outright lie? In the end she settled on the truth. "I was a lot older than him. And crippled."

"Not that much older," Hazel said. "He's what? Thirty-six?"

"Thirty-five." Six years younger than her yesterday—and nine years older today. She watched Gavain and Larkspur vanish from sight around the bend of Bluebell Brook.

"For what it's worth, you have my blessing," Hazel said. "There's no better man in the village."

There's no better man in the whole vale, Maythorn thought. She looked down at her hands and rubbed her thumbnail. "He may not be interested in me."

Hazel snorted. "You saw his face. He's interested."

A shuffling, thumping sound came behind them. Ivy, with her crutch. "The way he looked at you, Mother . . . Maythorn. It took my breath away."

It had taken Maythorn's breath away, too. Her chest constricted in memory.

"I've never seen two people look so poleaxed before," Hazel said. She turned back into the cottage. "You'll be married by midsummer. Mark my words!"

I hope so, Maythorn thought. But she didn't want to lie to Ren. And lie she must, if she was to win him. In fact, the first lies had already been uttered.

"You have my blessing, too," Ivy said quietly.

Maythorn turned to her. "Ivy . . ." She bit the tip of her tongue, uncertain how to say what she wanted to say.

Ivy gave a soft laugh. "Don't look so worried! I've never wanted to marry Ren."

Maythorn looked searchingly at her eldest daughter's face.

"I know you thought he might offer for me after Maud died—and of all the men in the village, Ren would make the best husband for a cripple like me; he is so *very* kind!—but the man I'll marry—if there *is* such a man—is no one I've yet met."

Ivy appeared to be telling the truth. Her gaze was level and serious and utterly candid.

A worry that had been lurking at the back of Maythorn's mind dissolved like a wisp of smoke blown in the wind. She reached out and took her daughter's hand. "I hope with all my heart that you find this man."

A smile lit Ivy's face. "So do I!"

CHAPTER 6

*I*t was tradition in Dapple Vale to usher in each summer with bonfires and dancing. Gone were the cold, dark days of winter, gone were the spring frosts and mud. The days were growing longer, the wildflowers blossomed, and the great trees in the forest were clothed in fresh green leaves. Summer beckoned, full of warmth and sunlight, ripening crops, and fat livestock. And to mark this—to *welcome* it—bonfires blazed high, animals were roasted on the spit, ale poured, voices raised in song—and not a few children were conceived.

On the afternoon of the last day of spring, Maythorn and her daughters put out their hearth fire, swept up the embers and ashes, and laid fresh kindling; they'd bring home a brand from the bonfire and light their fire for the year ahead. They bathed in the cool, clear brook, dressed in their most festive clothes, threaded flowers through their hair, and set out for the village. Bess stayed protectively close, but Bartlemay ranged joyfully ahead, his tail windmilling.

Their pace was slow—it always had been—but now it was only Ivy who struggled. *Six more weeks,* Maythorn told herself. *She will run again before midsummer.* But even so, she felt guilt. Guilt that she walked freely, and Ivy hobbled.

They walked alongside Bluebell Brook and across the

village common. The smell of roasting meat reached Maythorn's nose. Her guilt twisted into nervousness. Suddenly Ivy's pace seemed much too fast. This was it: the moment when she had to deceive her friends and neighbors.

They passed the millhouse, where Ivy and Hazel and Larkspur had been born, and the millpond where her husband had drowned. They passed the cottages of Humfrey Walleye and Alard Mason. Maythorn's stomach tied itself into a tight knot. *It's not too great a lie,* she told herself. *I truly am Maythorn of York.* They passed Dapple Bend's smithy. The great forge was quiet; Ren Blacksmith had put out his fire.

The smithy hound, a stiff-limbed brindled mastiff, uttered a gravelly bark and levered himself to his feet.

Bess and Bartlemay stayed at a prudent distance—ancient though he was, Tibald was still the largest dog in the village—but Maythorn crossed to the great hound and held out her hand. "I know I look different," she whispered, as Tibald sniffed her hand. "But I smell the same. See? It's me."

Tibald seemed to recognize her. His tail wagged.

Maythorn stroked his large head, and scratched behind his left ear, just how he liked it. Tibald groaned with pleasure and nudged her hand, a silent *Do that again.* "You're a great silly," Maythorn bent and whispered in his ear. "As big as your owner, and as soft-hearted."

Tibald wagged his tail in agreement and leaned heavily against her hip. Maythorn laughed softly, glanced up, and froze. Ren stood in the darkness of the smithy, watching her.

She stopped scratching Tibald's ear and straightened. Her chest was suddenly tight.

Ren crossed the smithy yard. He didn't wear his blacksmith's scarred leather apron, but instead his best tunic and hose. His jaw was newly shaved, his flaxen hair neatly combed. "I give you good day, Ivy," he said, with a dip of his head. "And you, Hazel, Larkspur." He turned to Maythorn last. "Maythorn."

Maythorn bobbed her head in return. Her throat was too

dry to utter any greeting other than a squeak, so she kept her mouth shut.

"Afternoon, Ren," Hazel said cheerfully. "Where's young Gavain?"

"Helping build the bonfire."

"Are you finished here? Come with us!"

"I'll be along shortly." Ren dipped his head again and turned back towards the smithy.

"You'll dance with us each?" Hazel called out.

Ren raised his hand in a silent *yes*, before disappearing in the shadowy gloom of the smithy.

"Good," Hazel said, and winked at Maythorn.

Maythorn didn't wink back. She felt queasy with nervousness. How could Hazel be so blithe, so unafraid?

They made their slow way past the smithy, past Robin Thatcher's cottage, past the home of the village alderman, old Phillip Whitelock, and turned the corner. Hazel was singing lightly, merrily, under her breath. In the market square, Maythorn saw a towering heap of firewood, saw people gathered round. Hazel's singing faded from her hearing. Her nervousness grew until she felt that she might vomit from it.

The bonfire drew close. Closer. Heads turned. She saw surprise on some faces, curiosity on others.

Maythorn's step faltered. She came to a halt. For a cowardly moment, she wanted to scurry back to the safety of her cottage. Larkspur halted, too, and Ivy. Hazel continued on two steps, and then swung back to look at them, her dark brows raised in query.

"They're our friends," Ivy said. "We have nothing to fear."

"*I'm* not afraid!" Hazel said.

Maythorn glanced at Larkspur. Larkspur's face was milk-pale. *She's as nervous as I am,* she realized.

Maternal instinct kicked in. Maythorn squeezed Larkspur's fingers and gave her a reassuring smile. "All will be well." And then she lifted her chin and stepped forward resolutely. Tonight she would be as calm as Ivy and as bold as Hazel.

41

It wasn't as terrible as Maythorn had feared. The lie came more easily the more often she told it, and it wasn't *really* a lie—she truly *was* Maythorn of York—and if a few of the older villagers exclaimed at the resemblance between her and the young Mistress Miller, most people seemed oblivious to it.

Maythorn slowly relaxed. A mug of ale helped. Stout, good-natured Mistress Thatcher waylaid them, full of cheerful conversation, and she relaxed still further. Ivy was right: these people were her friends. She tensed again when Ren Blacksmith arrived, but he made no effort to approach her. Maythorn watched him obliquely. Ren stood a good head taller than the other men. With his physique—the breadth of chest, the great slabs of muscle—he should have been intimidating, except that nothing about Ren was intimidating. He was simply too *Ren*.

When he'd been a young man, shortly after taking over Dapple Bend's smithy, word of his strength had spread through the vale. Men had come to Dapple Bend in ones and twos to test themselves against him. They'd tried to goad him into fighting, taunted him, even struck him—but Ren had simply turned his back on them all and walked away.

"You're staring," Hazel whispered in Maythorn's ear.

Maythorn jerked her gaze away, turned back to the conversation with Mistress Thatcher, and took a hasty gulp of ale.

"You never traveled all that way *alone*?" said Mistress Thatcher, her eyes round with alarm.

"Father came with me. My Aunt Miller went back with him."

"And you had no trouble?" Mistress Thatcher persisted. "The roads outside the vale are terrible dangerous, so I've heard!"

"No trouble at all," Maythorn said. And that wasn't a lie. Her journey all those years ago had been utterly without incident.

"But how did you find your way?" young Annis Thatcher asked, wide-eyed.

"My Aunt Miller sent a map and a pebble from the Dapple," Maythorn said, and that was the truth, too; she *had* sent a map and a pebble home to York, when she'd come to Dapple Bend as a bride. She didn't know whether her family had kept them or not. Certainly, no one had come to visit her. Or perhaps they'd tried, and failed to find the path?

"Ah." Mistress Thatcher nodded wisely. "The pebble, that's the trick."

Maythorn nodded, too, and sipped her ale. Her gaze slid back to Ren. He was built on a different scale than the men he was talking to, as if he had a drop of giant's blood in him. The only two men in the whole vale who matched him in size were the Ironfists of Dapple Meadow, father and son. They'd never tried to brawl with Ren; they were the Lord Warder's liegemen, sworn to stop fights, not start them.

She took another sip, not tasting the ale. Hazel was right; Ren was a fine-looking man. It wasn't just his height and build, it was the way he moved, the way he held his head, the directness of his gaze, the laughter lines at his eyes and mouth. Ren's face was good-humored and honest and kind. He wasn't handsome, the way her husband had been, but she wasn't a foolish girl to fall for good looks any more. She hadn't been that girl for a very long time.

"Staring . . ." Hazel muttered in her ear.

Maythorn flushed and brought her attention firmly back to Mistress Thatcher and her young daughter.

At dusk, the bonfire was lit. The flames roared up and the dancing began. They danced as a village—men, women, and children. Even the dogs joined in, bounding and barking, and young Annis's pet sheep.

It was a joy to dance again after so many years. Maythorn laughed out loud with the sheer pleasure of it. And then she glimpsed Ivy, sitting with old Dowse, and the laughter died in her throat. How many years had she sat to one side with Dowse and Ivy, clapping and smiling and wishing she could join in? Too many. And now she was dancing again—and Ivy was still sitting there, lame.

Ivy caught her gaze and grinned. It wasn't something Ivy did often, grin. There was no bitterness on her face that Maythorn could see, no sadness.

She's happy for me.

Maythorn smiled back, but her guilt didn't entirely vanish; a tiny nugget of it sat beneath her breastbone, as if she'd swallowed a plum stone—and then the dance swung her sideways and she found herself opposite Ren.

She stopped thinking about anything at all except remembering to breathe.

Ren held out his hands. His expression was serious, his gaze intent on her face.

Maythorn placed her hands in his. Her throat was dry, her heart thudded in her ears, and she felt as shy and awkward and tongue-tied as a young girl. She desperately wanted to say something to Ren, to make him smile, to make him laugh, to make him *like* her, but her mind was utterly blank. All she could think about was how large his hands were, and how his fingers seemed to burn her skin, and how she mustn't fall over her own feet.

The dance moved them on again. Ren went left and she went right, and the man facing her was beaming, grizzled Alard Mason. Him, she had no difficulty exchanging laughing comments with. Why couldn't she talk to Ren like that? Laugh with him like that? She'd been able to when she was Widow Miller; she should be able to now. She was the same person inside that she'd always been. And so was Ren.

Her question answered itself: because there were possibilities between her and Ren now that had never existed before.

Wondrous, terrifying, life-changing possibilities. The sort of possibilities that choked one's breath and paralyzed one's tongue and rendered one mute.

The sort of possibilities that one had to seize with both hands and hold on to with all one's might.

Next time the dance partners me with Ren, I'll say something, Maythorn vowed. Something about the bonfire. Something about the dance. About the village. About Gavain. About the coming summer and the spring that had passed. Something. Anything.

All too soon she found herself opposite Ren again. At the touch of his hands, the words she'd chosen dried on her tongue. Such large, competent hands. The hands of a blacksmith, strong and callused, marked with tiny burn scars. Hands that could gentle horses, and beat iron into ploughshares, and craft delicate cloak pins. Hands that could break jaws, if Ren chose to, or knock people senseless. But Ren never chose that.

No. That was wrong.

Ren *had* struck another person once. All Dapple Bend could remember that day: the day Swithin Broadback's horse had gone lame. Swithin had whipped the poor beast, trying to get it to move, and Ren had emerged from his smithy and torn the whip from Swithin's grip and given him such a hiding that he'd stayed abed for a week. Not long after that, Swithin Broadback had slunk away from Dapple Bend. Word was, he'd left the vale. Certainly, no one had seen him again. And, equally certain, no one missed him; Swithin's temper had been as foul as his back had been broad.

The dance moved her on again. Maythorn found herself opposite Alard Mason once more. Her tongue unfroze. She was able to speak again. *Fool!* she told herself. *Lackwit!*

But Ren hadn't spoken either. There'd been a frown of concentration on his brow, as if he'd been trying to remember the steps.

It's not only me who's struck dumb by this.

This realization gave Maythorn more confidence. When

the dance brought them together again, she smiled and said, "Such a fearsome bonfire! It roars like a lion."

Ren's lips twitched upwards. "Have you heard a lion roar?"

"No," Maythorn admitted. "But I'm sure it must sound like this. Loud and fierce and bellowing."

"Mayhap you're right." Ren's eyes crinkled at the corners in a smile.

Maythorn's breath caught in her throat. That smile. Those eyes.

She swallowed, and foundered for another comment: "I look forward to summer," and then mentally castigated herself. *What a stupid thing to say!*

But Ren didn't seem to think it stupid. "So do I," he said, and the smile faded from his face, leaving it utterly serious. "I think this summer will surpass all that have come before it."

Something in his tone, something in his gaze, caught her like a fish on a hook. Her awareness of the bonfire and the other dancers faded. The crackle of flames, the boisterous music, the laughter and voices, dwindled and vanished. The world narrowed to Ren. Ren and his serious, intent, gray-green eyes. Maythorn almost stumbled as her feet lost their place in the dance—and then Ren passed her to Alard Mason again, and the moment was gone.

They danced and feasted, danced and feasted. Most of the flowers she'd threaded into her hair were gone, though some still clung on precariously. Towards midnight, Maythorn requested the hand of six-year-old Gavain: "May I have this dance, kind sir?"

It was a rollicking dance around the bonfire, skipping and whooping. Gavain was shrieking with laughter by the end, his eyes bright with tiredness. Maythorn swung him up in her arms. "Let's dance this next one, too," she said, and pressed a kiss to his dark, silky hair.

This was a slower dance, the music—lute and pipes—was sweet and haunting and almost sad. Spring farewelled. The next dance would be bright and vigorous, welcoming summer.

Maythorn rested her cheek on Gavain's hair. She'd danced with Ivy like this, and Hazel. Young and warm in her arms. But she'd never been able to dance with Larkspur.

Grief touched her heart—grief for all the things she'd not been able to do with her children—and then the grief dissolved and her heart held only joy in this moment. Gavain's warmth and vitality. His trust. His arms around her neck, his legs around her waist, his sleepy laughter in her ear. Maythorn kissed his soft, warm cheek and breathed deeply of his child scent. *I love you, Gavain,* she whispered silently.

By the time the dance ended, Gavain was asleep. Maythorn carried him from the bonfire, to his father. Firelight cast a warm glow over Ren's face, but his gaze was dark and unfathomable. What was he thinking as he watched them approach?

"He's asleep," Maythorn said, in a low voice.

"About time." Ren gently took his son from her; their hands touched for a second, and then Gavain's warmth was gone from her arms.

Maythorn watched them go—father and son—and lifted her eyes to the bright stars in the sky overhead. "If it pleases you, merciful gods, let me have this man as a husband and his child as my son," she whispered.

Ren returned a few minutes later, a mug of ale in each hand. He gave Maythorn one.

"Have you put Gavain to bed?"

Ren nodded.

All the village children would sleep together this night, tumbled like a litter of puppies in Robin Thatcher's sweet-smelling strawloft. Her own girls had slept thus, many years ago.

Maythorn glanced across at her daughters. They were all watching her.

She looked hastily away, sipped her ale, and almost choked. She was intensely aware of Ren. Intensely aware of her daughters and their silent, smiling approbation.

The village musicians struck up another tune.

"Would you like to dance?" Ren asked.

I would like to live the rest of my life with you, Maythorn thought. "Yes," she said aloud.

They left their ale on a trestle table and joined the other villagers in a great ring around the bonfire. The music started at a sedate pace, like a horse ambling, and quickened to a trot, then a canter, then a romping gallop. People kicked up their heels and whooped and danced faster. Maythorn's awkwardness evaporated. The last of the flowers tumbled from her hair. She held on to Ren's hand and laughed up into his smiling face, and loved him with all her heart.

The dance ended with a great, joyous shout. The musicians laid aside their instruments—lute, pipe, rebec, tambourine, drums—and called for ale. She and Ren stood catching their breath, surrounded by red-faced, gasping dancers. Behind Ren, the bonfire was no longer roaring. The embers made a purring sound.

Ren offered her his arm. Something built between them as they walked back to the trestle table. Maythorn couldn't name it—a combination of anticipation and hope and expectancy. She felt it in her blood, in her bones. Ren felt it, too. She saw it on his face, felt it humming in his arm.

They both knew they were on the brink of something.

"Are you thirsty?" Ren asked. "Hungry?"

Maythorn shook her head.

"Shall we walk a little?"

Maythorn risked a glance at her daughters. None of them were watching her. "Yes," she said.

*C*HAPTER 7

*W*alk, they did. But not far. They halted at the bridge that crossed the River Dapple. Ren rested his forearms on the sturdy stone wall and looked down at the dark water. "Will you go back to York?" he asked quietly.

"York?" Maythorn's sense of ease faltered. York wasn't her home any longer. It hadn't been her home for many years. "York is crowded and noisy and dirty. I don't want to go back. I want to stay here." The people she loved most in the world were here. Ivy and Hazel and Larkspur. Ren and Gavain. She looked away from Ren and traced the groove between one block of stone and the next with a fingertip. *No more questions,* she begged silently. *Please. I don't want to lie to you.*

Fabric rustled against stone as Ren straightened and turned to face her. "Maythorn . . ." His voice told her he was about to ask another question.

A sick feeling gathered in Maythorn's stomach. She didn't want to lie to him. She stood on tiptoe and pulled Ren's head down and kissed him, pressing her lips softly to his.

For a brief second Ren held absolutely still—and then he pulled her into his heat and kissed her back.

The world seemed to swing dizzyingly sideways. Ren's kiss wasn't gentle; it was fierce, almost desperate. His mouth plundered hers, parting her lips, seeking her tongue.

Maythorn nearly lost her balance. She clutched Ren's arms. She'd initiated this kiss, but Ren was definitely the master of it. One large, strong hand burned at her waist, the other cradled the back of her head, fingers clenched in her hair, and his mouth . . . Merciful gods, his *mouth*.

Whoever would have thought that Ren Blacksmith could kiss like this?

It was no seduction, but something much more urgent. Ren's mouth demanded participation. *Kiss me,* his lips commanded. *Kiss me,* his tongue cried silently. *Kiss me.*

Maythorn needed no urging. She kissed Ren back quite as fiercely as he was kissing her, driven by a desperate, overwhelming desire to possess as much of him as she could. Lips, tongue, teeth. Hers. All hers. She lost track of time. Seconds melted into minutes.

Ren's mouth gentled. His hands eased their strong grip. He broke their kiss. His breath fluttered against her cheek, warm and ragged. "Maythorn, will you please marry me?"

The words flew past Maythorn's ears like moths in the darkness. It was several seconds before she heard them for what they were.

Marry Ren?

For a long moment she couldn't breathe. Shock held her utterly still. Marry Ren? Had he said that? Had he *truly* said it?

Ren drew back slightly. "Please marry me," he said again, and she heard the uncertainty in his voice. He thought she was hesitating, that she was about to refuse him.

"Tomorrow," Maythorn promised vehemently. "I shall marry you as soon as the sun rises in the sky."

Ren released his breath in a quiet sound like a sigh. He gathered her close. He kissed her brow, her eyelids, her jaw. Feather-light kisses, tender and reverent. Each one was a benediction, a wordless declaration of love. He found her mouth again and delved into it.

Maythorn leaned into the solid warmth of his body. Years,

she'd loved Ren. So many years. Year upon year upon year of hopeless, aching, silent love—and now he was holding her, kissing her, wanting to marry her.

She wanted to laugh with joy, cry with joy.

With the laughter, with the tears, came a jolt of arousal, intense and unexpected, something Maythorn hadn't felt for more than twenty years. She suddenly wanted—suddenly *craved*—to have Ren inside her. Her hips rocked against him of their own accord.

Ren's hips flexed instinctively back, and he tore his mouth from hers and said breathlessly, "Maythorn?"

The craving was deep and powerful, clenching in her belly, in her womb. Maythorn gave in to it, rocking against Ren again, this time deliberately.

Ren uttered a ragged groan. His body was trembling.

"Please . . ." she whispered.

Ren stood motionless and unyielding for a long, agonizing second—and then he groaned again, deep in his throat, and gathered her in a crushing embrace and kissed her, his mouth hot and urgent. "I am your most obedient servant." He released her abruptly, took her hand in a strong grip, and strode from the bridge.

Maythorn half-ran to keep up. Eagerness mounted in her blood with each step. She imagined peeling off Ren's clothing, imagined exploring his body, imagined touching him, tasting him, making him cry out with pleasure. They passed the dark shapes of thatched cottages, henhouses, stables. The glow of the bonfire drew nearer.

He was heading for his cottage, on the other side of the village.

Maythorn's eagerness shrank in on itself. No one would censure them, not tonight of all nights—the night when spring became summer, a burgeoning night, a night for procreation—but she could imagine the villagers shouting ribald comments as they passed, imagine Hazel grinning and Ivy watching gravely.

52

Maythorn halted.

Ren's forward momentum almost jerked her off her feet. He swung round. "What?"

She couldn't pass the bonfire.

Maythorn swallowed, and looked around. "Here. The hayloft."

Ren stood for a moment, panting. "Hayloft?" And then her words must have penetrated his brain, for he turned and tugged her down the pathway to the back of Wensel Red-head's cottage.

CHAPTER 8

Wensel had a cart, and two stalls for horses, and above that, a dark and fragrant hayloft. Maythorn scrambled up the ladder. Ren followed, muttered something and climbed back down, and returned a moment later. "Here." He pushed something at her, a blanket, smelling faintly of horse.

Maythorn spread the blanket on the hay and reached for Ren, pulling him closer. She kissed him—missed his mouth and found his smooth-shaven cheek instead—fumbled at his tunic and kissed him again—found his mouth this time and lost herself for a moment in the texture of his lips, the taste of him—roughly unlaced the tunic and yanked it over his head.

His torso was bared to her, but her eyes were blind in this darkness. Touch would have to suffice. Touch. Taste. Smell. She leaned into Ren and pressed her face against his shoulder and inhaled his scent, opened her mouth and nipped him lightly, tasted the salt on his skin with her tongue, felt the flex of muscle as he pulled away from her.

Maythorn made a noise of protest—and swallowed it as Ren began stripping her. She helped him as best she could, twisting this way and that. Scant seconds passed—and then she was naked, the kirtle and smock tossed away in the darkness.

Ren reached for her, one hand sliding down her arm, clasping her wrist, pulling her close.

"No." Maythorn slipped free, and groped for his ankle. She yanked first one soft leather boot off, then the other, peeled his hose swiftly and roughly down his legs, and then his braies. She flung the garments away and made a wordless sound of satisfaction. Now they were both naked.

She heard Ren's breathing in the darkness—harsh, ragged—and heard her own panted breaths.

"Maythorn . . ." he whispered, and his hand found hers.

This time she didn't slip free, but let Ren pull her to him. His hand slid up her arm, cupped the nape of her neck, drew her closer for a deep, fierce kiss. His other hand found her waist—those long, strong fingers burned against her skin— caressed her hip, slid up her ribcage to one breast.

Pleasure ignited inside her, like a smoldering ember abruptly bursting into flame. So long since she'd been touched like this. Too long. Maythorn pressed herself eagerly closer. Ren's erection prodded her belly, so hot it should brand her skin, making arousal jolt through her, making her gasp into his mouth. One large, callused hand slid down her back to cup her buttocks and pull her even closer. Another jolt of arousal scorched through her. Maythorn clutched his arms, her fingers digging in to the slabs of muscle, and kissed him more fiercely, her tongue clashing with his.

Urgency built between them until she was almost mad with it. Maythorn tore her mouth from Ren's, begged, "Now, please," and pulled him down with her.

Ren settled himself between her thighs. Maythorn arched her back, pressing as close to him as she could. She was on fire, frantic with need. Ren's cock burned at the entrance to her body—and then he slid into her in a long, vigorous thrust that made her cry out with pleasure.

Ren froze, buried deeply inside her. "Am I hurting you?" His voice was hoarse, strained, dismayed. She felt him trembling, felt the immense control it took him to hold still.

"No," Maythorn gasped. "Don't stop. Merciful gods, don't stop!"

Ren obeyed, withdrawing, thrusting even deeper. Their coupling became urgent, almost frenzied. Heat grew between them, a conflagration, an inferno. The pleasure, when it came, was so intense that Maythorn nearly fainted from it. It rocked through her like a thunderclap. She heard Ren cry out, felt his huge body spasm, felt his cock surge inside her as he spilled his seed.

Ren's weight came close to crushing her, before he groaned and rolled to one side. For a long moment, they lay panting, then Ren pulled her close, tucking her into his body, holding her.

Gradually their breathing slowed. The scorching heat between them cooled to a pleasant warmth.

One of Ren's hands lay on her hip. Maythorn covered it with her own hand, lacing her fingers between his. *He has asked me to marry him.*

The thought gave her pause. Ren wasn't rash; he considered his choices, made sensible decisions. To offer marriage to a woman he'd only just met . . . there was nothing sensible about that. Nothing prudent. It was impulsive, reckless, foolhardy. It invited disaster.

There could only be one reason why a mature, sensible, prudent man would make such an offer: he'd fallen in love with her.

But so fast?

It seemed impossible—unless Ren had sensed the bond they'd built over years of friendship? Sensed it, and acted on it without understanding why. Allowed instinct to rule, and not caution.

Ren's fingers flexed in hers. "Are you sure I didn't hurt you?" His voice was low, his breath ruffling her hair. "I'm usually . . . more restrained."

Maythorn tightened her grip on his hand. "You didn't hurt me at all."

The first time she'd lain with her husband, it had hurt. For all Gyles's careful tenderness, that coupling had been awkward and painful. Not so, with Ren. Tonight had been wondrous.

Gyles . . . Memory gave her a glimpse of her dead husband's face: the black hair, the brown eyes. She waited for a pang of grief—grief for the man she'd married and the man he'd become—but felt nothing. Gyles was so long ago. Twenty-one years since he drowned—and even longer since she'd lain with him, full to bursting as she'd been with Larkspur. Memory of him didn't hurt now that she had her youth back again—and Ren warm alongside her.

Maythorn released Ren's hand and shifted, turning to face him in the darkness. "I think we both needed that."

"It's a long time since my wife died," Ren admitted.

Maythorn knew precisely how long: two and a half years. She could remember the exact morning Maud had died, remember Ren's pale-faced, silent grief and little Gavain's bewilderment.

Her heart had broken for them both, that day.

She reached out in the darkness and found his chest, laid her hand over his heart and felt it beat beneath her palm, slow and steady. *I have loved you for such a very long time,* she thought.

She lifted her hand and pressed her lips where it had lain, above his heart. Kissed him once, twice, thrice. He smelled of woodsmoke and fresh sweat and something intensely and wonderfully male. She could get drunk on Ren's taste, on his scent.

Hay rustled beneath the blanket as Ren stirred. His hand stroked down her back, idled across her buttocks, caressed her hip.

Maythorn exhaled a low, sighing breath of pleasure. She found Ren's nipple, kissed it, licked it, nipped it.

"Again?" Ren whispered. His fingertips trailed lightly back across her buttocks, tickling.

"Again," Maythorn agreed.

This time they took it leisurely, tasting and teasing, learning what gave each other pleasure. Time flowed as slowly as warm honey. Maythorn's senses were overwhelmed by the delicious friction of Ren's callused hands on her skin, the sheer size of his body, his heat, the taste of his kisses, the intoxicating scent of his skin.

Their explorations climaxed in a long, slow coupling that crested in a wave of intense, rippling pleasure that seemed to linger endlessly. Finally, the ripples faded. Maythorn lay dazed, filled with a delicious lassitude. Ren rolled his weight off her and tucked her in to his side, one arm warm and strong and possessive around her.

They lay together quietly. Maythorn's body still tingled with the aftermath of their lovemaking. She slid her fingers around Ren's wrist and felt the throb of his pulse. *My heart used to ache whenever I saw you,* she wanted to tell him.

That ache had been a secret she'd kept hidden for more than a decade. A secret she'd concealed from everyone—her daughters, Ren, the villagers. A secret she'd tried to hide even from herself, hoping that if she could just ignore it long enough, bury it deep enough, it would go away.

It had seemed such a dark, shameful thing—to love a man younger than herself, a man who was married—but now she had another secret. A secret even darker and more shameful.

The deep, warm contentment of being in Ren's arms evaporated. Guilt squirmed beneath her breastbone.

What she did to Ren was a terrible and profound deception, a betrayal of trust. She'd tricked him into coupling with her. If he knew who she truly was, he'd push her from him with revulsion.

Maythorn squeezed her eyes shut. *I am not Widow Miller,* she told herself firmly. *I am Maythorn. I am young. I am whole. I am worthy to be Ren's wife.*

But in her heart, she knew she was still Widow Miller—and that what she was doing was wrong.

Maythorn opened her eyes and stared into the darkness.

She felt guilt burgeoning inside her, putting out tiny, creeping roots. She imagined pale tendrils worming around her heart, coiling up each rib.

She shoved the image aside and nestled closer to Ren. *I am Maythorn of York. I am worthy to be Ren's wife.* She slid her fingers up Ren's arm, trying to ignore the guilt, but the guilt refused to be ignored. It wriggled and grew inside her like the blind, white roots of a weed. Was it going to be with her for the rest of her life? Tainting everything? And if it was, wasn't that what she deserved for lying to Ren?

Maythorn shifted, rolling to face him, and laid her hand on his chest. Such a solid chest, such thick slabs of muscle. She traced his pectorals, ran her fingertips down to his navel and back up, circled first one nipple, then the other, light and tickling, making his sweat-damp skin quiver. Down to his navel again, and then lower, across his taut, flat abdomen. The muscles trembled faintly beneath her touch.

Maythorn slid her fingers lower, combed them through the nest of hair at Ren's groin and cupped his heavy balls in her hand. She stroked the thick length of his quiescent cock. No, not entirely quiescent. His cock stirred at her touch. Maythorn gave a low hum of satisfaction in her throat, and stroked him again, felt him stir again.

Her guilt was fading, subsumed by other emotions: love for Ren, pleasure that she was giving *him* pleasure. She bent her head and kissed the crest of Ren's cock, smelled the musk of their lovemaking, licked lightly.

Ren's whole body twitched. He groaned, deep in his chest, and said her name, his tone half-protesting, half-pleading, "Maythorn . . ."

Maythorn laughed, a light, delighted sound, and bent herself more fully to her task, teasing Ren's cock with her fingertips and her tongue, learning the contours and shape of him, learning the taste. She drew him into her mouth and sucked—felt Ren's body jerk, heard him groan again—and sucked more strongly.

It was decades since she'd last done this, but she hadn't forgotten the skill, hadn't forgotten the rhythm. Delicious minutes passed. Her guilt was gone, forgotten about. Ren's cock was hot and hard, straining in her hands, in her mouth. Maythorn sucked more strongly. She wanted to know what his seed tasted like.

"Enough!" Ren grabbed her shoulders and hauled her up his body. "Ride me."

She wanted to pleasure him, not herself, but if this was what he wanted, she would give it to him. *Anything and everything*, Maythorn told him silently. *Because I love you.* She spread her legs and straddled him. Ren's cock surged into her, making her gasp.

He gripped her hips urgently. "Ride me!"

Maythorn rode him, in the darkness, in the hayloft, her eyes squeezed shut. This was another rhythm she hadn't forgotten. Ecstasy built inside her until she almost burst with it.

Ren's fingers spasmed on her hips, his seed surged inside her, a groan tore from his throat. His climax triggered her own. Pleasure jolted through her, and then subsided in a slow spiral, like a feather floating to the ground. Ren sighed deeply, and slid his hands up her back, drawing her down to lie on his chest.

For long minutes, they lay bonelessly relaxed. Ren's cock was soft and warm inside her. Maythorn listened to his heart beating beneath her ear. *I hope we've made a child tonight,* she thought.

Ren stroked her back and settled his hand at her waist. "We should go back to the bonfire."

"Yes." But Maythorn couldn't bring herself to move. She wanted to stay like this forever: Ren inside her, his heartbeat in her ear, his scent in each breath that she took, the solid heat of his body warming her. And then she thought of her daughters—wondering where she was, perhaps worrying. She sighed, and pushed up to sit.

It took time to locate their clothes in the dark hayloft, and even more time to dress. Maythorn had no doubt that telltale strands of hay clung to her kirtle. She climbed slowly down the ladder. The joy faded. Guilt returned. She felt it in her chest, creeping, squirming, putting out roots.

Ren took her hand and guided her down the path past Wensel Redhead's cottage.

I will do all in my power to make him happy, she vowed. *Anything and everything. I will comfort him, pleasure him, love him.* But still the guilt persisted. If Ren knew she was Widow Miller, he wouldn't be holding her hand right now. He wouldn't have bedded her thrice in the hayloft. He wouldn't have asked her to marry him.

They walked slowly, silently. Cottages loomed on either side, shaggy thatched shapes in the darkness. Maythorn's guilt grew with each step, filling stomach and lungs, climbing her throat until she almost gagged with it. At the end of the street, the market square came into view. She saw the glow of the smoldering bonfire and the black figures of dancers, heard music and voices.

Ren halted. "Maythorn . . ."

Maythorn turned to him. He was nothing more than a vague shape in the darkness, but memory filled in his features: the flaxen hair, the gray-green eyes, the honest, open face. Ren Blacksmith. The kindest, truest, *best* man in all Dapple Vale. Love welled painfully inside her, bringing tears to her eyes.

"Maythorn . . ." Ren took both of her hands in his. "Please tell me what happened to you."

Maythorn's heart seemed to stop beating. It took several seconds to find her voice. "What do you mean?"

"It's Faerie magic, isn't it? They gave you your youth back."

The blood congealed in her veins. Ren knew she was Widow Miller?

Maythorn pulled her hands free.

"Maythorn . . ." Ren reached for her and found her wrist.

"Please tell me the truth. We have to trust each other. If we don't . . ." His voice trailed off. She heard his unspoken words: *If we don't trust each other, our marriage won't work.*

The full enormity of what she was doing broke over her. She loved Ren, yes, but she'd also done her best to deceive him. She was selfish, greedy, shameful.

Maythorn twisted her wrist free. "I'm sorry." Tears spilled from her eyes, choked in her throat.

She turned and ran.

*C*HAPTER 9

*H*er one thought was to get as far from Ren as possible, as far from the dreadful thing she'd done to him as possible, but she couldn't outrun her shame. It stayed at her heels, as tenacious as a huntsman's hound.

"Maythorn!" Ren cried.

Maythorn veered down the path beside old Dowse's cottage and burst out onto the starlit common.

"Maythorn!"

Maythorn fled across the common. Grass wrapped itself around her ankles. Sheep lurched out of her way. Glade Forest loomed ahead, blacker than the night sky. Behind her, Ren shouted her name again.

She ran harder, panting and sobbing. The forest closed around her, cool and dark and quiet. Without the faint starlight, she was blind. Maythorn blundered into branches, stumbled over roots, running, running, shame biting at her heels. She heard Ren shout once, in the distance, and then there was only the hoarse whistling of her breath and the crackle of underbrush and the scuffing of her feet.

Finally, Maythorn could run no more. She lurched to hands and knees, crying so fiercely she almost couldn't breathe, retching, painful tears that went on and on and on. There had been times in her life when she'd cried, but never like this, never with such deep and anguished despair—despair worse than any she'd felt during her marriage, worse than the despair of being crippled—because this, she had brought upon herself.

Eventually the tears came to an end. Maythorn lay on the leaf litter, raw-throated, swollen-eyed, curled up tightly, hugging herself. Her breath hitched with each inhalation, each exhalation.

What had she done?

She loved Ren—had loved him for years, a bone-deep, aching love—and yet she'd chosen to deceive him. Ren had tried to talk to her at the bridge and she'd turned his questions aside with kisses—and he had known. He'd *known*.

Maythorn squeezed her eyes shut. The joyous exhilaration of being youthful again was gone. In its place was shame.

The undergrowth rustled and something large bounded at her. A wet nose touched her cheek and a familiar dog voice whined in her ear.

Maythorn pushed up to sit, groggy with misery. "Bess? Bartlemay?"

The wriggling body was Bartlemay's, the wagging tail, the enthusiastic tongue. He tried to climb into her lap. Maythorn put her arms around him and wept into his shoulder. *I have ruined it all, Bartlemay.*

"Maythorn?"

Her head jerked up. She looked around blind-eyed.

A twig snapped, the bushes rustled again, and someone loomed over her in the darkness. The voice told her who: Ren Blacksmith. And here was Bess, pushing close, gently licking her neck.

The sense of being loomed over vanished. Boot leather creaked softly as Ren crouched. "Maythorn? Why did you run? What's wrong?"

What was wrong was that she wasn't worthy to be his wife.

Maythorn swallowed a sob. "I'm sorry," she whispered.

"What for?"

64

"For deceiving you." She closed her eyes tightly and pressed her face into Bartlemay's warm, bony shoulder.

"You didn't deceive me. I knew who you were the instant I saw you."

"I *tried* to deceive you. I *meant* to deceive you." Her voice cracked, and the tears were back, pushing their way up her throat, spilling from her eyes.

"Maythorn . . ." Ren's arm came around her shoulders. "Don't cry."

But now that she'd started again, she couldn't stop. She cried in great, gulping, painful, despairing sobs. *Please tell me the truth,* Ren had said, and she hadn't been planning to. She'd been planning to *lie* to him.

"Hush," Ren said, and he gathered her closer, both his arms around her now, rocking her gently.

Even endless tears eventually come to their end, and so they did. Maythorn inhaled a shuddering breath and tried to draw away from Ren. She wasn't worthy of him. She was selfish and greedy.

Ren's grip on her tightened. "Tell me what happened. Please, Maythorn."

"You were right," she whispered. "It's Faerie magic."

She tried to pull away again, but Ren didn't release her. "Tell me it all," he said.

Maythorn wiped her face with a trembling hand. Tears still leaked from her eyes, warm and salty. "I found a babe in the woods. A Faerie babe. I saved it from drowning and brought it home."

"Drowning? Was that why you were soaking wet that day?"

Maythorn nodded against his chest. "You carried the baby. It was in the basket."

She felt his body stiffen. "What? Why didn't you tell me!"

"Because I was afraid you'd want to help."

"Of course I would have helped!"

"You have a son, Ren. A son with no mother. And the Fey are dangerous."

65

Ren was silent for a long moment, then he released his breath in a sound like a sigh. "Tell me what happened after I met you."

"The girls looked after the baby all night. And the next day, I went to the border and gave it back to its mother—and asked for wishes for the girls and me."

"For your daughters? But Ivy—"

"She'll receive her wish on her birthday. They all will."

Ren was silent a moment. "They have summer birthdays, don't they?"

"Hazel first, and then Larkspur. Ivy's just before midsummer." Maythorn inhaled a hitching breath. "I wanted it to be now, but the Faerie was displeased and I . . . I was too much a coward to press for it."

"Not a coward," Ren said firmly. "By all the gods! Do you *know* how much danger you were in? She could have cursed you. Killed you!"

"I thought it worth the risk. I wanted to be whole again. I wanted Ivy to be whole." Maythorn's breath hitched again. She tried to draw away from him.

Ren's grip on her tightened. "Why did you run from me?"

Maythorn squeezed her eyes shut. She struggled to keep her voice steady. "Because you deserve a better wife."

"I do? Why?"

"Because I was going to lie to you."

"If I hadn't known who you were, that's exactly what you should have done. Of course you mustn't tell anyone! Gods, Maythorn, can you imagine? If folk knew you'd won Faerie wishes, they'd be out searching for the border tomorrow—and most of them would end up dead! You mustn't tell *anyone*." Ren paused. "Except the Lord Warder. It's Faerie magic, and he needs to know."

Maythorn shrank into herself. "Do you think . . . he'll expel me?"

"Dappleward? Of course not. But you may be certain he'll swear you to silence. He won't want anyone else trying to win wishes from the Fey." Ren bent his head. She felt him press a kiss into her hair. "You had no reason to run from me, love."

"I'm selfish and greedy, and you deserve better," she whispered.

Ren snorted a laugh. "Maythorn, anyone *less* selfish than you I have yet to meet." His grip on her eased. One hand found her chin and tilted her face towards him. He kissed her. His mouth was achingly gentle, achingly tender. "I deserve you," he whispered against her lips. "Only you."

Tears gathered in her eyes again.

"I remember the first time I saw you." Ren stroked her cheek, then slid his fingers into her hair. "I was nigh on fifteen. I came to Dapple Bend to visit my uncle."

"I don't remember you," Maythorn whispered, and felt a pang of regret.

"Why should you?" Ren stroked her hair, running the strands through his fingers. "I fell in love with you that week. Infatuation. You were the most beautiful woman I'd ever seen." His hand stilled. "And then five months later, Gyles beat you half to death."

Maythorn tasted blood in her mouth for an instant. She repressed a shudder. "I don't remember much of that, either."

Ren cupped his hand protectively around her head. "When my uncle offered me his forge, you were one of the reasons I took it. I had this foolish idea . . . I thought you might need a husband."

"What?" Maythorn stiffened in shock.

Ren made a sound, part grunt, part laugh. "Infatuation," he said. "Even after six years."

"Ren . . ." She drew back slightly, disturbed.

"Oh, I got over it quick enough. Got over it the first time I saw you again. Gods, Maythorn! I knew Gyles had hurt you, but I hadn't realized—" Ren's fingers clenched in her hair, a grip that was almost painful. His voice roughened: "If he'd still been alive, I swear I would have killed him."

Maythorn shivered. "Don't say that," she whispered.

Ren's grip on her hair relaxed. "It's true." And then he sighed. "It took me a while, but I learned to see past what Gyles had done to you, and I fell in love with you again. Only, it wasn't infatuation this time."

Maythorn shook her head. "Ren—"

"I wanted . . . I hoped . . . to marry you."

Maythorn pulled back. Ren's fingers slid from her hair. "But I was *years* older than you—"

"Only six."

"And I was crippled! My face—"

"It wasn't your face that made you beautiful; it was your heart."

The words silenced Maythorn. Her throat grew so tight she could barely breathe.

"My mother guessed, when she came to live with me. She saw how I looked at you. She begged me on her death bed . . ." He paused, swallowed. "Begged a promise of me, not to offer for you, begged me to marry one of the village girls."

"Ren . . ." Maythorn reached out in the dark and found his face, laid a comforting hand on his cheek.

"It's not that she didn't like you, it was just . . ."

"I was a cripple, and older than you. No wife for a young man. If you *had* asked me, Ren . . . I would have had to refuse."

"No." Ren shook his head.

"Yes." Maythorn laid her hand across his mouth, silencing him. "You deserved a wife who matched you, in youth and vigor and health. And that wasn't me. But I did love you. That, I can promise you."

She didn't remember Ren as a youth, but she remembered the man who'd come to take over the Dapple Bend forge. The young giant with more kindness and patience than any man she'd ever met.

"How could I not love you once I came to know you?" Maythorn whispered. "How could any woman not love you? The kindest man in the vale. The *best* man in the vale."

Ren huffed a faint, almost soundless laugh against her hand. "There are better men than I."

"No. It's not possible." She lifted her hand, leaned closer, kissed him. "Haven't you noticed how people respect you? How they listen when you speak? How they come to you when they've difficult decisions to make?"

"The Lord Warder—"

"You are as wise as Dappleward."

Ren opened his mouth to protest, and she kissed him again, softly, her lips clinging to his.

Ren's arms came around her. He gathered her close.

The kisses they'd shared at the bridge and in the hayloft had been hungry; this kiss was quiet and tender. It spoke of love, years of silent, overflowing love.

Time slowed. Their mouths slowed. They leaned into each other, holding each other, breathing each other's breath. *I love you*, she thought. *I will always love you.*

Faintly, far away, an owl hooted, and much closer, a hound scratched itself, grunting, tail thumping the ground.

Ren pulled away from her, and shuffled sideways, changing his position, and said "Here," and gathered her on his lap.

Maythorn nestled into his arms, pillowing her cheek on his chest. His heart thumped beneath her ear. "How did you know I was me, and not my niece?" she whispered.

Ren grunted a laugh. His breath stirred her hair, tickling. "Maythorn, have you never looked at yourself in a mirror? There is no one—*no one*—who has such a face as yours." Callused fingertips gently touched her cheek. "I knew it had to be magic of some kind. But I was afraid . . . I wasn't sure if you were still *you*, or if you'd altered inside in some way."

"Not altered. Just me as I always was."

"So I concluded."

"How?"

"Tibald, first. You walked up to him without fear, and you knew exactly where to scratch him—which told me that you *were* you and not some other creature wearing your face." Ren stroked her hair back from her temple. "And then there was Gavain . . . When you danced with him, when he fell asleep in your arms . . . I saw that you loved him—it was plain to see on your face—but it wasn't a scant day's worth of love, it was *years'* worth, as if you'd treasured him from the moment he was born."

"I have. I always have."

All children were precious, but Gavain especially so. Maud had suffered three miscarriages before his birth, and two afterwards, the last taking her life.

Poor Maud. So desperate to have children. And now dead. Maythorn closed her eyes. *I will look after them both for you, Maud,* she promised silently. *I will love them as much as you did.*

They sat in silence for several minutes, Maythorn nestled in Ren's lap, his hand stroking her hair. Was Ren thinking of his dead wife, too? "After Maud died, I thought—I hoped—you might offer for one of my daughters," Maythorn confessed in a low voice. "I could think of no better husband for them than you."

"Marry one of your daughters?" Ren seemed to recoil. His hand lifted from her hair.

Maythorn stiffened. "You don't like them?"

"Of course I *like* them. They're kind, good-hearted girls, but how could I marry one of them when it was their mother I loved? It would have been a terrible thing to do! A betrayal to them and myself."

"Oh . . ." Maythorn's stiffness eased. She rested her cheek on his chest again.

The deep peacefulness of Glade Forest settled around them. Ren stroked her hair, then cupped the back of her head in one large hand. Maythorn burrowed into his warmth. "When can we get married?" she asked. "Tomorrow?"

"I'd like to wait a week or two, if you don't mind. I want Gavain to have time to get to know you. I want him to think of you as a friend, not a stranger."

"Of course I don't mind." She wanted Gavain to be happy about having a new mother, not bewildered, not anxious.

Ren stroked her hair again. "And before we marry, you should speak to the Lord Warder. He needs to know what's happened."

Maythorn shivered. "Must I tell him?"

"Are you afraid of Dappleward? Don't be. He's a good man."

"I know." And she *did* know. But . . . the Lord Warder. Maythorn suppressed another shiver. "Will you come with me?"

"Of course I will."

CHAPTER 10

The River Dapple sprang from its source deep in Glade Forest and wandered almost fifty miles before flowing into the sparkling waters of Lake Dapple. Along its banks lay a dozen villages, the largest being Dapple Meadow, in the lower reaches of the vale, where the river meandered gently and the pastures were wide and fertile, and where the Lord Warder made his home. On the third day of summer, Maythorn set out with Ren to walk the thirty miles to Dapple Meadow. Hazel and Gavain came as far as Dapple Orchard, Gavain riding on patient Githa, and those miles passed merrily, but once Hazel and Gavain had turned back, Maythorn found herself growing apprehensive. It was all very well to say that Dappleward was a good man—for he was—but he was also Lord Warder of all Dapple Vale, and as such, he had the power to expel folk from the vale.

What if he banished her?

They'd intended to overnight at Dapple Weir, where Ren's brother was blacksmith, but when they reached Dapple Hollow in the lazy, bee-humming warmth of early afternoon, they discovered the Lord Warder and his liegeman Rauf Ironfist were in conference with the village alderman.

"We had a bit of trouble here the night of the bonfire,"

Dapple Hollow's thatcher told them, as they drank water at the village well. "Gilbert Baker got a mite too friendly with John Swineherd's daughter, which she didn't like overmuch, and John liked even less, and they got to fighting and John stuck Gilbert with a knife, except he didn't *mean* to—they was both drunk." The thatcher grimaced, and scratched his head. "So the Lord Warder's come to sort it out."

"Was Gilbert badly injured?" Ren asked.

The thatcher shook his head. "It's John we're all worried about. What if Dappleward banishes him? It don't warrant that!"

"Dappleward only banishes troublemakers," Ren said. "Is John Swineherd that?"

"Neither of 'em's troublemaking. It was just the drink."

"Then John Swineherd should be all right."

"I hope you're right," the thatcher said, and sighed gustily. "I hope you're right."

Not long after that, two men emerged from the alderman's house looking sheepish and relieved. Gilbert Baker and John Swineherd, Maythorn guessed. Shortly after that, two more men stepped out into the sunshine. She had no need to guess who they were. Guy Dappleward and Rauf Ironfist.

Ironfist was built on the same scale as Ren, but there the resemblance ended; Ironfist's face was tough and craggy, and he wore a huge sword belted at his hip.

Maythorn's stomach tied itself in a knot. Her mouth was suddenly dry.

Another man emerged from the house, gray-haired, with an alderman's chain hanging at his throat. Dappleward and his liegeman stood talking to the alderman for several minutes, and then Ironfist looked around and saw Ren. He gave a blink of surprise, and a nod of greeting.

Ren nodded back.

Ironfist detached himself from his liege lord and crossed to where they stood. The two men clasped hands. Ironfist was half an inch shorter than Ren, and slightly thicker in the chest. "Ren Blacksmith," he said, in a deep, gravelly voice. "What are you doing here?"

"We're on our way to see Dappleward. But our business can wait until tomorrow—"

"Dappleward?" Ironfist glanced from Ren to Maythorn, and back. Years lined his face and his ash-blond beard was turning gray, but his gaze was knife-sharp.

"Yes." Ren's hand closed lightly on Maythorn's shoulder. "This is Maythorn of York. She has a tale the Lord Warder needs to hear. Privately."

Ironfist's eyebrows rose. "He does, does he? In that case, let's not wait until tomorrow." He gave a short nod, and walked back to his lord. A brief, murmured conversation ensued, and Maythorn found the Lord Warder looking at her. Dappleward was shorter and leaner than his liegeman and he carried no sword, but somehow he was as intimidating as Ironfist. His grave gaze had *weight*.

The Lord Warder nodded, Ironfist beckoned, and the alderman opened the door to his house.

The knot in Maythorn's stomach twisted even tighter. "Can you tell them, please?" she whispered.

"If you need me to, I will." Ren smiled down at her, and touched her cheek gently with his fingertips. "But I don't think you will. You have more courage than anyone I know, Maythorn of York."

Dapple Hollow's alderman was its weaver. A tall loom dominated the main room and half a dozen finely woven tapets hung on the walls, but Maythorn had no eyes for them. She watched Dappleward pull out a stool at the long trestle table.

Ironfist gestured that they sit opposite the Lord Warder.

The alderman set out four pewter goblets and a jug of cider, said "You'll be quite private, my lord," and then left, closing the door firmly behind him.

Ironfist's sword clanked as he took a stool next to his liege lord.

Maythorn's heart climbed to the base of her throat, where it sat beating fast. She glanced at Ren, seated alongside her. He smiled, and she saw in his gray-green eyes that he loved her.

Dappleward folded his hands on the table, and gazed across at her. "Your name is Maythorn of York?"

Maythorn nodded mutely.

"Let me hear your tale."

Ren took her hand in a warm, reassuring grip.

Maythorn clutched it tightly, and gulped a deep breath. Ren believed she had courage. "My name is Maythorn of York, but it's also Widow Miller. Last week, when I was in the forest . . ."

Dappleward and Ironfist listened intently. Frowns gathered on their faces as she spoke. When she said she'd requested wishes for her daughters, Ironfist grimaced. When she said the Faerie had agreed to bestow wishes on her female bloodline, he grimaced again.

Maythorn held on to Ren's hand and finished her story. "Ren said I needed to tell you." She looked at the two frowning faces opposite her, and wished that she hadn't. They clearly weren't happy.

"Who, other than Ren and your daughters, knows of this?" the Lord Warder asked.

"No one."

The Lord Warder released his breath, and sat back on his

stool. He exchanged a glance with his liegeman. "It could be worse."

"It could be a *lot* worse." Ironfist raked a hand through his close-cropped hair. "If the secret can be kept . . ."

"If? An entire female bloodline?"

"We do the best we can," Ironfist said firmly. "Can't do any more than that."

"No." The Lord Warder studied Maythorn's face for a moment, and then smiled faintly. "Don't look so worried. I'm glad you came to speak with me." He reached for the jug, poured cider into two goblets, and pushed them towards her and Ren. "Something somewhat similar happened several centuries ago. A young stonemason in Dapple Reach. His wife was dying and he went to the Faerie border and offered an exchange of gifts."

"I've heard of that," Maythorn ventured hesitantly. "He offered his firstborn child."

Dappleward shook his head. "He offered a song. One song, sung with all his heart—and his gift was accepted."

"He had a particularly fine voice," Ironfist said.

"The Lord Warder at the time changed the story." Dappleward poured cider for himself and his liegeman. "It took two generations for the tale to stick. Thank the gods it finally did."

Maythorn bit her lip, and then asked, "Why?"

"Because the stonemason didn't keep his encounter with the Fey a secret," Ironfist said. "By the end of that first week, over a dozen people had set out from Dapple Reach to try to earn wishes for themselves. None came back—unless you count the donkey, who was probably the thatcher's son . . . only no one could ever be certain."

"The Lord Warder forbade anyone to approach the border." Dappleward said. "But the stonemason's tale spread down the vale and by the end of that year, upwards of three score people had tried to strike bargains with the Fey."

"Tried, and failed," Ironfist said grimly.

"The stonemason's first child *did* die," Dappleward said.

"And the Lord Warder took that fact and made a new story. One that deterred people from seeking out the Fey. But it took two generations and almost a hundred people missing. *That* is what I wish to avoid."

"No one knows about the wishes except Ren and my daughters," Maythorn assured him hastily.

He smiled at her again. "For which I thank your good sense." The smile faded, and his face became serious. "But I must ask for your word that you'll never reveal your secret— you and Ren Blacksmith both—and I'll need your daughters' words, too."

"Of course," Maythorn said.

"And their daughters and granddaughters and great-grand-daughters." Ironfist sighed, and shook his head. "Your *entire* female bloodline?"

"I'm sorry," Maythorn said, and discovered that Ironfist was hiding a small smile beneath his grizzled beard. She blinked. The dread warrior could smile?

"We do the best we can." Dappleward repeated Ironfist's earlier words. "Your situation is different from the stonema-son's—you *saved* one of the Fey, something I doubt anyone else will ever do—but I fear that people will be tempted to seek the border if they realize what you've won. Youth is a great prize."

"There's always someone willing to take a risk if the reward is great enough," Ironfist said, in his gravelly voice. "Human nature."

"Which brings us to my next concern." Dappleward paused, and sipped his cider. "What exactly did you ask for?"

"To be healed of my injuries, and to be fifteen years younger."

"Why fifteen?"

"I didn't want to be younger than my daughters. It didn't feel right."

The Lord Warder exchanged another glance with his liege-man. "I think you're extremely lucky you phrased your wish as you did. I think that if you'd asked for your youth back, there's a strong chance you'd have found yourself an infant—and as an infant, you'd have died out there in the forest . . . unless someone found you."

Maythorn stared at him.

"The Fey are cruel. If they can harm us, they will—unless they have a whim not to. They're *dangerous*. I need to talk to your daughters, not just to obtain pledges of secrecy, but to warn them to choose their wishes very carefully."

Maythorn shook her head, aghast. "I didn't want to *endanger* them!"

"Of course you didn't." Dappleward's face relaxed into a brief smile. He gestured at the pewter goblet in front of her. "Drink."

Numbly, she reached for the goblet. The cider fizzed tartly on her tongue and almost choked in her throat.

"In addition to a pledge of secrecy, I will need a pledge from your daughters that they'll choose wishes that aren't . . ." Dappleward's brow furrowed as he sought a word. "Aren't obviously Faerie magic. Which brings me to another problem. Your eldest daughter. I understand that her wish will be to heal her lameness?"

Maythorn clutched her goblet. "Ivy's been lame for *twenty-one* years." Tears gathered in her eyes. "You can't ask it of her! She *has* to walk again!"

Dappleward held up one hand, halting her words. "Widow Miller . . . Maythorn . . . I'm not asking that she remain lame—I'm asking how we can conceal that it's Faerie magic."

"There's a way—there's always a way. We just have to find it." That deep, rumbling voice was Ironfist's.

Maythorn blinked back her tears.

The room was silent for a long moment, and then Ren said, "My grandfather told a tale about a woodcutter who lost his sight—a branch fell on him—and three years later he fell over and hit his head and he could see again."

"I heard that, too," Ironfist said.

"Could Ivy not fall over?" Ren said. "And be bedridden several days, and then find she can walk again?"

Maythorn wiped her eyes. "Perhaps."

"Or . . ." Ironfist said musingly. "Or the gods could visit her in a dream and tell her that her fortitude—her patient and uncomplaining fortitude—of the last twenty-one years is being rewarded, and her lameness healed. It'd be magic, but not Faerie magic."

There was another long moment of silence, and then Dappleward said, "Either could work. If your daughter is prepared to dissemble."

Maythorn thought of her eldest daughter—grave, thoughtful, wise. She could no more imagine Ivy acting out a lie than she could imagine her running whooping through the village. "She won't like it, but she'll understand why it's necessary." She looked across the table at Dappleward. The Lord Warder was a man of fifty, with a bony face and high-bridged nose, but he reminded her strongly of Ivy. "She's very like you, my lord." They both had the same quiet manner, the same observant gaze, the same fleeting, solemn smile.

"I look forward to making her acquaintance. Now tell me, when are their birthdays?"

"Hazel in a couple of weeks, Larkspur ten days later, and Ivy two weeks after that."

"Ah . . ." the Lord Warder said. "Soon." He frowned down at his goblet for a moment. "I'll come to Dapple Bend this week and talk with them."

Maythorn hesitated, and then said, "My youngest, Larkspur, she's . . . she's very shy. Please don't frighten her too much."

"I try not to frighten young maidens," Dappleward said gravely, and then his eyes crinkled at the corners in another faint smile. "Do have some more cider."

They sat drinking cider, and the men discussed the new bridge at Dapple Hollow, and Maythorn found herself slowly relaxing. Dappleward was the most powerful man in the vale, and Ironfist the most dangerous, but there was more to them than their reputations had led her to believe. Dappleward wasn't just stern and wise, he was kind. And for all Ironfist's brawniness and the sword belted at his hip, he was as astute as the Lord Warder, and just as kind.

When their goblets were empty, Dappleward climbed to his feet, and Maythorn and Ren knelt before him and took oaths of secrecy.

"I pledge, upon pain of banishment from Dapple Vale, to never speak of my Faerie wish, or of my daughters' wishes, to anyone barring a Dappleward or an Ironfist." The words had a dreadful weight. *Banishment from Dapple Vale.* Maythorn shuddered inwardly.

Dappleward helped her to her feet and took both her hands in his. "If you should ever need to discuss any of this, and if Ironfist and myself are away, both my sons will know of this matter, and Ironfist's son. That will be the extent of it: you and Ren Blacksmith and your daughters, Rauf and I and our sons."

Maythorn nodded soberly.

The Lord Warder released her hands. "I shall see you in Dapple Bend in a few days."

"Thank you." She dipped a curtsy. "I'm sorry you have to come all that way for us."

"I should have had to come soon regardless; I need to speak to your alderman on another matter." Dappleward paused, and seemed to be considering his next words. He glanced at Ironfist.

The liegeman shrugged. "Now's as good a time as any."

The Lord Warder turned his gaze to Ren. "Whitelock has requested to step down from his duties as Dapple Bend's alderman—he's feeling his age—and the person he'd like to replace him is you, Ren Blacksmith."

Ren rocked back on his heels. "Me?"

"Whitelock feels—and Ironfist and I agree—that you would make an excellent alderman. You've got a sound head on your shoulders."

Ren looked stunned. "But . . . I'm not old enough. Surely Alard Mason or—"

"I don't select aldermen because of their age, I select them because of their good sense, and Whitelock says you have the best sense of anyone in Dapple Bend."

Ren opened his mouth to protest, and closed it again.

The Lord Warder turned his shrewd gaze to Maythorn. "Do you agree with Whitelock's estimation?"

"Everyone in Dapple Bend would agree with it."

Dappleward nodded. He turned back to Ren. "I'll talk it over with you and Whitelock later this week, answer any questions you've got. You don't have to make a decision immediately. Whitelock's not stepping down until after the harvest, so you've got most of summer to think about it." He held out his hand.

Ren shook it, looking dumbfounded.

Ironfist clapped Ren on the shoulder. "See you in a few days."

$\mathcal{A}$FTERWARDS

$\mathcal{D}$appleward and Ironfist rode into Dapple Bend four days later. After stabling their horses, they strolled through the village to stretch their legs, and then across the common, and then across a meadow to where a little cottage stood.

Maythorn invited the Lord Warder and his liegeman inside, and introduced her three daughters.

Dappleward stayed for twenty minutes. When he departed, her daughters all looked extremely thoughtful.

Later that day, Dappleward and Ironfist spent several hours with old Phillip Whitelock and Ren. Ren emerged from that meeting also looking extremely thoughtful.

One week later, on a golden afternoon, Ren Blacksmith married Maythorn of York, witnessed by the folk of Dapple Bend village. Their handfasting took place beneath an ancient spreading oak. They exchanged simple rings Ren had made, and young Gavain solemnly bound their hands together with a cord, and then they spoke their vows to each other in the cool, green shade beneath the leafy boughs.

"So mote it be," the alderman said, and Gavain gave his new mother a shy, delighted grin.

After that came dancing, and after that, feasting. And after that, Maythorn sat with her husband's arm around her shoulders and Gavain warm and sleepy in her lap. Her fortunes had come full circle, from young bride, to crippled widow, to young bride again.

Maythorn's gaze rested on her eldest daughter. Soon, Ivy would be able to cast away her crutch. She imagined Ivy dancing at midsummer, kicking up her skirts, laughing joyously. *One more month, love,* she thought. *One more month.*

Her gaze slid to Hazel, to Larkspur. What gift would Hazel choose next week? What would Larkspur choose?

Dusk gathered in the sky, mauve tinged with orange and gold. Gavain yawned, and snuggled deeper into her embrace. Maythorn rested her cheek on his soft, tousled hair. "I love you, Gavain," she whispered.

Ren pressed a kiss to her temple. "Shall we go home?"

Home. With Ren and Gavain.

Maythorn smiled with pure happiness. "Yes. I would like that above all things."

Hazel's
PROMISE

A Baleful Godmother

Novella

ONCE UPON A TIME

In the northern reaches of England lay a long and gentle valley, with villages and meadows and wooded hills. Dapple Vale was the valley's name, and the woods were known as Glade Forest, for many sunlit glades lay within their cool, green reaches. Glade Forest was surrounded by royal forest on all sides, but neither it nor Dapple Vale were on any map, and the Norman king and his foresters and tax collectors and huntsmen knew nothing of their existence.

Within the green, leafy expanse of Glade Forest lay the border with the Faerie realm, where the Fey dwelled. The boundary was invisible to the human eye; nothing marked it but a tingle, a lifting of hair on the back of one's neck. Wise men turned back when they felt the tingle, and unwise men continued and were never seen again.

Despite its proximity to Faerie—or perhaps because of it—the sun shone more often in Dapple Vale than elsewhere in England, and the winters were less harsh. The Great Plague bypassed Dapple Vale, and the Great Famine, too. Crops flourished, animals were fat and sleek, and the vale's folk were hale and long-lived.

One road led to the vale, but few travelers discovered it. No Romans found Dapple Vale, nor Vikings, and England's

latest invaders, the Normans, hadn't found it either. Even folk born and bred in the vale had been known to leave and never find their way back, so well hidden was Glade Forest. Shrewd inhabitants took a pebble worn smooth by the clear, sweet waters of the River Dapple with them if they ventured from the vale, to be certain of returning.

The folk of Dapple Vale didn't take their good fortune for granted. They had heard of plagues and famines, heard of marauding soldiers and starving serfs and murderous outlaws. Each was careful to respect the forest that sheltered them, and most careful of all was the Lord Warder of Dapple Vale, who went by the name Dappleward. Dappleward and his sons and his liegemen, the Ironfists, knew the location of rings of standing stones where the Fey had danced in olden times. They knew where to find the great stone barrow that held the grave of a banished Faerie prince, and they knew of the dark and narrow crevice wherein lay a hoard of abandoned Faerie gold. They knew these places, and guarded them carefully.

All tales must have a beginning, and our tale begins in Dapple Bend, in the crook of Dapple Vale, where there once lived a miller's widow and her three beautiful daughters. The widow was half-blind and half-lame, but she had whole-hearted courage, and when she came upon a Faerie babe drowning in a deep, dark pool in the forest, she flung herself into the water to save it.

Now the Fey are dangerous and capricious and cruel, and the folk of Dapple Vale know better than to attract their attention, but Widow Miller went searching for the border with Faerie and called the babe's mother to her.

The Fey dislike humans, and dislike even more being in-debted to them, and the babe's mother was deeply in Widow

Miller's debt, so she granted the widow a wish, and each of her daughters a wish, too, and their daughters in turn.

Widow Miller entered Glade Forest half-lame and half-blind; she left it supple-limbed and clear-eyed and with a girl's spring in her step, and two weeks later she married the blacksmith she had secretly loved for years.

Her three daughters were to receive their wishes on their next birthdays, and those birthdays were soon. As spring ripened into the golden days of summer, the widow's daughters waited with joyful hearts for their birthdays to come.

Thus begins our story . . .

CHAPTER 1

*T*am Dappleward shucked off his boots. The creek burbled at his feet, clean and cold. A wash, a shave, clean clothes,
and then home. Home. After five months, *home*.

He pulled his stained, faded tunic over his head, and
began peeling out of his fraying hose—and stopped as his ears
caught the scuff of footsteps on the road.

He was in Glade Forest now. There were no outlaws here.
But even so . . .

Tam pulled up his hose and reached for his stave. The
donkey stopped cropping grass and lifted her head, ears
pricked, alert.

Together, they watched a figure come into view between
the trees. Tam's tension eased. Just a lad, slim, youthful, and
alone, with a small sack slung over his shoulder.

Tam put down the stave. "I give you good day," he called
out.

The lad jerked around, eyes wide and startled beneath his
brown hood. Tam saw him take in the tethered donkey, the
small fire with its pot of simmering water, himself half-naked
at the creek—and relax fractionally. "Good day." He was even
younger than Tam had thought; his voice hadn't yet broken.

"May the gods speed your journey."

"And yours." The lad gave a courteous nod and continued along the road.

"Go back to your grass, Marigold," Tam told the donkey. "He was no one to be alarmed about." Unlike the man he'd met an hour ago. A villain, if ever he'd seen one. But Tam had been taller than him, and armed with the stave, and the man had done nothing more than eye the donkey and pass on. And if he tried to follow . . . Well, no outlaws ever found their way into Glade Forest.

Tam peeled off his hose and braies, tossed them aside, and stepped into the creek. Cold water lapped his ankles.

He glanced down the road at the retreating figure. The lad had no stave, no weapon of any kind. *I should have warned him*, he thought uneasily.

The lad was striding briskly, too far away to call out to. Tam frowned, watching him. There was something about the way he walked, something . . . not wrong, exactly, but not quite right, either. The way his hips moved, almost swaying . . .

"He's a girl!" Tam said, his voice loud and startled. And then, "Shit!" He scrambled out of the creek and dragged on braies, hose, boots, tunic. The girl was out of sight, now. Tam doused the fire hurriedly, took two hasty strides down the road, and looked back at his packsaddle. Too precious. He daren't leave it. Which meant he had to take Marigold, too.

Even working as fast as he could, it was nearly ten minutes before Tam had the donkey loaded again. "Hurry, Marigold. Hurry!" he said, half-dragging the donkey down the road. "If he sees her, if he realizes she's not a lad . . ."

Not just robbery, but rape, too.

Tam convinced the donkey to trot, and ran alongside her, his stave in his hand. The girl had been walking fast. How far ahead was she now? Half a mile? More?

Another ten minutes, and they passed out of Glade Forest. There was no sign declaring this fact, no fence or marker of any kind, but Tam knew—just as he'd known when he'd crossed into the forest less than an hour ago. His nose told him, his eyes told him, even his blood told him.

The narrow cart track from Dapple Vale intersected the broad, dusty road to York. The junction was clear to his eyes, but few travelers noticed it. Only if one carried a pebble from the River Dapple could one be certain of seeing it.

Tam halted, panting. Where was the girl? Had she gone left, or right?

Marigold's ears pricked. Her head swung left.

"Voices?" Tam said. "Yes. I hear them."

Marigold was reluctant to trot again. Tam dragged her with him, around the bend. Fifty yards ahead, he saw three scuffling figures, the girl and two men.

"Ah, shit!" Tam dropped Marigold's rope.

The men had realized their victim was female; he saw that even as he ran. They weren't going for her sack; they were going for her clothes, trying to rip off tunic and hose. The girl was fighting back, kicking and biting. Her hood came off. A long plait of dark hair tumbled free. One outlaw snatched at the plait, caught it in his fist, yanked backwards. The girl lost her balance with a sharp cry.

Tam ran even faster. The girl tried to tear her hair free. The other man was closing in, reaching for her legs, evading her kicks.

A shout swelled in Tam's throat. He choked it back. Twenty yards, ten yards . . . and he was upon them.

He swung his stave at the man gripping the girl's hair. The outlaw looked up at the last instant, his mouth opening in a cry.

The stave hit the man's skull with a bone-jarring *crack*.

The outlaw dropped as if dead. The girl dropped, too, rolled, scrambled to her feet.

Tam spun to face the second man, wielding the stave as if it were a spear—a mighty jab, right at the outlaw's sternum. Again, he heard the crack of bone.

The man staggered back and fell heavily.

Tam raised the stave again, but the outlaw didn't get up. He lay stunned, his breath coming in rattling gasps.

Tam lowered the stave. He turned to the girl, panting. "You all right?"

Her face was starkly white, smudged with dirt. Blood daubed her chin. Her eyes were wide, dark, and frightened. Her plait was unraveling. Glossy nut-brown hair tumbled down her back.

"Are you all right?" Tam asked again.

"Yes," the girl said, but her voice betrayed her, wobbling. She took a deep breath and lifted her chin. "Yes," she said, more strongly. "I'm unharmed."

"There's blood on your face."

"Not mine." The girl wiped her mouth and chin. "I bit one of them." She looked at the blood on her fingers, and then met his eyes. "Thank you. I'm very much in your debt."

Tam shook his head. "The fault was mine. I should have warned you. I passed that one . . ." he pointed to the man he'd struck first, "not an hour ago. If I'd thought to tell you, if you'd turned back—"

"I wouldn't have turned back," the girl said.

Marigold ambled up and nudged Tam's thigh. He caught her trailing rope. "You have to. You can't go on alone—"

"I'm not turning back," the girl said, folding her arms. "I've waited *ten* years—and I am *not* turning back!" Some color was returning to her face. Tam realized, belatedly, that she was remarkably beautiful. And older than he'd thought. Close to his own age, if he guessed right. A woman, not a girl.

He eyed her. "How far are you going?"

"Mottlethorpe. It's only twenty miles from here."

Tam thought of his father's letter, hidden in his packsaddle. *I don't anticipate trouble, but Faerie wishes have a way of going awry, and I confess I'd like you home as soon as possible, son. I know I have three good shoulders to lean on, but I would be glad of your shoulder, too, should anything go wrong.*

His father wanted him home. But his father would also expect him to protect this woman.

Tam looked at her folded arms and stubborn jaw and

determined, dirt-smudged face, and weighed his father's request for his swift return against the danger she faced on these roads. Twenty miles to Mottlethorpe, twenty miles back. It would add less than two days to his journey.

"Very well," Tam said. "Marigold and I will escort you."

The woman blinked, looking startled. "I don't need an escort." And then she looked at the two men lying on the road and had the grace to blush. "I don't *want* an escort," she said, in a smaller voice.

"Tough," Tam said cheerfully. "This isn't the vale; it isn't safe for a woman alone." Especially not one as beautiful as this woman was.

She hesitated, and then asked, "Where were you headed?"

"Mottlethorpe."

She rolled her eyes. "Where were you headed . . . *truly?*"

"Truly?" Tam shrugged. "The vale."

The woman shook her head. "Thank you, but no. I can't let you go so far out of your—"

"And *I* can't let you go on alone," Tam told her bluntly. "You won't turn back. I doubt you'd let me drag you back. Therefore, I go to Mottlethorpe with you."

She bit her lip, and looked down at the two outlaws sprawled on the road. Emotions flitted across her face: determination, despair.

"And besides," Tam said lightly. "Marigold insists, and she's a stubborn creature." He scratched the donkey's head.

The woman gave a small, reluctant laugh, and then sighed. "Thank you. I would be doubly in your debt." She rubbed her face, found a smear of dirt, rubbed it again. For a moment, she looked tired and vulnerable. Her lips quivered as if she was going to cry, but then she blinked fiercely and took a deep breath and lifted her chin.

Tam should have been relieved; instead, he was disappointed. He imagined holding her in his arms while she cried, imagined stroking that glossy hair, wiping tears from her cheeks, offering a kiss or two in comfort. Her lips would be warm, soft, salty.

"What shall we do with them?"

Tam blinked, and followed the direction of her gaze. The outlaw he'd struck in the head was clearly dead. The second man was unconscious. "The dead one in the ditch," Tam said. "The other one . . . off to the side of the road." He handed Marigold's rope to the woman, took the dead man's ankles, and hauled him to the ditch. A leather purse was tied to the man's belt. Tam ignored it. Let someone else steal the coins.

He dragged the second outlaw off the road. The man didn't stir.

"Will he live?" the woman asked.

Tam looked at the pallor of the man's face, heard his rattling breath. "Mayhap," he said. But he thought it unlikely.

He glanced at her. By all the gods, she was lovely—lustrous brown eyes, elegant cheekbones, delicious mouth—but it was the sharp intelligence in her gaze that he liked the most. The stubbornness of her jaw.

No ordinary woman, this. Strong-minded. Stout-hearted. Determined.

If he hadn't come along, they'd be raping her by now.

For a brief second, bile rose in his throat. Tam turned away, swallowed hard, and crossed to her sack, lying abandoned in the dirt.

It was half empty. Clothes, he guessed. Maybe a blanket. Maybe some food. Tam strapped it on Marigold's back.

"It seems unfair to make your poor donkey carry my belongings."

"Marigold doesn't mind, do you, girl?" Tam patted the donkey's rump, and turned to pick up his stave. "What's your name?"

"Hazel. Of Dapple Bend."

I think I could fall in love with you, Hazel, Tam thought. He placed one hand over his heart and bowed with a flourish. "Tam. Of Dapple Meadow." He almost wanted to tell her his full name—Wistan Dappleward—and watch her manner change when she realized who his father was.

95

No. If she was to fall in love, let it be with *him*, not his name.

He took Marigold's rope from her. "To Mottlethorpe, then."

CHAPTER 2

"What's so important about Mottlethorpe?" Tam asked, once they'd put a mile between themselves and the outlaws.

Hazel glanced at him. Her lips pursed, as if she were deciding what to tell him.

"The truth, please."

Hazel gave a rueful laugh. "Am I so transparent?" And then she sighed. "Very well, the truth."

Tam waited, while they walked another dozen yards. The twenty miles to Mottlethorpe seemed suddenly a gift. Twenty miles to get to know this woman.

"I'm betrothed," Hazel said finally. "To a man who left the vale ten years ago to earn his fortune and never returned. I gave him a pebble from the Dapple, so he could find his way back, but he must have lost it. And yesterday I learned that he was in Mottlethorpe, so I've come to find him."

Tam tried to look as if her words weren't a kick in the stomach. "Betrothed?" Curse it. He'd been halfway to falling in love. He glanced sideways at her, and frowned. "You must have been young."

"Thirteen."

Very young.

"Who is he?" Tam asked.

She glanced at him assessingly. "You might have known him. He's from Dapple Meadow. Drewet's his name."

Drewet . . . Tam cast back through his memory—and almost stumbled. "Not Drewet Ilbertson!"

Hazel's face lit with eagerness. "You knew Drewet?"

"Tall. Black hair. Good-looking."

"You *did* know him!"

"I did," Tam said grimly. "He's a . . ." A son of a bitch, was what Drewet was. But he couldn't tell Hazel that. He searched for something else to say. "He's a lot older than you." At least fifteen years older, if he remembered correctly.

"I know," Hazel said seriously. "That's what made it so special. And then he never came back—" She swallowed, and lifted her chin. "But I know why, now. He must have lost his pebble and he couldn't get back into the vale. And so *I've* come to find *him*."

"You're certain he's at Mottlethorpe?"

Hazel nodded.

Dear gods, she was beautiful. It was easy to imagine her at thirteen, fresh and lovely and innocent. And trusting. Trusting *Drewet*, of all people. Lecherous, shallow-hearted, cheating Drewet. Drewet, who went where his cock led him, casually seducing, casually discarding. Hazel would have been a sweet and tantalizing morsel for him.

He wondered if Drewet had seduced her virginity from her. Knowing Drewet, he had.

Rage curdled in Tam's chest. If Drewet truly was at Mottlethorpe, he might have to castrate the man.

"So, tell me about Drewet," he said, tugging on Marigold's rope. "How did you meet him?"

"He came up from Dapple Meadow to help with the harvest. And we fell in love, and pledged ourselves to each other." A frown furrowed her brow. "And then he left the vale to seek his fortune and never came back. I knew something had happened! I *knew* it. He'd *pledged* himself—" She took a breath, gathered herself. "And yesterday I learned where he was. So, I set out to find him and bring him back."

Braving thieves and rapists and murderers.

Drewet did *not* deserve her.

"Ten years is a long time," Tam said mildly.

Hazel grimaced. "I know."

Suddenly, Tam made the connection. Hazel. Dapple Bend. He almost missed his step. "You're one of Widow Miller's daughters!"

Hazel halted. "What of it?"

Tam halted, too. He thought of his father's letter, tucked away in his packsaddle. *Widow Miller has won Faerie wishes for herself and her daughters. She has taken her wish already, with discretion, and her daughters are due their wishes on their birthdays. The eldest, of course, will choose to be rid of her lameness; the younger two have promised to choose discreetly. I have sworn them all to secrecy, on pain of expulsion from the vale. I don't anticipate trouble, but Faerie wishes have a way of going awry, and I confess I'd like you home as soon as possible, son.*

"What of it?" Hazel said again.

"Uh . . . nothing." Questions crowded on Tam's tongue. Had she chosen her Faerie wish? Was that how she knew where Drewet was? But there was no point asking them; Hazel had sworn an oath of secrecy, and she was clearly a woman who held to her word.

Hazel put her hands on her hips. "My mother's a cripple, is that what you've heard? Or have you heard that my sister's lame? It's true—and it doesn't make them less than anyone else!"

"Of course I don't think that!" Tam said, stung.

"Then what?" Hazel asked, narrow-eyed.

Tam hesitated. He *had* heard of Hazel Miller, and not just from his father's letter.

"What?" she demanded again.

"I've heard of you," Tam admitted. "Hard-hearted Hazel, who spurns all suitors to her hand."

Hazel sniffed and turned her head away. She began walking again. Towards Mottlethorpe. Towards Drewet. "Not all suitors."

Evidently not. Tam gritted his teeth. He pulled on Marigold's rope, and strode after her. "How is it your family allows you to travel so far alone?"

"I didn't tell them. They don't know about Drewet. No one knows about Drewet."

"You kept your betrothal a secret?"

Hazel flushed faintly. "Drewet said it was best that way. He said people would try to convince me he was too old for me."

Tam managed not to snort. That hadn't been the reason. Drewet hadn't wanted to be chased off before he got what he wanted. "But didn't your family suspect? Didn't your mother ever ask why you wouldn't take a husband?" Vale girls usually wed any time after sixteen, and Hazel was long past that age.

"Mother encouraged us to wait. She says, the older we are, the better decisions we'll make."

Widow Miller was correct. Gods, if she knew her thirteen-year-old daughter had been seduced by Drewet Ilbertson . . . Tam winced inwardly.

"She says it's better to never marry, than to marry the wrong man."

Belatedly, Tam remembered that Widow Miller had been beaten half to death by her drunken husband. Her advice to her daughters had been hard-won.

"But I've found Drewet now, so I don't have to wait any longer." Hazel's step became buoyant. A smile lit her face.

Tam eyed her narrowly. Had Hazel had her birthday? Did she *know* Drewet was in Mottlethorpe, or only *think* he was?

He walked fifty yards trying to think of a subtle way of finding out. "So, you're twenty-three? You don't look it."

Hazel shrugged. "I am."

"You look younger."

"I'm not."

Tam gave up trying to be subtle. "When was your birthday?"

Hazel glanced at him. "Yesterday. Why?"

"Uh," Tam said, and thought: *She used her Faerie wish to find Drewet.* "Uh . . . just making conversation." And then, because Hazel didn't look as if she quite believed him, he hastily said, "So you didn't tell your family you were leaving the vale? They'll be worried."

"They won't be worried. They think I'm visiting my cousin in Dapple Orchard." Hazel's gaze dropped. She looked shamefaced. "It wasn't well done of me to sneak off, but if I'd told them where I was going, they'd have made me wait until Ren or one of the other men could come with me, and I couldn't wait even a day longer! I've been waiting *ten years!*" Those last words burst from her, full of pent-up frustration.

Tam studied her face. How hard had those years been? She must have come close to despair many times. And yet she'd stood firm to her pledge, had looked at no other man.

She wasn't hard-hearted Hazel, he realized, but faithful Hazel. Ten years, faithful.

"Not long now," Tam told her. And when they found Drewet, he was going to wring the man's neck.

CHAPTER 3

They halted an hour before dusk. Hazel wanted to push on—Mottlethorpe was only seven miles away—but Tam was adamant. "It's too dangerous to travel at night. We need to find somewhere safe to sleep while it's still light."

Since she was already deeply in his debt, Hazel forbore to argue.

They turned off the road into the forest, following the course of a small, burbling creek. "How about here," Hazel said, after they'd gone a dozen yards in. "It's flat."

Tam shook his head.

He rejected the next site Hazel pointed out, too. After that, she kept her mouth closed. "Here," he said finally. "This'll do."

Hazel looked around. The road was well out of sight, well out of earshot. No one would hear their voices, see their fire, smell the smoke.

Tam unloaded his donkey and rubbed the beast down. Hazel watched him obliquely. He was as tall as Drewet, but leaner. Not thin, though. Not handsome, either, but he had merry blue eyes, with more than a glint of mischief in them, and a mobile, smiling mouth. He looked like a man who liked to laugh.

He also looked extremely scruffy. His tawny hair needed

a good comb, his beard was scraggly, and his clothes were threadbare, filthy, and—truth be told—smelled strongly of sweat. But he'd saved her. And he was escorting her to Mottlethorpe. Scruffy and smelly, then, but also honorable.

Hazel was uncomfortably aware that the debt she owed him was greater than she could ever repay. She was also aware that Tam wasn't the only one of them who was the worse for wear after today's exertions. "I'm, um, going to wash," Hazel said, gesturing at the creek.

Tam glanced up and nodded.

Hazel didn't go far, just out of sight of the campsite. She washed swiftly—not because she didn't trust Tam, but because this wasn't Glade Forest and it didn't feel safe to be alone. When she returned, Tam had built a fire. He put a pot of water on to boil, then rummaged in his packsaddle. "My turn to wash. Won't be long." He disappeared down the creek, a jaunty whistle trailing in the air behind him.

Hazel fed more wood onto the fire and frowned at the flames. *I was a fool to attempt this journey by myself,* she thought. But when she'd received her Faerie wish, when she'd learned that Drewet was only twenty miles from Glade Forest . . . The euphoria of knowing he was alive had pushed her into recklessness. The things she'd dreamed of for ten years—dreamed and despaired of—had suddenly seemed within reach. A loving husband. A home of her own. Children.

"Fool," Hazel muttered to herself, poking another stick into the fire. "Reckless fool." Better to have been patient, to have asked Ren Blacksmith to come with her, to have waited a few days.

Tam returned, dressed in clean—if shabby and patched—clothes. His damp hair was tidy. He no longer smelled of sweat. "Water hot yet? Ah, good." He fished a sliver of mirror from his packsaddle and a broken-handled razor, and proceeded to rid himself of his beard. "Much better," he said, once he'd finished.

Hazel had to agree. Tam cleaned up well. He still wasn't handsome—his face was too bony for that—but he was surprisingly attractive. It was the angular cheekbones, she decided, and the grin, and the gleam of humor in his eyes.

She found herself feeling almost shy in his company, and busied herself going through her sack, pulling out a loaf of bread and a shank of cold meat.

"Ah, you *do* have food." There was relief in Tam's voice.

Hazel glanced up. "You don't?"

"A crust of rye, only."

"Then please eat my food." Hazel pushed the cloth-wrapped bundles towards him. "Have all of it!"

Tam laughed, and pushed the bundles back towards her. "I don't need it all. A few bites will suffice."

"You could eat it all, and I'd still have done nothing to repay you," Hazel said frankly.

Tam glanced at her, the laughter fading from his face. His eyes were remarkably astute. "It makes you uncomfortable?"

It made her feel ashamed of herself.

"You were right," Hazel said bluntly. "I should have turned back. It was foolish of me and . . . and reckless, and selfish. You risked injury for me, and now you're going *two days* out of your way—"

"Stop," Tam said, laughing again. "It's not as bad as all that."

Yes, it was.

Tam smiled kindly at her. "The debt you owe is much smaller than you think, Hazel Miller. It's Marigold who insists on accompanying you, and all she asks is a good rub and some grass in exchange. As for myself . . ." The smile became speculative. "I slew your dragons; I will be content with a kiss."

A kiss?

For a long moment Hazel couldn't breathe, and then she tried to laugh. "A kiss?"

"One kiss," Tam said. "In exchange for two dragons."

Hazel hesitated. "Drewet . . ."

"Drewet wouldn't begrudge it. A maiden's kiss is fair reward for slaying dragons."

Hazel chewed on her lower lip. She thought about Drewet, and she thought about the two outlaws, and she thought about Tam saving her.

Tam watched her, his head cocked to one side.

If there'd been anything predatory about him, anything even slightly threatening, she would have refused. But there was amusement in Tam's eyes, and a half-smile hovering on his mouth, and his voice had held a note of laughter.

Hazel tossed her head. "Very well."

Tam's smile broadened, showing a gleam of white teeth. "Good," he said, and then he busied himself with laying out their meal, unwrapping the bread and cold meat.

He didn't want to kiss her now? Hazel didn't know whether to be relieved, or piqued. After a moment, she rummaged in her sack again and pulled out a handful of nuts.

Tam's face lit up. "Vale walnuts? Those, I've missed. There are none sweeter in England." He took a knife from his belt and began slicing bread and meat. "Nor juicier apples. I can't tell you how I've *longed* for a vale apple."

Hazel eyed him curiously. "How long have you been gone?"

"Five months."

"Why?"

Tam shrugged with his shoulders, with his face. "Wanted to see a bit of England before settling down."

"Settling down as what?"

Tam grinned. "As my father's son."

Hazel sniffed. That was no answer. "What's your family name?"

"If you guess right, I'll tell you." He reached for the walnuts. "May I have one of these?"

"Have all of them, if you wish."

Tam chose a walnut and cracked it between his fingers. He held both halves out to her. "Like some?"

Hazel shook her head.

Tam ate the walnut, not greedily, but slowly, savoring the taste. After he'd swallowed, he uttered a sigh of pleasure. "The best in all England."

Hazel studied him while he cracked more nuts. His hands were as lean and strong as the rest of him. A blacksmith's hands?

Tam didn't look like a blacksmith. Or a thatcher or mason or baker.

But did she look like a miller's daughter?

Tam laid the shelled nuts in a neat pile. "Bread, nuts, meat. And—" he flashed a grin, "I have some cider to wash it down with." He delved into his packsaddle, pulled out a battered pewter flask and placed it alongside the food, then gave her a half-bow. "Shall we dine, milady?"

Night closed around them. It didn't feel dangerous; it felt cozy: the firelight, the shadows, the woodsmoke. The bread was fresh, the meat tender, the nuts sweet, the cider tangy. Tam had been hungry—she could tell by the amount he ate— but he didn't shove the food into his mouth; he ate neatly, unhurriedly.

Good manners, but poor. Who was he?

Hazel reached for the pewter flask. The cider was stronger than she was used to. It fizzed on her tongue and warmed her blood. "Which is your family?" she asked.

Tam glanced at her, chewed, swallowed, grinned. "If you guess right, I'll tell you," he said again.

Hazel rolled her eyes. Did he know how irritating he was?

She took another sip and watched Tam eat. Firelight and shadows flickered across his face. There was something vaguely familiar about the shape of his nose, the shape of his forehead. "Do you have a brother?" Hazel asked abruptly.

"One."

"Older or younger?"

"A year and a half older. He's twenty-six."

"What's his name?"

"Hugh."

Hazel tried to remember if a Hugh had ever offered for her hand. "Do you look like him?"

Tam shook his head. "He's dark. Takes after our mother. I look like Father."

Hazel tilted her head, studying his face. Had she met Tam's father? Was that the resemblance she saw? And if she *had* met his father, when and where?

Tam looked like a peddler with his worn, travel-stained clothes. He walked like one, too, a ground-eating stride with a hint of merry swagger. And he had the glib tongue of a peddler.

Hazel frowned, and drank more cider.

There *was* a family of peddlers in Dapple Vale. Twice a year the men ventured from the vale and returned bearing spices, wines, fabrics, and news. Tam wasn't one of them—she knew Dapple Vale's peddlers by name—but he behaved like them. Would it offend him to hear that?

"You dress like a peddler," Hazel said. "You walk like one, you talk like one, therefore . . . I say you're Tam Peddler."

Tam gave a hoot of laughter. "A peddler? Me?"

No, not offended. Hazel sighed in exasperation.

"Tam Peddler," Tam said, rolling the words around in his mouth. "Has a nice ring to it, don't you think?"

"It sounds ridiculous," Hazel told him. She put the pewter flask down with a thunk.

Tam's grin widened. He knew she was annoyed.

Hazel sniffed and looked away.

"Don't frown, sweet Hazel."

To her annoyance, Hazel felt herself flush. "I'm not sweet," she said shortly.

"Tart Hazel, then. Prickly Hazel. Cross Hazel."

She was all of those, right now. And she knew why: the kiss Tam had asked for. She wanted it over with. *Hurry up, curse it!* She blew out a breath. It was foolish to be prickly about something as minor as a kiss. So what if she'd not kissed anyone since Drewet? So what if it felt like a betrayal of sorts?

Tam had saved her life; if he wanted a kiss, she owed him one.

She just wished he'd hurry up and get it over with.

Hazel fished in the sack for her blanket. The kiss was unimportant. Tomorrow she'd see Drewet again. Ten years since they'd pledged themselves to each other. Ten years since he'd left the vale. Ten long years of hoping and waiting and silently despairing.

"You want any more food?"

She glanced at Tam, shook her head, and looked for a flat spot to spread her blanket. Her thoughts returned to Drewet. So handsome, with his green eyes and curling black hair, so mature, so wise. She longed to hear his voice again, longed to be held by him. *Tomorrow,* Hazel told herself, brushing a twig out of the way.

When the blanket was spread to her satisfaction, she turned back to the fire. Tam had rewrapped the bread and meat in their cloths. "Here." He held the pewter flask out to her. "There's still a mouthful left."

"You have it," Hazel said, feeling ashamed of her prickliness.

Tam drank the last of the cider and rinsed the flask in the creek. The back of her head ached, Hazel realized. She fingered her scalp. It was tender.

"Sore?"

She glanced up to find Tam watching her. There was no amusement on his face now. He looked grim.

"A little. It's nothing."

Tam's lips tightened, but he didn't say anything. He dried his hands on his tunic and sat down again.

Hazel watched him across the fire. She owed him so much. Perhaps Drewet could pay him? Money was a better reward than a kiss, and Tam clearly *needed* money.

The cider hummed in Hazel's veins, making her warm and drowsy. She rubbed the back of her head again. When she looked up, Tam was watching her, his face grave, his eyes dark and unreadable. They stared at each other for a long moment, and then Tam said quietly, "I'll take that kiss now."

*C*HAPTER 4

*H*azel's mouth was abruptly dry. "Now?"

Tam shrugged with one shoulder. "If it pleases you."

If it *pleased* her? Hazel flushed. "Now is fine," she said primly. She climbed to her feet, walked around the fire, and knelt beside Tam. Her heart was beating faster. She felt suddenly shy and self-conscious. *It's just a kiss*, she told herself.

She glanced at Tam's face. Her gaze skidded away from his dark, watchful eyes and settled on his mouth. As mouths went, Tam had a nice one. Well-shaped. It would be no hardship to kiss him.

Hazel inhaled a shallow, nervous breath, and leaned closer to Tam. She pressed her lips to his for several seconds, and drew back.

Tam tutted under his breath. "That doesn't qualify," he said, capturing her chin in his hand.

Hazel stiffened in alarm.

"Relax," Tam said. "I don't bite." And then he leaned closer and kissed her.

His lips were warm and surprisingly gentle. There was nothing forceful about his kiss. It was slow, tender, comforting.

Hazel relaxed. She was safe with this man. She closed her eyes and let Tam kiss her.

Seconds slowly passed. A minute trickled by. Tam's hand slid along her jaw to the nape of her neck, pulling her closer. The mood of his kiss changed, became less comforting and more playful. He teased open her lips and delved into her mouth, touching her tongue with his.

Pleasure shivered through her. Tam must have felt her tremble, for he kissed her more deeply, more persuasively. It was impossible not to respond to that invitation. Impossible not to kiss him back.

Heat built between them. Tam cradled her nape with one strong, warm hand. His grip wasn't tight. She could pull free, if she wanted to. But she didn't want to. What she wanted was to relax into Tam's embrace, to have him hold her close and not stop kissing her.

Hazel almost protested when Tam finally released her. She stared at him, breathless and dazed.

Tam grinned. The glint of mischief was back in his eyes. "Your debt is paid, sweet Hazel."

Hazel lurched back on her heels, dismayed. She'd let him kiss her almost witless. She scrambled hurriedly to her feet. Her lips were hot and tingling, her cheeks burning.

She walked around the fire on weak legs and sat, struggling to pull her dignity around her. The nape of her neck felt cold without Tam's hand there. She rubbed it with trembling fingers. She wanted to rub her lips, too, wanted to stop them tingling.

To her shame, she realized that she hadn't thought of Drewet from the instant Tam's lips had touched hers.

It was the cider, she told herself. *I drank too much of it.* But in her heart of hearts, she knew that wasn't true. It was Tam's mouth, Tam's tongue, Tam's skill at kissing that had stripped her of caution and common sense. Not the cider.

Pride kept her sitting at the fire, when all she wanted to do was crawl into her blanket and pull it up over her head. She tried to look unconcerned and nonchalant, as if Tam's kiss had been merely commonplace, as if she weren't shaken to her very core.

Tam wasn't shaken. He was spreading out a blanket on the other side of the fire, whistling under his breath.

Hazel rubbed her lips surreptitiously with the back of her hand. It didn't erase the tingle.

Tam turned back to the fire and sat, cross-legged. Hazel found herself unable to look at his face. "I think I'll turn in," she said, and was pleased with how casual she sounded.

"Good night," Tam said cheerfully, as if absolutely nothing had happened.

CHAPTER 5

$\mathcal{H}$azel found it difficult to meet Tam's eyes in the morning. She was embarrassed by their kiss. Embarrassed, and ashamed. How could she have responded to Tam when it was Drewet she loved?

Tam wasn't embarrassed. He whistled jauntily as he folded up his blanket and stowed it in the packsaddle.

Hazel folded her own blanket, not looking at him as he strapped the packsaddle onto Marigold's back. She buried the blanket in her sack and yanked the drawstring tight.

"Toss that over here," Tam said, holding out one hand.

Hazel hugged the sack to her chest. "You needn't come any further. Mottlethorpe's only two hours from here. I'll be fine by myself."

"We're coming," he said, and gestured with his hand for the sack.

Hazel hugged it more tightly. "I'd rather you didn't."

"Tough," Tam said. He crossed the small clearing in three strides, pulled the sack from her grip, and returned to Marigold.

Hazel followed him. "I *said* I'll be fine by myself!"

"And I told you yesterday that Marigold's a stubborn beast. She's got her heart set on Mottlethorpe. Don't disappoint her."

"I'm not joking!" She reached for the sack.

The cheerfulness faded from Tam's face, leaving it serious. "Nor am I. It's too dangerous for you to travel alone. I'm coming with you."

"I don't want you to," she said stiffly.

"Is this because of last night?" Tam strapped the sack in place. "It was just a kiss, Hazel. Forget about it." He reached out and ruffled her hair. "Come on, let's go. I'll tell you about London, if you like." And his manner was so casual, so *brotherly*, that she felt foolish.

By the time Tam had told her about London—the cantilevered bridge and the great wall with its gatehouses, the beauty of St Paul's Cathedral—Hazel had mastered her embarrassment. She was able to look Tam in the eye again.

"What would you like to hear about next?" he asked cheerfully. "Coventry? Lincoln? York?"

"My mother grew up in York. What did you think of it?"

"York?" Tam shrugged. "It's much like any other city."

"You didn't like it?"

"I prefer Dapple Vale. Cities are so full of bustle that you can't hear yourself think. They're filthy. They stink. The buildings are all crammed together. There's no *space*. The vale is . . . it's green and peaceful." Tam thought for a moment, and added: "And safe. When you enter York, at the city gates there are heads stuck on poles, and crows sit on them eating out the eyes. And there are arms and legs hung on ropes."

Hazel shivered. Her mother had lived in a city with heads at the gates? "Why the heads? Why the arms and legs?"

"Criminals," Tam said.

Hazel pondered this answer. Glade Forest kept the vale safe from outside dangers—outlaws and famine and plagues—but not from human pettiness. The vale had its share of drunkards and brawlers. Occasionally men were brought before the Lord Warder accused of thieving, sometimes even manslaughter or worse. But Dappleward didn't cut such men's heads off and put them on poles for the crows to pluck out the eyes; he expelled them from the vale.

"I'm glad we live in Dapple Vale," Hazel said somberly. She looked around. They'd come out of the king's forest. Fields lay on either side of the dusty road. Many were planted with grain crops; some lay fallow, grazed by sheep and cattle. To her eyes, the crops looked sparse and the livestock scrawny.

"Not far to Mottlethorpe now," Tam said. "Once we get to the top of that rise, we'll see it."

Hazel's pulse doubled its pace. "I have a smock and kirtle with me," she said, suddenly nervous. "I'd like to change before . . ."

Before meeting Drewet again. Drewet. After ten years, *Drewet*.

"Change behind that oak tree," Tam said. "Marigold and I'll wait here."

Mottlethorpe was no city such as Tam had described, but even so, it stank. The smell assaulted Hazel's nose long before they reached the first houses. A wooden bridge crossed a shallow creek that was clearly the town cesspit. Excrement lay in stinking piles, tumbled together with animal bones and offal. Flies swarmed and maggots crawled and filthy pigs rooted among the waste.

A hundred yards past the creek was Mottlethorpe, houses crammed together as closely as dirty teeth in a mouth. The skyline was a bewildering jumble of gables and rooftops and crooked chimneypots. Several derelict cottages lay between the stinking creek and the town. Their timbers had been removed and the cob walls were collapsing in on themselves. Hazel eyed the ruins as they passed. Had the owners died of plague? Starvation? Murder?

"There's someone *living* in that one," she said, horrified.

Tam followed her gaze, and grimaced. "Makes you appreciate the vale, doesn't it?"

Hazel nodded soberly. No one slept in roofless hovels in Dapple Vale, not even the very poorest folk—among whom her family numbered. And no one ever starved to death.

Compared to these people, her family was wealthy beyond measure.

They entered the town proper. Ramshackle buildings lined narrow, squalid streets. Hazel stepped closer to Tam, glad he was with her. Mottlethorpe didn't feel dangerous, but neither did it feel safe.

"You know where Drewet lives?" Tam asked.

Hazel nodded. Her Faerie gift told her exactly where Drewet's house was. "It's on the other side of the market square," she said, and then hastily added: "So I was told."

Tam accepted this with a nod, and Hazel felt a twinge of guilt for lying to him.

They set off down a street that was almost as filthy as the reeking creek had been. Hazel stepped carefully, holding up her hem. Her throat was tight with nervous excitement. Drewet. After ten years, *Drewet*.

"Market day," Tam said, when they reached the end of the street.

Mottlethorpe's square was a swarming, seething mass of people. Hundreds of people. People past counting. Hazel almost recoiled. The din was overwhelming, a roar of voices like a river in flood, above which dogs barked and livestock squealed and bleated. Musicians played somewhere. Song spilled from an alehouse.

"On the other side?" Tam said.

"Yes."

Tam stepped into the market square, leading Marigold.

Hazel reluctantly followed. People jostled her on all sides, more people than she'd ever seen in her life, townsmen and women, merchants, tradesmen, farmers, peasants, all pressing close and shouting to be heard. Smells filled her mouth and nose until she thought she would gag: cow dung, singed leather, a whiff of roasting meat, the stench of sewage, rank human sweat. An elbow caught her in the ribs, a boot nipped her toes, someone butted into her, knocking her a step sideways. A tiny spark of panic kindled in Hazel's chest. She was close to being crushed in this mob, close to suffocating.

Tam glanced back, and halted. "You all right?"

No. She'd just discovered she wasn't as brave as she'd thought she was. Hazel lifted her chin. "Of course I'm all right."

"Best not get separated." Tam took her hand. His smile was kind, brotherly. "Come on."

Hazel felt foolish—but she held on tightly to Tam. That firm, warm, strong handclasp was an anchor. She no longer felt as if the mob was going to swallow her whole. It became easier to breathe. She found herself able to look at the wares for sale: candles and spices, lengths of fabric, metalware, leather goods, slabs of bloody meat. "Hot peascods!" someone cried shrilly, and someone else: "Hot sheep's feet!"

On the other side of the market square, Tam released her hand. "Where now?"

Where is Drewet's house? Hazel asked silently, and the Faerie gift led her down a street to a tall, narrow house.

"Drewet lives here?" Tam looked dubious.

Drewet had left the vale to make his fortune. It seemed that he'd succeeded. The house was three stories high, leaning out over the street, the plaster newly whitewashed, the timbers freshly painted. Some of the windows were even glazed.

"Are you *certain* he lives here?" Tam said.

"Yes. Um . . ." Hazel groped for a reason that didn't involve magic. The door knocker caught her eye, shaped like a lion with an iron ring in its mouth. "I was told a three-storied

116

house with a lion as the door knocker," she said, and flushed for her lie.

Tam still didn't look entirely convinced.

Hazel moistened her lips. Her heart was banging against her breastbone. She drew a deep breath, stepped forward, raised the knocker, and rapped on the heavy oak door.

CHAPTER 6

$\mathcal{A}$ woman answered the knock. Tam could tell with one glance that she was a servant.

"I wish to see Drewet Ilbertson," Hazel said.

Tam gritted his teeth. He wanted to grab hold of her arm and yank her away, tow her back to the vale. He curled his fingers into his palms.

"Drewet Ilbertson? Ain't no Drewet Ilbertson lives 'ere," the woman said. "It's Drewet Blacklock as lives 'ere."

Hazel lifted her chin. "Then it is him I wish to see."

"He's stepped out," the servant said. "Missus is in, if you want to see 'er."

Hazel lowered her chin. "Missus?"

"Widow Mercer, as was."

Hazel's brow creased. "Widow Mercer?"

"Widow Mercer, as was, 'til she married Drewet Blacklock," the woman explained, her tone patronizing and impatient.

Hazel paled. Her hands clutched one another. "It's not the right Drewet."

Yes, it is, Tam told her silently. *He found himself a wealthy mercer's widow to marry.* His relief was dimmed by the expression on Hazel's face: bewilderment, despair. She looked as if her dreams were collapsing around her.

Ten years of dreams, Tam reminded himself. Ten years of holding faithful to her pledge. While Drewet married a wealthy widow.

I will kill him for this, Tam vowed silently.

"Here's master," the servant said, with a nod up the street.

They both turned to look.

A man strolled towards them. Tam struggled to recognize him. The cocky strut was Drewet, the black hair, but everything else . . .

Tam raised his eyes heavenward. *Whichever god is responsible for this, thank you.*

Drewet had been muscular ten years ago; now he was . . . the only word for it was *fat.* He had enough flesh for two men. His paunch strained against his belt as if he were pregnant.

"Master." The servant bobbed a curtsy. "These people wish to speak with you."

Drewet glanced at them, taking in the donkey and their clothing, dismissing them.

"Drewet?" Hazel whispered.

Drewet blinked, and looked at her more closely. "Hazel?" He tipped his head back and laughed. His paunch wobbled like suet pudding beneath the over-stretched doublet. "Well, I never. Hazel Miller. I never thought to see you again."

"We had a *pledge.*" Hazel's voice was tight. Tam glanced at her hands. They were curled into fists.

"My dear girl, that was years ago. Don't tell me you've held to it? How amusing." Drewet's fleshy jowls quivered, as if he suppressed another laugh. He looked Hazel over, his eyes lingering on her breasts, her hips. "You've matured well."

Tam handed Marigold's rope to Hazel. "Hold this."

Hazel didn't take the rope. He thought she wasn't even aware of his presence. Her face was bloodlessly pale, her jaw clenched, her eyes burning.

"Hold it," Tam said again, taking one of her hands and wrapping her stiff fingers around the rope. He turned to Drewet. "You and I need to talk."

"And who might you be?" Drewet said, arrogantly.

Tam stepped closer, until they were nose to nose. "We've met," he said, his voice a low hiss, just loud enough for Drewet to hear. "Wistan Dappleward."

Drewet recoiled a step. "You?"

"Yes," Tam said, and punched Drewet as hard as he could.

Drewet's head snapped back. Blood sprayed from his nose.

Tam hit him again. And again. Punches that had all his weight behind them. Drewet staggered back, and collapsed. Tam followed him to the ground and kneed him in the groin. Drewet screamed breathlessly. "That's for Hazel," Tam told him, panting, blood roaring in his ears. He kneed Drewet again, even harder. "That's for Hazel, too." And again. He was going to *smash* the man's balls. He'd never bed a woman again.

Drewet stopped screaming. His eyes rolled back in his head. Behind him, Tam heard the servant shrieking.

Hard fingers clenched in Tam's hair, yanking his head up, almost pulling his hair from his scalp. "Get up!" The voice was Hazel's.

Tam blinked, and focused on her face. It was as fierce as her voice.

"Get off him." Her fingers clenched even tighter, hauling him backwards.

"Ow," Tam said. "Ow!" He staggered to his feet, trying to loosen her grip on his hair. He still had to castrate the bastard.

"We're leaving," Hazel said. "Now!"

She towed him through Mottlethorpe's backstreets, fast, almost running, her hand fisted in his hair. Tam was forced to bend almost double. Buildings flashed past, half-glimpsed. Marigold trotted at their heels. "You can let my hair go," Tam said, when they reached the stinking creek outside the town. He peered awkwardly up at her. "Please."

Hazel halted and looked at him. He saw fury on her face, and tears in her eyes.

The tears undid him. The last of his rage evaporated. In its place was contrition. "I'm sorry, Hazel."

Hazel released his hair. "What would have happened if you'd killed him? *What?*" The tears spilled from her eyes. "They'd have hanged you for murder!"

"I'm sorry," Tam said again, straightening, rubbing his aching scalp. "When he spoke to you like that, when he looked at you like that . . ." He'd wanted to kill Drewet.

He pulled Hazel into a hug, and held her close. "I'm sorry."

Hazel rested her head against his chest. "We have to get back to the vale. As fast as we can. If they send people after you—"

"They won't," Tam said, with a certainty he didn't entirely feel. Hazel was right: he could be hanged as a common criminal. His name meant nothing outside Dapple Vale. "But you're right; we'd best get going." He stroked Hazel's hair once, resisted the urge to kiss her, and released her. He took Marigold's rope and held out his hand. "Come on."

"Your knuckles are bleeding." The fury was gone from Hazel's voice. She sounded weary and defeated.

"I'll survive."

He knew he should be ashamed of himself, but he wasn't. Satisfaction hummed in his chest. He'd broken Drewet's nose, and he was pretty certain he'd done a lot of damage to his balls.

Hazel's smile was faint and miserable. She gave him her hand.

Tam gripped it firmly. "Come on," he said again. "Back to Dapple Vale."

CHAPTER 7

*H*azel's thoughts kept returning to the expression on Drewet's face when he'd recognized her, the amusement, the contempt. And then memory showed her Drewet reeling from Tam's first punch, his nose spraying blood, his eyes wide with astonishment. "Thank you for hitting him," she said, after they'd gone a mile.

"It was my pleasure."

Hazel kicked a stone off the road. She was mortified with herself. No, more than mortified—furious. Drewet, handsome Drewet, wise Drewet, wonderful Drewet, the man she'd given her body to, pledged her heart to, the man she'd held faithful to for ten years—*ten years*—was shallow and fickle and faithless. "I can't believe I fell in love with him."

"You were thirteen."

"Thirteen and *stupid*." Another stone, another kick. "He made the village boys look so callow! I was flattered by his attention. Flattered!"

"Stop wallowing."

"Wallowing?" She looked at him indignantly.

"You made a mistake. You were only thirteen. You hadn't the experience to recognize Drewet for what he was."

"A mistake I held on to for ten years," Hazel said bitterly.

"Because you honored your pledge. That's something to be proud of, Hazel."

Hazel kicked another stone. She wasn't proud of herself.

"If you met a man like Drewet now, you'd see who he was in an instant," Tam said. "Be glad he didn't make you pregnant. Be glad you didn't run off with him."

Hazel glanced at him.

"It could be a lot worse. As it is, no real harm came from it." And then Tam grinned. "Unless you count all the hearts you've broken."

Hazel tossed her head. "No one's heart was broken. It was my face they fell in love with, not me."

"Then it's just as well you refused them all, isn't it?"

She gave a half-laugh, and then scowled at him. "Damn you for making me laugh."

Tam's grin widened. He pulled her close for a quick hug. "Be glad it's not worse." And then he kissed her forehead, a light, brotherly, affectionate kiss. "Come on. Let's see if we can reach Glade Forest before dark."

At this reminder, Hazel cast a fearful glance over her shoulder. The road was clear behind them, but dread sat in her belly like a fist with sharp, bony knuckles. It was all too easy to imagine Tam hanging from a gallows, the lean body dangling, the laughing mouth silenced. Crows would peck out his eyes.

She pushed the image resolutely out of her mind, and lengthened her stride, walking faster. Tam was right: it could have been worse. Much worse.

She was free of her pledge. She could marry whomever she wished. And this time she'd choose well. Someone she could trust. Someone who wouldn't flatter her, or lie to her.

Someone like Tam. Who made her feel safe. Who made her laugh. Who would slay her dragons for her.

Tam, with his shabby clothes and tousled tawny hair and laughing blue eyes.

Tam, whom she liked a lot.

She'd used him poorly, dragging him all the way to

123

Mottlethorpe and back. He'd looked after her, risked his neck for her.

"Thank you," Hazel said contritely. "You've been so very kind to me, and . . . and *patient* and honorable and—"

"Honorable?" Tam cast her a startled, frowning glance. "That, you can't lay at my feet."

"Of course you're honorable!"

Tam halted. "Hazel, have you forgotten last night?"

She blinked, not sure what he meant—and then memory came tumbling back. Tam had kissed her.

A blush rushed to her cheeks. She looked hastily away.

"I talked you into a kiss you didn't want. That I knew you didn't want. An honorable man wouldn't have done that."

Hazel glanced at him.

"I apologize for kissing you last night," Tam said. "I wanted to make you doubt your commitment to Drewet, and that was the only way I could think of doing it. So don't call me honorable, because I'm not."

"Make me doubt my commitment?" She frowned at him. "Why?"

"Hazel, Drewet Ilbertson seduced at least half a dozen girls in Dapple Meadow. Made several of them pregnant."

Hazel opened her mouth, and then closed it again. "How do you know?"

"Some of the villagers went to my . . . to the Lord Warder. They wanted Drewet expelled from the vale. He left of his own accord, so it came to naught."

"Almost *expelled*? I never . . . I didn't know . . ."

"Of course you didn't."

"Why didn't you tell me!"

"Would you have believed me?"

Hazel bit her lip. She'd have taken him for a liar.

Tam must have seen the answer on her face, for he nodded. He turned away and started walking.

Hazel followed half a step behind him, digesting his confession. "So, you didn't really want to kiss me last night?" Mortification congealed in her belly.

Tam glanced back at her. "I wanted to."

The words, the glance, almost made her miss her step. Hazel's mortification vanished. How could three words, spoken mildly, make her blush so hotly, make her feel so tongue-tied?

CHAPTER 8

$\mathcal{I}$t was noon by the time they reached the king's forest. "Best if you change into that tunic and hose again," Tam said. "Just in case."

Hazel nodded silently.

Tam cut her a stout, strong stave while she changed. His bruised knuckles were stiff, making it awkward to wield the knife.

Hazel emerged from behind a tree. The brown hood covered her long hair.

"Another fifteen miles to Glade Forest," Tam said, handing her the stave. "Five hours. Four, if we hurry."

Hazel nodded again.

They walked fast. The road wound its way through the forest, rutted and dusty. Every hundred yards or so, Hazel cast a glance back over her shoulder. Her expression was anxious, a frown pinching between her eyebrows.

She was worried about pursuit. Worried that he'd end up on the gallows.

"They'll not come after us," Tam said.

"They might." Her pace became faster.

Even dressed in men's clothing and with her hair hidden, Hazel was remarkably beautiful. Beautiful. Bold. Brave.

Tam remembered the softness of her lips, the heat of her mouth. His cock stirred. *Down, boy,* he told it. He'd razed his chances, confessing to her. But it was better than Hazel thinking him better than he was.

Honorable. *That* had stung.

Hazel glanced over her shoulder yet again.

"They won't come after us," Tam said.

Hazel flicked him a glance and walked even faster. Tam lengthened his stride. Marigold trotted to keep up.

Hazel had scarcely spoken to him since his confession. He could understand that. He'd *earned* that. But it still hurt.

He could tell her his full name. She'd speak to him, then. Probably. Young women usually treated him differently once they learned who he was. Some were flustered, some stiffly shy, some flirtatious, hoping to get into his bed, and thence his family.

He couldn't imagine Hazel as any of those. Scornful, perhaps?

Tam stifled a sigh. *You were the lackwit who confessed,* he told himself.

Their pace ate up the miles. Dusk was still several hours away when they passed an alder that had fallen alongside the road. Tam recognized it. "Only a mile now," he told Hazel.

Ten minutes after that, Hazel slowed. "I need to pee."

They were the first words she'd spoken to him in two hours. Tam choked back an ironic laugh. "Choose your tree," he said. "Marigold and I will wait at that bend."

The bend was twenty yards ahead. Beyond it, the road stretched for a quarter of a mile before curving out of sight again. Recognition was like a sharp kick in his stomach. That distant curve was where Hazel had been attacked. Where he'd killed a man.

Only yesterday. It seemed like a week ago.

Marigold fell to cropping grass, chewing noisily.

Was the second man dead? Alive? Had thieves found the bodies and stripped them naked, taking clothes, shoes, weapons, purses?

Tam grimaced. They'd find out in a few minutes.

Footsteps crunched lightly in the dirt behind him. Tam turned. "Haz—"

It wasn't Hazel. It was a man. A bear of a man, burly and shaggy-haired, with a thick, matted beard. He wore a mismatch of filthy clothes and carried a cudgel.

Uh, oh.

Tam held up one hand placatingly and took a prudent step backwards. "I don't have any money. But I have half a loaf of bread you're welcome to."

More footsteps scuffed behind him. Tam spun around. *Shit, two more of them.*

He released Marigold's rope and hefted his stave in his hand, flexing his fingers around it, gripping it tightly. Should he shout for Hazel to run? *Could* she outrun these men?

Hide, Hazel, he urged her silently, while aloud he said, "Back off. Unless you want your blood on the road."

Bear man didn't back off. Nor did the other two. They moved closer. One had a cudgel, the other a stave. Tam eyed the stave. He needed to get rid of that first, before dealing with the cudgels.

He raised his own stave and took a step forward, but the bear man rushed at him, cudgel uplifted.

Tam sidestepped and swung his stave, a heavy blow to the man's ribs, making him stagger and grunt—and caught a flicker of movement out of the corner of his eye.

He ducked just in time. The outlaw's stave missed his skull and glanced off his arm instead.

Tam staggered and half-fell. His arm went numb. His fingers lost their grip on his stave.

CHAPTER 9

$\mathcal{H}$azel had truly lost her temper only once in her life. She'd been occasionally annoyed, cross, piqued, peeved, and irritated, but true rage had only occurred once, when she'd found some village boys idly shying stones at a brood of day-old ducklings. The rage had been instant, and utterly consuming—and the boys had taken one look at her face and fled.

When she came out of the trees and saw Tam facing a hulking man wielding a cudgel, it wasn't anger that overcame her, but fear. Hazel froze, half behind a tree, her throat choking tight. And then Tam turned, and she realized there were three men, not one, and they were all attacking him at once. Caution and self-preservation fled. In their place was an overwhelming and uncontrollable rage.

She saw Tam stumble, saw the stave fall from his hand— and then she was upon them, flailing with her own stave, fury roaring in her ears. What followed was a blur. Rage left no space in her head to think clearly. The world narrowed to one thing: hitting. Hitting and hitting and *hitting*. She felt the shock of each impact jar up her arms, smelled blood, heard the crack of bones breaking.

Someone caught her around the waist, lifting her off her feet. "Hazel, *stop*," a voice said in her ear.

She swung the stave—and realized that the arms and the voice belonged to Tam. Her awareness of the world expanded again. Road and trees and donkey. And men. Two lay on the road, a third scrambled away on hands and knees.

Hazel lowered the stave, panting, gulping for breath.

Tam set her back on her feet. "Glade Forest," he said. "Run!"

They ran, towing Marigold—down the long, dusty straight, around the curve—then veered into the forest, following the narrow cart track to Dapple Vale. Yesterday, Tam had been worried he might miss this track—it was so easily missable, the subtle Faerie magic of Glade Forest hiding it from human view; today it never occurred to him they might miss it. He knew it was there; and there it was, as plain to see as the road to York.

Tam slowed to a walk, panting. He shook out his right hand. His fingers were beginning to come to life, stinging painfully.

Hazel swung back to face him. "Don't stop!" she cried. "There might be more of them!"

"We're safe. Can't you feel it?" Glade Forest surrounded them. The colors were richer, the air more fragrant, and there was a faint tingle in his blood that said *home*.

Hazel lifted her head and looked around sharply. He saw the tension ease from her jaw, from her shoulders. She'd sensed it, too.

Tam touched his cheekbone and found a shallow cut there. "Thank you," he said. "I think you just saved my life."

Hazel turned to look at him. She seemed unharmed. Frightened, yes—her eyes wide, her face starkly pale—but uninjured. "You were magnificent," Tam told her.

To his astonishment, Hazel burst into tears.

"Don't cry." Tam crossed to her hastily, put his arms around her, and pulled her close. "It's over. We're fine."

"I thought they were going to kill you," Hazel sobbed against his chest.

Tam tightened his embrace. "Well, they didn't," he said firmly. "A few scratches, some bruises . . . that's all." Her hood had fallen off. Glossy nut-brown hair tumbled down her back. He stroked it gently, and then cradled the back of her head with one hand. A strange feeling filled his chest: bittersweet tenderness, protectiveness, love.

Hazel pulled back. "I'm sorry," she said gruffly, not meeting his eyes. She sniffed, and rubbed her face with her sleeve. "I never cry. It's just . . . There were *three* of them, and they were going to kill you."

"Well, they failed," Tam said. "I'm fine."

"You're bleeding."

He touched his cheekbone again, and brought his fingertips away bloody. "There's a creek ten minutes from here. Come on."

It was disconcerting to be back at the creek again. Yesterday, he'd been about to bathe here when a stranger had passed by . . . and now here he was, back again, with that same stranger. Except she wasn't a stranger any more. Was it *really* only yesterday? It felt as if time had distorted itself, cramming several days' worth of experiences into only a few hours.

Hazel washed his face ruthlessly with a scrap of blanket, and then examined the cut. "It doesn't need sewing up. In fact, I don't think you'll even get a black eye."

"Good." Tam flexed his right hand. The fingers no longer tingled. A bruised arm and a cut cheek . . . If those were the only mementos he carried away from the fight, he was astonishingly lucky.

"Two outlaws yesterday, and three today . . . Is the road normally so dangerous?"

"No," Tam said. "There must be a gang of them. Happens from time to time."

"Should we tell Dappleward? I know they can't enter Glade Forest, but—"

"I will definitely tell Dappleward," Tam said. "He'll send some men to clear them out." Tam among them, probably.

He looked at Hazel. She was extraordinarily lovely—the elegant cheekbones and soft, full mouth, the lustrous brown eyes. "I've never seen anyone fight like you. You were . . ." Terrifying, was what she'd been. "I think you're a berserker."

Hazel blinked and sat back on her heels. Her brow creased. "Me? A berserker?" She shook her head. "I don't think so."

Tam thought so, but he didn't argue the point. He climbed to his feet. "We've still got another hour or two of daylight. Let's keep going."

Hazel stood. "I slew your dragons for you."

"Believe me, I know," Tam said, reaching for Marigold's rope. "I can't thank you enough."

"You owe me a kiss."

Tam froze, and then turned his head to look at her. "What?"

"A kiss," Hazel said again.

Tam tried to read her expression. "Um . . . it's not necessary, you know."

Hazel's face tightened, as if he'd slapped her. "You don't want to kiss me?"

"Well, yes, but *you* don't want to kiss me."

Hazel frowned, her dark eyebrows winging together. "Why don't I want to?"

"Because you don't fully trust me anymore. And you don't much like me either."

"I don't? Why?"

"Because I told you why I kissed you last night."

Her face cleared. "Oh, that."

Yes, *that*.

132

Hazel crossed her arms and studied him. "So, you think I don't trust you? Or like you overmuch?"

Tam nodded.

"Why?"

"You stopped talking, after I told you."

"I stopped talking because we were walking too fast. My opinion of you didn't change."

"Oh." Tam began to feel more cheerful.

Hazel examined his face, her eyes slightly narrowed, as if she wanted to see inside his skull. "Is there any reason why I shouldn't trust you?"

Tam shook his head. "No," he said emphatically. "I'd never do anything to hurt you. Ever."

A smile lit her face. "Then you owe me a kiss."

"Now?" Tam said hopefully.

Hazel grinned, and turned towards the road. "I'll let you know when."

Tam grabbed Marigold's rope and followed her. There was a buoyant spring in his step. He felt like laughing out loud.

Hazel wanted to kiss him.

*C*HAPTER 10

A berserker, Tam had said. Hazel turned the word over in her head and worried at it like a squirrel worrying a nut. *Me? A berserker?*

Her memory of the fight was vague. She'd lost control, *that* she knew. Lost her temper, lost control. Maybe that was what it meant to be a berserker?

Yesterday, when she'd been attacked, it hadn't been anger that had consumed her, but terror. The outlaws had overcome her easily. Today, rage had obliterated fear and she had seriously injured—perhaps even killed—two men. That was sobering. *Very* sobering. But she wasn't sorry for it. Not if it meant that Tam was alive.

She glanced at Tam, sauntering alongside her, whistling under his breath. The cut made a thin, red slash along his cheekbone.

Tam caught her glance, and grinned. "I have time for that kiss now."

To her annoyance, Hazel felt herself blush. "I don't," she said, and lengthened her stride.

Tam whistled a few bars of a song, and then said, "I have time now, too."

Hazel cast him a stern glance. It bounced off Tam like an

arrow bouncing off a breastplate. He gave her a wide, innocent smile.

They walked another hundred yards. "Still got time . . ." Tam said.

Hazel smacked him on the arm. "I get to choose when."

"We'll not make it to Dapple Reach before dark," Tam said. "May as well stop here."

Hazel looked around. A creek ran alongside the cart track, and on the other side of the creek was one of Glade Forest's dells, the grass studded with wildflowers. It looked a good place to spend the night.

She gathered firewood while Tam tended to Marigold. Now that they'd stopped, she realized how weary she was. And hungry. They'd not eaten anything since morning.

Hazel crouched and dumped an armful of twigs and branches on the ground and glanced across at Tam. He looked weary, too.

She watched as he tethered the donkey, as he scratched between her ears.

Tam had a very nice face, full of kindness and patience and laughter. The face of a man you could trust.

Hazel narrowed her eyes. There was something extremely familiar about the wide forehead, the high-bridged nose, the angular cheekbones. Where had she seen that nose before? That forehead?

He said he had his father's looks. Therefore, she must have seen his father somewhere.

When? Where?

Tam knelt at the creek and washed his hands, cupped them and drank, wiped his mouth—and looked up and caught her watching him.

He grinned, and the weariness vanished from his face. "I have time now."

Hazel considered this statement for a moment, then came to a decision. "All right."

She almost laughed at the astonishment on Tam's face, and then the astonishment vanished and his expression changed, becoming intent, and she found herself suddenly nervous.

Tam climbed to his feet and crossed the grass.

Hazel's heartbeat doubled, then tripled. She hastily stood.

Tam halted, close enough to touch her. "Are you certain, sweet Hazel?" His face was serious, but there was a smile in his eyes.

Hazel nodded, not trusting her voice.

Tam reached out and cupped the nape of her neck with one hand, drew her closer, and bent his head.

His kiss was gentle and sweet.

Hazel's nervousness evaporated. She relaxed and let him slide one arm around her waist and gather her closer, let him coax open her lips with his tongue.

The kiss deepened, became less gentle. Hazel pressed herself even closer, reveling in the taste of Tam's mouth, the strength of his arm around her waist, the heat of his long, lean body.

Tam broke the kiss, releasing her.

"What—?"

"Don't worry," Tam said. "Not finished yet. Not by a long shot." He sat on the grass and reached up for her hand, tugging her off balance and onto his lap—laughed at her surprise—and put his arms around her and tipped himself backwards until he was lying down.

Hazel froze, startled by the intimacy of it. His chest was beneath her. Her legs straddled his hips.

Tam laughed up at her. "Come on," he said. "Kiss me."

He was giving control to her, she realized. *She* was on top. *She* had the power.

Hazel bent her head and pressed a light kiss to one corner

of Tam's mouth, then the other. Such a wonderful mouth. Perfect, in fact. She nipped Tam's bottom lip gently, then licked where she'd nipped.

Tam's arms came around her waist, gathering her closer.

Hazel nipped his lip again, and this time Tam opened his mouth, inviting her inside.

Hazel closed her eyes and sank into the kiss, losing herself in Tam's taste, in the play of his tongue against hers.

The large, hard lump pressing against her belly, she abruptly realized, was Tam's erection.

Alarm jolted through her. She broke the kiss.

"What?" Tam said.

Hazel stared down at him. He was flushed and breathless, his lips rosy from their kiss, his blue eyes dark and almost dazed.

She could trust Tam. He wasn't going to fling her on her back and rape her.

"Nothing," Hazel said. She bent her head again, kissed him again.

Now that she was aware of his erection, it made the kiss more exciting. Heat and tension built in her body. She rocked her hips, pressing closer to him.

Tam groaned. His whole body seemed to jerk.

Hazel laughed, husky, breathless. "Like that?" she whispered against his mouth, and rocked again.

Tam groaned again, and shuddered. "Yes."

The kiss deepened, becoming almost frantic. Hazel rocked against Tam, kissed him, rocked, kissed. So much heat, so much pleasure, so much tension building inside her—

Tam tore his mouth free. "Stop, or I'll spill in my braies."

"It's my kiss," Hazel told him. "I get to say when we stop." And she laughed into his mouth and rocked against him again.

Tam's hips bucked helplessly. He uttered an inarticulate cry and rolled from under her, fumbling with his hose, scrambling to his knees. She caught a glimpse of his penis, ruddy and engorged, before his hand closed around it and he turned away from her. His seed spurted into the grass.

Hazel bit her lip. She'd taken her teasing too far. She should have stopped when he asked. She nervously watched Tam straighten his clothes. Would he be angry? Embarrassed?

Tam turned his head and looked at her. His lean cheeks were flushed, his eyes so dark they were almost black, and his stare . . .

Not angry or embarrassed.

Hazel's heart began to thump loudly in her chest.

There was nothing mischievous, nothing teasing, in Tam's eyes. His gaze was intent and hungry.

He wanted to bed her.

Muscles she didn't even know she had clenched in her womb, in her belly.

She saw Tam draw in a deep breath, saw him struggle to master himself—and then he breathed out, a long exhalation, and he was the Tam she knew again. The alarming intensity was gone from his eyes.

He pushed to his feet and crossed to the creek, crouched, and washed his hands. Hazel watched, soberly. What Herculean effort had that taken him?

Tam stood, wiped his hands on his tunic, and turned back to her.

Hazel stood, too. "I'm sorry," she said awkwardly.

"Don't be." Tam's smile was easy, cheerful. He slung an arm around her shoulders, gave her a quick, friendly hug and a kiss on the brow, and released her. "Let's get that fire going. I'm so hungry I could eat poor Marigold, and that would be distressing for both her and me."

Hazel huffed a laugh. Her awkwardness vanished. It was one of the things she loved most about Tam: the way he made her laugh.

She turned to follow him—and came to a halt, rerunning her last thought in her head: One of the things she loved most about Tam.

One of the things she *loved* about him.

Hazel stared at Tam as he crouched at his packsaddle and rummaged for the tinderbox.

Did she *love* him?

Darkness fell. They ate sitting on either side of the fire—half a loaf of bread and the last of the cold meat. Hazel tried to eat slowly, to not wolf her food down. She glanced at Tam. Firelight and shadows flickered over his face.

Had she fallen in love with him? Tam No-Name?

The emotion that she felt for Tam wasn't infatuation, breathless and dizzying. It was deeper and more solid than that, a sense of *rightness*, deep in her bones.

This man was *right* for her. Being with him made her happy.

It didn't matter that Tam was poor. She'd been poor all her life. She knew how to forage for food in the woods, how to stretch a meal from one night to three, knew how to patch and re-patch clothes, and re-patch them yet again.

It didn't matter that she didn't know his full name, or how he earned his keep. Thatcher, weaver, swineherd . . . it was unimportant. What mattered was Tam himself. And Tam himself was someone she had come to love, someone she wanted to be with, not just for two days, but for *ever*.

Hazel rested her gaze on him, on the bones and hollows of his face. A lively, merry, intelligent face. A face that was a pleasure to look at.

Except that Tam didn't look merry, right now. He was chewing slowly, deep in thought, more serious than she'd yet seen him.

Recognition teased at her. The high-bridged nose, the serious frown . . . Where had she seen that before?

Tam looked up and caught her watching him. The impact of his gaze made Hazel slightly breathless. "Is something wrong?" she asked.

Tam's frown didn't ease. If anything, it deepened.

"What?"

Tam put down his slice of bread. His expression, the way he drew in his breath . . . He looked like a man preparing to jump off a cliff.

"What?" Hazel said again, alarmed.

"Hazel . . . will you marry me?"

CHAPTER 11

$\mathcal{H}$azel had been proposed to before, but never so unexpectedly. She gaped at Tam for a moment, her mouth open in shock. "You want to marry *me*?" Her voice rose on the last word.

"Yes."

Her heart seemed to have climbed up her throat, where it sat beating rapidly. Hazel swallowed and managed to say, "Why?"

"Why?" Tam half-laughed, and shook his head. "Hazel, you're unlike any woman I've ever met. You're . . . You're faithful and true-hearted and courageous. You're not meek and timid, and you're definitely not boring. You're strong-minded. You take risks. You've got *spirit*. You're stubborn and fierce and brave and determined and . . . and being with you makes me feel more alive than I've ever felt."

Hazel stared at him, stunned. No suitor had ever said anything so astonishing to her before, anything so heartfelt.

And he hadn't said a word about her face.

She realized her mouth was open again. She closed it hastily.

"I think we suit each other," Tam said seriously. "I think we'd have an interesting marriage. A good marriage."

Hazel thought that, too.

Tam was watching her intently. No laughter gleamed in his eyes. She saw tension in his face, tension in the set of his shoulders. Did he think she'd refuse him? Was he bracing himself for rejection?

Hazel found her voice. "I think you're right. We do suit each other."

"Is that a yes?" Tam asked cautiously.

"Yes." Laughter bubbled up her throat. "Yes, I'll marry you, Tam No-Name."

"Truly?" Joy and disbelief mingled on his face.

"Truly."

Tam grinned widely. "Now would be a good time for another kiss, Hazel Miller."

Hazel scrambled to her feet and went to him.

Tam met her halfway. He caught her face in his hands, his fingers cradling her jaw, his thumbs warm on her cheeks. "Hazel . . ." he said. "Sweet, tart Hazel. I love you." And he bent his head and kissed her.

"I love you, too," Hazel told him, when they came up for air. "You make me laugh more than anyone I know."

"That's why you're marrying me? Because I make you laugh?" Tam sounded taken aback.

"One of a great many reasons." She stood on tiptoe and pressed her lips to his.

Tam cupped the back of her head in one hand and kissed her again. When he finally lifted his mouth, she was dazed, dizzy.

"Tam Goodkiss," Hazel said, trying to catch her breath. "That's what I'm going to call you."

"Goodkiss?" Tam grinned down at her. "I could live with that." And then he kissed her again, even more thoroughly. They ended up lying on the grass—Hazel lost track of exactly how—but Tam's body was long and lean and warm beneath her, and her fingers were buried in his hair, anchoring his head, and she was kissing him as if he were air and water and life itself, and without him she'd die.

She became aware of Tam's erection, pressing against her belly. A delicious shiver went through her. She rocked her hips, felt Tam shudder, heard him gasp. "This time we're not stopping," she told him breathlessly.

"We're not?" Tam said, equally breathless.

"No."

"Well, in that case, we're wearing far too many clothes . . ."

Hazel had lain with Drewet twice. Both times had been hasty and furtive, the first time painful, the second merely uncomfortable. Sex with Tam was none of those things. Sex with Tam was laughter and teasing and pleasure. So much pleasure. Pleasure until Hazel was almost drowning in it.

Tam laid a blanket on the grass and peeled off her clothes, kissing the skin he bared. Shoulders, breasts, midriff. And then her inner thighs, his mouth tickling, making her quiver and squirm. His hands stroked up her legs, and his fingers roamed into the thatch of hair and delved inside her, and then his mouth wandered there, too.

Hazel gasped his name, shocked.

Tam chuckled and kissed her there again. His fingers coaxed, his tongue teased, his teeth nipped. Hazel heard herself moan—and then waves of pleasure came and she did drown for a moment.

When she swam back up, Tam was laughing.

He settled himself between her legs and braced his arms on either side of her. His erection pressed hot and hard and insistent against her entrance. "Ready?"

"Yes."

There was no pain when Tam sank into her; instead, there was a jolt of pure, raw pleasure. Her back arched, her hips rose to meet him, and a groan came from her throat.

Some time later, Hazel drowned again.

Afterwards, lying in Tam's arms, the ability to think slowly returned. Hazel became aware of her surroundings: the coarse wool blanket and cool night air, the heat of Tam's body, his arms around her, his breath stirring her hair. The burble of the creek and the chirp of night insects. The red glow of the dying fire.

"Well?" Tam whispered in her ear.

"That was . . ." She searched for a word to do it justice. "Phenomenal."

Tam laughed. "Phenomenal? You use big words, Hazel Miller."

She needed big words to describe what had just happened.

"Better than Drewet, huh?"

Tam sounded so smug that Hazel was tempted to lie, to say, *Actually, no. I doubt any man could equal Drewet.* Instead, she said, "A hundred times better."

"Only a hundred? We'll have to practice some more. See if we can do better."

"It can't get any better than that."

"It can, if we practice. And we're going to practice a lot. Every day."

"Twice a day."

Tam nipped her earlobe. "Thrice a day."

Hazel stroked the back of Tam's hand, tracing the ridges of his knuckles, the lines of his tendons. She'd rather live in a one-roomed cottage with him than in a manor house with any other man.

Tam pressed a kiss into her hair. "I have to eat," he said. "Or you'll marry a corpse."

They rekindled the fire and finished their meal. Hazel hugged her blanket around her bare shoulders, hugged her happiness to herself. She hadn't realized it was possible to be this happy. She was happy right down to the marrow of her bones.

She watched Tam eat, enjoying the play of firelight over his face. Such a wonderful face, strong and good-humored. The flickering shadows made his brow more prominent—

Suddenly, Hazel knew where she'd seen that forehead before, that high-bridged nose. The shock of recognition made her gasp.

Tam looked up. "What?"

Everything fell into place. The older brother named Hugh. Tam's knowledge of Drewet's near-expulsion from the vale.

For a moment, Hazel's tongue refused to work, and then she blurted: "You're the Lord Warder's son. You're Wistan Dappleward!"

CHAPTER 12

*T*am's grin became wary.

"Why didn't you *tell* me?" Shock was replaced by indignation, and a swift, stinging hurt.

"Hazel . . ."

"Why didn't you tell me!"

Tam put down his bread. "I didn't tell you because it gets in the way. People treat me differently when they know who I am."

Hazel's indignation grew. "You thought I'd *throw* myself at you?"

"No," Tam said firmly. "I didn't think that at all."

Hazel narrowed her eyes, not sure whether she believed him or not. "Then why didn't you tell me?"

Tam sighed. He pushed his hair back from his brow, looking suddenly weary. "I wanted to be Tam with you. Just Tam."

"Why?"

"Because I thought I could fall in love with you." Tam's smile was wry.

Hazel snorted. "You introduced yourself two minutes after we met. You didn't even know me!"

"Hazel, I could see very well who you were. You were brave and determined and strong-minded and not at all like most women I know."

146

Oh. Hazel bit her lip.

"And then you told me about Drewet." Tam grimaced. "Gods, I couldn't believe it. *Drewet,* of all men!"

Hazel winced inwardly.

"I was determined to do anything I could to stop you marrying him. Anything! But it turned out I didn't need to. Drewet did it all himself.

"By then, I knew I loved you. And I knew you were poor and you were proud, and I thought that if I told you my name, you'd be so determined to show me that you *weren't* going to throw yourself at me that you'd do the exact opposite."

"Oh." Hazel looked down at her hands. Tam was probably right.

"I didn't want you to keep your distance. It was as if the gods had given me a gift, meeting you like this. I wanted to see what would happen. Without my name getting in the way."

She glanced up and met Tam's eyes. The expression in them took her breath away.

"I love you, Hazel Miller," Tam said softly. "I will always be true to you."

I love you, too, she wanted to say, but she couldn't utter the words because foolish tears were choking her throat. Hazel blinked fiercely, and sniffed, and swallowed.

"Come here," Tam said, and when she did, he put his arms around her, hugging her close.

Hazel sniffed again, and wiped her eyes on his blanket. Tam No-Name. Tam Peddler. Tam Goodkiss. Wistan Dappleward. "Do people call you Tam?" she asked, once she was certain she had control of her voice. "Or did you make it up?"

"My family calls me Tam. And my oldest friends."

"Why?"

"Hugh couldn't say Wistan, when I was born. Tam was the closest he could get."

Hazel snuggled closer to him. His blanket was threadbare beneath her cheek, and beneath that, his chest was warm and solid. "Why are you walking?" she asked. "Why are your clothes little better than rags? Did someone rob you?"

"No. I sold my horse and sword and most of my clothes."

"I thought you might be Tam Swineherd," she whispered teasingly.

Tam chuckled. "Swineherds are very respectable people, I'll have you know."

"I know. I wouldn't have minded if you were one."

The full import of Tam's heritage burst on her. He was *Dappleward's* son. His father was the Lord Warder, the most powerful man in all Dapple Vale. The man who'd sworn her to secrecy about her Faerie wish.

She couldn't tell Tam her secret, but Dappleward could.

Tears of relief pricked Hazel's eyelids.

"I bought a gift for my father," Tam said. "It cost more money than I had, but with the horse thrown in, and my sword and best clothes . . . I could just afford it."

Hazel rubbed her eyes. "What gift?"

"Let me show you." Tam released her and climbed to his feet. He rummaged in his packsaddle and pulled out a large, cloth-wrapped object, and then hesitated and put it down and reached for something else instead: a piece of folded parchment. "Actually . . . um, first I should probably tell you . . . my father wrote me a letter. He sent one of the Ironfists to York with it. It was waiting for me when I got there." He glanced at her diffidently. "I know about your mother and the Faerie wishes."

Hazel blinked in astonishment. Tam already knew?

Tam didn't say anything more. He stood, holding the letter in both hands, watching her.

Did he think she might be angry?

Hazel released her breath. "Good," she said. "I'm glad."

"You are?"

She nodded firmly. "*Very* glad. It means I don't have to hide my gift from you any longer."

Tam's eyebrows rose. "Your gift? You mean . . . you wished for more than just finding Drewet?"

"I can find anything," Hazel said. "Any person, any object."

Tam's eyebrows climbed higher.

"I was only going to wish to find Drewet," Hazel admitted. "And then I got to thinking. You remember that little boy who went missing from Dapple Orchard last year? The one who almost died before they found him? I thought that if I chose to know where anyone was, I could find people like him. So I decided that's what I was going to wish for—to be able to find people—and then the day before my birthday I lost my thimble, and I spent half the morning looking for it, and it was in my basket—and I'd already looked there *twice*—so I decided to ask to be able to find any*thing* as well as anyone."

Tam looked bemused. "A useful gift."

"And a gift I can hide. Your father said it was important to keep it secret."

"Very important. If folk start trying to win Faerie wishes for themselves . . ." Tam grimaced. "That's how people die."

"I know," Hazel said soberly. "Your father told us the story of the stonemason's wish."

"Good." Tam crouched and tucked the letter into his pack-saddle. He picked up the cloth-wrapped bundle, came back to the fire, and sat beside her, so close their shoulders touched.

Hazel looked at him. Tam Dappleward, wearing nothing more than a ragged blanket. Her heart clenched in her chest. She loved this man. "I'm glad I don't have to keep my gift a secret from you. It would have pained me to lie to you."

Tam laid two fingers on her cheek, a light touch. "No lies between us."

"No lies between us," Hazel said firmly.

Tam smiled, and held the cloth-wrapped object out to her. "This is what I bought Father."

Hazel took it carefully. It was heavy and rectangular. A jewelry box? It seemed unlikely. The Dapplewards didn't flaunt what wealth they had. Whenever she'd seen the Lord Warder, he'd been plainly dressed.

The first layer was oiled cloth. Hazel unwrapped it and laid it neatly aside. Next came two layers of sturdy cotton, and then a layer of fine linen. She peeled the linen back and exhaled in wonder. "It's a *book*."

"Open it," Tam said.

"I don't dare!"

"It won't break. Go on, open it."

Cautiously, reverently, Hazel opened the book.

The vellum was smooth and creamy. The writing was in black ink, line after line of it, more ornate than her mother's handwriting. The first letter on the page, an *S*, was fully as long as her thumb, flourishing and elaborate, the two ends curling in on themselves into a figure eight. Curlicues of blue and red ink decorated the page border.

Page after page. Hundreds of words. *Thousands* of words. And illustrations, too. Knights in armor and ladies in fine gowns, men hunting and doing battle, strange beasts and fantastical landscapes, all drawn in colored ink.

"It's the most beautiful thing I've ever seen," Hazel said, awed.

"I thought so, too, when I bought it," Tam said. "But I've since changed my mind."

Hazel touched a page with a reverent fingertip. "Nothing could be more beautiful than this."

Tam's hand slid under her hair, cupping the nape of her neck. "You are more beautiful," he whispered against her temple.

Men had told Hazel she was beautiful before, dozens of times, scores of times, so many times that it had come to annoy her. *I'm more than my face,* she wanted to snap at whichever fool uttered the words. *If that's all you see, then you don't know me.* But coming from Tam, it was no longer a shallow, empty, easy compliment. When Tam looked at her, he saw her inside and out. And he found her beautiful.

Sudden tears stung her eyes. She blinked them back.

Tam kissed her temple, and released her. "Father has a library. He likes books. We often have someone read aloud in the evenings."

Hazel tried to imagine it: the Lord Warder's great hall, shutters closed against the night, a fire burning in the huge hearth, candles flickering, people leaning back in their seats, listening.

One of those people would be her, soon. Dappleward Manor would be her home. It was . . . not daunting, exactly, but it was definitely disconcerting.

Hazel ran a fingertip over the words on the open page—each letter was beautifully formed—loop of *g*, bold stroke of *l*—then closed the book and wrapped it back up: fine linen, sturdy cotton, and oiled cloth. Tam was like this parcel. On the outside he was plain, unassuming Tam No-Name, but beneath the layers of Tam Peddler and Tam Goodkiss was hidden Wistan Dappleward. And when you opened Wistan Dappleward and looked inside him, there was the greatest treasure of all: Tam Trueheart.

Hazel tilted her head and looked at Tam. "It's a very fine gift; your father will be pleased to have it." She reached out and touched his face, ran her fingers lightly over his cheek, felt the prickle of his whiskers. "But the gift you're giving me is even finer. *You* are a gift beyond price."

To her amusement, Tam blushed.

Hazel laughed. "I love you, Tam Dappleward," she said, leaning over to kiss him. "And I pledge myself to you *forever*."

Ivy's
CHOICE

A Baleful Godmother

Novella

ONCE UPON A TIME

*I*n the northern reaches of England lay a long and gentle valley, with villages and meadows and wooded hills. Dapple Vale was the valley's name, and the woods were known as Glade Forest, for many sunlit glades lay within their cool, green reaches. Glade Forest was surrounded by royal forest on all sides, but neither it nor Dapple Vale were on any map, and the Norman king and his foresters and tax collectors and huntsmen knew nothing of their existence.

Within the green, leafy expanse of Glade Forest lay the border with the Faerie realm, where the Fey dwelled. The boundary was invisible to the human eye; nothing marked it but a tingle, a lifting of hair on the back of one's neck. Wise men turned back when they felt the tingle, and unwise men continued and were never seen again.

Despite its proximity to Faerie—or perhaps because of it—the sun shone more often in Dapple Vale than elsewhere in England, and the winters were less harsh. The Great Plague bypassed Dapple Vale, and the Great Famine, too. Crops flourished, animals were fat and sleek, and the vale's folk were hale and long-lived.

One road led to the vale, but few travelers discovered it. No Romans found Dapple Vale, nor Vikings, and England's

latest invaders, the Normans, hadn't found it either. Even folk born and bred in the vale had been known to leave and never find their way back, so well hidden was Glade Forest.

The folk of Dapple Vale didn't take their good fortune for granted. They had heard of plagues and famines, heard of marauding soldiers and starving serfs and murderous outlaws. Each was careful to respect the forest that sheltered them, and most careful of all was the Lord Warder of Dapple Vale, who went by the name Dappleward. Dappleward and his sons and his liegemen, the Ironfists, knew the location of rings of standing stones where the Fey had danced in olden times. They knew where to find the great stone barrow that held the grave of a banished Faerie prince, and they knew of the dark and narrow crevice wherein lay a hoard of abandoned Faerie gold. They knew these places, and guarded them carefully.

All tales must have a beginning, and our tale begins in Dapple Bend, in the crook of Dapple Vale, where there once lived a miller's widow and her three beautiful daughters. The widow was half-blind and half-lame, but she had whole-hearted courage, and when she came upon a Faerie babe drowning in a deep, dark pool in the forest, she flung herself into the water to save it.

Now the Fey are dangerous and capricious and cruel, and the folk of Dapple Vale know better than to attract their attention, but Widow Miller went searching for the border with Faerie and called the babe's mother to her.

The Fey dislike humans, and dislike even more being indebted to them, and the babe's mother was deeply in Widow Miller's debt, so she granted the widow a wish, and each of her daughters a wish, too, and their daughters in turn.

Widow Miller entered Glade Forest half-lame and half-blind; she left it supple-limbed and clear-eyed and with a joyful heart, and two weeks later she married the blacksmith she had secretly loved for years.

Her three daughters were to receive their wishes on their birthdays. First to wish was the widow's middle daughter, and she asked for the gift of finding people and things, and with that to guide her she embarked on a hazardous journey, where she met Dappleward's youngest son and won his love.

Second to wish was the youngest daughter, and alas, her wish went awry. But the time has not yet come to tell her tale.

Third to wish, as the long golden days of midsummer approached, was the eldest daughter, who was the wisest of the widow's daughters, and who also was lame.

Thus begins our story . . .

CHAPTER 1

$\mathcal{I}$vy limped through the forest, leaning on her crutch. Her sister Hazel walked alongside her, a basket slung over one arm. Ahead, the derelict woodcutter's cottage peeped through the trees, a lopsided building with crooked shutters and threadbare thatching. Ivy glimpsed her youngest sister, Larkspur, sitting on the mossy doorstep, two large red-brown hounds at her feet.

"I see her," Hazel said.

As if she'd heard Hazel, Larkspur turned her head and looked into the forest, directly at them.

She can't see us yet or hear our voices, Ivy thought. *But she senses us.*

"Go ahead," Ivy said. "Don't wait for me."

Hazel nodded, and picked up her skirts and ran ahead, the basket bouncing and swinging on her arm. "Larkspur!"

The hounds surged to their feet, barking.

Ivy hobbled as fast as she could, awkwardly navigated the gnarled roots of an oak, and came out into the sunlit clearing.

Larkspur ran to meet her.

Ivy hugged her sister tightly, while the hounds frisked around them like puppies.

Larkspur drew back. Tears were bright in her eyes.

Ivy smoothed Larkspur's pale hair away from her face. "How are you, love?" She didn't need to say the words aloud; Larkspur could hear them just as clearly unspoken as spoken. "The cottage hasn't fallen down around your ears yet?"

Larkspur shook her head. Her face was thin, her cheeks almost hollow, her skin translucently pale except for the dark shadows beneath her eyes.

The Faerie gift was killing her.

Ivy tried to smother the thought, but it was too late. Larkspur had heard it. Her lips twisted in silent agreement.

"Five more days and it will be undone," Ivy said.

Larkspur didn't argue. She'd stopped arguing a week ago, driven half-mad by everyone's thoughts pushing into her head.

Ivy limped across to the doorstep and awkwardly sat, stretching out her stiff leg. Larkspur and Hazel sat, too. The hounds settled at their feet. This should have been a happy moment, sitting in the sunshine with her sisters, but it wasn't; the silence between them was strained and anxious, tense with everything that lay unsaid between them.

"No one's found you?" Ivy asked finally.

Larkspur shook her head.

I hate that you're sleeping here alone, Ivy thought.

"I'm not alone," Larkspur said. "I have the dogs. It's quite safe. You think I wouldn't know if anyone were nearby? How can I *not* know?" There was a bitter note in her voice.

Ivy put an arm around her sister's thin shoulders. *Don't hate yourself,* she thought to Larkspur. *The Faerie tricked you. It's not your fault.*

She glanced at Hazel. Hazel was silent and tight-lipped. Ivy didn't need to have Larkspur's gift to know that she was angry.

Larkspur bowed her head. "I'm sorry."

"It's not your fault," Hazel said flatly. "It's that bale-tongued creature's, and I'll *kill* her if I—"

"Hazel," Ivy said.

Hazel shut her mouth, but anger still blazed in her eyes. Larkspur would be able to hear it. No wonder she was going mad.

"You think I'd rather be without my sister than my crutch?" Ivy shook Larkspur gently. "Silly. Of course I wouldn't!"

"I wanted you to walk." Larkspur's voice broke on the last word. She began to cry.

Both hounds sat up, anxious.

Ivy tightened her arm around Larkspur's shoulders. "I'm used to this leg of mine. I never thought I'd be able to walk properly."

"You did think so for the last month," Larkspur sobbed.

"And not for the past twenty-one years," Ivy said firmly. "Stop crying, love. It's upsetting the dogs."

Larkspur drew in a shuddering breath and wiped her eyes with her sleeve.

The misery on her face tore at Ivy's heart. "I love you," she said. "And when my birthday comes I shall be *glad* to use my wish for you. It will give me more joy than anything else could."

Larkspur's lips twisted bitterly. She could read Ivy's thoughts; she knew she wasn't lying.

"Eat," Hazel said abruptly. "I want to see you eat something." Her voice was rough and her eyes suspiciously bright, as if she was trying not to cry.

"I'm not hungry."

"Eat!" Hazel shoved the basket towards Larkspur, her face fierce.

Larkspur obediently rummaged in the basket. She pulled out a slice of rye bread and nibbled on it.

They sat in silence while Larkspur ate. Ivy tried to bury her worry, so Larkspur wouldn't sense it. She focused on the little clearing, on the summer-green grass and the buttercups nodding their bright heads in the faint breeze, on the warble of birdsong. Such a beautiful, golden summer's day. Not long to her birthday. Five days. Five days until she received her Faerie wish.

Larkspur's wish had been a disaster, but Ivy would undo it. All would be well again.

Larkspur finished the piece of bread. She rubbed her fingers on her skirt. "When Mother and Ren return from Dapple Weir . . ." she said, and then fell silent.

Ivy exchanged a glance with Hazel.

"Please don't tell her."

"We can't hide this from her," Ivy said gently.

"She'll be so upset." Larkspur pressed her hands to her head, her fingertips whitening with the pressure. "I couldn't bear it if she came to see me!"

"We shan't bring her," Hazel said hastily. "I promise."

Ivy nodded. *I promise, too,* she said silently.

Larkspur lowered her hands. Her face was wan and miserable. "I wish—" She stiffened, and lifted her head, and stared intently at the forest. "There's a man coming."

Hazel stood hurriedly. "Someone we know?"

"I don't think so."

Ivy reached for her crutch and levered herself to her feet. "Whoever he is, we know he's not an outlaw."

Hazel cast her a grim look. "You think every man in the vale is trustworthy?"

"No. But I don't think there's a man in Dapple Vale foolish enough to go up against Bess and Bartlemay."

Both hounds were on their feet, ears pricked and alert.

"Maybe," Hazel said. "Maybe not." She ducked into the cottage and emerged with a thick wooden stave in her hand.

"Something terrible has happened to him." Larkspur pressed her hands to her temples as if trying to push the man's thoughts out. "He's mad with panic."

"Is he dangerous?" Hazel demanded.

Ivy heard the crackle of someone blundering through the undergrowth. Bess took a stiff-legged step forward, her hackles up, a low growl rumbling in her chest.

"He's terrified." Larkspur's eyes were squeezed shut, her face set in a grimace.

"Then he needs our help," Ivy said. "Bess, Bartlemay—down!"

The hounds obeyed her, but their hackles didn't lower, nor did their growling abate.

The snap and crack of breaking twigs came closer. Ivy saw a dark shape lurch between the tree trunks. She gripped her crutch tightly. *There's nothing to be afraid of,* she told herself firmly. *Whoever this man is, he needs our help.*

But the creature that burst into the clearing wasn't a man. It was a deer.

Ivy stared at the animal. It was a young roebuck, chest heaving, eyes showing their whites, staggering, clearly close to collapse.

Hazel lowered her stave. "That is *not* a man."

"It is!" Larkspur was weeping, clutching her head. "It's a man inside. *It's a man.*"

*C*HAPTER 2

"*B*ess, Bartlemay, stay," Ivy said. She limped towards the roebuck, leaning on her crutch, and lowered her voice: "It's all right. We'll help you."

The young buck shied back, stumbling to one knee.

Ivy paused. "Don't run," she said, quietly. "We mean you no harm."

The roebuck staggered up to all four legs again. She saw how labored his breathing was, how his muscles trembled.

"You can trust us." Ivy took a small step forward. "We want to help you." Another small step. "I promise we'll do you no harm."

This time, the buck didn't shy from her. He stood motionless, panting, watching her slow approach with wary eyes.

When she was close enough to touch him, Ivy halted. She gripped the crutch tightly with her right hand, and reached out with her left.

The buck flinched at her touch, but didn't bolt. His coat was wet, filthy. A rank animal scent came from him: sweat and fear.

"It's all right. You're safe with us."

His ears twitched. Did he understand her words?

Ivy felt his body heat, the tension in his muscles, his

trembling exhaustion. She stroked his shoulder soothingly. There was a man inside this skin. A terrified, panic-stricken man. "We'll go to the Lord Warder," she told him softly. "He knows more about Faerie magic than anyone. If it's possible to restore you to yourself, he'll know."

Perhaps the buck did understand her. He leaned against her hip. A sound came from his throat. A groan? A sob? Ivy had no word for the sound, but she heard the anguish in it. She bent and hugged him gently. "It will be all right," she whispered into his damp, mud-flecked ear. "I promise."

"He needs to go," Hazel said behind her, her voice urgent. "*Now.* Larkspur can't cope with this."

Ivy straightened and glanced back at the cottage. Larkspur sat hunched on the doorstep, her head buried in her arms. Her body was taut with distress—elbows, wrists, white-knuckled fingers.

"Look after her," Ivy said. "I'll take him home."

Ivy was almost at the forest edge before Hazel caught up with her. "Larkspur's asleep and the dogs are on guard." Hazel was red-cheeked and panting. She caught her breath and turned her attention to the buck. "Faerie magic, hmm? I wonder what he did to deserve this?"

"Whoever he is, whatever he's done, he's been punished enough."

"Or maybe not. He could be dangerous, Ivy."

"Not now, he isn't. He's suffering. And he needs help."

Hazel ducked beneath a branch and ceded this with a shrug.

"Can you find his home? Find his family?"

"Oh! I hadn't thought of that." Hazel halted. Her eyes narrowed and became slightly unfocused.

Ivy leaned on the crutch, watching her sister's face.

Hazel blinked. Her brow creased. "Odd. There's just . . . nothing. My gift can't find his home or even where he was born. It's as if he doesn't exist."

"The man he was no longer exists."

Hazel grimaced agreement. She started walking again. "I'll take him to Dappleward. Will you be all right alone tonight?"

"I won't be alone," Ivy said, hobbling alongside her sister. "He'll stay with me."

Hazel frowned. "But he's a *man*."

"He won't make it to Dapple Meadow. The Lord Warder will have to come to him."

They both looked at the buck. He walked with his head hanging, stumbling over the tree roots, each step a small lurch.

Hazel blew out a breath. "I don't like it," she muttered.

They came to the edge of Glade Forest. A sunlit meadow lay before them. On its far side was a small thatched cottage with a henhouse, a beehive, and a privy. "Home," Ivy said aloud, and patted the roebuck's shoulder.

The animal halted, lifted his head, and stood swaying on unsteady legs.

"We could take him to the village," Hazel said. "Let someone there look after him."

"We'd have to tell them about Larkspur, else they wouldn't believe us."

Hazel pressed her lips together. She didn't say what they were both thinking: *We have sworn oaths to Dappleward not to reveal our Faerie wishes to anyone.* Conflicting emotions wrestled on her face. "If only Mother and Ren were here!" she burst out.

"They're not, so we do the best we can," Ivy said. "It's not as terrible as it seems. Larkspur will be rid of her gift shortly, and the Lord Warder will know how to help this poor creature."

Hazel glanced at her crutch, but didn't say the words: *And you will still be lame.*

Ivy pretended she hadn't seen the glance. "And think, you'll see Tam tomorrow."

Happiness usually lit Hazel's face when the Lord Warder's youngest son was mentioned. This time, it didn't; she frowned at the roebuck.

Ivy set off across the meadow. "He stinks," Hazel said, when they neared the little brook. "If he's coming inside, he needs a wash."

"He's coming inside."

"Well, then . . ." Hazel turned to the buck, hands on hips. "Into the water with you."

The buck glanced at the brook, flicked his ears, and obeyed, picking his way cautiously over the stones. So, he *did* understand what was said to him.

Hazel fetched a bucket and scrubbing brush and washed the roebuck ruthlessly. The animal didn't resist, just stood motionless, his head down, exhausted. Each of his ribs was visible. Had he eaten since his transformation into an animal?

Ivy limped into the cottage. The hearth fire was almost dead. She fed twigs into the embers until they flamed again. "Burn well for us," she said, laying dry wood on the fire. "We need you."

She went to the door and watched Hazel and the roebuck emerge from the brook. Hazel was almost as wet as the deer. She'd done a good job; the buck's coat was clean and sleek.

Hazel upended the bucket, laid the scrubbing brush on top, and entered the cottage, her tread brisk. "I'll get changed," she said over her shoulder, vanishing into the bedchamber, "then be off."

The buck followed cautiously, placing his hooves with care, flicking wary glances around. Ivy tried to see the room as he did: small and shadowy, furnished with a trestle table and stools, with two small unglazed windows tucked under the eaves.

Did it feel safe to him, or did it feel like a trap? She thought the man in him would find it safe; the beast, a trap.

"Lie down by the hearth," Ivy told the buck. "Get dry."

He obeyed, bending his legs awkwardly, lowering himself to the rush-covered floor.

"Are you hungry?" she asked.

The buck glanced at her with liquid brown eyes, and dipped his head in a nod.

Ivy looked at him thoughtfully. "I'm guessing you can't eat meat in that form . . . and that you'd prefer milk to grass. Shall we see?"

They kept their milk cooling in a pail in the brook. It required balance to haul the pail out, leaning on the crutch, and care to lug it inside without slopping milk. Ivy set it down by the hearth. "Goat's milk," she said. "See if you can drink that."

The roebuck sniffed the pail, his black nostrils flaring, and staggered to his feet. He bent his head and lapped eagerly.

Ivy eased down to sit on a stool. She watched him, and kneaded her aching kneecap. Yes, he'd been hungry.

When the pail was empty, the roebuck lifted his head and looked at her. He heaved a huge sigh and came across to her and nudged her arm gently with his nose.

"Are you saying thank you?" Ivy stroked his damp, velvety head. His antlers were short and unbranched, only a few inches long. "You're welcome. There's plenty more where that came from. I'll warm it for you next time, and sweeten it with honey."

The roebuck sighed again. She heard his weariness, his despair.

Ivy put an arm around his neck and hugged him. "We'll do all in our power to help you, I promise. Now, go lie down by the fire. Rest."

The buck went back to the hearth and curled his long legs up under him, laying his chin on the rushes.

Hazel emerged from the bedchamber with her wet smock and kirtle over her arm. Her gaze skipped to the empty pail. "He drank all that?"

"He was hungry. I'll hang those out to dry." Ivy held out her hand for the clothes. "Go."

"Not yet."

"He needs help!"

"And so do you. You need firewood. And what are you going to feed him? More milk? Then I need to milk the goats."

Ivy bit her lip. Hazel was right; she needed help. She always would. *If not for this wretched leg of mine* . . . Ivy shoved the thought hastily aside, glad Larkspur hadn't been close enough to hear it.

It was an hour before Hazel consented to leave. Several days' worth of firewood was chopped and stacked beside the hearth and two full pails of goat's milk sat cooling in the brook. "I'll be back as soon as I can," Hazel said. "The day after tomorrow. Be careful!"

"And you."

Ivy watched until Hazel was out of sight, striding briskly. Merry, laughing, confident Hazel—who hadn't laughed once in the past week. None of them had. Ivy stifled a sigh, and closed the door and latched it. She turned to look at the roebuck. He lay by the fire, curled up tightly, watching her with solemn eyes.

Ivy limped across to him. "Don't look so worried," she said, bending to pat him as if he were a dog. His damp pelt shivered beneath her touch. "You're cold, poor creature."

She fetched a blanket and laid it over him. "Go to sleep. Don't worry; everything's going to be all right."

*C*HAPTER 3

*I*vy woke abruptly. Darkness surrounded her. Her straining ears heard only silence. No soft breathing from her sisters. No snorts from the dogs. Was she alone in the cottage?

A sound cut the air, a breathy, agonized gasp, almost a scream.

Ivy sat bolt upright. Memory returned in a fierce flood: the roebuck.

"I'm coming," she cried, fumbling for her crutch. "I'm coming!"

The fire had died down to a bed of embers, casting a warm glow. The roebuck writhed on the hearth. His long neck arched back, his slender sharp-hooved legs kicked out, the gasping scream came again, torn from his throat. Was he convulsing? Dying?

Ivy hurried to him, avoiding the flailing legs. She couldn't kneel, so she flung herself down on the rushes behind him. "Roebuck!" she cried, reaching for him. Beneath his pelt, his muscles were rigid. A shudder tore through him. He twisted, writhed, screamed again.

Ivy held on to him, her arms around his heaving ribcage. If he was dying, at least he'd have the comfort of not dying alone.

A huge convulsion wracked the roebuck's body. She felt

his muscles knot and twist. His very bones seemed to wrench apart. He screamed again—a human sound, raw with agony. Abruptly, it was no deer's pelt beneath her hands, but smooth human skin. The ribcage she hugged was a man's, not an animal's.

Ivy inhaled in wonder. The spell was broken!

The man, whoever he was, lay gasping for breath, shuddering—and stark naked. Ivy was suddenly aware that she wore only a thin linen smock, and that she was alone in the cottage with this stranger. There were no dogs to protect her. No Hazel.

Fear prickled up her spine. She stopped hugging him and tried to inch back on the rushes, but the man turned and caught her wrist.

Panic flared in her chest—and then Ivy recognized his face in the glow from the embers. "Gods," she said, involuntarily.

She'd last seen this man less than a fortnight ago. Then, she'd thought him unnervingly attractive, with his quiet composure and alert, intelligent gaze. He'd been reserved, almost stern—until one saw the hint of a smile in the watchful gray eyes. Composure and reserve were stripped from him now; in their place were confusion and distress.

No, this man wasn't dangerous. Just suffering almost beyond human endurance.

Ivy relaxed her wrist in his grasp. "It's all right," she said. "I know it hurts, but you're human again."

He released her. His face twisted. Tears tracked down his cheeks.

"Hush," Ivy said softly, gathering him in her arms. "It's all right."

He didn't pull away. He leaned into her and cried like a child, deeply, utterly, and without inhibition. Ivy held him tightly, rocking him, stroking his hair, stroking the nape of his neck, whispering soothing words. *Hush, hush, it's all right now.* Gradually the tremors wracking his body eased; slowly his breathing steadied. The sobs quieted. He lay limp and exhausted in her arms. Ivy pressed a silent kiss into his tousled dark hair. "Go to sleep," she whispered.

"Where am I?" His voice was hoarse. "*Who* am I?"

"You don't know who you are?"

"No." He pulled away from her. His cheeks were damp, his eyelashes spiky with tears. "Do you?"

"You're Hugh Dappleward."

His brow creased. "Who?"

"Hugh Dappleward. Eldest son of Guy Dappleward, Lord Warder of Dapple Vale." At his blank look, she went on: "Do you remember Tam? Your brother?"

He shook his head—and froze. She saw it on his face: memory rushing through him like an avalanche.

Hugh clutched his head and doubled over. Ivy gathered him in her arms again. His body shook helplessly. His breathing was short, gasped. She tried to imagine what it must be like for him—the flood of memories forcing their way into his head, layer upon layer of people and places and names and events. It would be dizzying, painful, overwhelming. "Lie down," she told him. "Lie down, Hugh."

He obeyed, still clutching his head.

Ivy stretched out on the rushes alongside him and held him close. She didn't speak, didn't whisper soothing words. Silence was what he needed, while this deluge of memory engulfed him. She held him and waited.

The embers in the fire stirred and subsided with sighing sounds. Gradually Hugh's body stopped shaking. His breathing became easier. Was he sorting through his memories? Putting them in order in his head?

"I know you," he said, after several minutes. "Don't I?"

"We've met once. Almost two weeks ago. Your brother is marrying my sister at midsummer."

Hugh was silent for another minute, and then said, "Ivy. Widow Miller's daughter."

"That's right."

"Ivy . . ." His voice was hoarse, bewildered. "Ivy, what's happened to me?"

"You don't remember?"

"No."

Ivy stroked the nape of his neck comfortingly. "Some kind of Faerie magic. We found you in the woods today. You were a roebuck."

"A roebuck?" Hugh sounded even more bewildered.

"You changed back into a man, just now."

"That's why it hurt so much." He shivered in memory. "Gods, it *hurt*."

"It's over now." She pressed a kiss to Hugh's cheek, tasting the salt of his tears, and then caught herself. He was no child to be comforted with kisses. She drew back, but Hugh's arms came around her. His mouth sought hers.

Ivy's heartbeat tripped over itself, then sped up.

Hugh kissed her roughly, fiercely, desperately. He tasted of tears, of salt and anguish—a taste that made her heart clench in her chest. Ivy tilted her face to him and returned his kiss shyly.

Whenever she'd let herself imagine what her first kiss might be like, she'd imagined sunshine. Sunshine, and a kiss that was soft and gentle and sweet. Hugh's kiss was no soft, sweet, sunshiny kiss; it was fumbling and passionate and exciting, a clash of mouths in the almost-dark. A minute sped past. A second minute. Ivy learned to delve into Hugh's mouth with her tongue, learned to match each deep, breathless kiss with one of her own.

Urgency grew between them. Hugh's kiss became fiercer, more desperate. He rocked his hips against her. Pleasure jolted through Ivy. She uttered an incoherent sound and pressed herself closer to him.

The kiss became even fiercer. Hugh rocked against her again—once, twice, thrice. More pleasure jolted through her. Ivy gasped for breath, and rocked urgently back. *Bed me,* she thought. *Bed me, Hugh Dappleward.*

As if he'd heard her, Hugh tore his mouth free and rolled her under him, pushing up her linen smock.

Oh, *yes*. Ivy arched herself against him.

Hugh settled himself between her thighs, one arm around her waist, tilting her hips to him. Ivy felt his organ, hot and hard, nudging for admittance. Anticipation shuddered through her.

Oh, yes. She may have uttered those words aloud, breathless and eager—or she may not have. She felt feverish, almost witless, consumed with a frantic, burning passion.

Hugh drove into her.

There was an instant of pain, but Ivy had lived with pain most of her life, and this pain was sharp and swiftly over, and after the pain came pleasure, a primitive, animal pleasure that made her groan. Hugh's weight on her, the thrust of his organ inside her, the rhythm he set . . .

The wild, primitive pleasure built until Ivy felt that she might burst with it—and Hugh drove deeply into her again—and again—and she splintered with a pleasure so intense it could almost be called pain, bucking under him, her fingers digging deeply into his biceps.

Ivy lost herself for a few moments. Dimly, she heard Hugh groan, dimly, she felt him shudder. Clarity slowly returned. Hugh lay relaxed on her, warm and heavy. His breath was ragged in her ear.

She felt almost like crying. With wonder. With joy. Here, on the rushes, with Hugh Dappleward, she didn't feel lame at all. She felt like a woman, not a cripple. She felt *whole*.

Ivy tilted her head and pressed her face to the curve of Hugh's neck, inhaling his scent.

Hugh caught his breath and stiffened, and then he pushed abruptly away from her, scrambling back on the rushes. "Gods—I didn't mean to— Oh, gods!"

Ivy's joy congealed into a cold, hard lump in her belly. She pulled the linen smock down over her knees and sat up. *Don't be embarrassed by what just happened,* she told herself firmly. *If you're not embarrassed, he won't be.* "It's all right," she said.

"All right? Gods, I *forced* myself on you!"

Ivy blinked. "Nonsense."

"I'll marry you," Hugh said, his voice frantic. "Of course I'll marry you!"

Marry Hugh Dappleward? *Oh, yes,* said a wistful voice in her head. "Don't be absurd," Ivy said aloud.

"But I *forced*—"

"Hugh Dappleward, calm down." She wanted to take him by the scruff of the neck and shake him; instead, she caught his wrist. "I wanted that as much as you did."

The room wasn't so dark that she couldn't see Hugh shake his head, couldn't see the repudiation on his face. "Not that rough."

Had it been rough? It had certainly been animal and primitive, but not brutal, not violent. "I didn't think it was rough." Ivy released his wrist and found her crutch and climbed to her feet.

Hugh watched her stand. His mouth became tighter. "I hurt you, didn't I?"

"No." Ivy flicked her plait over her shoulder. "Are you hungry?"

"Hungry?" Hugh gave a flat, bitter bark of laughter.

Ivy leaned on the crutch and looked down at him. "Well? Are you?"

He was silent a moment, his head bowed. "I'm starving," he said, in a low voice.

*C*HAPTER 4

*I*vy lit fresh rushlights and added more wood to the fire. Hugh sat silently on the floor while she warmed some pottage. His expression was closed, hiding his thoughts as the blanket hid his nudity. When the pottage was hot, Ivy ladled it into a bowl. Peas and oats, bacon and herbs. "Here," she said, placing it on the table.

Hugh climbed to his feet, staggered, and almost fell.

"Hugh!" Ivy said, reaching for her crutch.

"I'm fine," he said, in a hoarse voice. "Just need to get my balance."

He stood for a moment, swaying, and then walked to the table, each step almost a lurch.

"How long were you a roebuck?" Ivy asked, as he sat carefully. He looked like a drunk man, his movements cautious and over-large.

"I don't know," Hugh said, not looking at her. "I don't remember."

"Your face is clean-shaven."

"It is?" He raised a hand and touched his cheek. "I don't . . . remember when I did that."

"Eat," Ivy said, handing him a spoon.

Hugh took it silently. After a moment, he dipped it in the pottage.

He'd claimed to be starving, but he made no move to lift the spoon to his mouth. "What's wrong?" Ivy asked. Had he forgotten how to use a spoon?

"Wrong?" Hugh shoved the bowl away. "Ivy, I practically raped you, and now you're sitting here feeding me as if nothing happened!"

Ivy placed the bowl in front of him again, calmly. "You're being nonsensical."

"Curse it, Ivy, I know what just happened!"

"No, I don't think you do. I wanted to have sex with you, and I enjoyed it as much as you did, and there is nothing more to say about it. Now eat, before your food goes cold."

"I didn't even *ask* you!"

"Yes, you did." He'd asked her with his body—with his kisses and the rocking of his hips—and she had answered him the same way.

Hugh blinked. Confusion crossed his face. "I did?"

"Yes," Ivy said. "Now, eat."

Hugh blinked a second time. After a moment, he picked up the spoon again. He hesitated, then dipped the spoon in the bowl.

Hugh ate silently. Ivy sat at the table with him and looked down at her folded hands and gave herself a brisk talking to. She was a grown woman; why should she not enjoy physical congress with a man? *I am not embarrassed by it*, she told herself. *And I do not regret it.*

What she did regret was that Hugh regretted it.

She glanced at him out of the corner of her eye. Hugh Dappleward. She'd known him by reputation for years. Men spoke of him highly. He was like his father, it was said. A man who took his responsibilities seriously. A man who listened

176

and observed, who thought before acting. A man people respected.

He hadn't thought before acting tonight, but then neither had she.

Ivy suppressed a sigh. She studied her hands for another minute—and then glanced at Hugh again.

She'd seen him from a distance when he'd visited Dapple Bend with his father, but only met him twelve days ago, on the occasion of Hazel and Tam's betrothal. He'd been surrounded by his brother and father and cousin and his father's liegemen, the Ironfists, but he'd drawn her attention. She'd liked him far too much. Liked his stern, dark face, his watchful gray eyes, his reserve—and especially liked his rare smile. When he'd smiled, it had made her heart turn over in her chest.

The Hugh who sat at her table dressed in a blanket was a different Hugh entirely, weary and haggard, a man pushed almost to his limits by pain and anguish. And shame. Shame because he'd had frantic, desperate, unthinking sex with her on the rush-strewn floor.

Ivy let her gaze rest on his face. He looked heartbreakingly vulnerable, his disheveled dark hair falling forward over his brow.

Hugh Dappleward, I could easily love you, she thought.

But she could never marry him. Hugh would be Lord Warder of Dapple Vale one day. A huge responsibility. A burden, even. The last thing he needed was a cripple for a wife. Hugh needed a strong woman, a woman he could lean on, a woman who would be able to help him—not one who needed help herself.

Ivy looked down at the tabletop. If Larkspur's gift hadn't proved so disastrous—

No, she wouldn't think of that, wouldn't allow herself to fall into regret and bitterness, any more than she would allow herself to fall into useless embarrassment.

Hugh laid down the spoon. The bowl was empty.

"Would you like more?" Ivy asked.

He shook his head, not meeting her eyes. "No, thank you."

Ivy leaned her elbows on the table. "Hugh . . . how did you become a roebuck? What happened?"

Hugh pushed the empty bowl away. "I don't remember."

"It's Faerie magic," Ivy said. "But *you* of all people wouldn't have done anything to earn a punishment like that!"

Hugh glanced at her and grimaced slightly, but said nothing.

"Can you think of anyone who wishes you ill? Someone who might know about Faerie magic?"

"No one who wishes me ill . . . that I know of." He rubbed his face.

"And people who know about Faerie magic?" Ivy persisted.

"Outside of my family, and the Ironfists . . . no one."

"The Ironfists?" Memory gave her a picture of the Ironfists, father and son: big, bearded, brutal-looking men. "Could it be one of them? Cadoc?"

"Cadoc? No!" Hugh shook his head sharply. "Cadoc isn't capable of something like this. I trust him as I trust my brother." He closed his eyes. He looked utterly exhausted.

"You need to sleep." Ivy reached for her crutch and stood. "We've four beds."

Hugh pushed slowly to his feet—she thought she almost heard his bones creak with weariness—and walked to the bedchamber, each step a half-lurch, and hesitated in the doorway.

She saw the room through his eyes for a moment—a small, cramped, dark space with four narrow straw mattresses side by side on the floor, and a wooden chest crammed into the corner.

"I can't sleep in here with you," Hugh said quietly.

"Well, *I* can't shift those mattresses, and neither can you right now; you can barely stand!"

Hugh turned away from the door. "I'll sleep by the fire."

"Hugh . . ." But there was nothing Ivy could do to halt him. All she could do was watch helplessly as he walked back to the fire and slowly lurched to his knees in front of the hearth.

"Go to bed, Ivy. I promise I won't disturb you."

Ivy jerked awake. The bedchamber was dark. The echo of a scream seemed to ring in her ears. Dream? Or reality?

She sat up, disquieted, groping for her crutch.

The scream came again, raw with pain—and very real.

"Hugh? Hugh!" Ivy scrambled from the bed and lunged for the door, moving as fast as the crutch allowed her. "Hugh!"

Hugh lay in front of the fire, his body jerking in helpless agony. His back bowed, he screamed again—and a roebuck lay on the rushes, flailing its legs.

"No!" Ivy cried. She hobbled across the room.

The buck convulsed, writhed, screamed an animal scream.

"No!" Ivy cried again. She threw herself down beside the roebuck and flung her arms around him.

The buck's thrashing stilled. Deep tremors racked his body. His breathing was labored.

"Hugh . . ." Ivy hugged him. "Hugh . . . please come back!" But words had no power to alter what had happened. Light crept through the cracks in the shutters. Day broke. And Hugh remained a roebuck.

CHAPTER 5

$\mathcal{I}$vy picked her way slowly through the forest, leaning on her crutch, a basket of food hooked over her left arm. Beside her, very subdued, walked the roebuck. "Mother saved the life of a Faerie child. In return, she was granted wishes, and one of them was that we—Hazel and Larkspur and I—would each receive a Faerie wish on our next birthdays. Your father knows. He swore us to secrecy." Ivy bit her lip, and glanced at the roebuck. "Did he tell you? Do you remember?"

Hugh dipped his head in a nod.

Ivy released her breath in a sigh and ducked under a low-reaching branch. "For her wish, Hazel chose to be able to find people and things, and Larkspur . . . Larkspur is wary of marriage. Mother was crippled because Father beat her, and it was Father who broke my leg, and Larkspur's afraid she'll make the same mistake Mother did and choose the wrong husband. She wished for a Faerie gift that would let her know her suitors' true natures, and the Faerie . . . the Faerie *tricked* her, gave her the ability to hear people's thoughts, and it's driving Larkspur *mad*—" Ivy made herself pause, made herself take a deep breath and continue calmly. "The gift came in slowly. Larkspur was all right the first day, but the second

180

day it grew stronger, as if it needed to take root before it could flower properly, and since then . . .

"She hears everyone's thoughts, whatever they're thinking about, memories, emotions, everything. She can't shut it out. It drove her half-mad, before we thought to take her into the woods. She's been living in an abandoned woodcutter's cottage this past week. Hazel and I visit her each day. It's where we found you. Larkspur heard your thoughts. She knew you were a man."

The roebuck glanced at her with dark, liquid eyes. What was Hugh thinking, trapped inside that body?

"Only Hazel and I know about Larkspur's . . . problem. Mother left for Dapple Weir the day after Larkspur's birthday—her new husband has family there, and they've gone to visit." Ivy eyed the roebuck. "You know about my mother's transformation? She has her youth back and she's married Ren Blacksmith."

Hugh nodded again, and picked his way delicately over the tree roots.

Ivy blew out a breath. "My birthday's in four days. Mother will be back for that." Her mother would be back because she wanted to see Ivy walk freely again—which wasn't going to happen. "I shall use my wish to save Larkspur."

They came to a tiny creek, barely more than a trickle of water. Hazel always stepped lightly over it. The roebuck did, too. Usually Ivy managed to cross with dry feet, but today, with the basket of food, she was more awkward than usual. She gave up trying to keep her shoes dry and hobbled through the shallow water, embarrassed by her ungainliness, feeling her cheeks flush.

The roebuck watched solemnly. What was Hugh thinking?

"If Larkspur finds your presence upsetting . . . would you mind waiting for me in the woods? I promise I won't leave you there."

Hugh ducked his head in a nod.

"Thank you." Ivy peered ahead through the trees. "The cottage is just past that oak. Don't be afraid of the dogs. We won't let them attack you."

Larkspur was waiting beneath the oak tree. How long had she known they were coming? One minute? Five minutes?

"Keep hold of the dogs, love," Ivy called, and then saw that Larkspur was already gripping each hound by the scruff of its neck.

She limped as fast as she could, anxiously assessing her sister. Larkspur had always been slender, but in the past week she had gone from slenderness to a frightening, hollow-cheeked fragility.

Ivy put down the basket and hugged Larkspur. *Know how much I love you,* she thought. *Know that I would do anything for you.* She released her sister, and smoothed the white-blonde hair back from her face. "How are you, love?"

"Fine."

Hugh had halted half a dozen steps back. He eyed the red-brown hounds warily. They eyed him back with the tense eagerness of hunters seeing prey.

"Bartlemay, Bess . . ." Ivy waited until she had both hounds' full attention, then pointed to the roebuck and said firmly: "Friend."

The hounds lost their taut-muscled intentness.

"Stand still," Ivy told the roebuck. "Don't run." And then, to Larkspur, she thought, *Release them.*

The hounds advanced on Hugh, Bess suspicious, Bartlemay with eager curiosity. They were both as large as the roebuck.

Hugh stood very still, his ears pricked stiffly, his eyes wide. The hounds circled him, sniffing. Satisfied he was no threat, Bess trotted back to Larkspur. A moment later, Bartlemay followed suit.

"Does his presence disturb you? He'll wait back in the forest, if it does."

Larkspur shook her head. "He's much calmer today." And then her eyebrows rose sharply. "He's Hugh Dappleward?"

182

Whose head had Larkspur plucked that knowledge from? "Yes," Ivy said. "He returned to his own shape for a few hours last night." And, despite her best efforts not to think of it, memory of their frenzied lovemaking leapt to the forefront of her mind.

Larkspur's eyes widened with alarm. Her lips parted.

Don't! Ivy said silently. *Don't speak of it.*

Larkspur closed her mouth and bit her lip. She glanced warily at the roebuck.

What was Hugh thinking right now? That he'd forced her into something she hadn't wanted? That he'd been rough and unrestrained? That he'd hurt her?

He is ashamed of last night, but he has no reason to be, Ivy told Larkspur silently. *I wanted it as much as he did, and I enjoyed it as much as he did.* And even though she tried not to feel embarrassed making that admission, she did.

She looked for censure on Larkspur's face, and instead found deep worry.

Don't worry about me, Ivy thought firmly. She held out the basket, and managed a smile. "I brought some food. Are you hungry?"

They stayed for only an hour; an hour was the longest Larkspur could cope with having other people's thoughts filling her head. "Do you think Hugh will change into himself tonight?" Larkspur asked, when Ivy reached for her crutch.

"It's possible." Ivy looked at the roebuck. He lay curled up in the sunshine, watching them. "I don't know whether to hope for it or not. It *hurts* him so."

"If he does . . . will you be all right?"

Ivy glanced at her, and saw anxiety in her eyes. "I shall be perfectly safe," she said, giving her sister's cool fingers a reassuring squeeze. And if Hugh did become human again, and if he had the same fierce need for sex, she would be glad of it.

Larkspur eyed her uncertainly.

It's true, Ivy told her silently. She felt her cheeks grow warm with embarrassment, but along with the embarrassment was an edge of defensiveness. Why should she not enjoy sex? She was a grown woman.

"Take one of the dogs. Please."

"No."

"But—"

"If he *does* change . . ." She remembered Hugh's agonized screams, the way he'd flailed, thrashed, convulsed. "It would terrify the dogs. Best that they stay here with you, love."

Larkspur's face became even paler. "Is it that bad?" she whispered.

Ivy grimaced. "Yes." She climbed to her feet. "Take care of yourself, love. I'll come and see you tomorrow. And remember to *eat.*"

Larkspur stood, too. So did the hounds. So did Hugh.

Ivy hugged Larkspur tightly. "Only four more days."

C HAPTER 6

$\mathcal{H}$ e was dying, being ripped apart, his skin flayed from his flesh, his muscles shredding, bones snapping. Hugh screamed, and screamed, and screamed again.

After an eternity, the agony waned and became merely pain. Hugh lay panting, gasping, sobbing.

The pain faded until only an ache remained.

Hugh's senses sorted slowly through his surroundings. He lay on a floor in a dimly lit room, curled up on his side. Rushes pressed against his right cheek. Someone held him from behind, arms around his ribcage, hands splayed across his chest, forehead pressed to his shoulder blade.

Where was he? *Who* was he?

His breathing steadied—and his awareness of himself firmed. He knew who he was, knew where he was. And he knew who was holding him so tightly.

Hugh swallowed. His throat felt raw from screaming and his voice, when he spoke, was little more than a hoarse whisper. "Ivy?"

"Hugh?" Her breath caught in a sob. She sat up and leaned over him. "Are you all right?"

He rolled over slowly, stiffly, trying—and failing—to choke back a groan. Every muscle in his body hurt. He saw Ivy's face in the firelight, wet with tears. "Don't cry," he whispered.

"It was worse that time, wasn't it?"

His mind flinched from the question. He didn't want to think about how much worse it had been. "Don't cry," he said, reaching for her.

Ivy didn't recoil from him. She came into his embrace and let him gather her in his arms.

Hugh held her, while the ache faded into nothing. His body began to wake up. He was aware of Ivy's cheek pillowed on his chest and her soft hair tickling his throat.

He couldn't stop himself stroking her hair. Such beautiful hair. The color of midnight, dark and mysterious. Silky soft. He pictured Ivy's face—her ivory skin, her cool, green eyes, her full, sweet mouth. Heat flushed through his body. His cock stirred.

Hugh stopped stroking her hair. He released her and turned away, fumbling for the blanket on the floor. "Ivy, go back to your room."

"Why?"

"Because I said so." Hugh drew the blanket around him, hiding his nudity. His cock stirred again, and began to harden. It had been like this last night, too—the uncontrollable arousal, as if his body had thought itself dying, and now finding itself unexpectedly alive, wanted sex. Affirmation of life at its most basic.

Hugh gritted his teeth. He might not have control over the arousal, but he had control over whether he surrendered to it or not. "Ivy, go to your room."

Ivy didn't move. "Do you . . . um, do you need sex?"

"No," Hugh said firmly. "Please go to your room."

Still, Ivy didn't move. He heard her take a deep breath. "Because if you do need it—if you *want* it . . . I wouldn't mind."

Hugh squeezed his eyes shut. *Gods,* but it was tempting. His cock was fully hard now, rising from its nest of hair. He thought of the sweet slenderness of Ivy's body, thought of her mouth, so soft, so kissable.

And then he remembered last night. He'd rutted her like an animal, straining for release, rougher than he'd ever been with any woman in his life.

Shame rose in him. "No," he said harshly. "Go, Ivy."

Ivy still didn't move. "We're both adults. Why shouldn't we do it, if we both want to?"

Because his need was too urgent. Because he was afraid he'd be rough again. Because even though he wore his own body, a remnant of the beast still lingered in him.

"There would be no obligation between us."

Hugh opened his eyes and turned his head and stared at her in disbelief. No obligation? His obligation to Ivy was already more than he could repay. He owed her shelter and food, safety and sanctuary. He owed her kindness. He owed her physical pleasure that was sweet and tender.

He owed her marriage.

The muscles in his groin and abdomen clenched. His balls contracted with painful need. Hugh gritted his teeth and struggled to breathe.

"You think that what happened last night is something to be ashamed of," Ivy said seriously. "Well, it's not. It was something perfectly natural that both of us enjoyed." Her cheeks flushed, and her gaze dropped slightly. "I see no reason why we shouldn't do it again tonight . . . if . . . if both of us wish to." Her blush deepened, and she looked down at the floor and picked up a rush and turned it over in her fingers, and said diffidently, "Do you wish to?"

Yes, he did. More than anything in the world.

Hugh unclenched his jaw and dragged a ragged breath into his lungs. "The beast is still in me a little."

Ivy looked up and met his eyes. "You didn't hurt me last night. Or frighten me. And you won't tonight."

Hugh spread the blanket on the rushes. His hands trembled and his heart beat fast in his chest. He knelt and looked at Ivy, seated in front of the hearth, watching him. Gods, but she was beautiful—the sweet mouth and cool, dark eyes, the quiet composure. His body craved her. His heart craved her. His soul craved her.

Hugh swallowed the lump in his throat and reached for her slowly, giving her the chance to draw back. She didn't.

He dipped his head and kissed her.

He'd kissed Ivy last night—that, he remembered—but his kisses had been fierce and unrestrained. Tonight, he kissed her as she deserved to be kissed: softly, lovingly.

Ivy kissed him back with shy, trusting eagerness. The shyness, the trust, almost undid him. How could Ivy trust him when he barely trusted himself?

Gods give me strength, Hugh prayed silently, and pressed his lips to Ivy's mouth, her cheeks, her throat. His trembling need became more urgent. He laid Ivy down on the blanket. *Slow, slow, slow,* he told himself, but slowness was beyond him; the best he could do was to dampen his urgency to polite, fumbling haste.

He slid the linen smock up, baring her slender legs, the triangle of dark hair, the curve of her waist. His cock strained. *Slow, slow, slow.* Hugh ignored the temptation of those dark curls and laid one trembling hand on Ivy's midriff. Such smooth skin.

He pushed the smock higher, choking back a groan at the sight of her breasts. Never had he seen more perfect breasts, beautifully rounded, gilded by firelight.

Hugh touched one of them with reverent, shaking fingers, stroked up the soft curve to the taut pink nipple, and bent his head and kissed where his fingers had been. The scent of Ivy's skin pushed him close to the edge of his fragile self-control. Urgency overtook him. He kissed her breasts greedily, using his teeth, his tongue. He kissed her belly, her hipbone, her inner thighs. Muscles fluttered beneath her skin. Hugh slid his fingers through the dark, curling hair—*slow, slow*—parted her nether lips and delved inside her. She was hot and tight and slick with juices.

Gods give me strength, Hugh prayed again, silently, and bent his head and tasted her with his tongue.

Ivy's scent, her sweet-salty flavor, forced a groan from him. His cock lunged against his belly, straining with need. The last shreds of Hugh's control deserted him. He settled himself between her legs, slid one arm around her waist, tilted her hips to him.

Their lovemaking was frantic, almost wild, their bodies striving together. Hugh lost all sense of time and place and who he was, or even what he was—man or beast or both. Dimly, distantly, he felt Ivy convulse beneath him, and then a brutal orgasm wrenched through him, almost making him scream.

Afterwards, he lay panting, shuddering—and ashamed of himself. That hadn't been how he'd wanted to make love to Ivy.

So, do it over, a voice whispered in his head.

Hugh considered this while his breathing steadied. He felt fully in control of himself now, as if that painful climax had driven the last of the beast from him.

Ivy stirred, and pulled away. "Are you hungry?"

"No."

"Not hungry? But you've hardly eaten all day. You need—"

"Not yet." Hugh cupped her nape in his hand and kissed her gently.

This time, it went how he wanted. He drew out Ivy's pleasure, making her whimper and gasp. She climaxed three times, once to his mouth, once to his fingers, and once with his cock inside her. His own climax, when it came, rolled over him endlessly, until he thought it would never stop.

At last, the echoing tingles of pleasure dissipated. Hugh gathered Ivy close and bowed his head so that his brow touched hers. Emotions swelled in his chest: tenderness, a sense of wonder, and something more. Love. He loved Ivy Miller. "When this spell is broken, I'll marry you," he said. "I promise."

Ivy stiffened beneath him. "No." She pushed at his shoulder.

Hugh rolled off her. "Ivy—"

"No obligation. Don't you remember?" She pulled down her smock.

"But—"

"You didn't marry that widow in Dapple Meadow, did you?"

"What?"

"That pretty widow you were friendly with. You didn't marry her."

Hugh stared at Ivy in appalled disbelief. "How do you know about her?"

"The whole vale knew about her. You're the Lord Warder's son. People talk about you. You and Tam both."

Heat rose in Hugh's face. "I didn't marry Beatrice because she didn't want me to." Beatrice had wanted a lover, not another husband. She'd made that clear from the start.

"Well, neither do I. Where's my crutch?"

Hugh handed it to her, and tried to gather his scattered wits. The whole of Dapple Vale had known about Beatrice?

With effort, he stopped his thoughts from veering down this track. Beatrice had been more than two years ago. What was important, right now, was Ivy.

Ivy climbed to her feet. "Would you like some food?"

What he wanted was to marry her.

Hugh stood, lurched, and almost fell. For a moment, the floor tilted alarmingly beneath his feet—and then everything settled into place: trestle table, stools, fireplace. He bent cautiously and picked up the blanket, shook it out, and wrapped it around himself, swaying slightly.

"Would you like some food?" Ivy asked again.

His balance became more firm. "Yes. Look, Ivy—"

"No."

"But I *owe*—"

"No, you don't." Ivy calmly ladled pottage into a bowl.

"But—"

"I'm not the wife for you, Hugh Dappleward." Ivy placed the bowl on the trestle table, and laid a spoon alongside. "A Lord Warder shouldn't have a cripple for a wife. Eat."

Hugh crossed silently to the table. How could Ivy be so cursed calm about this? He sat and picked up the spoon and turned it over in his fingers. "What if you're pregnant?"

"I doubt I am. But if I am, then we deal with it later. Don't worry about it now, Hugh. You have problems enough as it is."

When he'd eaten the pottage, Ivy sliced rye bread and cold meat. "Eat," she said, placing it in front of him.

Hugh eyed the plate. "I don't know that I can."

"You need to. You're thinner than you were—and who knows how long this spell will last?"

Soberly, Hugh ate the bread and meat. "When do you think Hazel will return?"

"Some time tomorrow. Or rather, today."

Hugh pushed his empty plate away. "I've been trying to remember . . ." He rubbed his brow. "I've been bespelled for three days. I think. I seem to remember . . . I think I've been a man three times. Twice here, and once in the woods." His mind flinched from the memory: "It was dark, and I didn't know where I was, or who I was, or even *what* I was, and . . . and it hurt and I was panicking and . . . I think it's too real to be a nightmare. I think it happened. And I think . . ." Hugh took a deep breath. "I think Aleyn Fairborn did this to me."

"Your *cousin*?" Ivy's expression was aghast. "Surely not! He's little more than a boy!"

"Eighteen."

Ivy shook her head. He saw on her face that she didn't want to believe him.

"You met Aleyn two weeks ago. What did you think of him?"

"He's very handsome. And polite. Charming."

"And . . . ?" Hugh prompted.

Ivy hesitated, and blew out a breath. "Truth be told, I thought him rather arrogant. It seemed to me that his smiles were all on the surface, that he didn't mean them. That he thought Hazel too lowly a bride for a Dappleward."

Hugh nodded, relieved she was so perceptive. "His mother was a vain woman. She thought very highly of herself. Aleyn caught the trick from her."

"And his father?"

"Died when he was an infant."

Ivy frowned, and traced a seam on the tabletop. "Will Aleyn become your father's heir, if you and Tam die?"

"If we die, and if my father doesn't remarry and have more sons . . . yes."

Ivy's frown deepened. "You and Tam and your father, you have humility. I'm not sure Aleyn does. If he became Lord Warder of Dapple Vale, he might make decisions for his own good, not the good of the vale. If he were Warder . . . I'd be afraid."

She'd have good cause to be afraid. Hugh grimaced, and kept that thought to himself.

Ivy rubbed the frown from her brow and shook her head. "Arrogant or not, Aleyn's your *family*. I can't believe he'd do such a thing! It must be someone else. Some other reason."

"It's not just his arrogance, Ivy . . . The last thing I remember, before this happened—" Hugh gestured to his body, "—was riding out with Aleyn. We went as far as the triple oaks, and I remember Aleyn offering me his flask, and I remember drinking . . . It tasted like blood. After that, all I remember is being a roebuck."

Ivy held his gaze for a long moment, and then nodded. Her face was pale and grave. "So . . . it probably was Aleyn."

Hugh nodded back.

"If it was Aleyn, he'll likely come with your father. He'll want to know whether you have your wits about you. He must fear you'll be able to . . . to *indicate* that he's to blame."

"I think I could—if I had to." He wouldn't need speech for that; he could do it with his behavior.

"So, if Aleyn *does* come . . ." Ivy steepled her hands and pressed them to her lips, thinking.

Hugh watched her. Gods, she was lovely—the arch of her eyebrows, the high cheekbones—but far more than he admired the structure of her face, he admired her composure, her intelligence. Ivy Miller wasn't a woman to be overset by problems. She'd never fall into hysterics; she'd think her problems through, as she was thinking now, calmly and rationally.

He was one of her problems. And she was one of his. Not his biggest problem at this moment, but his second biggest. One that baffled him almost as much as his bespelling.

Why had Ivy willingly lain with him?

Not because she wanted to marry him; she'd made that quite plain.

Hugh remembered the taste of her in his mouth, remembered her gasping and shuddering as the climax took her—and then he remembered Ivy saying, cool and unflustered, *I am not the wife for you.*

He strongly disagreed. Ivy Miller possessed every quality he wanted in his wife.

Why wouldn't she marry him? Her passion had matched his, she clearly felt warm emotions for him—and yet she had rebuffed his offer. Twice.

A Lord Warder shouldn't have a cripple for a wife, Ivy had told him. Surely she didn't believe that? Her lameness was unimportant. It was Ivy's quiet strength, her compassion, her astuteness, that had captured his heart. Whether or not she used a crutch was irrelevant.

Ivy lowered her hands. "If your cousin comes, we need Larkspur. She'll know whether Aleyn did it or not. He won't be able to hide it from her. And if there's a way of reversing the spell—if he *thinks* of it in her presence—she'll know that, too."

Her words focused Hugh's attention absolutely. He allowed himself a moment's cautious hope. "Will she do it? *Can* she do it? You said it was driving her mad."

"It is. But it would only take a few minutes. I'll ask her first thing in the morning."

"Thank you." Hugh rubbed his face. Stubble rasped beneath his hand, a half-day's growth of whiskers.

"You should sleep," Ivy said.

"Sleep?" Hugh shook his head. "I can't sleep. Not knowing what's coming." How long until he changed back into a deer? One hour? Two? His stomach tightened at thought of the pain that lay ahead. He regretted the food he'd eaten.

Ivy didn't argue, she just nodded. "Very well," she said. "Let's discuss the most obvious eventualities and plan for them. What do we do if your cousin comes? What do we do if he doesn't? Or if he *does* come, and Larkspur says it wasn't him who did this to you?"

Hugh looked at her. *I love you,* he wanted to say. But he didn't. Instead, he leaned his forearms on the table and gratefully bent his mind to the questions she'd posed.

CHAPTER 7

$\mathcal{H}$ ugh watched from the forest edge as four riders approached Widow Miller's cottage. He let his gaze rest on each rider. His brother, Tam. Hazel Miller. Cadoc Ironfist. And Aleyn Fairborn.

His father hadn't come, but Tam and Cadoc had, and they were every bit as competent as the Lord Warder. They'd save him, if anyone could. He found it suddenly much easier to breathe, as if his lungs and ribcage had expanded.

Tam swung down from his horse and turned to help Hazel dismount. Hugh saw Ivy limp from the cottage, saw the people and horses mill. To his deer's eyes the late afternoon sky was an odd shade of blue and the meadow a dull green, blotched with gray and white flowers. The horses, the riders, and the clothes the riders wore were varying shades of gray, from off-white to almost black, except for Cadoc's blue hood, which stood out clearly.

Ivy went into the cottage. So did Hazel. Then a minute later, Tam and Aleyn together. Cadoc took the horses to the brook to drink.

Several minutes passed, then Hazel emerged from the cottage. She headed briskly for the forest.

Hugh's pulse picked up. Their scheme was underway.

Hazel crossed the meadow, and paused just inside the cool gloom of Glade Forest, looking around.

Hugh stepped out onto the path.

Hazel put her hands on her hips and stared down at him, lips pursed, frowning. "So you're Hugh Dappleward?" And then the frown dissolved. "Poor soul." She bent and hugged him. "We'll do all we can, Hugh."

Hugh leaned his head against her, a silent *thank you*.

It took twenty minutes to reach the woodcutter's cottage. Hazel walked fast, almost running. Larkspur waited for them at the edge of the clearing, a piece of rope in her hand. Hugh stood back and watched Hazel hug her sister fiercely, then hold her at arm's length. "Are you sure you have the strength for this, love?"

Larkspur nodded, and glanced at Hugh. *Thank you*, he told her silently, and knew that she, at least, heard.

"Ivy said Hugh's going to pretend to do something—but then Aleyn came in and she couldn't tell me what. What?"

"He'll pretend not to recognize anyone, and he'll pretend to be mad."

"Why?"

"Because it's safer for him—if it *is* Aleyn who cast this spell."

"Oh." Hazel's brow cleared. "Of course. A mad Hugh is no threat; a sane one *is*. Tam's no fool. If Hugh tried to tell him something—even if he couldn't speak—Tam would figure it out."

"Ivy was afraid Aleyn might try to kill Hugh. This way, he has no reason to."

"None at all!" Hazel said firmly. She took the rope from her sister. "Come on. Let's be off to the bluebell dell."

They walked more slowly, now. Hazel held Larkspur's hand. She radiated an intense, anxious protectiveness. The two red-brown hounds came. Bess stayed close to the women, but Bartlemay cast in circles around them, his tail wagging. Twice, he came up to Hugh and pranced, inviting him to play.

After ten minutes, Hazel called Bartlemay to her in a low voice and took hold of his scruff. "Can you hear them yet?" she asked her sister.

Larkspur walked forward cautiously and halted beneath a young alder. She grimaced, and nodded.

"Clearly?"

Larkspur nodded again.

"Can you cope?"

"For a few minutes, yes."

"Bartlemay, Bess—sit, stay." When the hounds had settled themselves at Larkspur's feet, Hazel tied the rope around Hugh's neck in a loose halter. "Let's make this quick," she told him. "Ivy couldn't get Tam aside. He doesn't know the truth yet. He's *frantic* with worry about you." She checked the halter, making sure it wasn't too tight. "Ready?"

Hugh dipped his head in a nod. Tension was tight in his belly.

Hazel blew out a breath. "Very well, let's act out this charade."

⸎

Hazel led him into the bluebell dell. Ivy was there, leaning on her crutch. Tam and Cadoc. And Aleyn.

Hazel halted.

Hugh halted, too. He stood with his legs splayed, his body shaking, his head hanging lopsided. He heaved his lungs so that breath whistled from his mouth, and rolled his eyes, and examined the three men looking at him: Tam, his face drawn and worried; Cadoc, bearded and equally worried; and Aleyn, staring intently at him.

Tam, Hugh thought. *Cadoc*. Emotion squeezed his ribcage. It took all his willpower not to tear free and run to them.

"It's a man? Are you certain?" Tam came closer and went down on one knee. He looked more serious than Hugh had ever seen him. No levity on his face today, just deep worry.

Hugh's ribcage squeezed even tighter. *Tam.* He rolled his eyes wildly again, dropped one hip, and canted to the left.

"Yes. Larkspur was able to tell that much," Ivy said. "But she can't tell who he is. He's quite mad, poor thing. Being in our cottage distressed him. He's much calmer in the forest."

Tam reached out to touch him.

Hugh wanted to lean into his brother's hand; he made himself flinch and half-rear, almost tugging the rope from Hazel's grip.

Tam lowered his hand and clenched it on his knee. "It's not Hugh, is it?" His voice was low and controlled, but Hugh heard the fear in it.

"We don't know who he is," Ivy said. "Larkspur can't tell."

Tam looked up at Hazel. He swallowed, and moistened his lips. "Can *you* tell if it's Hugh?"

"My gift can't find Hugh," Hazel said. "He's . . . gone. Nowhere."

Hugh rolled his eyes again. He saw grim compassion on Cadoc's face—and glee on Aleyn's.

"There must be some way of returning him to his true form," Ivy said.

Tam stood. "Not necessarily. If this is a punishment laid on him by the Fey, it's unbreakable."

"Could it not be a spell cast by a human?" Ivy asked.

"Cast by whom?" Tam shook his head, and turned to Cadoc and Aleyn. "We'll take him back to Dapple Meadow, though I doubt anything can be done for him."

"But if it *is* a spell, he *could* be returned to his true form?" Ivy persisted.

"Probably," Tam said. "But it's not a spell. Who could have cast it? No, it's a Faerie punishment." He looked at Hugh, and sighed. "What did you do to deserve this, poor creature?"

Nothing, Hugh thought. Then he made himself shudder and roll his eyes wildly. Cadoc still looked grimly compassionate. Aleyn looked smug.

"It's so sad," Hazel said. She leaned against Tam.

Tam hugged her.

Hazel whispered something in his ear and stepped back.

Tam gave her a sharp glance, and turned to Cadoc and Aleyn. "We're getting nowhere here. Go back to Dapple Bend, both of you, get us beds at the alehouse, see if you can hire a wagon. We'll take this creature back to Dapple Meadow tomorrow."

Cadoc nodded gravely and turned to go.

"I'll stay with you," Aleyn said.

"No, no," Tam waved him off. "There's no point. Go."

Aleyn hesitated, and glanced at Hugh.

Hugh rolled his eyes, and stood splay-legged and askew, chest heaving, shaking as hard as he could. *I'm mad. Quite mad.*

Aleyn shrugged, and followed Cadoc.

When both men were gone from sight, Tam swung to face Hazel. "What did you mean, get rid of Aleyn and Cadoc?"

Hugh straightened and stopped shaking.

"Just that," Hazel said, slipping the halter from Hugh's neck. "Tam, the roebuck's not mad; he's just pretending."

"Pretending?" Tam directed a fierce, suspicious frown at Hugh. "Hazel, what's going on?"

"This is Hugh."

Tam's face drained utterly. "Hugh? *No!*"

"He's not mad," Hazel repeated firmly. "He was pretending."

There were tears in Tam's eyes, and pale horror on his face. He lurched to his knees and held his arms out.

Hugh went to him, butting his head into Tam's chest.

Tam hugged him fiercely. "Hugh? Oh, gods, *Hugh.*"

Hugh closed his eyes and leaned into his brother. Tam's chest was shaking, his breath hitching. He was crying? Hugh tried to burrow closer to Tam, tried to climb into his lap. *Don't cry, Tam. Please, don't cry!*

"It was Aleyn," a thin, breathless voice said.

Tam's grip slackened slightly. "What?"

"It was Aleyn."

Hugh looked out from under Tam's arm. Larkspur stood at the edge of the bluebell dell. Her face was deathly pale. She leaned against Bartlemay, looking close to collapse.

Their distress was *her* distress.

Hugh tried to control his agitation.

"Hazel, get her away from here," Ivy said.

Hazel ran to obey, looping an arm around her sister's waist, taking her weight. "Come on, love," she murmured.

"I can carry her," Tam said, scrambling to his feet, one hand still gripping Hugh.

"No," Ivy said.

Tam swung to face her. Tear tracks were wet on his face. "She can barely walk—"

"Your emotions are hurting her. You're too upset. She needs to get *away* from you."

Tam closed his mouth. He inhaled a shaking breath, visibly trying to control himself.

CHAPTER 8

They made a slow procession back to the cottage: Tam Dappleward, the roebuck, and herself. Ivy explained matters as best she could. Tam walked with his hand on the roebuck's neck, his expression growing grimmer with each step he took. "I'll kill Aleyn for this," he said, when Ivy had finished, and there was such murderous rage on his face—jaw clenched, nostrils flared—that she believed him.

"Not yet," Ivy said, placing her hand on his arm. "You mustn't do anything, Tam. Wait until Larkspur's told us what she learned. Wait until you've spoken to Hugh."

A muscle jumped in Tam's jaw. He inhaled a harsh breath—and released it slowly. His jaw unclenched, but anger still burned in his eyes. "Midnight to dawn? Is that correct?"

"Come an hour after midnight. Your brother's transformation is . . . unpleasant. If you witness it, you'll be upset. Too upset to be in the same room as Larkspur afterwards."

Tam's jaw tightened again. After a moment, he said, "Larkspur's coming?"

"She has pledged to."

They came to the edge of Glade Forest. Ahead, the cottage nestled in the meadow. Low evening sunlight cast long shadows and tinted the grass golden.

Ivy halted. "When Larkspur comes, you must control your emotions, regardless of what she tells us. Your anger and distress hurt her. She's very close to breaking."

"Hazel told me." Tam turned to her. The anger was gone from his face; in its place was concern. "I'm so sorry, Ivy. If there's anything I or my father can do to help—"

Ivy smiled reassuringly at him. "Thank you, but there's no need. In three days, the gift will be taken from her."

Tam flicked a brief glance at her crutch, but said nothing.

"Tell Cadoc Ironfist, too, please," Ivy said, ignoring the glance. "No emotion. You must remain calm."

"I'll tell him." Tam looked across the meadow at the cottage. "We'll be here one hour after midnight."

"Take care Aleyn doesn't wake and follow you."

"He won't." Tam snorted, a contemptuous sound. "Cadoc can drink him under the table without even trying."

Tam Dappleward was as good as his word. He and Cadoc Ironfist arrived an hour after midnight. Ivy unlatched the door and let them in. Tam looked past her eagerly. "Hugh?"

Hugh stood, steadying himself on the trestle table, one blanket knotted around his waist, a second draped over his shoulders. "Tam?" he said hoarsely.

Tam brushed past Ivy, stumbling in his haste. Ironfist entered more slowly, ducking his head. When he straightened to his full height, he loomed in the room, his head almost touching the ceiling. His face was tough and craggy beneath the close-cropped beard.

The brothers hugged for a long time. Tam, when he released Hugh, was unashamedly weeping. Ironfist then stepped forward and embraced Hugh. Ivy was astonished to see that his eyes were damp, too. Clearly, he wasn't as tough as he looked.

"Aleyn?" Hugh asked, sitting again.

"We left him snoring." Tam sat alongside Hugh and gripped his hand.

Side by side, the similarities between the brothers were obvious. They had the same height, the same lean muscularity, the same high-bridged nose, but Hugh's jaw was wider than Tam's, his cheekbones blunter, his hair black instead of honey brown. His eyebrows were strong, dark slashes. The combination of jaw, cheekbones, eyebrows, and nose gave his face an innate sternness.

Tam peered around the tiny room, and glanced at the door to the bedchamber. "Where's Hazel?"

"Gone to fetch Larkspur. They'll be here soon."

Tam nodded, and turned his attention back to his brother. "You're thinner."

Hugh shrugged the comment aside. "How's Father?"

"Beside himself with worry—and trying not to show it. He wanted to come, but I got down on my knees and begged him not to. He's been short of breath the last two days. I was afraid if he came I'd lose both of you in one week." Tam's grip on Hugh's hand tightened, his knuckles whitening.

"He thinks I'm dead?"

"He thinks you've been called to Faerie. We all did."

"Faerie?" Hugh's eyebrows climbed up his forehead. "Me?"

"Aleyn said . . . he told us that a man had ridden up to you both in the forest, mounted on a horse the color of fresh-minted gold. The man had a terrible, cold beauty and his eyes were as black as midnight. One of the Fey, obviously. Aleyn said the man asked you to accompany him—just you, not Aleyn—and that the two of you rode off into Glade Forest. The inference was clear."

"We searched the woods around Dapple Meadow," Ironfist said, his voice rumbling deep in his chest. "Found your horse, but no sign of you."

"Aleyn said you told him you'd be back soon." Tam's mouth twisted. "Soon? What does that mean? Especially in Faerie.

Everyone knows time runs differently there. Soon could be *years*."

"Clever of Aleyn," Hugh said, his voice dispassionate.

"Very." Tam's mouth twisted again. "I was setting out to fetch Hazel, when she arrived. I asked her to find you—and she couldn't. You were nowhere on this earth, Hugh. *Nowhere*. She couldn't find you alive *or* dead. We took it to mean you truly were in Faerie." Tam paused, swallowed, and continued: "When Hazel told us about the roebuck . . . I didn't know whether to hope it was you or not. Dapple Bend's so far from Dapple Meadow, it seemed unlikely, but . . ."

Ironfist's rough-hewn brow furrowed in a frown. "How did you get here, Hugh? It's all of thirty miles."

"I ran. I think." Hugh grimaced. "It's not very clear in my head . . . but I do remember running."

"He was exhausted when we found him," Ivy said. "Close to collapse."

There was silence for a moment. Tam's face was bleak, Ironfist's grim. Their rage was palpable. Ivy could almost taste it on her tongue, acrid.

"What I want to know is how Aleyn did it," Ironfist said harshly. "And how to reverse it."

"I hope Larkspur can tell us," Ivy said. "She'll be here soon. I know you're both angry, but please try to calm yourselves."

Ironfist gave a flat laugh. "Angry? Yes." He unclenched his huge fists and blew out a breath. "What shall we discuss instead?"

~⚬⚬⚬~

The anger had almost dissipated by the time Hazel and Larkspur arrived, the hounds crowding on their heels. The small room shrank even further.

Ivy stood and anxiously examined Larkspur's face. *Are you all right?* she thought.

Larkspur gave a faint nod.

"Crowded in here," Hazel said. "Bess, Bartlemay—out!"

They sat around the trestle table, elbow to elbow. Ironfist, at the far end, loomed like a giant. His back was to the fire, casting his face in shadow. He looked like an outcrop of rock, not a man.

Ivy clasped Larkspur's cool, slender fingers. "What can you tell us, love?"

"Aleyn did it, and it's not just a spell, it's a . . . a *bargain*."

Tam's eyebrows arrowed together in a sharp frown. "A bargain with whom? Or what?"

Larkspur shivered. "Something evil. It's not fully alive."

"Not alive?"

"It has no body."

"Is it in a barrow?" Ironfist asked, leaning forward.

Larkspur shook her head. "Not a barrow; a cavern, deep in the forest. There's an altar there, with blood on it."

All three men recoiled. "Dréor," Tam spat. "He made a bargain with the dréor!"

Ivy saw open-mouthed horror on Hugh's face.

"What's the dréor?" Hazel asked.

"A creature that was expelled from Faerie thousands of years ago," Tam said flatly. "In the old days, men would offer up sacrifices to it in exchange for power. The early Warders couldn't kill it—it's a creature of spirit, not flesh—but they managed to bind it. Its cavern became its prison."

"I've never heard of it," Ivy said, disturbed. She'd always thought Glade Forest was safe.

"Knowledge of the dréor is forbidden. Only the Warder and his most trusted men know where the cavern lies, and they're under strict orders never to venture there."

"Aleyn was entrusted with this knowledge?" Ivy asked.

Hugh and Tam exchanged a glance. "I thought not," Hugh said.

"He had access to the old Warders' journals. I saw him reading the scrolls often enough," Ironfist said.

Hugh rubbed a hand over his face. "Yes, he did, didn't he? The past few months, particularly." He grimaced, and shook his head. The look on his face—bleak, weary—made Ivy's heart turn over in her chest. The urge to reach out and touch him was so intense that she curled her fingers into her palms.

"Sacrifices?" Hazel said.

"Human sacrifices." Ironfist's gravelly voice made the words sound even more terrible than they were. "Larkspur, please continue. What else did you learn from Aleyn?"

"He hates Hugh and Tam for being the Dappleward heirs, and he hates you for your loyalty and your integrity. He enjoyed seeing Hugh's suffering. It . . . delighted him."

Ivy glanced at Hugh. He looked as if he tasted bile in his mouth.

"Does he know Hugh changes back into a man for a few hours each night?" Ironfist asked.

Larkspur shook her head. "He seemed not to." She looked at Hazel. "He's afraid of you."

"Me? Why on earth?"

"Because no one's asked you the right question."

Tam leaned forward. "What's the right question?"

"Instead of asking where Hugh is, you should have asked where to find the man who harmed him."

Tam's gaze fastened on Hazel. "Where, Hazel? Where is that man?"

Hazel blinked. Her eyes widened. "Oh . . . Oh, it *is* Aleyn."

Tam settled back on his stool, grim satisfaction on his face.

"How does Aleyn know about our Faerie gifts?" Ivy asked. "Your father said he'd only tell you and the Ironfists."

"Oh . . ." Tam grimaced, and rubbed his face. "It was when Hazel arrived. Aleyn was so desperate to help find Hugh and he *begged* to be allowed in on that meeting, and . . ." He blew out his breath. "We decided to tell him. He *is* family."

"Is Hazel in danger?" Ivy asked.

Tam looked sharply at Larkspur.

Larkspur hesitated. "Aleyn is worried she'll expose him."

Ivy took that as a *Yes.* From the expression on Tam's face, so did he. He reached for Hazel's hand across the table. "Hazel—"

"I'm in no danger," Hazel said. "Not with you and Cadoc here."

Tam didn't look reassured. Nor did he release Hazel's hand. "If Aleyn offers you anything to drink—"

"Of course I shan't drink it!"

Ironfist leaned forward. "Larkspur, did you learn anything else about the spell that binds Hugh?"

"The bargain isn't complete yet. Aleyn sacrificed a roebuck on the altar and mixed its blood with water. Drinking that made Hugh change shape, but Hugh won't be fully bound until a second sacrifice is performed. A human sacrifice."

"What's Aleyn waiting for?" Tam asked. "Is it the human sacrifice? Can't he bring himself to do it?"

Larkspur shook her head. "He's waiting because he wants to get you, too."

Tam flinched slightly. "Me?"

"Tam . . ." Hazel said, and there was a note in her voice that Ivy had never heard before: fear.

Tam lifted Hazel's hand and turned it over and kissed her palm. "Don't worry about me."

Ivy's chest contracted in a moment of intense envy. To have a man look at her the way Tam was looking at Hazel.

No, not any man: Hugh.

She glanced at Hugh. He was staring at her, and the expression on his face, even shadowed as it was . . .

Her lungs stopped working. The breath dried up in her throat.

Ivy broke the glance hastily and stared down at the table. *I am not the wife for Hugh Dappleward,* she told herself. *He needs a stronger woman than I.* The regret, at that moment, was excruciating.

And then she remembered Larkspur, sitting alongside her. Ivy's thoughts lurched to a frozen, horrified halt.

"Can the spell be broken?" Ironfist asked.

Ivy focused intently on the question—*Could* the spell be broken?—and shoved the regret to the very back of her brain.

There was a brief pause before Larkspur answered Ironfist's question. "Yes. By killing Aleyn, or . . . something to do with a dead Faerie prince and a barrow. I didn't understand that."

From the men's faces, Ivy thought they understood.

"Killing Aleyn will do it?" Hazel said.

Larkspur nodded. "Aleyn promised to sacrifice his first-born child to the dréor. He sealed the pact with his own blood. If he dies before making the sacrifice . . . the bargain is void. The spell breaks."

"His first-born child!" Hazel said, her voice sharp with horror.

"A son. Born two months ago."

"A son?" Hugh sounded baffled. "Aleyn doesn't have a son."

"Born to someone in your household," Larkspur said. "She died in childbirth. I think her father might be one of your grooms."

"Oh." Understanding dawned on Hugh's face. "Rosamund. She never said who the father was. Her parents were distraught when she died."

"Aleyn plans to kill Rosamund's child?" Ironfist's voice was soft—and yet it made hairs prick upright on the back of Ivy's neck.

He's dangerous, Ivy thought.

"Yes." Larkspur's head drooped. She closed her eyes. Her fingers trembled in Ivy's grasp.

I think you've had enough, love, Ivy told her silently. She caught Hazel's eye. "Time to take her back."

Hazel stood.

"One final question, Larkspur . . . if I may?" Ironfist's voice was still soft, but no longer terrifying. He sounded gentle, not dangerous.

Larkspur raised her head and looked at him.

"If Hugh's in deer form when Aleyn dies, will he change back into himself? Or will he be stuck?"

Tam shot him a sharp glance.

"He'll change back."

"Are you certain? Absolutely certain?"

Larkspur hesitated. "Aleyn seemed to think that would be the case."

"Seemed to think . . ." Tam grimaced and shook his head. "Let us err on the side of caution. We do it when Hugh's human."

"Now?" There was a note of disquiet in Ironfist's gravelly voice. "Cut Aleyn's throat while he's asleep? That's too much like murder for my liking."

Tam grimaced again. He glanced at Hugh. "Tomorrow night at Dapple Meadow. A closed court—and an execution. Justice, not murder. If you can wait another day?"

"I can," Hugh said.

Ivy looked down at the table. Two more agonizing transformations . . . Could he cope?

But Ironfist was correct. Cold-blooded murder was no way to undo this unholy bargain.

"I don't want Father to witness me changing shape," Hugh said. "Promise me you'll keep him away."

"I promise," Tam said.

She looked up to see Tam stand and bow to Larkspur. "Thank you," he said, formally. "My family is very much in your debt. If you ever need our help in any matter, you have only to ask."

Hazel held out a hand to Larkspur. "Come on, love. Let's get you back to the woodcutter's cottage."

Larkspur released her grip on Ivy's fingers. She pushed slowly upright. She looked frail, almost elderly. The shadows under her eyes were as dark as bruises.

Ironfist stood. "I'll come with you." He made a bow to Larkspur. "That is, if my presence won't disturb you?"

CHAPTER 9

T am, Ironfist, and Aleyn carried the roebuck off in a wagon. Ivy stood on the doorstep with Hazel and watched the wagon trundle out of sight. *May the gods protect you, Hugh Dappleward,* she prayed silently.

Calmness wasn't a quality she possessed this morning. Anxiety and worry were the emotions that rode her. Anxiety and worry—and a foolish, wistful sense of loss that tightened her throat and made her heart ache in her chest.

She wanted to be on that wagon with Hugh. She wanted to protect him.

"What if Aleyn manages to bespell Tam?" Hazel's voice was agonized, her hands clenched. "Or finds some way to kill him? Or—"

"Ironfist is with them." Ivy managed to find a shred of calmness. "He's more than a match for Aleyn. He'll keep Tam safe. And Hugh."

"But—"

"You'll know where Tam is every mile of the journey. You can ask yourself where he is once an hour—once a minute, if you need to."

"I do that all the time anyway." Hazel unclenched her fists and scrubbed her face with her hands. "Gods, I'm tired." She sat on the doorstep, her shoulders sagging. "A midsummer wedding? I was a fool to agree to wait. I should have married him two weeks ago."

"I'm glad you didn't," Ivy said. "If you hadn't been here to help me with Larkspur . . ."

They exchanged a sober glance. Hazel pushed wearily to her feet. "Let's go see her now."

"You don't want a nap?"

Hazel shook her head. "I'm too worried to sleep."

So was Ivy. "Where's Tam?" she asked.

Hazel's eyes unfocused slightly. "Crossing the bridge." She blew out a breath and smiled wryly. "Crossing the bridge, alive and well. As are Hugh and Cadoc. And . . ." Her eyes unfocused again. "And Larkspur's awake. Come on, let's go."

They sat together on the mossy doorstep, the three of them, with the hounds basking in the sunlight at their feet. Another beautiful, golden day. Ivy gazed across the little glade, at the summer-green grass and the wildflowers nodding in the breeze. This was how they'd sat three days ago. She had an odd, unsettling sense that they'd slipped back in time. Any moment now a roebuck would come crashing from the trees . . .

She remembered Hugh as he'd been then: filthy, shaking with exhaustion, half-mad with terror. Her heart clenched in her chest. And then she told herself—and Larkspur—silently and fiercely: *I do not love Hugh Dappleward.*

Larkspur slipped her hand into Ivy's. "He'll be free of the spell soon."

Ivy looked at her sister. Anxiety jolted through her. Larkspur's cheeks were even more hollow today, the shadows under her eyes darker. Guilt followed swiftly on the heels of anxiety. "We shouldn't have asked it of you. It was too much—"

"No, it wasn't. I'm fine."

Ivy reached for her crutch. "I think we should go. You need to rest."

"I'm *fine,*" Larkspur repeated.

"Last night, you were too weak to walk," Hazel said. "Cadoc carried you."

Ivy's guilt intensified.

"Don't!" Larkspur said sharply. "Don't feel guilty! How could I not help after what I've done to you!"

"You've done nothing to me," Ivy said, climbing to her feet. "It was Father who broke my leg, not you."

Larkspur's lips twisted. "He broke it because I was born."

"He broke it because he was a drunkard and a fool," Hazel said, standing.

Ivy glanced at her, and wondered how much Hazel remembered of that day. Nothing, she hoped. Her own memory was mercifully disjointed; she remembered her first glimpse of Larkspur—wrinkled and pink—but not their father's drunken rage.

"My lameness is *not* your fault," she told Larkspur firmly. "Not then, and not now."

Larkspur shook her head.

Father may not have wanted another daughter, Ivy thought to her. *But if he had lived, he would love you now.* Ivy reached down and touched Larkspur's shining hair. "You regret your wish, love, but remember this: because of it you've saved two lives."

"She's right," Hazel said bluntly. "If you couldn't hear people's thoughts, Hugh would have died a roebuck. And Tam, too. And Aleyn would likely be Dapple Vale's next Warder. We should thank the gods you wished as you did!"

Ivy stroked a strand of hair back from Larkspur's cheek and tucked it behind her ear. "Hazel's right. We should thank the gods for your gift."

Hazel bent, and hugged Larkspur fiercely. "Make sure you eat everything we've brought! And that you *sleep.*"

"We'll be back tomorrow." Ivy hugged Larkspur, too.

She tucked the crutch into her armpit and hobbled across the glade. The crutch would be with her forever, but she didn't regret it. If it meant Larkspur and Hugh were safe, she would willingly be lame the rest of her life.

*C*HAPTER 10

H ugh sat in one of the huge oak chairs in a corner of his father's work chamber. His legs were too weak to stand for long, his hands too weak to shave the stubble from his face, but he was home, home and human, and about to be free of Aleyn's spell.

He glanced around the shadowy chamber: the long table, the chairs and stools, the shelves of scrolls and books. He would work in this room one day, pass judgments here one day. But not, he hoped, for a very long time.

He looked at his father and Tam, seated at the far end of the table, closest to the fire and the candles. Light and shadows flickered across their faces. For a second, it was almost impossible to tell them apart; they had the same bony faces, the same strong noses, the same unruly hair, and then the light shifted and the difference was clear: his father looked old. Older than Hugh had ever seen him. This affair had aged him.

Rage flared anew in his chest. Rage at Aleyn. How *dared* he do this?

Next to Tam sat Cadoc, huge and bearded and grim. None of the men talked. They waited silently. Gravely.

Behind Hugh, the door opened. "But I was *asleep*," he heard Aleyn say petulantly. "I don't see what's so urgent!"

"Your uncle will explain it," Rauf Ironfist said. His voice was the same deep rumble as his son's.

Hugh tensed. He sat motionless as Rauf Ironfist and Aleyn entered the room. Rauf shut the door and turned the key in the lock. Hugh heard it *snick* firmly.

Aleyn strode across the floor to confront his uncle and cousin. "What's so urgent?" he demanded. "I was sleeping."

Rauf crossed to stand alongside Aleyn, moving quietly for a man of his size; like his son, he was light on his feet. Cadoc stood. Between the two Ironfists, Aleyn seemed as small and slight as a twelve-year-old boy.

"What?" Aleyn demanded again.

Hugh's father gestured silently towards the dark corner where Hugh sat.

Aleyn swung round and peered into the shadows. "What?"

Hugh pushed to his feet and stood swaying.

"Who—?" Aleyn froze. Shock and disbelief were clear to see on his face.

Hugh braced himself for what was to come—Aleyn's pretense of joy, the protestations of ignorance and righteous innocence—but instead of feigned delight, Aleyn's lips pulled back from his teeth in a snarl. "You!"

So, there'd be no pretense. Hugh was relieved.

Rauf gripped Aleyn's right shoulder; Cadoc took hold of his left arm.

"This is a trial," Hugh's father said, his voice low and sad. "A closed trial. The charges are—"

Aleyn moved—snatching the dagger from Rauf's belt, burying the blade in Cadoc's upper arm.

It happened so fast that Hugh barely had time to blink: the flash of the dagger in the candlelight, Cadoc's yelp of pain, Aleyn wrenching free.

Aleyn charged at Hugh, dagger raised, his face contorted with hatred.

Rauf moved fast for a man in his fiftieth year. He caught Aleyn before he'd gone three paces. Aleyn fell headlong, with a thump Hugh felt through the floorboards. There was a quick tussle, Rauf and Aleyn rolled over one another, the dagger flashed in the candlelight again, the thrashing bodies stilled—and then Rauf pushed up slowly from the floor. He turned to Hugh's father. "He's dead, Guy."

Hugh looked at his brother and father, both standing open-mouthed in shock, at Cadoc, gripping his arm tightly, blood leaking between his fingers, at Rauf, standing over Aleyn's body, and lastly at Aleyn.

The hatred was gone from Aleyn's face. He looked handsome in death—the high brow, the aquiline nose, the chiseled features.

Hugh lifted his gaze, and swallowed, and tried to make his tongue work. "Why did he hate me so much? What have I ever done to him?"

"You've been yourself," Rauf said, in the gravelly Ironfist voice. "Which is a better man than he could ever be. And he knew it. We all knew it."

Hugh swallowed again. He sat shakily in the great oak chair.

A faint sighing breath came from Aleyn's mouth. His body seemed to deflate, like a wineskin that had been uncorked. His muscles lost their tension and became flaccid.

Aleyn was dead. Truly dead.

Hugh doubled over in sudden agony. His intestines writhed in his belly. His joints seemed to crack open, his muscles to pull apart. A scream tore from his mouth.

CHAPTER 11

$\mathcal{M}$idmorning, when Ivy was packing a basket of food for Larkspur, Hazel ducked her head in through the open door. "Mother's here," she said, before disappearing again.

Ivy limped hastily across the room. Yes, Maythorn was coming across the meadow, holding up her skirts, running, her hair as bright as gold in the sunlight. Behind her strolled her new husband, Ren Blacksmith, with his six-year-old son on his shoulders.

Ivy stood on the doorstep and watched Hazel run to meet their mother, watched them embrace. She heard Maythorn's laughter, a joyous sound, and then Maythorn released Hazel and picked up her skirts and ran again. "Ivy, love!"

Ivy hobbled down from the doorstep to meet her. Maythorn hugged her fiercely, laughing and crying. Ivy hugged her mother back. But Maythorn didn't feel like a mother; she felt like a sister, a beloved friend.

"I missed you, my Ivy. Very much." Tears of joy were bright in Maythorn's eyes. She shone with youth and health. No one, looking at her, would believe that last month she'd been the crippled, graying Widow Miller. Maythorn looked around. "Where's Larkspur? Where are the dogs?"

Ivy met Hazel's eyes briefly, then glanced at Ren and

217

Gavain, approaching across the meadow. "Come inside," she said to Maythorn. "There's something I need to tell you. You and Ren both. Hazel, stay out here with Gavain. Play with him. He doesn't need to hear this."

Ivy told the tale of Larkspur's gift as succinctly as she could. The happiness drained from Maythorn's face. The tears in her eyes were distress now, not joy.

"Tomorrow everything will be put right," Ivy said. "I shall ask the Faerie to take Larkspur's gift back. That will be my wish."

Maythorn shook her head. Tears spilled from her eyes and tracked silently down her cheeks.

Ivy's throat tightened. She knew the one thing her mother most wanted was for her to walk again.

Ren gathered his wife in his arms and held her close. The expression on his face—tenderness, love, grief—made Ivy's throat tighten further. She looked away, out the open door, to where Hazel and Gavain were playing hoodman blind in the meadow.

Ivy took a deep breath, and continued. "There's more to tell you. Several days ago, we found a roebuck in the forest . . ."

The tale sounded fantastical, even to her ears, and yet Ren and Maythorn believed her; she saw it on their faces—their astonishment, their growing horror. "So, you see, Larkspur's wish was a *good* thing. Without it, Hugh and Tam Dappleward would both soon be dead."

Maythorn wiped her cheeks and inhaled a shaky breath. "I want to see Larkspur."

"We promised her we wouldn't bring you. I'm sorry."

Maythorn's brow creased in fresh distress. "But—"

"Your grief would be too much for her to bear."

218

Ren hugged Maythorn close again and pressed a kiss into her hair. "You'll see her tomorrow, dear heart. Once she's restored to herself."

Ivy met his eyes and gave a nod of thanks.

Maythorn washed away her tears and put on a smile for Gavain's sake, but grief shadowed her face and her eyes were dark with misery.

"Time to go, young scamp," Ren said, swinging his son up onto his shoulders again. He looked at Ivy, at Hazel, his expression grave. "If you need anything—anything at all—we're only five minutes away."

"We know," Ivy said. "Thank you, Ren."

Ren nodded, and put an arm around Maythorn, gathering her close. "We'll come tomorrow."

Ivy watched them cross the meadow. Gavain, laughing and joyful, perched atop his father's shoulders. Ren—tall, dependable, and kind. And Maythorn. Maythorn's youthful grace was gone; she walked as if she were weighed down. She looked like Widow Miller again, burdened with sorrow.

"Thank the gods she has Ren to comfort her," Hazel said quietly.

Ivy turned back to the cottage with a sigh. "Let's visit Larkspur. The basket's ready."

Ivy struggled with her crutch today. It seemed to catch every tree root, every fallen branch. Three times, she tripped and nearly fell. Her shattered kneecap began to ache fiercely. Frustration built in her. Frustration, and something close to anger.

"I'm sorry," she said at last, halting in a tiny glade dappled with sunshine. "I'm not calm enough to visit Larkspur. I need to rest for a few minutes."

Hazel turned to look at her, her gaze searching. "Is it Maythorn?"

Ivy nodded, even though that was only partly the truth. "You go ahead. I'll follow shortly."

Hazel hesitated.

"Go. I just need to sit for a moment, clear my head." Ivy began to lower herself to the soft, sunlit grass.

"Here, let me help." Hazel put down the basket and slid an arm around Ivy's waist, taking most of her weight, settling her gently on the grass.

Ivy hated being so helpless. For a moment she almost wept with rage and self-pity.

Hazel's brow furrowed with concern. "You don't look at all like yourself. I'll stay with you—"

"No." The word came out sharply. Too sharply. Ivy took a deep breath and forced herself to speak calmly. "I'm fine. I just need a few minutes alone. Please, Hazel."

Hazel gave her a long, frowning look, and then a dubious nod. She picked up the basket again and stepped towards the trees, looking back over her shoulder.

Ivy made herself smile. "Go."

Hazel did, still frowning.

When she could no longer hear Hazel's footsteps, Ivy lay back on the grass. It was Maythorn's grief, yes, but it was far more than that. It was her lameness, the crutch, Hugh Dappleward, Larkspur, everything. Emotions stewed in her breast: frustration, bitterness, regret. *I want it all,* she thought. *I want Larkspur back. I want Hugh Dappleward as my husband. I want not to be lame.*

But she couldn't have all of those things. It wasn't possible.

Ivy took a deep breath, and released it. *Calm,* she told herself.

She stared up at the sky—blue sky with a wisp of white cloud trailing across it—and listened to the beating of her heart and concentrated on her breathing—slow inhalation, slow exhalation—and waited for her agitation to fade and calmness to take its place.

In winter, when her knee ached almost too much to bear, she did this—brought her awareness back to breath and heartbeat—until the pain became manageable. And sometimes in spring she did it, too, when the flowers blossomed and she wanted to run through the meadow with her arms outstretched, and frustration at her lameness built inside her until she felt she would *burst* from it.

It usually helped, usually brought calmness.

Inhalation. Exhalation. The slow thump of her heart.

Gradually, the bitterness unraveled into nothing. The frustration dissipated like the wisp of cloud was doing above her, fading until it vanished entirely. The regret took longer to deal with. A stubborn knot of it remained, like a clenched fist beneath her breastbone. Regret that she'd never walk freely. Regret that Maythorn grieved. Regret that she'd allowed herself to fall in love with Hugh Dappleward.

But at least Hugh lived. He and Tam both.

Tomorrow was her birthday. Tomorrow they'd get Larkspur back. That was the most important thing in all this: Larkspur.

At last, the knot loosened and the regret was gone, too. Only calmness remained. Ivy sat up, and reached for her crutch, and levered herself to her feet.

CHAPTER 12

$\mathcal{H}$ ugh drifted back to consciousness. For a long time, he was too weary to open his eyes. Why was he so tired? Memory escaped him; he knew he was exhausted, but not why.

Finally, he mustered the energy to lift his eyelids.

He was in his own bed, in his own room. His father sat on a stool alongside the bed, his face weary and unshaven. Sunlight streamed through the open window. The shadows it cast told Hugh that it late afternoon.

Memory grudgingly returned. Nighttime. His father's work chamber. Aleyn.

"What happened?" Hugh whispered. His voice was hoarse, his throat painfully raw, as if he'd been screaming again.

His father's head jerked up. "Hugh!" He pushed hastily off his stool and leaned over the bed and gathered Hugh in his arms as if he were a child again. "Son . . . Oh, gods, *son.*"

Hugh tried to return the hug, but his arms had no strength in them.

His father laid him carefully back on the bed and returned to the stool, wiping moisture from his eyes. "I began to fear you'd never wake."

"What happened?" Hugh whispered again.

His father grimaced and looked away and rubbed one hand over his face, making the stubble rasp. "When Aleyn died, you changed into a roebuck again, and then back into yourself, and then into a roebuck . . . A dozen times at least. Gods, you were screaming! Woke the whole manor. You fainted before it ended, else you'd have woken the whole vale. I thought you were dying . . ." Guy Dappleward swallowed, and rubbed his face again.

"I'm fine," Hugh whispered hoarsely. He found the strength to untangle one arm from his bedclothes and reach out and take his father's hand.

"When your mother died, I felt helpless," his father said, in a low voice. "But this was a thousand times worse. You were in such pain and there was nothing I could do—" His voice cracked. He swallowed again, hard.

Hugh tightened his grip on his father's hand. "Father, I'm unharmed."

His father reached out and stroked the hair back from Hugh's brow, as if he were six years old, not twenty-six. "Thanks be to the gods—and Widow Miller's daughters."

Ivy.

Hugh let go of his father's hand and tried to raise himself up on one elbow. "Father, I have to go to Dapple Bend. I need to speak with Ivy Miller."

"Not today." His father pushed him gently back down onto the mattress. "Not for several days. You're as weak as a newborn kitten. You'd fall right off your horse."

"But I have to see Ivy Miller!"

"You shall. And so shall I. I need to thank those girls personally." Guy Dappleward stood, tall and lean, and bent over the bed and stroked Hugh's hair again and kissed his brow. "I'm glad to have you back, son. More glad than I have words for." And then he straightened and cleared his throat, and blinked several times, and said, "I'll fetch you some broth. And tell Tam and Cadoc you're awake. They're desperate to see you, been haunting this room all day."

CHAPTER 13

Jvy's twenty-fifth birthday dawned clear. She packed bread and cheese into a basket, and her sewing. "I'm going to the bluebell dell," she told Hazel. "To wait for her."

"I'll carry the basket."

"She won't come if you're with me. She only came when you and Larkspur were alone."

"I'll carry the basket and then leave." Hazel's tone brooked no protest. "It's difficult for you with the crutch, carrying something."

It always would be difficult.

The words echoed in the small room, as if they'd been spoken aloud. Or was she the only one who thought them?

No, Hazel's lips were compressed; she was thinking the same thing.

"I shall be glad to have Larkspur back," Ivy said, turning away and limping to the door. "And Bess and Bartlemay. The cottage is so empty without them." It would be even emptier soon. Hazel would be gone, married to Tam.

Tam, whose brother was Hugh. *No, don't think about Hugh, either,* Ivy told herself as she hobbled over the doorstep.

They crossed the meadow and entered the trees. Glade Forest was cool, green, quiet. At the bluebell dell, Hazel set down the basket and hugged Ivy. "I love you," she said, her voice tight, as if she were trying not to cry, and then she released Ivy and turned and ran back along the path.

Ivy lowered herself awkwardly to sit. She unpacked her sewing, threaded the needle, and bent her concentration to placing the stitches. Her thoughts tried to bend themselves in directions she didn't want them to go, but by focusing absolutely on each stitch, on its placement, on the tautness of the thread, she managed to hold them back.

Morning ripened slowly towards noon. The dew dried on the bluebells, bees buzzed and hummed, the breeze grew warm—and Ivy sewed calmly and methodically.

When the sun was high overhead, she laid aside her sewing and ate a slice of bread with cheese, and then sat for a long moment, enjoying the quiet beauty of the dell—the rich blue flowers, the lazy murmur of insects, the breeze bearing mossy forest scents. Somewhere, a squirrel chittered.

The skin at the back of Ivy's neck prickled sharply. She glanced around. Nothing had changed. Bluebells nodded in the breeze. Birds sang. Bees hummed. The prickling became stronger, climbing up her scalp. Someone—something—was watching her.

"I know you're there," she said quietly.

A piece of shadow detached itself from a rowan tree and stepped into the dell. For a moment, Ivy saw right through the shadow to the trees behind it, and then the shadow firmed, solidified, sharpened into focus.

The Faerie was as her mother had described: slender and imperious and inhumanly beautiful. She had marble-white skin, ebony hair bound with pearls, a gown as red as blood—and eyes that were as black as night.

Ivy's heart beat faster. *Calm,* she told herself, but it was hard to remain calm when confronted by such cold, cruel, perfect beauty. She reached for her crutch and slowly stood. "Good day."

The Faerie made no answer, just stood and stared haughtily at Ivy, contempt glittering in her black eyes.

She despises me, Ivy realized. *Because I'm human, a crude, lowly creature.* The knowledge didn't cow her; it stung her pride. She lifted her chin. "I hope your daughter is well?" she said, coolly polite.

Again, no answer.

Very well, let them dispense with courtesies. "I want you to remove the gift you gave my sister Larkspur," Ivy said bluntly. "That is my birthday wish."

The Faerie blinked, and then suddenly smiled, revealing sharp, white teeth. "That's not what you truly want."

Ivy gripped her crutch. "Yes, it is."

The Faerie stepped gracefully across the dell, bluebells bending themselves out of her way. She halted in front of Ivy, close enough to touch. Her smile glittered cruelly. "You want to be rid of that crutch."

"I want Larkspur as she was," Ivy said, firmly. "Take back the gift you gave her."

The Faerie's eyes narrowed. She seemed to stare into Ivy's skull for a moment. "Ah . . . You're in love with the Lord Warder's son." She laughed, a tinkling, disdainful, bell-like sound, her sharp teeth glinting. "Shall I give him to you as a husband? I know that's what your heart craves most . . ."

Ivy tightened her grip on the crutch and matched the Faerie stare for stare. The woman was playing with her as a cat played with a mouse. Well, Ivy was no mouse. "Take back Larkspur's gift," she demanded. "Now."

The Faerie lost her smile. Her cheekbones were suddenly knife-sharp beneath her pale skin. Her black eyes glittered with pure malevolence.

Ivy's throat dried.

They stared at each other for a long, breathless moment. Ivy's lungs were frozen. Her heart scarcely dared to beat. And then the Faerie shrugged lightly and turned away. "As you wish." She snapped her fingers carelessly.

Between one blink of Ivy's eyelids and the next, the Faerie vanished, as utterly as if she'd never existed. The dell was empty. The scalp-prickling sense of being watched was gone.

Ivy released a slow, trembling breath. She loosened her grip on the crutch. "Merciful gods . . ." she whispered.

Ivy left the basket and sewing where they lay. She hastened through Glade Forest, hobbling over tree roots, ducking beneath low branches, her heart beating loud and fast with hope, with fear. She splashed heedlessly through the little creek near the old woodcutter's cottage, hurried past the oak tree, and burst out into daylight.

The cottage dozed in the sunshine beneath its threadbare roof of thatching. Ivy looked around frantically, panting. Where was Larkspur? Where were the hounds?

"Larkspur?" she cried, breathlessly. "Larkspur!"

The crooked, sagging door swung open. The hounds jostled each other in the doorway, and behind them was Larkspur, pale and wraith-like.

Bess and Bartlemay bounded out, barking welcome, and on their heels was Larkspur, running. "I didn't hear you," Larkspur cried. "I didn't hear you!" And then she flung her arms around Ivy and burst into tears.

Ivy held her sister tightly, while Larkspur sobbed and the hounds milled around them, anxious.

There was no regret in Ivy's heart. None at all. Maybe the regret would come later, but right now, there was only love for Larkspur and sheer, utter relief that the Faerie had granted her wish.

At last the storm of tears died. Larkspur sniffed and drew back and inhaled several shaky, hiccuping breaths.

"Can you hear my thoughts at all?" Ivy asked.

Larkspur shook her head and wiped her face on her sleeve. Her cheeks were flushed from crying, her eyes bright with misery.

Ivy smoothed tangled strands of hair back from Larkspur's damp cheeks. "I love you," she said softly. "Very, very much."

"I love you, too," Larkspur whispered. "And I'm so *sorry*—"

Ivy touched two fingertips to her sister's lips, silencing her. "Don't say it. Don't even think it. None of this was your fault, love. You were tricked into wishing for your gift." She held Larkspur's eyes. "You helped care for her daughter, she *owed* you, and she despised you for being human, and so she tried to harm you. She has a baleful heart and a baleful tongue. If blame lies with anyone, it's with *her*, not you."

Larkspur's gaze fell. Her lips compressed faintly.

What did that slight movement of Larkspur's mouth mean? Repudiation? Or acceptance?

Acceptance, she hoped.

"And if I'm still lame, remember that you saved two lives. Hugh and Tam Dappleward would soon be dead, if not for the gift you chose. Remember *that*."

Larkspur glanced up.

Ivy smiled at her, and took her hand. "Come on, love. Let's go home."

*C*HAPTER 14

H ugh rode through Dapple Bend and across the village common, with his father and Tam and the Ironfists. The meadow opened out in front of him, golden-green, scattered with wildflowers. Hugh's eyes fastened on the whitewashed little cottage. Five days since he'd left its safety. Five days since he'd trundled away in a wagon, guarded by Tam and Cadoc. Five days since he'd last seen Ivy.

His throat was strangely tight. It was stupid to be nervous, and yet he was more nervous than he'd ever been in his life, his hands sweating on the reins, his heart beating unnecessarily fast. Gods, please let him say the right thing.

He saw a young boy running across the meadow, followed by the two huge red-brown hounds, heard peals of childish laughter and deep joyful barks.

A cluster of people stood in front of the cottage. Hugh squinted, trying to pick them out. The tall, hulking man was Renfred Blacksmith, a man with a reputation for integrity, good sense, and for never losing his temper. A man his father hoped would accept the post of Dapple Bend's alderman, when the aging incumbent stepped down this autumn.

"There's Hazel," Tam said, and his horse pranced two steps sideways and flicked its tail, as if Tam's eagerness had transmitted itself down the reins.

Hugh narrowed his eyes. Yes, there was Hazel, her hair gleaming rich brown in the sunlight, and there were Maythorn and Larkspur standing alongside her. He spared a moment's concern for Larkspur—was she fully recovered?—before searching for Ivy. Where was she?

Ah . . . There, she was. Standing in the doorway, leaning on her crutch.

Hugh's heart clenched in his chest, his hands clenched on the reins, and his horse snorted and tossed its head. Gods, what should he say to her? The words he'd spent the last thirty miles practicing suddenly seemed terribly inadequate.

Tam nudged his horse into a canter. Hugh followed more slowly, his gaze on Ivy. He scarcely saw Tam leap down, swing Hazel up in his arms, and kiss her soundly; all his attention was focused on Ivy. She was even lovelier than he remembered—the ebony hair, the clear green eyes. She had the same elegant bone structure as her sisters, but her beauty was quite different from theirs. She reminded him of Glade Forest—her hair the deep, mysterious shadows, her eyes the dark green moss. And Ivy's calm, quiet strength, her cool serenity were Glade Forest, too. No wonder his heart yearned for her.

Hugh dismounted alongside his father. His gaze skimmed the watching faces and settled on Ivy again. She gave him a small, polite smile, as if they'd never kissed, never made love.

Hugh narrowed his eyes at her. *No,* he told her silently, *we are not going to ignore what happened.*

Beside him, his father was thanking Larkspur. Hugh dragged his attention from Ivy and added his voice to his father's. Larkspur wasn't as terrifyingly frail as she'd been when he'd last seen her, but she was still far too thin. "I can never thank you enough," Hugh told her. His gratitude was heartfelt; he hoped she saw it on his face, heard it in his voice. "You risked your sanity for me and my family."

His father turned to Ivy next. "My son says he wouldn't have survived, but for your care of him."

"Your son exaggerates, sir."

"No, I don't," Hugh said. The words he'd practiced began to pile up urgently on his tongue. He closed his mouth and tried to swallow them back, but they pressed against his teeth, demanding to be let out. Gods, he was going to spill his soul in front of everyone. "Ivy, we need to talk," he said abruptly. "Now. Privately." He ignored his father's blink of surprise, ignored the sudden flare of curiosity on Hazel's face, ignored Tam's raised eyebrows, and gestured towards the brook.

Ivy hesitated for a moment, and then gave a slight nod.

They walked at Ivy's slow, limping pace. Behind them, conversation started again, haltingly. Hugh didn't need to look back to know that everyone was watching them.

They reached the brook and stopped. Ivy turned to face him. Hugh had the impression that she braced herself slightly. "Yes?" she said.

Now that the moment had come, Hugh's carefully worded proposal evaporated from his tongue. The silence stretched.

"What is it?"

Hugh swallowed the lump in his throat. *Just spit it out,* he told himself. "Ivy, will you please marry me?"

Ivy's head jerked back, as if he'd slapped her. "I told you, you don't owe me anything!"

"I owe you a lot, but that's not why I'm offering for you. Ivy . . ." He took one of her hands. "Ivy, I love you."

Ivy repossessed her hand. "You're confusing guilt and gratitude with love."

"No, I'm not," he said, stung.

"I'm not the wife for you, Hugh Dappleward."

"*I* think you are."

"Think, Hugh!" Ivy said sharply. "You'll be Lord Warder one day. You need a strong wife, someone who can support you, not a cripple!"

"Tam and Cadoc are all the muscle I'll need. What I need in my wife is a strong *mind.*"

Ivy looked away. "There are many women who have that."

"But they're not *you,*" Hugh said, frustrated. "It's not obligation, Ivy. Curse it, I love you!"

Ivy was silent for a moment, staring at the brook, at the pail of goat's milk cooling in the water. Hugh wished he could read her mind, wished *she* could read *his* mind and know he spoke the truth.

A fleeting shadow seemed to pass over Ivy's face. Sadness? She came to a decision; her jaw firmed and her lips compressed slightly. She turned her head. He saw the *No* in her eyes.

Hugh held up his hand, silencing her before she'd even drawn breath. "Stay here. Don't move."

Ivy's brow creased. "What?"

"Please stay," Hugh said, and then he turned and ran back to the cottage. Everyone stopped speaking. Hugh ignored their bright-eyed curiosity and took Larkspur by the hand. "Larkspur, I need you a moment."

He towed Larkspur back to where Ivy stood. "Tell her," he said. "Tell Ivy why I want to marry her. Tell her it's not guilt or gratitude or obligation!"

Larkspur crossed her arms and stood for a moment, her head tilted to one side, staring at him. Her blue eyes were narrow and unfocused. Hugh knew she wasn't seeing him; she was remembering his thoughts. He held his breath, and waited.

At last, Larkspur blinked, and shifted her gaze to Ivy. "He was very upset about what happened between you that first night. He felt that he'd behaved like an animal, not a man. He was deeply ashamed."

That wasn't what she was meant to be telling Ivy. Hugh opened his mouth to protest.

"And he most certainly is grateful—profoundly grateful—to all of us. And he does feel a strong sense of obligation."

"Larkspur!" Hugh said desperately.

Larkspur ignored him. "And he loves you as much as Tam loves Hazel."

Hugh closed his mouth. He held his breath. *Tell her, Larkspur,* he urged silently.

"When we were sitting around the table that night, there was very little difference between his thoughts about you and Tam's about Hazel—except that Tam knew he had Hazel's love, and Hugh was afraid he didn't have yours. His uncertainty and anxiety and hope were . . . painful." Larkspur touched her chest, above her heart.

Hugh released the breath he was holding.

Larkspur turned her head, meeting his eyes. "She loves you, too, you know. But she thinks you'll have responsibilities enough as Lord Warder, and you don't need another burden."

"You wouldn't be a burden!" Hugh said, appalled. "Gods, Ivy, how could you think such a thing!"

Ivy flushed faintly. Her gaze dropped.

"He doesn't care that you're lame, Ivy. He never thought about it, not once. It doesn't *matter* to him."

Ivy bit her lip. She didn't look cool or calm; she looked as if she was trying not to cry.

There was a moment of silence, and then Larkspur said: "I think it was love at first sight; you both have extremely vivid memories of meeting each other." And then she said, astutely: "I'll go now."

CHAPTER 15

Jvy stared at the brook, at the sunlight dancing on the water, the rippling reflections. When she was certain—well, *almost* certain—she wasn't going to cry, she lifted her gaze to Hugh. He was watching her, an expression of cautious hope on his face.

They looked at each other for long seconds, and then Hugh smiled at her. "Ivy, will you please marry me?"

The urge to cry ambushed her again. Ivy bit her lip and nodded.

Hugh's smile broadened into a grin. "Thank you. *That* was the answer I wanted." He stepped closer, gathered her in his arms, and kissed her gently.

Ivy closed her eyes and leaned into Hugh's kiss. Her crutch fell unheeded to the ground. Hugh's arms were strong, his mouth tender, and he loved her. Hugh Dappleward didn't care that she was lame. He *loved* her.

Abruptly, Ivy came to her senses. She drew back and glanced at the cottage. Eight people stood there in absolute silence, staring at her and Hugh, their expressions variously surprised and amused.

A hot blush suffused Ivy's face.

Hugh chuckled, deep in his chest. He tucked her close to his side. "Ivy and I are getting married," he called out.

There was a surge of movement towards them, an excited babble of noise. Ivy saw joy on Maythorn's face and sincere delight on Guy Dappleward's. Tam and Cadoc were grinning, and even grim, craggy Rauf Ironfist was smiling, and Larkspur . . . Larkspur looked truly happy for the first time in days.

For several minutes it was chaos. Ivy was kissed and embraced and exclaimed over. The hounds bounded across the meadow and joined in, barking loudly. "Get married at midsummer with us!" Hazel begged, and Tam swung Ivy up in a laughing, dizzying, rib-crushing hug, set her carefully back on her feet, and repeated the invitation.

Gradually, the chaos settled. Ivy had no idea where her crutch was, but it didn't matter; Hugh's arm was around her, warm and strong.

Guy Dappleward took one of her hands and held it in both of his. His face was kindly and smiling. "Welcome to the Dappleward family, Ivy. I'm very glad to have you as a daughter."

"Not half as glad as I am to have her as a wife," Hugh said, tightening his arm around her shoulders.

Tears pricked Ivy's eyes. She had Larkspur back, *and* she had Hugh, and now the gods were giving her a father, too.

Hugh pressed a kiss into her hair. "A midsummer wedding?"

Ivy looked at the smiling faces around her, and lastly at Hugh's face, at the joy in his eyes, and felt her happiness swell until she thought she might burst from it. The future stretched before her, better than anything she could have wished for.

No Faerie gift could have brought her this much joy.

"A midsummer wedding," she said.

Larkspur's
QUEST

A Baleful Godmother

Novella

$\mathcal{O}$NCE $\mathcal{U}$PON $\mathcal{A}$ $\mathcal{T}$IME

$\mathcal{I}$n the northern reaches of England lay a long and gentle valley, with villages and meadows and wooded hills. Dapple Vale was the valley's name, and the woods were known as Glade Forest, for many sunlit glades lay within their cool, green reaches. Glade Forest was surrounded by royal forest on all sides, but neither it nor Dapple Vale were on any map, and the Norman king and his foresters and tax collectors and huntsmen knew nothing of their existence.

Within the green, leafy expanse of Glade Forest lay the border with the Faerie realm, where the Fey dwelled. The boundary was invisible to the human eye; nothing marked it but a tingle, a lifting of hair on the back of one's neck. Wise men turned back when they felt the tingle, and unwise men continued and were never seen again.

Despite its proximity to Faerie—or perhaps because of it—the sun shone more often in Dapple Vale than elsewhere in England, and the winters were less harsh. The Great Plague bypassed Dapple Vale, and the Great Famine, too. Crops flourished, animals were fat and sleek, and the vale's folk were hale and long-lived.

One road led to the vale, but few travelers discovered it. No Romans found Dapple Vale, nor Vikings, and England's

latest invaders, the Normans, hadn't found it either. Even folk born and bred in the vale had been known to leave and never find their way back, so well hidden was Glade Forest.

The folk of Dapple Vale didn't take their good fortune for granted. They had heard of plagues and famines, heard of marauding soldiers and starving serfs and murderous outlaws. Each was careful to respect the forest that sheltered them, and most careful of all was the Lord Warder of Dapple Vale, who went by the name Dappleward. Dappleward and his sons and his liegemen, the Ironfists, knew the location of rings of standing stones where the Fey had danced in olden times. They knew where to find the great stone barrow that held the grave of a banished Faerie prince, and they knew of the dark and narrow crevice wherein lay a hoard of abandoned Faerie gold. They knew these places, and guarded them carefully.

All tales must have a beginning, and our tale begins in Dapple Bend, in the crook of Dapple Vale, where there once lived a miller's widow and her three beautiful daughters. The widow was half-blind and half-lame, but she had whole-hearted courage, and when she came upon a Faerie babe drowning in a deep, dark pool in the forest, she flung herself into the water to save it.

Now the Fey are dangerous and capricious and cruel, and the folk of Dapple Vale know better than to attract their attention, but Widow Miller went searching for the border with Faerie and called the babe's mother to her.

The Fey dislike humans, and dislike even more being indebted to them, and the babe's mother was deeply in Widow Miller's debt, so she granted the widow a wish, and each of her daughters a wish, too, and their daughters in turn.

Widow Miller entered Glade Forest half-lame and

half-blind; she left it supple-limbed and clear-eyed and with a joyful heart, and two weeks later she married the blacksmith she had secretly loved for years.

Her three daughters received their wishes on their birthdays. First to wish was the widow's middle daughter, and she asked for the gift of finding people and things, and with that to guide her she embarked on a hazardous journey, where she met Dappleward's youngest son and won his love.

Second to wish was the youngest daughter, and alas, she let the Faerie trick her into a wish that almost sent her mad. But if her wish brought harm, it also brought good, for Dappleward's eldest son had been cruelly bespelled, and it was she who learned how to break the spell that bound him.

Third to wish was the eldest daughter, who was the wisest of the widow's daughters, and who was lame, and she used her wish to restore her youngest sister to health, and she won the love of Dappleward's eldest son, but she was still lame.

The marriages were to be celebrated in Dapple Meadow, in the lower reaches of Dapple Vale, where the River Dapple meandered gently and the pastures were wide and fertile, and where the Lord Warder made his home. The widow's youngest daughter wanted more than anything for her sister to walk freely, but she had no Faerie wish to wish away her sister's lameness.

However, she *did* know how to earn one.

Thus begins our story . . .

*C*HAPTER 1

C adoc Ironfist strolled across the hillside paddock. Two mares grazed with their foals: one filly, one colt. He inhaled the meadow scents—clover, ryegrass, wildflowers, horse dung—and squinted up at the sun riding high in a sky the color of robins' eggs. Two days short of midsummer.

Cadoc dug a couple of last year's withered, sweet apples from his pocket and gave a whistle. The mares lifted their heads and ambled in his direction. He gave them the apples and looked them over while they crunched happily. Both well.

The foals let him examine them, too. He'd been present for their births, more than two months ago, and spent time with them whenever he could, getting them used to being handled. They stood quietly now while he touched them from head to tail, picked up each leg, tapped the bottom of each hoof. Next came the soft halter, and a turn being led around the paddock. Neither foal balked.

Lastly, he picked the foals up. *Prove to them you're bigger than them, and they'll always believe it, even when they stand taller than you,* Dappleward's old horse master had told him. It was a practice he continued, now that he was horse master himself.

"Won't be able to do this with you much longer," Cadoc

told the young colt. "You're getting heavy." The stab wound in his right biceps twinged slightly. He set the colt carefully down and rubbed his arm. Memory of last week's events came flooding back: the darkened chamber, Aleyn's frenzied hatred, Hugh Dappleward's agonized screams as his body changed from human to roebuck to human repeatedly.

Cadoc grimaced, pushed the memories aside, and bent his attention to the colt. It was a dark bay, large-boned and gangly. Not many horses could carry his weight comfortably at a gallop, but this one looked like he might be able to when he was fully grown. "Keep eating. You need to grow a barrel chest, if I'm to ride you." He scratched between the colt's ears, then headed for the stables.

He whistled as he walked, enjoying the sunshine, the blue sky, the sense that everything was right in the world. The Dappleward manor was spread before him: stables and smithy and kennels, kitchen and bakehouse, storerooms, the great hall where everyone gathered for meals. Upwards of fifty people lived here: Guy Dappleward's family, his retainers, his retainers' families. The manor was almost a village in itself, buildings and courtyards laid out on the hillside, basking in the sun—and half a mile distant, nestled in the curve of the valley, was the village proper, Dapple Meadow, largest settlement in Dapple Vale, home to nearly a thousand souls.

In the meadow between orchard and river, men were digging fire pits for the upcoming celebrations: midsummer, and the weddings of Dappleward's two sons. And up on the slope behind the orchard was the quiet, sunny graveyard where the Dapplewards and the Ironfists buried their dead. His mother rested there, and Guy Dappleward's wife.

Cadoc stopped whistling, and touched two fingers to his brow in a gesture of respect. *Salute, Mother,* he said silently. *Salute, milady.*

The clash of wood on wood brought his gaze back to the sprawling manor. In the nearest courtyard, two men trained with wooden staves. One was a hulking bear of a man with grizzled hair: his father, Dappleward's weapon master. Cadoc halted for half a minute, watching. Rauf Ironfist was fifty now, but age hadn't shrunk him yet, nor slowed him; he was still light on his feet, still fast. His opponent was half his age, strong and lean—and struggling to hold his own.

Cadoc winced in sympathy as his father disarmed Dappleward's younger son, Tam. He could sense Tam's frustration from here, fifty yards away. *Give over, Tam,* he thought. *You'll never beat him. Even I only manage one time out of three.* Rauf Ironfist had been the best warrior in Dapple Vale for the past thirty years, and would probably remain so for another ten.

Cadoc grinned and shook his head and entered the stables. He paused just inside the wide door, letting his eyes adjust to the dimness. The stables were cool and shadowy and fragrant. Cadoc inhaled deeply. He loved this smell: horse, straw, dung. Loved it far more than the metal-and-wood smell of weapons. Horses were vibrant and warm and alive; weapons were hard and cold and brought death.

He had a flash of memory: Aleyn Fairborn lying dead on the floor.

Cadoc touched the dagger belted at his waist, half unsheathed it, felt the sharp coolness of the blade. Aleyn had been worse than a murderer. He'd dared to harness Faerie magic to serve his own twisted purpose, had planned death upon death, driven by nothing more than his own greed for power. He'd deserved to die.

Cadoc grimaced. Yes, Aleyn Fairborn had deserved to die. But even so . . .

Ironfists were warriors, sworn to guard the peace. They were the shoulder the Lord Warder leaned on. Wherever there was a Dappleward, an Ironfist wasn't far away.

But even so . . . Cadoc did not like killing.

He slid the dagger back into its sheath and strode between the horse stalls. He was an Ironfist, he'd fight if he had to—kill if it was necessary—but this was what he preferred: horses.

"Cadoc?" a female voice said.

He jerked around, blinked, and saw a woman standing shyly in the shadows. A young woman, too slender, with hair as pale as moonbeams and a face that was luminously beautiful.

Recognition was like a physical blow. Larkspur Miller.

His lungs seemed to tighten. The muscles in his belly definitely did tighten.

Cadoc tried to look as if he weren't helplessly attracted to her. He gave her a courteous nod. "I give you good day, Larkspur."

"And you."

Five days, she'd be here at Dappleward Manor. Five days only. Was that enough time to court her? Would she even want him to?

He knew Larkspur was wary of men, and he knew she'd been afraid of him the first time they'd met. She'd stayed as far from him as possible, unnerved by his size or his face or his reputation as a warrior, or all three. But she wasn't afraid of him now.

Therefore, he would court her. He was twenty-five, past time for marrying. And Larkspur was the wife he wanted. Beneath her quiet shyness, she was strong and courageous. She had risked her sanity to help save Hugh Dappleward.

"Would you like to look around the stables?" Cadoc asked politely, and then thought, *No, better to show her the foals. She'll like that.*

"No, thank you." Larkspur stepped closer. Her hands were clasped, her gaze intent on his face. The light was too dim to clearly see the color of her eyes, but he knew they were blue, a blue as vivid as the flower she was named after. "Cadoc, may I talk privately with you, please?"

"Of course. Uh . . . there's no one here—the grooms are helping build the midsummer bonfires—or we can go outside—"

"Here's fine."

Cadoc nodded, and studied Larkspur's face. She was still

245

far too thin, not fully recovered from the Faerie gift that had nearly driven her mad. For two long weeks she'd had the ability to read people's minds—two weeks when every thought, memory, and emotion her companions experienced had pushed relentlessly into her head. That gift was gone now, and Larkspur was privy to only her own thoughts, but something was still clearly wrong; there was a sharp crease between her eyebrows, anxiety in her eyes, and her lovely mouth was tightly compressed.

"What's wrong?" Cadoc said gently. "If I can help, I will."

"I know," Larkspur said, and she smiled at him, suddenly and blindingly. "That's why I came to you."

Cadoc's lungs became even tighter. He swallowed, and found his voice. "Then tell me."

Larkspur looked away from him. She moistened her lips. "Cadoc . . . that night we all met to find a way to help Hugh . . . there were two ways to save him. One was killing Aleyn Fairborn, and the other was something to do with a Faerie prince buried in a barrow."

"Yes," Cadoc said cautiously. That Faerie prince, that barrow, were the most secret of secrets. What did Larkspur know about them? *Everything*, a voice said in his head. *She could read your thoughts then, remember?*

Larkspur took a deep breath. "Ivy shouldn't be lame. She *deserves* not to be lame!"

"Yes," Cadoc said again, even more cautiously. Where was Larkspur going with this?

Larkspur clenched her hands more tightly together. "Will you please go to the barrow with me and help me earn a wish for Ivy?"

"What?" Cadoc recoiled. "Gods, Larkspur! Of course I can't!"

"Why not?"

"Because I'm sworn to Guy Dappleward! I gave my word *never* to approach that barrow, let alone enter it and . . . and . . ."

"Please," Larkspur begged.

"Larkspur, I can't!"

"Ivy's still lame because of me." Tears glistened in Larkspur's eyes. "She gave up her wish for me. I have to find a way to give it back to her!"

"You can't," Cadoc told her gently. "You have to accept that."

"No!" Larkspur's voice was fierce. "I know where that barrow is, and I know what I have to do to . . . to *earn* a wish. And if you won't go with me, I'll find a man who will!"

Cadoc blenched. "Larkspur . . . do you know what the Faerie prince demands in return for his gifts?"

Larkspur flushed, and raised her chin. "Yes. You all thought of it, all three of you. Tam even thought that maybe Hazel would go with him. And you . . ."

Cadoc wanted to shut his eyes in a wince.

"You thought it was dangerous, but doable. And that it was most likely to succeed with a virgin, because the prince is said to prefer virgins."

Cadoc did shut his eyes in a wince.

"*I'm* a virgin, and I'm prepared to do it. But I need a man to do it with."

Cadoc cautiously opened his eyes. Larkspur's stare impaled him. "You're my first choice," she said. "I *trust* you. But if you say no . . . I'll find someone else."

"Larkspur, I'm loyal to Dappleward," Cadoc said desperately.

"And *I* am loyal to Ivy."

"You can't tell me she asked you to do this!"

"Of course not. She's resigned to being lame for the rest of her life. But *I'm* not resigned to it!"

"I gave Dappleward my word never to enter that barrow," Cadoc said helplessly. Fidelity had been bred into him. He couldn't alter it if he tried. Ironfists were loyal to the Lord Warder. They were *always* loyal.

247

"You gave me your word, too. Last week. You said that you owed me for Hugh's life. That if I ever needed anything, all I had to do was ask."

They'd all said it: Guy Dappleward, Tam, Hugh, he and his father. But he'd never imagined *this* request.

"If you won't do it for me or Ivy, then do it for Hugh. I know you love him as a brother. Think how much joy it would give him if Ivy were to walk freely again!"

Cadoc hesitated.

Larkspur stepped closer. "You would have done it for Hugh. You *thought* of doing it."

"He's a Dappleward," Cadoc said lamely.

"Ivy will be, too, the day after tomorrow!"

"Larkspur . . ." He couldn't bear the sight of her face any more, the sight of those unshed tears in her eyes, her desperation. He turned away from her. "Larkspur, I can't. I gave Guy Dappleward my *word*."

There was a long moment of silence. Cadoc stared at the nearest horse stall, feeling sick.

"Very well," Larkspur said quietly. "Be loyal to Dappleward. I shall find another man to help me, someone who doesn't have your scruples. And he'll learn about the barrow and what may be earned there."

Cadoc turned around and stared at her. "That's blackmail."

Larkspur's gaze fell. "I don't intend it to be." And then, to his horror, she dropped to her knees in front of him. "Cadoc, *please.*"

"Gods," Cadoc said, appalled. "Get up. Get up!"

He hauled her to her feet, but as soon as he released her, Larkspur knelt again. "Please, Cadoc."

Cadoc's throat tightened until breathing was impossible. He stared down at Larkspur's thin, beseeching face. Her desperation and determination were clear to see. If he refused, she would ask someone else. She would ask until she found a man who would go with her, and that man would defile her in the darkness of the Faerie prince's barrow.

His hands clenched into fists. Helpless rage choked in his chest.

"Please." Larkspur begged again.

If Larkspur went with another man, they'd get *into* the barrow, but there was no guarantee they'd ever get *out*. People had died in there.

And if they *did* get out . . .

Someone other than the Dapplewards and the Ironfists would know about the Faerie prince's barrow—and unlike a Dappleward or Ironfist, that man wouldn't be sworn to serve the best interests of Dapple Vale. He'd serve himself. And that was dangerous. *Very* dangerous.

"Larkspur . . ." As Cadoc uttered her name, he knew he'd surrendered. *Gods help me,* he thought as he slowly knelt. On his knees, he was almost eye to eye with her. "I'll do it."

"You will?" Relief transformed her face.

Cadoc nodded. Shame sat heavily in his belly. Whose interests was he serving now? The vale's or his own?

"Thank you," Larkspur said, and she flung her arms around his neck and hugged him.

Cadoc froze. She was so feminine, so slender. He wanted to wrap his arms around her and hold her tightly to him, wanted to kiss her silky hair, kiss her soft lips. He held himself very still.

Larkspur released him and sat back on her heels. "Thank you," she said again. Tears spilled down her cheeks. She brushed them impatiently aside.

Cadoc nodded dumbly.

"Can we go today, please? This afternoon?"

He nodded again.

Larkspur climbed to her feet. "In half an hour. I need to find my sisters. I'll tell them I'm going riding with you. They won't worry until dusk, and by then it will be too late for them to come after us!" She bent and shyly kissed his cheek. "*Thank* you."

A blush suffused Cadoc's face. Larkspur didn't see it; she

was already heading for the door, almost running. Her hair shone like silver in the sunlight, and then she was gone.

Cadoc touched his cheek where Larkspur had kissed him. Gods, what was he doing? And then he pushed to his feet and went to saddle two horses.

CHAPTER 2

Larkspur found her sister Hazel watching Tam Dappleward and Rauf Ironfist train with wooden staves. "Hazel?"

Hazel glanced at her, grinning. "Poor Tam. Ironfist is slaughtering him." And then her grin became wider. "And once he's finished with Tam, Ironfist is going to teach *me*."

Larkspur nodded. "Hazel, I'm going riding with Cadoc."

A loud clatter of staves drew Hazel's attention back to the combatants. She winced. "Poor Tam." But there was laughter in her voice, and from her eager expression, she was looking forward to her turn on the training ground.

"I'm going riding with Cadoc," Larkspur said again.

Hazel transferred her gaze to Larkspur. Her eyebrows quirked slightly upwards. "What?"

"I'm going riding with Cadoc," Larkspur said, a third time.

"With Cadoc?" Hazel's eyebrows rose higher.

Larkspur felt herself blush. "Yes. We might be out quite late. Can you please tell Mother and Ivy?"

"Cadoc Ironfist." Hazel tilted her head to one side. Her long nut-brown plait slithered forward over her shoulder. She flicked it back. Her gaze became speculative. "Do you like him?"

I love him, Larkspur thought. Her cheeks grew hotter. "He's nice."

Laughter leapt into Hazel's eyes, but she forbore to tease. "Very well, you're going riding with Cadoc. I'll tell the others. Where are you going and when will you be back?"

"Oh . . . Just into the forest. There are some places Cadoc wants to show me. We might be several hours. Don't look for us until dusk."

The laughter faded from Hazel's face, leaving it serious.

"What?" Larkspur said, apprehensively.

"You always were a terrible liar."

"I'm not lying! We *are* going into the forest!"

"And?"

"And nothing!" But she heard with her own ears that her voice was pitched slightly too high.

"With anyone else, I'd say you were sneaking off for a quick tumble, but you're too cautious for that and Cadoc's too decent." Hazel put her hands on her hips and fixed Larkspur with a stern stare. "What exactly are you up to, Larkspur Miller?"

Nothing, Larkspur wanted to say, but she knew Hazel would hear the lie in her voice, so she told the truth: "Something important that I can't tell you about."

Hazel's eyes narrowed. "Important?"

"*Very* important. But Cadoc swore an oath not to tell anyone, and I only know about it because I heard him think about it, and you *must* see, Hazel, that I can't tell anyone!"

Hazel thought about this for a moment, and then asked, "Is it dangerous?"

Larkspur hesitated. "It might be. I don't know."

"Then I don't care whether it's secret or not, I'm coming with you."

"No!" Larkspur took a deep breath and found a voice that was just as firm as Hazel's. "There's nothing you can do to help. This is something only Cadoc and I can do. You would only be in the way."

Hazel's eyes became even narrower.

"If it's dangerous, Cadoc will protect me better than you ever could."

Hazel pursed her lips.

"Please don't tell Mother or Tam or anyone," Larkspur said urgently. "Or try to follow us." And then, because Hazel's Faerie gift was to be able to find people, she added, even more urgently, "And *please* don't try to find out where we've gone until it's dark."

Hazel looked at her for several long seconds, her eyes sharp and astute. "When do you expect to be back?"

Larkspur bit her lip, and then admitted, "Tomorrow."

"Tomorrow? Gods, Larkspur! I can't let you—"

"Cadoc will be with me. You *know* he'll keep me safe!"

Hazel stared at her for a long moment, her lips pursed, then her gaze turned to Tam, clashing staves with Rauf Ironfist.

"You left Dapple Vale all by yourself, and you faced *outlaws*. I'll still be in Glade Forest, and I'll have Cadoc."

Hazel's gaze came back to her. "What does Cadoc think of this?"

"That it's dangerous, but doable."

Hazel grimaced. "If *Cadoc* thinks it's dangerous—"

"But doable! He thinks it's doable!"

Hazel glanced at Tam again. She wanted to call him over; Larkspur could see it on her face.

"Don't you trust me?" Larkspur said desperately.

Hazel looked back at her. "Of course I trust you."

"Then, please, trust that I'm doing the right thing!"

Hazel hesitated.

"I wouldn't do it if it weren't important."

"But you won't tell me what it is?"

Larkspur shook her head.

"Larkspur—"

"Cadoc will keep us both safe. You know he will!"

She held her breath, while Hazel stared at her narrow-eyed, and then her sister huffed out a sigh and lifted her hands in a shrug and said, "All right."

"Will you tell everyone we've gone riding and won't be back until late? *Please*, Hazel."

Hazel sighed again. "All right."

"Thank you." She hugged Hazel swiftly.

Hazel hugged her back, and said in her ear, "By all the gods, be careful, little sister, or I will personally flay you alive!"

*C*HAPTER 3

*L*arkspur had ridden horses a few times, but never with reins and a saddle and stirrups. The horses she'd ridden had been working horses, stolid, amiable creatures used to pulling ploughs or wagons, as far removed from the mare she rode now as a farmer's crude scythe was from a perfectly balanced sword.

Cadoc Ironfist looked utterly at ease in the saddle. His horse was a huge beast, twice the size of the dainty mare she rode. It could easily pull a plough, but it was no workhorse; even her inexperienced eyes could see that. The horse was agile in its muscularity, and there was nothing placid about it. It was obedient to Cadoc's slightest wish, but there was spirit in the way it held its head, and intelligence in its dark, liquid eyes.

Cadoc looked at ease on the horse—but not at ease in himself. His face was even grimmer than it usually was, his jaw tight beneath the short-clipped beard. There was tension in his wide shoulders, tension in his strong thighs. His hands, gripping the reins, were white-knuckled.

Larkspur grimaced and looked away. Guilt would overwhelm her, if she allowed it to.

No, that was wrong. Guilt had already overwhelmed her. In doing this, she was merely exchanging one guilt for another.

But hopefully this guilt would be easier to bear.

She glanced at Cadoc Ironfist again. When she'd first met him, at Hazel and Tam's betrothal, she'd been so intimidated by his towering height, his brawniness, his apparent fierceness, that she'd scarcely dared to look him in the eye. The second time she'd encountered him, she'd had her Faerie gift and Cadoc's mind had been laid bare to her. His thoughts hadn't matched his exterior at all. She'd realized that he wasn't a man to fear; he was a man to *trust*.

The third time she'd met Cadoc, she'd fallen in love with him—and she'd learned of the dead Faerie prince in his barrow and the gifts he could bestow, and how to earn those gifts. And she'd known that Cadoc was the one man she could face that ordeal with.

But Cadoc didn't want to do this.

Guilt tightened its grip on her innards. She wished she could tell Cadoc she loved him, but to do so *would* be blackmail. *I love you, and I'll marry you if you'll do this one thing for me* . . . No, she wouldn't stoop that low.

The trail they followed was narrow, and then no trail at all. Cadoc's mount slowed, its glossy haunches bunching as they climbed steeply, winding their way up a heavily-wooded gully along which a stream poured in a froth of white water. The incline lessened and they emerged into a sunny clearing that Larkspur recognized; Hugh and Tam Dappleward had pictured this place in their minds. And Cadoc.

At the far side of the clearing was a huge, rounded mound overgrown with grass and wildflowers. The mound was taller than she was, taller than Cadoc. Massive, ancient stones ringed its base, gray with lichen. The dead Faerie prince's barrow.

Larkspur's mouth was suddenly dry.

Cadoc dismounted and turned to help her. His lips were tightly compressed. He didn't meet her eyes.

Larkspur slid down from her saddle. She wanted to beg Cadoc's forgiveness for asking this of him—but if she did that, if she faltered in her purpose, they'd never enter the barrow, and she *had* to enter the barrow, or Ivy would forever be lame.

Today—tonight—was for Ivy, but after that, everything would be for Cadoc.

Cadoc unsaddled the horses, watered them, and hobbled them. "We should eat," he said, still not meeting her eyes directly.

"Oh, but—can't we just get this over with?"

Cadoc's lips compressed further. His gaze flicked to her and away again. "Time could run strangely in there. What seems like minutes could actually be hours. Or days. It's best that we eat now."

Cadoc had brought bread and cheese. They ate in awkward silence, not looking at each other, not talking. Larkspur didn't taste the food; it was merely fuel to get her through what was going to happen next.

Fear shivered through her . . . and a tiny flicker of curiosity.

She glanced at Cadoc out of the corner of her eye. His hands were huge, strong, and tanned. And clean. Huge, strong, clean hands.

The rest of him was huge, too. He was massive, a warrior who'd wield a battleax as easily as he would a spoon. Larkspur looked down at her rye bread and salty, crumbling cheese, but she saw Cadoc clearly in her mind's eye: the ash-blond hair, the steely gray eyes, the bearded, square-jawed face, the shoulders as broad as an ox's, the deep chest from which his voice came with a gravelly rumble, the legs as strong as tree trunks. He was a man composed of heavy bones and thick slabs of muscle. A rugged, brutal, dangerous man—until one saw inside his head and realized that Cadoc wasn't dangerous at all.

Larkspur ate the last of her bread and brushed the crumbs from her lap. Long, golden twilight was falling. Cadoc stood. She glanced up at him towering above her. "Now?" Her stomach tied itself in a knot.

"No. I want to wash first."

Wash? Now? And then she realized why: Because he'd be lying with her soon.

257

Color rushed to Larkspur's cheeks, but Cadoc was already turning away, making for the creek.

She watched him go. His hair was cropped as sternly short as his beard. Did he grow that short-clipped beard in an attempt to soften his appearance? To hide the harsh, craggy bones of his face? If so, it didn't work. The beard made him look older than he was, older and grimmer. *No*, Larkspur realized with a sudden moment of insight. *He has the beard because it makes him look forbidding. It makes men think twice about going up against him.* And Cadoc didn't like fighting.

Cadoc returned ten minutes later. "Um . . . I'll wash, too," Larkspur said, and sidled past him, heading for the creek. She found the little pond he'd used—one of the rocks bore his damp footprint—and stripped off her clothes and washed hastily. Would Cadoc kiss her? Would he touch her? Or would it be a hurried copulation, quick and rough and painful?

No, not rough. Not Cadoc. And it would be as painless as he could make it. Cadoc didn't like to hurt people, but more than that, he had affection for her. The night they'd all met to save Hugh Dappleward, Cadoc had carried her back into the forest. His thoughts had been like a blanket wrapped around her: protectiveness, tenderness, a blossoming love. No, Cadoc would do his best not to hurt her tonight.

His footprint was still on the rock when she finished bathing. Larkspur placed her own bare foot alongside. His print was twice the size of hers. *Gods, so big.* She suppressed a twinge of fear. Whatever pain there was would be worth it. *Any* amount of pain would be worth it, if it meant that Ivy would walk again.

Back in the clearing, Cadoc was examining the barrow. It was as large as the great communal hall at Dappleward Manor, thickly overgrown with grass. Had the Faerie prince already sensed their presence? And how could a dead prince know he had visitors, let alone bestow gifts on them?

Larkspur shivered. "Why is he buried here, not in Faerie?"

"Punishment for something. Only the Fey know what for."

The weathered gray stones ringing the barrow were taller than Cadoc, except to the north, where there was a low archway blocked by a single slab of rock. Cadoc halted in front of the slab. It was no higher than his shoulder, as weathered as its neighbors, pitted with lichen. Her eyes judged it no match for him.

"If he's dead, how can he grant wishes?"

"He's not truly dead; he's *mostly* dead." Cadoc ran his hands around the edge of the slab, looking for handholds. "His body's long rotted, but whatever makes him Fey is still alive. And bound here."

Larkspur shivered again. *Gods, what a fate.*

Cadoc glanced at her. "Are you certain you want to do this?"

Larkspur swallowed her fear. "Yes."

Cadoc grimaced slightly, as if he'd hoped she might have changed her mind. He turned back to the slab and found solid handholds. She saw his jaw clench, saw the tendons in his throat stand out.

Cadoc didn't try to rip the rock from its resting place; he shook it slowly free. At first, the slab moved grudgingly, half an inch, an inch, and then grit and dirt began to shower down. Cadoc's movements became more forceful—a black hole yawned behind the slab—more dirt cascaded down—and then Cadoc grunted and eased the slab down onto its side against the mound.

Larkspur eyed the hole. It was low and narrow, pitch-black. Cadoc would have to bend in half to get inside.

The barrow looked quite benign, round and grassy as it was, but the darkness inside seemed . . . threatening.

She shivered again, and glanced back over her shoulder. To the west, the sun was setting. They would soon be missed. And as soon as they were missed, someone would ask Hazel where they were, and Hazel, with her Faerie gift, would know exactly, and even if she didn't understand the significance, the Dapplewards would.

Night would slow any pursuers, but there were barely six hours of darkness, this close to midsummer. The Lord Warder could be here by dawn.

Cadoc wiped his hands on his tunic and turned to look at her. "You certain about this? People have died in here."

"Died?"

Cadoc nodded.

Larkspur stared up at his rough-hewn face. She could risk her own life in this, but not Cadoc's. "Do you think we'll die?"

Cadoc hesitated, and then said, "No," and she saw on his face that he wished he could lie to her and turn her from this path, but that he couldn't bring himself to do so.

Her love for him increased, and so did her guilt. "Then I'm certain."

Cadoc sighed. He turned away and walked to where the saddles and bridles lay and picked something up: a rolled blanket that had been tied behind his saddle. In a flash, she understood. The blanket was for them to lie on.

Larkspur's stomach tightened in apprehension. She began to regret the meal she'd eaten.

Cadoc unrolled the blanket. Inside were two beeswax candles and a bronze chamberstick. Larkspur blinked. Why hadn't she thought of candles?

Because it was the getting here that had consumed her; she'd shied away from thinking of anything beyond that.

No, that was untrue. She'd imagined what it would be like afterwards: Ivy walking, running, dancing at her own wedding. It was what would happen in the barrow itself that she'd not dared to think of.

Cadoc had thought about it, though. He'd had scant minutes to prepare, and he'd brought food, light, and a blanket. Her respect for him rose even higher.

Cadoc dug into the leather pouch hanging from his belt and pulled out a tinderbox. He lit one candle and placed it in the chamberstick, tucked the second candle and the tinderbox into his pouch, and came to stand alongside her, the blanket slung over his shoulder. His face was very grim.

I love you, Larkspur wanted to say. She bit her lip to stop herself uttering the words. Not now, not while they could be construed as an attempt at manipulation. Once this was all over, she would tell him.

She slipped her hand into his. "Thank you for doing this, Cadoc."

Cadoc's lips compressed. He looked away from her, towards the setting sun. "It'll hurt. You know that, don't you? You're a virgin, and I'm . . . not small."

"I don't mind if it hurts."

Cadoc's jaw tightened. "I mind."

"Don't," Larkspur said vehemently, tightening her grip on his hand. "Please don't! Don't even think about it! It's not important at all. What's important is Ivy. Whether you hurt me or not is irrelevant!"

Cadoc grimaced.

"Cadoc, you're the one doing *me* a favor. If *I* don't care whether it hurts or not, *you* shouldn't either!"

Cadoc glanced at her, and then away again. Did he believe her? From the set of his jaw, the tightness of his mouth, she thought not.

Gods, she shouldn't be doing this to him.

Remorse swept through her. Larkspur stared up at Cadoc's profile, torn between him and Ivy—and then resolve kicked in. Tonight was for Ivy. There was no turning back.

Cadoc exhaled his breath in a sigh. He released her hand and turned to the entrance of the barrow. "I'll go first."

CHAPTER 4

$\mathcal{I}$t was a tight squeeze. Cadoc's shoulders brushed rock and dirt on either side, dislodging showers of grit. He walked half a dozen yards bent double, before the passage opened out. Cautiously, he stepped into a dark chamber and straightened to his full height. Leather shoes scuffed softly behind him, and then Larkspur came to stand at his side.

Cadoc raised the candle high. The barrow was larger than it had appeared from outside; the candlelight didn't reach the far walls.

The air wasn't stale. There was no whiff of decay. The chamber was neither cool nor warm, and smelled only of earth.

A stone casket sat squarely in the middle of the space. The casket was massive, taller than Cadoc, big enough for a draft horse. It was fashioned from a dense black stone that seemed to suck up the candlelight. Was it his imagination, or did the casket radiate a silent malevolence?

Other than the casket, what he could see of the chamber was empty.

Cadoc had no urge to explore; his one impulse—deep and instinctive—was to get out of the barrow as fast as possible.

He glanced down at Larkspur. She met his gaze soberly.

She trusts me to bring us safely through this.

Cadoc cleared his throat, took a deep breath, and spoke: "Pardon us for disturbing your rest, Prince, but we wish to strike a bargain with you."

His voice echoed in the chamber, coming back again and again and again, until it seemed that a dozen men had spoken. Gradually, the echoes died away. Silence returned.

A tiny flicker of hope kindled in Cadoc's chest. It had been centuries since anyone had last breached this tomb. Perhaps the Faerie prince had truly and irrevocably died? No lingering magic, no dubious gifts to be earned, just . . . nothing.

Cadoc swallowed his hope, and spoke more loudly. "Sire? Pardon us for disturbing you. We wish to make a bargain with you."

Again, the echoes of his voice died into silence.

His hope strengthened. The barrow was empty. No Faerie prince rested here in a state of not-quite-death, bound in punishment for sins committed millennia ago.

He didn't dare glance at Larkspur, lest she see his hope. Instead, he took another breath and spoke again: "Sire?"

A low, rustling whisper susurrated around the chamber walls. It sounded like leaves stirring in a breeze, like the dry skittering of insects' legs.

Cadoc's words dried on his tongue. His throat clenched in a moment of deep-seated terror. *Get out of here!* a voice cried in his head. *Now!*

Something touched his hand. His whole body jerked in an instinctive recoil before he realized it was Larkspur.

Cadoc swallowed, and gripped her hand tightly back. Her fingers were trembling. She was terrified.

That knowledge stiffened his spine. "Pardon us for disturbing your rest, sire, but we wish to strike a bargain with you." His voice wasn't as loud as it had been the first three times—fear had squeezed the air from his lungs—and nor did it echo. The darkness swallowed his words whole.

After a moment, the dry, rustling whisper came again. This time Cadoc recognized it for what it was: an exhaled breath.

"A bargain?" The voice was faint and wispy. Each word

seemed to disintegrate as it was spoken, its edges fraying into nothingness.

"A bargain. Our . . . our copulation—for your enjoyment—in exchange for a wish."

"What wish do you seek?" wheezed the voice. Cadoc's ears strained to catch the words before they faded.

"A healing," Cadoc said.

"No . . ." The whisper grew stronger. "It's not you who wishes to bargain with me. Let the woman speak."

Cadoc glanced at Larkspur. He saw muscles work in her throat as she swallowed. Her chin lifted. "My sister is lame." Her voice was clear and strong. "I wish for you to heal her."

"Lame . . ."

"Her leg was broken when she was a child. Her name is Ivy. She's at Dappleward Manor."

The silence drew for a long time before a sighing breath rustled across the dirt floor. "Yes, I can heal her."

"Then we have a bargain?"

"Perhapsss . . ." The *s* dwindled to the very edge of Cadoc's hearing, then more words came: "You have been Fey-touched. Recently."

Larkspur hesitated. "Yes."

"By whom?"

"I don't know her name." Larkspur paused, bit her lip, and offered: "My sister Hazel calls her Baletongue."

"Baletongue?" The voice was growing stronger, the words no longer fraying at the edges. "Why did this Baletongue come to you?"

"My mother saved Baletongue's daughter from drowning. In exchange, we were granted wishes."

There was a full minute of silence. Even the rustling breaths died away. Cadoc strained his ears, listening.

"You have taken your wish. Why did you not use it to heal your sister?"

Cadoc glanced at Larkspur. Her face was tense and miserable. "My wish came before Ivy's. I thought . . . I thought she would use her wish for herself."

"She didn't?"

"She used her wish to save me." In the candlelight, Cadoc saw a tear track down Larkspur's cheek.

A low chuckle rolled around the chamber walls, and wheezed into silence.

Cadoc tightened his grip on Larkspur's hand. "A bargain," he said firmly. "Our copulation, for your enjoyment, in exchange for Ivy's healing."

There was a long moment of silence, and then the voice spoke slyly, "Perhaps I don't feel like it?"

You feel like it, Cadoc thought. *But you're a Faerie; you want us on our knees, begging.*

"How many years has it been since someone last had sex in here?" he said, out loud. "More than three hundred? You want it." Some of his anger, his contempt, leaked into his voice.

An ill-tempered hiss slithered around the chamber, sibilant and snake-like. The sound made the hairs rise on Cadoc's scalp. He managed not to shiver.

The hiss died away. Silence filled his ears. The candle flickered faintly. A drop of hot wax trickled down the shaft and pooled in the bronze cup of the chamberstick. Cadoc tried to hold on to his anger—better to be angry than afraid—but the longer the silence drew out the more worried he became.

"It seems a poor bargain," the voice said finally, making Cadoc start. Another drop of hot wax slid down the candle. "One copulation in exchange for an act of great magic . . ."

What was the Faerie prince hoping to force them into? Multiple acts of sex? Cruel degradations?

No, he wouldn't allow that.

"One copulation in exchange for one healing," Cadoc said firmly. "As bargains go, it's perfectly balanced."

"I disagree."

"I'm a virgin," Larkspur said clearly.

A sharp breath skittered around the chamber walls and across the arching ceiling. Larkspur's fingers clutched Cadoc's convulsively.

"A virgin . . ." the disembodied voice breathed.

"Yes," Larkspur said.

"I do like virgins . . ." The Faerie prince made a low humming sound, almost a purring. Cadoc's ears recognized the noise for what it was: sexual excitement.

The hairs on his scalp rose again. This time, he couldn't prevent a shiver. "Then we have a bargain," he said loudly. "One act of copulation, in exchange for one act of healing."

There was a long pause, and then the Faerie prince said, "A bargain."

"We want your word," Cadoc said firmly. "Your word that you will heal Ivy as soon as we do this for you. Heal her completely and everlastingly. You will not delay. You will not attempt to renegotiate."

"You have my word," the dead prince said grudgingly.

"Say it," Cadoc said, a hard edge to his voice. "Say what you are agreeing to."

The prince hissed a sharp, venomous breath. "Once your act of copulation is over, I will permanently heal this woman's sister of her lameness."

"The *moment* it's over."

"The moment it's over. My word on it."

"Then we have a bargain." Cadoc released Larkspur's hand and unslung the blanket from his shoulder.

*C*HAPTER 5

*C*adoc had had precisely two lovers in his life. Both had been older than him, both widows, both women who'd known what they wanted in bed. They'd chosen him because of his physique, made their interest known, and he'd surrendered willingly. There, the similarities had ended. Elinor had cheerfully stripped him of his virginity and then taught him how to pleasure women. That relationship had spanned more than a year and he'd enjoyed every minute of it. If Elinor hadn't remarried, they might still be lovers. With Elinor, sex had been fun.

Sex with Meg had been deeply unsatisfying. More than that, it had been disturbing. He'd lain with her three times, and each time he'd known that he'd failed to please her. She wanted him to be rougher. She wanted him to *hurt* her. They had parted with mutual relief.

Meg had been two years ago. Since then, he'd been celibate. He'd wanted the next woman he lay with to be someone he loved.

But not like this.

Cadoc placed the chamberstick on the dirt floor and spread the blanket carefully. He straightened to his full height. He couldn't bring himself to look directly at Larkspur. He averted his gaze and stared into the shadows. What now? Should he undress himself? Undress *her*?

A snigger scurried around the chamber walls.

You're enjoying this, you bastard, Cadoc thought. He bent and snuffed the candle with his fingertips. The blackness was instant and utter.

He stood slowly. At least Larkspur would have the privacy of darkness. It was the only thing he could give her.

The wick flared alight. "Oh, no . . ." the Faerie prince whispered gleefully. "I want to see it all. You may disrobe each other now."

Cadoc cast Larkspur an agonized glance.

Larkspur crossed to where he stood. Her eyes were grave, her hair shining like moonlight. She smiled at him, faint and reassuring, and reached for his belt. "It's all right," she whispered, unfastening the heavy bronze buckle. "It's all right, Cadoc."

It was *not* all right, but he'd agreed to this bargain; he wouldn't renege on it. Cadoc captured Larkspur's hands, halting her. "I'll undress myself."

"No, no," came the susurrating whisper. "Let her do it."

"We are not your puppets." He gave Larkspur's hands a reassuring squeeze, and released them. "We undress ourselves."

A displeased hiss echoed around the walls. Cadoc ignored it. He took several steps back from Larkspur and began to strip, calmly and methodically and with as much dignity as he could muster.

"I want her hair loose."

Cadoc glanced at Larkspur, and then quickly away. He focused his attention fully on himself. Belt, boots, tunic, hose, braies. The clink of his buckle and the rustle of fabric were loud in the silence. He placed each item neatly on the floor. When he was naked, he paused for a moment, staring at his bare toes, then took a deep, bracing breath and lifted his gaze to Larkspur.

She was naked, too.

Gods. The muscles in his throat and abdomen clenched in a reaction that had nothing to do with fear or dread. His balls clenched, too, in shameful anticipation.

Cadoc let out a shallow, shaky breath. Larkspur was even more beautiful than he'd imagined. Still too slender after her ordeal, but not lacking in curves. His mouth dried as he took in the dip of her waist and gentle flare of her hips, and her breasts . . .

Her breasts were pert and perfect, tipped with rosy nipples.

For a moment, Cadoc lost the ability to breathe.

Larkspur's skin was a warm ivory in the candlelight and her hair was silver-bright, hanging down past her waist. The triangle of hair at her groin gleamed brightly, too. It was like a beacon, calling to him.

Cadoc wrenched his eyes upwards, to Larkspur's face. She was watching him.

She looked shy and nervous and determined, but not—that he could see—repulsed by him.

"What are you waiting for?" Eagerness edged the disembodied voice.

Cadoc swallowed. He stepped reluctantly towards Larkspur. One step, two steps, three. He halted, close enough to reach out and touch her. He felt overlarge and clumsy alongside her slender beauty. Gods, he must weigh twice what she did.

Larkspur was still watching him, her gaze holding his. Cadoc felt as if she were staring into his head, that all his thoughts were laid bare to her.

She couldn't read his mind now, but she'd been able to, once. She knew he wasn't indifferent to her.

No, not indifferent. Despite his reluctance, despite their

audience, he wanted to touch Larkspur, wanted to bend his head and kiss her, make love to her. He felt heat begin to build in his loins.

Cadoc's sense of shame deepened. How could his body want this?

"Get on with it," the voice said impatiently.

Cadoc swallowed. He reached out and touched Larkspur's shining hair with careful fingers.

Larkspur gave him another faint, comforting smile. "It's all right, Cadoc," she said again.

He studied her face. What he saw reassured him. Larkspur was shy and apprehensive, but not afraid of him. She *trusted* him.

Cadoc swallowed. He'd done nothing to earn Larkspur's trust, but he'd prove to her it wasn't misplaced.

So, do it, he told himself. *Get it over with. Get her out of here.*

*C*HAPTER 6

C adoc had given a lot of thought to this moment. The whole three hours in the saddle, he'd thought about nothing but how to cause Larkspur the least distress. He wanted to bed her fast and painlessly, but that was clearly unachievable. She was a virgin; the faster he did this, the less time he spent coaxing her body to arousal, the more it would hurt her. Even done slowly, it would still hurt her.

Fast and painful, or slow and not as painful?

Slow. It had to be slow.

An hour into the ride he'd realized he should have brought some strong mead with him. A slug or two of that, and Larkspur would relax whether she wanted to or not. But that realization had come too late.

Cadoc took a deep, resolute breath. "Um, let's lie down." Because lying down, he wouldn't loom over her so much, wouldn't be quite so intimidating.

Larkspur moistened her lips, and nodded. She stepped onto the blanket and sat. Cadoc followed suit, except he wasn't nearly as graceful as she was. Powerful, yes. Graceful, no.

Larkspur lay back. Her hands made an involuntary movement, as if to shield her breasts and groin from his eyes, then fell to her sides, not clenched, but not relaxed. Her gaze was fixed intently and apprehensively on his face.

Cadoc tried to smile at her. He had a feeling it came out more like a grimace. "I'm going to have to touch you, Larkspur, to, um . . . get you ready." Touch, but not grope. He'd do his best not to disgust her. He wanted her to walk away from this not feeling dirtied or demeaned, or worse, afraid of sex.

Larkspur nodded, quite seriously.

Cadoc blew out his breath. "If anything hurts or is uncomfortable, please tell me, because it's not meant to be. Not yet. It's meant to be . . . it's meant to feel good."

Larkspur gave him a sudden smile. She lifted her hand and touched his cheek lightly. "Don't look so worried, Cadoc."

Cadoc swallowed. How could he not be worried?

"Get *on* with it," the voice prodded impatiently.

Cadoc snarled inwardly—and obeyed. He reached out and touched one of Larkspur's breasts, allowing his fingertips to trail across the smooth, soft skin, teasing and tickling. He thought perhaps her nipple, already taut with bashfulness, became tauter still. He flicked a glance at her. She was watching his face intently.

Cadoc blushed and looked hastily away, focusing on his task, circling her breasts lightly with his fingertips, stroking and teasing. He bent his head and kissed where his fingers had been. Yes, her nipples were definitely tauter. He licked first one and then the other, drew them into his mouth, nipped very lightly with his teeth.

He heard his own breathing, and the thumping of his heart, and heard Larkspur's breathing, too—short and light and quick—and heard a low rumbling note of impatience reverberate from the chamber walls.

Cadoc shifted his attention to Larkspur's midriff, stroking his hands lightly over her smooth skin, down towards the pale, glinting hair. He didn't dare look at Larkspur's face again. He caressed her first with his hands, then his mouth. Muscles fluttered beneath her skin. Arousal, he hoped, not tension.

Breasts, midriff . . . But not her mound next, no. Next he stroked up her inner thighs, drawing his fingertips from her knees to the bright, gleaming hair. He wished his hands were softer, smoother, not bearing a swordsman's calluses.

The dead prince hissed his impatience, a sound that scurried sharply around the chamber. Cadoc ignored it and bent to kiss where his fingers had just explored—up, up, up, until Larkspur's feminine scent filled his nose. Gods, but she smelled *good*.

Arousal pulsed through him. His cock surged upwards, stiffening. The Faerie prince's hiss died.

Cadoc inhaled a shallow, shaky breath. "Try to relax," he said, not looking at Larkspur's face, and he slid his fingers into that soft, crinkling, moon-bright hair, parted her nether lips, and bent his head to taste her.

Larkspur tasted even better than she smelled. His balls tightened convulsively and his cock gave another surge.

Cadoc bent to this task, licking and sucking, nibbling, teasing. Larkspur trembled beneath his ministrations. Her body shifted helplessly. He heard her breath: short and gasping. He slid a finger inside her and was relieved to find her hot and damp. Her sleek inner muscles clenched eagerly around his finger. Cadoc inserted a second finger. Gods, she was tight—but still not tensing in pain.

When he slid a third finger inside her, she stiffened.

"Does that hurt?" he asked.

"A little," Larkspur said breathlessly.

Could he get her to climax? He'd thought it would be impossible, given the circumstances—the hard floor, the malevolent presence in the chamber, her virginity—but Larkspur was surprisingly responsive. She seemed close to climaxing.

He bent his head again, flexed his fingers inside her, licked—and felt a sudden, agonizing sensation, as if someone grabbed the scruff of his neck, pinched hard, and shook him. He yelped with pain and pulled away from Larkspur, rearing up to sit.

"Enough of this play. *Get on with it.*"

Larkspur pushed up on her elbows, her expression alarmed. "Are you all right?"

Cadoc rubbed the nape of his neck. "Yes."

"You're too slow," the prince hissed, his voice scurrying like spiders over the chamber walls. "Bed her now."

"We're not your puppets," Cadoc snarled. "You'll have to *wait.*"

"You said copulation, not play." The invisible fingers tightened again, forcing another choked cry from his throat, making his eyes water. "This isn't the bargain we made."

"Cadoc, just do it," Larkspur said, her eyes wide and frightened.

Cadoc rubbed his throbbing neck, and looked at her face and knew that he wouldn't be able to bring her to climax. Not now that she was afraid.

He wasn't sure whether he could climax, either. The agonizing grip on his neck had brought his erection to half-mast.

The Faerie prince hissed his impatience. Something close to pain jolted through Cadoc's loins. His cock reared up again, as if it had been stung.

"*Do it,*" the dead prince hissed.

"Do it," Larkspur said urgently.

Cadoc gritted his teeth. "Lie down," he told her.

Larkspur lay down again. Her expression was anxious, worried.

She was concerned about *him*, Cadoc realized. Not herself. He almost huffed a humorless laugh. This was so warped, so *wrong.*

"Hurry *up*," the dead prince snarled. Invisible fingers bit painfully into Cadoc's neck again. "Mount her."

Cadoc eased Larkspur's thighs apart with one hand and settled himself between her legs, bracing his weight on his forearms. He bowed his head, unable to look Larkspur in the eye. There was a tight feeling in his chest, as if a wail of anguish were trying to get out.

A cruel sense of anticipation filled the chamber. Cadoc felt it sting his skin, as sharp as a knife blade. The prince wanted penetration. He wanted a virgin's pain.

Cadoc reached down and positioned his cock. It pressed

274

against Larkspur's damp, tight entrance with shameful eagerness. "I'm sorry," he whispered in her ear.

Her hand rose to touch his shoulder blade lightly. "Don't be."

Cadoc took a deep breath and flexed his hips, thrusting deeply into her.

He felt Larkspur's whole body clench with pain, heard the hissing exhalation of the Faerie prince's delight.

Gods, but it felt marvelous to be inside a woman again. A silent groan of pleasure reverberated in Cadoc's throat. His cock wanted to thrust again and again. He forced himself to stay motionless, braced above Larkspur, his teeth clenched, his muscles trembling. The stab wound in his right biceps twinged slightly.

"What are you waiting for?" the prince snarled.

He was waiting for Larkspur's pain to ease.

"Continue!" The grip on the back of Cadoc's neck tightened. At that same moment, he felt Larkspur relax slightly beneath him. "Now!"

Cadoc obeyed, a slow, gentle withdrawal and thrust.

"Harder," the dead prince said. His fingers pinched tighter, digging in deeply, making Cadoc's eyes water. "Faster!"

He obeyed half the order: faster, but not harder. His body fell into its rhythm.

The fingers eased their grip, but didn't release him. It felt as if he had someone perched on his shoulders, holding him down, riding him. Cadoc gritted his teeth. *Get off me!* he shouted silently.

A chuckle sounded in his ear. "You don't like it?"

He hated it, hated it more than he'd ever hated anything in his life. Pain, he could endure, but not this sense of having someone crouched on his back, breathing in his ear, enjoying his shameful coupling with Larkspur.

He had to get this over with *fast*.

"No, no, no," the Faerie prince crooned, as if he'd heard

Cadoc's thoughts. The grip on his neck tightened. "Make it last."

Cadoc ground his teeth together, squeezed his eyes shut, and did his best to appear that he was obeying. Another minute, two minutes at the most, and he'd pretend to lose control. He counted the seconds desperately in his head.

At fifty seconds, Larkspur's sleek inner muscles clenched around his cock. Her hips lifted to meet him.

Cadoc felt a spark of wonderment.

For several astonishing minutes, their lovemaking became real—the slide of his body over hers, the slide of his cock inside her. He was sweating, panting, and Larkspur was, too, her skin smooth and slick beneath him, her hips rising to meet each thrust, her breath coming in eager gasps. Their pace quickened. Cadoc heard Larkspur inhale sharply, felt her shudder, and then his own release came. He groaned, his whole body jerking helplessly.

Cadoc slowly rolled off her. He wanted to hold Larkspur close; instead, he gave her space, shifting sideways on the blanket until their bodies no longer touched. He lay panting, trembling with exertion, deeply astonished, deeply relieved. Larkspur had actually *climaxed.*

Once he'd caught his breath, he sat up. "Have you healed Ivy?" he demanded.

"Yes." The voice sounded like dead leaves stirring, dry and dusty. Dry and dusty—and disgruntled.

Cadoc reached for Larkspur's clothes, handing them to her without looking at her, and then climbed to his feet and quickly dressed. His fingers fumbled in his eagerness to be gone from this place; he almost dropped his belt twice.

When he was fully clothed, he glanced at Larkspur. She was fastening her shoes. Her hair hung down, pale and shining, almost to the floor. She straightened, and flicked it back over her shoulder. Cadoc looked hastily away. He rolled up the blanket, slung it over his shoulder, and picked up the chamberstick. "Ready?" he said, not looking Larkspur directly in the eye. His pulse beat an urgent tattoo: *Get out of here, get out of here now.*

"Yes."

Cadoc crossed to the passageway, the thick shadows parting for the candlelight, and found that he'd misjudged: only a rough rock wall met his eyes. He stepped sideways, and sideways again, finding only more rock. "Must be back that way," he said to Larkspur, heading in the other direction, but the candlelight revealed no low, dark, narrow passage.

Cadoc swallowed his disquiet. He'd got turned around, that was all. The passage was on the other side.

By the time he'd circled the whole chamber, his heart was beating hard and fast in his ears. His muscles were taut with anger—and beneath the anger was an edge of panic. Now was not the time to remember that people had died in here.

Cadoc halted, and turned to the huge casket. "You *feculent* son of a whore."

A wheezing, delighted giggle rolled around the chamber, climbing the walls and echoing off the ceiling.

"Let. Us. Leave," Cadoc said, biting off each word with his teeth.

"Leaving wasn't part of our bargain," the dead prince said gleefully.

Cadoc glanced at Larkspur. Her face was starkly pale, her eyes wide and dark.

He took her hand. Her fingers were cool, and trembled slightly. "It'll be all right," he told her, giving what he hoped was a comforting smile.

The candle blew out.

Blackness pressed against Cadoc's eyes. His lungs told him there was no air in the chamber.

He had a moment of pure panic, a moment when he couldn't think, couldn't breathe, when he knew he was going to die in this darkness—before he recaptured his self-control. He inhaled a shaky breath. He had to keep his wits. Panic would kill them.

"Relight the candle and we'll bargain," he said, as calmly as he was able.

The candle flickered grudgingly alight.

Cadoc looked at Larkspur. "You all right?"

She nodded. Her face was even paler than before, her eyes larger and darker, but she was holding on to her composure.

He released her hand, put his arm around her shoulders and hugged her reassuringly, and spoke to the Faerie prince. "Very well, we'll strike another bargain. One act of copulation in exchange for—"

"No," the voice whispered. "Something different this time."

Unease crawled up Cadoc's spine. "What?"

A low hum echoed around the chamber. It buzzed in Cadoc's ears, full of malice and anticipation. "I was always most partial to a woman's mouth . . ."

Cadoc flinched slightly. Not that. Not here. Not with Larkspur. "No."

"Then you may share my tomb with me." The candle blew out again.

Cadoc's heart beat loudly in his chest. *Don't panic,* he told himself. *There's a way out of this. There has to be.*

"What does he want us to do?" Larkspur asked. She hadn't understood the prince's request; she sounded baffled and anxious. "Cadoc? What?"

Cadoc swallowed. "He, uh, he wants us to, uh . . ." Gods, he couldn't say it out loud.

"What?" Larkspur said, more urgently.

Cadoc's eyes winced shut. "He wants you to use your mouth on my, uh . . . my penis."

"Oh." There was a long moment of silence, and then Larkspur said cautiously, "You mean kiss you there?"

"Kiss, and um, suck." An image of that act flashed into his mind: Larkspur on her knees, himself with his braies down around his ankles. To Cadoc's mortification, his cock responded to the image, twitching. "And we are *not* doing it. It's too . . ."

"I'll do it," Larkspur said.

"No," Cadoc said flatly. "I won't allow—"

"I believe we have a bargain," the Faerie prince purred. The candle sprang to life again.

*C*HAPTER 7

"*L*arkspur, no," Cadoc said. "We are absolutely *not* doing that. It's . . . it's too . . ."

"Too what?"

Cadoc swallowed. He removed his arm from Larkspur's shoulders and looked away from her. "It's too intimate. It's something lovers do, not . . ."

Not people such as himself and Larkspur.

Larkspur was silent a moment. "Surely no more intimate than what you did to me earlier?"

Memory gave him a glimpse of that gleaming triangle of hair, gave him her scent, her taste. "No, but—"

"It's a bargain. We're doing it. And then we're getting out of here. Right?" That last word wasn't spoken to him; it was directed at the dead Faerie prince. "Your *word* on it."

"My word on it." There was a gloating, gleeful chuckle in the disembodied voice. "Use your mouth on him, and I shall release you."

"Once," Cadoc said, still not looking at Larkspur. "She does this *once* only, and you release us both, immediately."

"Agreed."

Cadoc kept his head turned from Larkspur. Oh, gods. This was worse than his worst nightmare. Gods, if only it *were* a nightmare.

"You will have to tell me what to do," Larkspur said seriously.

Cadoc squeezed his eyes shut.

"Cadoc, the sooner we do this, the sooner we get out of here!"

Cadoc opened his eyes. He put the chamberstick on the floor and unslung the blanket from his shoulder. He spread it on the hard-packed dirt again, still not looking at Larkspur. He'd lie down for her—she would *not* kneel at his feet.

His tunic hung down past his hips. He tucked the excess fabric up under his belt. Slowly, reluctantly, he loosened the ties that held his hose up, but he couldn't bring himself to pull them down.

Elinor had used her mouth on him many times, sometimes excruciatingly slowly, sometimes so fast it had left him dazed. Fast was the only way he would consider teaching Larkspur to do it. Could he climax in less than a minute? Perhaps. If he tried really hard to.

Cadoc dredged back into his memory. What had Elinor done to make him respond so swiftly?

Recollection broke over him. His cock began to stiffen. He told himself that was good—the harder he was now, the quicker it would be for Larkspur. Cadoc dwelt on memory of Elinor as he slowly eased down to sit on the blanket. He spread his legs. "Um . . ." He thought desperately of Elinor. Her clever tongue, her deft fingers. His cock obliged nicely, pushing eagerly against his hose, tenting the fabric.

Cadoc turned his head to one side, utterly unable to look Larkspur in the face. "If you kneel, um, there . . ."

Larkspur knelt between his legs.

Cadoc's breathing became constricted. *No, no, no . . .* a voice cried in his head. He fumbled with his hose and braies and pulled them down to expose his loins. Freed, his cock stood up stiffly from its nest of hair.

His sense of shame increased sharply, and—to his mortification—so did his arousal.

"What do I do?"

Cadoc closed his eyes tightly. "If you . . . if you, um, stroke at the same time as you suck."

"Stroke?" One of her fingertips tentatively touched the sensitive crown of his cock.

Cadoc flinched. His eyelids sprang open.

Larkspur drew her hand hastily back. "I'm sorry. Did that hurt?"

Cadoc swallowed past the tight constriction in his throat. "No." Gods, he had to get this over with. Fast. He took both her hands in his. "Like this," he said matter-of-factly, not meeting her eyes. He wrapped one of her hands firmly around the base of his cock, and the other halfway up the shaft.

His cock pulsed with pleasure.

"Squeeze, and stroke." He demonstrated the pressure, the rhythm, not looking at Larkspur's face. "And at the same time, um, take the head in your mouth and suck as strongly as you can. Only, don't let me feel your teeth. Just, um, just your lips and tongue." He squeezed his eyes shut again, more ashamed than he'd ever been in his life. "It should be over quickly."

"Not too quickly," the Faerie prince breathed.

Want to bet? Cadoc snarled silently.

He lay down and stared up at the dark ceiling, intensely aware of Larkspur's hands gripping his cock. After a long moment, he felt the touch of her lips on the crown, the silky tickling of her long hair sliding over his bare upper thighs. A groan strangled in his throat, mercifully silent. Another hesitation, and then Larkspur opened her mouth and drew him inside. Moist heat and the most wonderful softness enveloped him. Oh, gods, her *tongue*.

Larkspur sucked once, tentatively, and a second time, more strongly, and began moving her hands as he'd shown her, stroking firmly up his shaft.

A loud hum reverberated within the chamber: the dead prince expressing his pleasure.

Cadoc stared desperately at the ceiling. The temptation to

touch Larkspur was almost overwhelming. He wanted to slide his fingers through her silky hair and cradle her head gently in his hands. Instead, he laced his hands behind his aching neck. He wouldn't look at her. Wouldn't touch her. Wouldn't move so much as an inch. *Climax,* he ordered himself. *Climax, curse it!*

"A little faster with your hands," he told her hoarsely. "And you can squeeze a bit harder."

Larkspur obliged. Gods, it was *perfect*—the rhythm of her hands, the rhythm of her mouth. Cadoc choked back another groan. His hips wanted to buck. He held himself utterly still.

It took more than a minute, but not more than two. His balls clenched—and then, weeping inwardly with shame, he climaxed helplessly in her mouth.

CHAPTER 8

*L*arkspur let Cadoc's organ slide slowly from her mouth. The taste of his seed was . . . interesting. Slightly salty, a little bitter, but not unpleasant.

She released her grip on him and moved back on the blanket, wiping her lips with her fingers. Her hands smelled of him, musky and masculine. The smell evoked a visceral response deep inside her, as if her womb pulsed with pleasure.

Cadoc scrambled to his feet and turned away from her, pulling up his braies and hose, tying them, hauling his tunic down. "Open the cursed door," he snarled.

Larkspur stood.

The Faerie prince gave a dry, rustling chuckle. "As you wish."

Larkspur's ears caught the grating sound of stone shifting against stone, the patter of falling dirt.

"Let's get out of here," Cadoc said, not looking at her. He bundled the blanket over his arm. "You go first." He snatched up the chamberstick and held it out to her. The tiny flame wavered and danced, almost blowing out.

Larkspur took the chamberstick.

Cadoc didn't meet her eyes, didn't even look at her. He stood clutching the blanket, his face turned from her.

"I've enjoyed your visit," the dead prince whispered. "Do come again . . ."

Larkspur crossed quickly to the passageway, ducked her head, and entered, aware of Cadoc's bulk behind her. The passage was only a dozen steps in length. Halfway along, the darkness of the barrow gave way to daylight with the suddenness of a curtain being drawn aside.

Larkspur emerged into the open, blinking. A clear, pale dawn sky arched overhead.

How could so much time have lapsed?

It felt as if she'd been in the barrow for less than an hour, the candle was barely a quarter melted, and yet out here, a whole night had passed. More than six hours.

Larkspur shivered, and blew out the candle, and turned to watch Cadoc heave the rock slab back into its place, sealing the barrow.

They'd done it! She'd erased her terrible mistake. Ivy was no longer lame.

Larkspur felt as if the weight of the barrow had lifted off her shoulders. She wanted to laugh, to cry, to dance, to fling her arms around Cadoc and hug him.

Cadoc turned away from the barrow. He averted his head, but not before she'd glimpsed his expression.

Larkspur's joy shriveled. She'd never seen such silent, anguished shame on a person's face before. Gods, were those *tears* in his eyes?

She put down the chamberstick hastily and followed him to where the saddles lay. "Cadoc?"

"What?" He kept his head turned from her as he sorted through the leather straps, separating the two bridles. Every muscle in his body seemed tense. Tense with shame?

"Cadoc, please sit down. I need to talk with you."

"We need to get back to the manor."

"Cadoc, *sit*." And then she tempered that command with a soft, "Please?"

He hesitated for a long moment, and then released the bridles, and turned to face her. Face her, but not meet her eyes. He looked past her shoulder.

"Please sit," Larkspur said, and she lowered herself to sit cross-legged on the grass.

For a moment, Cadoc towered above her, and then he took a step back and sat, too, not cross-legged, but hugging his knees. The rigid lines of his arms, the sharp jut of his elbows, were like a barrier between them. She'd never seen anyone project *Keep away from me* so strongly before. His face was tight and closed, utterly expressionless. "What?"

Now was clearly not the time to hug him and tell him she loved him.

Larkspur moistened her lips. Where to start?

At the very beginning. She'd explain it all to him.

Larkspur took a deep breath. "My father didn't want a third daughter. When I was born, he got drunk and beat my mother half to death, and he hurt Ivy, too. Lamed her."

Cadoc nodded stiffly. He probably knew that sad, sordid story; half the vale did.

"I don't think my father was evil exactly, he was just . . . flawed and . . . and violent. He wasn't the man my mother thought she'd married." Larkspur looked down at the ground. She plucked a blade of grass. "A number of men have asked me to marry them." Heat stole into her cheeks. Did she sound conceited, making that statement? "I was afraid I'd make the same mistake Mother did, choose someone who appeared nice on the outside, but wasn't inside. I thought . . . I might never marry." She glanced up at Cadoc. His posture hadn't changed; it still told her to keep away from him. His expression hadn't changed either: closed, tight, his eyes looking past her, not at her.

"And then Mother saved that baby, and we were given Faerie wishes, and I thought—I hoped—I could use mine to see who people truly were, and then I'd *know* if I was choosing the right husband. That's what I wanted. I didn't want to read people's minds, I just wanted to . . ." She sighed, and threw the grass blade away. "I wanted to *know*, and the Faerie offered me that gift, and I took it, and it was . . . a mistake." A dreadful, disastrous mistake that had almost driven her mad. Her mind lurched away from remembering, and she hurried on. "Do you remember the day we met? When you came with the Dapplewards and Aleyn Fairborn and your father?"

Cadoc gave another stiff nod, still not looking at her.

"I thought Aleyn was pleasant. Charming and friendly. I didn't like you. You looked tough and . . . and violent." She watched Cadoc's face as she said those words. Did his lips compress even more tightly? "And then I received my gift, and the next time you and Aleyn came, I could read your thoughts, and you were both so . . . so *utterly* unlike what I'd thought you were. Aleyn was ugly inside, full of greed and malice." She shivered. "And you were the complete opposite. There was no violence in you at all. You were compassionate and loyal and kind, and you had so much *integrity*."

Cadoc's jaw clenched even tighter. He turned his face away from her.

"That night, when we met at the cottage, I had you all in my head, you and Tam and Hugh, and my sisters. You were dreadfully, *terribly* worried about Hugh, but, um . . . I could hear what you thought of me, too. Especially afterwards, when you carried me back into the forest."

Why did that make him wince? He'd known, then, about her gift. And there'd been nothing shameful in his thoughts, nothing ugly or carnal. Cadoc's feelings for her had been warm, tender, respectful. He'd been worried and protective, not lustful. His thoughts had made her feel safe, so safe that she'd fallen asleep while he carried her.

"Cadoc . . ." Larkspur climbed to her feet and walked to where he sat—head averted, arms locked around his knees, elbows jutting out like fortifications on a battlement. "Cadoc, when I saw inside your head, I fell in love with you." She reached down and touched his close-cropped ash blond hair.

"That's why I asked you to come here with me, not just because I trust you—which I *do*—but because you're the only man I ever want to lie with." She knelt and put her arms around his shoulders and hugged him fiercely. "I'm sorry. I'm sorry I made you come here. I'm sorry it upset you so much. I'm *sorry.*"

Cadoc stayed stiff in her embrace for several seconds, and then his rigidity eased fractionally. He bowed his head into his arms.

"What is it, Cadoc?" Larkspur whispered, still hugging him. "What's upset you so much? Is it what we did last? I didn't mind about that, truly!"

The dead prince's presence and Cadoc's obvious distress had made it an uncomfortable experience, but in other circumstances she thought it would have been quite pleasurable. "It was no more than what you did to me. And that didn't upset you, did it?" What had he said? *It's too intimate.* And it had been intimate. Exhilaratingly intimate. She'd wished for privacy and more light and a lot more time. She'd wanted to see Cadoc clearly—the heavy testicles, the strong, muscular, and surprisingly silky-skinned penis. Was his penis a dusky rose color, or something darker? It had been difficult to tell in the candlelight. She'd wanted to explore his genitals, to discover the different shapes and textures and scents.

"I liked how intimate it was," Larkspur confessed. She could still smell him faintly, still taste him on her tongue. "I *like* how you taste." She tightened her arms around him and pressed her face into his hair. "Marry me, Cadoc. Please."

The last of Cadoc's stiffness—resistance or shame or both—seemed to melt. She felt his muscles relax. He didn't raise his head, but he lifted one hand and cradled the back of her skull.

Sudden tears rushed to Larkspur's eyes. "I love you," she whispered.

"I love you, too," Cadoc said, his voice a low, deep rumble in his chest.

Larkspur stayed kneeling, hugging him, for several minutes. She didn't want to pull back, didn't want to lose the touch of his hand on her head, large and warm and gentle. Finally, reluctantly, she released him and sat back on her heels. "Cadoc . . ."

Cadoc lifted his head. For the first time in what seemed like hours, he met her gaze. The impact of his steel-gray eyes momentarily stopped the air in Larkspur's lungs. She swallowed, and found the breath to speak. "I'm sorry. I'm sorry I made you come here. I'm sorry I made you take part in that bargain. I'll never do anything like that again. *Never.* I promise, Cadoc. I give you my word."

Cadoc stared into her eyes for a long moment, and then nodded, as if formally acknowledging her words.

"Thank you for coming here with me."

Cadoc nodded again, and then he sighed and rubbed his face. "If Ivy can walk again, it was worth it. I just wish . . ." His mouth twisted in a grimace. "I just wish your first time had been different. Better."

"It wasn't *bad*," Larkspur said. The experience had been awkward, embarrassing, painful, and a little frightening—but also surprisingly pleasurable. "Um . . . I meant what I said. I *do* like how you taste."

Cadoc blushed crimson. He looked away from her, and cleared his throat, and climbed to his feet. "Let's get back to the manor. They'll be worried about us."

Larkspur climbed to her feet, too. "I half expected the Dapplewards to be here, waiting when we came out." She glanced around the glade. The blue of the sky had intensified while they'd talked.

"We'll probably meet them on the way." Cadoc bent and began separating the bridles again.

Larkspur went to stand beside him. *Her* Cadoc. She touched his hair lightly, running her fingers through the short ash-blond locks. His hair would curl, if he let it grow longer.

Cadoc's nape was bare, tanned—and marked with fresh plum-red bruises. "Cadoc, there are bruises all over the back of your neck!"

Cadoc stood, a bridle in each hand. "Not surprised."

"Did the prince do that to you?" Gods, no wonder he'd cried out with pain.

Cadoc nodded. The blush had faded from his face. He stood for a moment, gazing down at her. His expression altered slightly. She saw intention form in his gray eyes. He was going to kiss her.

Larkspur's heart began to beat faster. Foolishly, she felt shy. She'd had sex with Cadoc, taken his organ in her mouth, but not kissed him.

Cadoc let the bridles drop to the ground again. He took her by the waist and lifted her to stand on his saddle. Larkspur's heart beat even faster. Her cheeks heated. Now *she* was the one who was blushing.

Cadoc held her steady, his hands warm and strong, almost spanning her waist. Their eyes were nearly level.

Larkspur gazed at him. Such a tough, craggy face—and such a generous, compassionate, honest heart beneath that forbidding exterior. She touched his lips lightly with a fingertip, and then slipped her arms around his neck and shyly kissed him.

Cadoc gathered her closer. His mouth was just as warm and gentle and marvelous as she'd imagined.

*C*HAPTER 9

*T*hey rode single file, picking their way down the gully, the stream leaping and splashing alongside them. Larkspur kept her eyes on Cadoc, on his broad back and strong shoulders and bruised neck. *Her* Cadoc. They left the gully behind and rode half a mile, and then Cadoc halted in a little glade, with a brook and a swath of grass studded with bright buttercups. "We should eat. We've a couple more hours ahead of us."

This time, Cadoc didn't unsaddle the horses; he let them graze at the brook's edge. He laid out bread and cheese, and spread the blanket on the grass for them to sit on.

Larkspur sat as close to him as she could, and felt the warmth and solidness of his thigh pressing against hers, and ate hungrily. She hadn't tasted the food properly yesterday, but today she did. It was the most delicious meal she'd ever eaten, and this morning was the best morning of her life. She was brimming with happiness, overflowing with happiness, and the world was a marvelous place and everything in it was marvelous—the clear, burbling brook, the early morning sunshine on her face, the tall trees with their outspread branches and green leaves—and Cadoc was the most marvelous thing of all.

When they'd finished eating, she took his hand. Such a

huge hand, twice the size of hers, with a swordsman's calluses ridging the palm. The love she felt for him grew so intense that her heart ached in her chest. "I love you," she told him.

Cadoc's hand flexed in hers, and he leaned closer, and Larkspur tilted her face to him, and he kissed her.

They kissed, and kissed some more, and then they lay down on the blanket and made love in the gentle morning sunshine. A quick tumble, Hazel had said, but this was no quick tumble, this was slow and perfect, Cadoc's hands stroking over her, his voice whispering in her ear, and when she asked if she could touch his organ, he let her, and after that it became less languid, but no less perfect, but it still wasn't a quick tumble; it went on for long, intense minutes and the waves of pleasure were almost painful. Larkspur heard herself gasping, heard herself crying out, and she heard Cadoc panting and groaning, and then his body jerked convulsively and she knew his seed was spilling inside her, and in that moment her love for him was so strong that she almost found herself weeping.

Afterwards, when they'd both caught their breath, Cadoc kissed her again and said, "That's how it's meant to be."

CHAPTER 10

T hey retraced their route through the forest, riding single file between the trees. The way was unmarked for the first hour, but Cadoc rode without hesitation; he was as much at home in these woods as he was at Dappleward Manor.

When they reached the main trail, he reined back to ride at Larkspur's side, holding out his hand to her. Larkspur's smile was shyly radiant. She tucked her hand into his. There was a glow in her cheeks and her eyes were luminous and she was so different from the woman who'd found him yesterday in the stables that Cadoc almost couldn't believe it.

She had shed a heavy burden.

He'd done the right thing, breaching the barrow. He just hoped Guy Dappleward would think so, too.

The trail wound through deep forest and sun-dappled glades. Gods, but he'd been tense when they'd ridden this way yesterday afternoon. He didn't feel tense, now. He felt buoyantly happy, buoyantly joyful—although worry lurked in the back of his mind.

How was the Lord Warder going to react to this?

"We'll meet the Dapplewards before we get to the manor," he predicted out loud.

"I thought they might have ridden through the night to try to stop us."

So had he. Maybe the delay in pursuit was tacit approval of his actions? Or perhaps they'd been worried about breaking the horses' legs in the darkness. "Hmm," Cadoc said neutrally.

Larkspur glanced at him, and tightened her grip on his hand. "Hugh and Tam love you as if you're their brother. They won't be angry with you."

"We are brothers, almost." There was less than eighteen months' difference between the three of them. They'd grown up like puppies from the same litter, playing together, training together. He'd been in the middle, younger than Hugh, older than Tam. It had been a warm, happy place to be.

"They won't be angry with you," Larkspur repeated. "And if their father is, I'll tell him it was my fault. If he's angry with anyone, it should be *me*, not you!"

"Hmm," Cadoc said again.

It wasn't the Warder's anger he feared, but his disappointment, his loss of trust. Ironfists were known for their unbreakable loyalty to the Dappleward family—and Cadoc had broken his oath.

They came to a small dell. White and yellow wildflowers starred the grass. Ahead, through the trees, Cadoc saw a flicker of movement. Horsemen.

He halted, his mouth unaccountably dry. "Here they come."

One, two, three . . . a whole cavalcade slowly came into view. He easily recognized his father and the Dapplewards, but it took a moment to recognize the others, patterned as they were by sunlight and shade: Larkspur's sisters, Ivy and Hazel. Her mother, Maythorn, and Maythorn's new husband, Ren Blacksmith.

"Ivy?" Larkspur released Cadoc's hand and slid from her horse.

The cavalcade halted. Hugh Dappleward dismounted and swung his bride-to-be down from her saddle and steadied her for a moment.

No crutch, Cadoc noted.

"Ivy?" Larkspur said again, hope urgent in her voice.

Ivy laughed. She didn't walk to meet Larkspur, she *ran.*

Cadoc dismounted. He led the two horses across the dell, crushing lush grass and starry wildflowers underfoot, trying to discern Guy Dappleward's expression. Tam was grinning, Hazel and Maythorn were laughing and crying at the same time, Hugh's eyes were suspiciously bright, and even Ren was wiping away tears—but then, the huge blacksmith had known Ivy since she was a child. But he couldn't see his father's face, or Guy Dappleward's. They stood back under the trees, in shadow.

Cadoc swallowed the lump in his throat. He released the horses' reins and stepped beneath the trees. His gaze went first to his father. Rauf Ironfist looked grim, but then he usually did.

Cadoc turned to Guy Dappleward. "Sir?"

The Lord Warder's face was grave and deeply troubled. Tears glimmered in his eyes. Not tears of happiness; not with that expression on his face.

Cadoc's throat constricted, his lungs constricted, his belly constricted. *He's going to dismiss me from his service.*

They stared at each other for a long, frozen moment. From behind them came laughter, and joyful voices. Those sounds shrank until they were no louder in his ears than the distant buzzing of insects. His own heart thumped loudly, a slow drumbeat of dread.

Cadoc bowed his head and waited.

"Cadoc Ironfist . . ." The Lord Warder's voice was deeply regretful. "You have broken your oath to me. I must ask you to . . . to . . ."

Gods, the Warder was going to cry. "I'll go," Cadoc said hurriedly. "I'll leave the manor. Today."

"No!" said a female voice.

Cadoc turned his head. "Larkspur—"

"No." Her hands gripped his left arm tightly, but all her attention was directed at Guy Dappleward. "You know you can trust Cadoc. He'd *die* for you and your sons. You *know* that!"

Guy Dappleward sighed, a sad, heavy sound. "Cadoc's oath—"

"Cadoc only broke his oath because he was redeeming his word to me." Larkspur had forgotten her shyness. Her expression was urgent. "And I ask *you* to redeem your word to me now, too. You said I could ask for anything within your power to give . . . well, I ask you to keep Cadoc as your liegeman."

Hugh stepped up on Cadoc's right. "I second that," he said firmly.

"And I," said Tam, equally firmly.

"And I." Rauf Ironfist's voice was a low, emotion-choked whisper. "Please, Guy."

Guy Dappleward looked away. He blinked several times. Muscles moved in his throat as he swallowed. And then he inhaled and looked back at Cadoc.

Cadoc met the Lord Warder's eyes. Kind, wise eyes.

I can't serve him if he no longer trusts me.

Cadoc loosened Larkspur's clasp on his arm and sank to one knee in front of Guy Dappleward, bowing his head. "If you wish me gone from your service, I'll go. I yield to your judgment."

He closed his eyes and waited. Nine people stood around him, but no one spoke. It seemed to his ears that no one even breathed.

The Lord Warder's hand touched his hair, and rested there lightly. "My judgment is . . . that I no more want you to leave than I want my own sons to."

Cadoc raised his head and looked up at Guy Dappleward.

Dappleward smiled at him. "Stay at my side, Cadoc Ironfist. That is what I wish from you."

CHAPTER 11

*C*adoc leaned his shoulders against the sun-warmed wall and looked across the courtyard to where Maythorn stood with her daughters. If he didn't know for a fact that two months ago Maythorn had been the crippled, graying Widow Miller, he would never have believed it. She was young and ripe and golden, glowing with happiness.

Seen together, the four women astounded the eye. Each of them was lovely in her own right, but all *four* of them . . . Dazzling.

None of them looked alike, though. Larkspur was palely luminous, her hair like spun moonbeams, whereas Hazel's coloring was more vivid: the lustrous brown hair, the bright, merry eyes. Ivy's beauty was the quietest, but by no means the least. She drew one's gaze, with that fall of midnight-dark hair and the solemn green eyes. But she wasn't solemn today. Ivy was laughing, her happiness obvious to see.

It had been worth it—the barrow, the dead Faerie prince, the awkward, anguishing sexual acts with Larkspur—to see Ivy walk again, to see her laugh like that. Cadoc had no regrets.

Hugh Dappleward crossed the courtyard towards him, smiling, dressed in his best doublet. He propped up the wall alongside Cadoc.

For a moment they leaned there silently, enjoying the sunshine, enjoying the view, and then Hugh said, "We'll have beautiful children."

"Yes. We will."

Silence fell again. Cadoc wasn't sure that he'd ever felt this happy in his life. His whole chest felt warm. The future stretched blissfully before him. The next few hours were clear: the three weddings—Hugh's, Tam's, and his own—then the midsummer dancing and feasting. Not too much feasting, though, and very little alcohol, because after the dancing and feasting came his wedding night. He and Larkspur, alone in his bedchamber, with candlelight and a soft bed. And after tonight came tomorrow, and the day after that, and the one after that, all blurring together into a long, golden future.

"I don't understand how I came to be so lucky," Cadoc said at last. "This is so much more than I ever dared dream of."

"Me, too." Hugh's gaze rested on Ivy, and then moved to Larkspur. "You know, when I first met Larkspur, I thought she was a shy, timid little thing."

"She has a lot of courage. She's tougher than she looks."

Hugh nodded, and settled back into contented silence. He was relaxed, smiling, the habitual graveness gone from his face. He looked like a man deeply in love.

Guy Dappleward entered the courtyard, with Rauf Iron-fist and Ren Blacksmith. The three men were absorbed in conversation. Ren's young son rode on the blacksmith's broad shoulders. The pure happiness on the boy's face seemed a reflection of Cadoc's own joy.

Cadoc watched Ren swing his son down, watched the boy run across the courtyard to Maythorn, skipping like a lamb in spring. Maythorn stroked the boy's hair back from his brow, and he laughed up at her, and she laughed back and bent and kissed him. *She loves him as if he's her own child*, he realized.

"Cadoc?"

"Mmm?" He turned his head to look at Hugh.

Hugh pushed away from the wall. "I can never thank you

enough for what you did for Ivy. If there's any way I can ever repay you—"

"No." Cadoc held up a hand, halting the words. "No one owes anyone anything. All words have been redeemed. Let's leave it at that. Let's just . . . be happy."

Tam Dappleward strode over to them. Tam usually had a smile on his face and a spring in his step, but today his grin was wide and exhilarated and he walked as if he had winged boots on his feet. "Are you ready to be married?"

"More than ready." Cadoc straightened to his full height.

Together, they walked across the courtyard to their brides.

$\mathcal{A}$FTERWARDS

$\mathcal{T}$o Maythorn's profound delight, she bore Ren Black-smith three children, all boys as great-hearted as their father. What with raising their four sons, and Ren's blacksmithing and his duties as Dapple Bend's alderman, they lived a full and happy life together.

Ivy, Hazel, and Larkspur also presented their husbands with children, a dozen between them, as many sons as daughters. Dappleward Manor rang to the sounds of laughter and play, as it hadn't for many years.

The six sons grew into fine, strong men and served Dapple Vale with integrity and honor, as their fathers and grandfathers and great-grandfathers had before them.

The six daughters were all kind-hearted girls, but apart from their kind hearts were as different from each other as one might expect. They were variously shy and bold and serious and merry and stubborn and wise. But however much they differed from each other, they all shared a common secret: in adulthood, each was visited by a baleful Faerie and granted one wish.

As the years passed, and kings and queens succeeded one another on the English throne, one thing remained unchanged: the daughters in Maythorn's female line received Faerie wishes. And those wishes changed their lives.

$\mathcal{T}$HANK $\mathcal{Y}$OU

Thanks for reading *The Fey Quartet*. I hope you enjoyed it!

If you'd like to be notified whenever I release a new book, please join my Readers' Group, which you can find at www.emilylarkin.com/newsletter.

I welcome all honest reviews. Reviews and word of mouth help other readers to find books, so please consider taking a few moments to leave a review on Goodreads or elsewhere.

The Fey Quartet novellas are the prequel to the Baleful Godmother historical romance series. The first six books in the series are set in Regency England. Their titles are *Unmasking Miss Appleby, Resisting Miss Merryweather, Trusting Miss Trentham, Claiming Mister Kemp, Ruining Miss Wrotham,* and *Discovering Miss Dalrymple.*

I'm currently giving a free digital copy of *Unmasking Miss Appleby* to anyone who joins my Readers' Group. If you'd like to join, here's the link: www.emilylarkin.com/free-uma.

To read the first two chapters of *Unmasking Miss Appleby,* please turn the page.

UNMASKING
Miss Appleby

On her 25th birthday, Charlotte Appleby receives an unusual gift from the Faerie godmother she never knew she had: the ability to change shape.

Penniless and orphaned, she sets off for London to make her fortune as a man. But a position as secretary to Lord Cosgrove proves unexpectedly challenging. Someone is trying to destroy Cosgrove and his life is increasingly in jeopardy.

As Charlotte plunges into London's backstreets and brothels at Cosgrove's side, hunting his persecutor, she finds herself fighting for her life—and falling in love . . .

It is a truth universally acknowledged,
that Faerie godmothers do not exist.

CHAPTER 1

October 10th, 1805
London

$\mathcal{M}$arcus Langford, Ninth Earl of Cosgrove, strode down the steps of Westminster Palace. Clouds streamed across the face of the moon.

"Excellent speech, sir," his secretary, Lionel, said.

Marcus didn't reply. His mind wasn't on the address he'd made to the Upper House, it was on the sniggers he'd heard as the debating chamber emptied, the whispers that followed him down the corridor. *Cuckold Cosgrove.*

A black tide of rage swept through him. "We'll walk back," he said abruptly, and lengthened his stride. The icy wind gusted, making the torches flare in their brackets, almost snatching his hat from his head, filling his mouth with the stink of the Thames.

Lionel tucked the satchel of papers more firmly under one arm and trotted to keep up. "Did you see Hyde's face, sir? He was so angry, he went purple. I thought he'd have apoplexy, right there in the chamber!"

"I wish he would." St. James's Park loomed dark on their left. "We'll cut through here."

The clatter of carriage wheels faded behind them. The fetid smell of the Thames receded, overlain by the scents of dank soil and dead leaves. Gravel crunched beneath their boots.

"You're correct, sir," Lionel said, puffing faintly alongside him. "It's the best course. Abolition of the trade, not of slavery itself. Slavery will disappear as a natural consequence."

Marcus grunted. He spread his hands wide, clenched them. He needed an outlet for his anger. A bout with Jackson or—

"Did you hear that?" Lionel swung back the way they'd come. "Sir . . . I think someone's following us."

Marcus half-turned. He saw leafless branches whipping in the wind, saw shadow and moonlight patterning the ground. "There's no one—"

His ears caught the faint crunch of gravel.

There. Not half a dozen yards distant, in the deepest shadows: three men, mufflers hiding their faces.

Footpads.

His pulse kicked, and sped up.

"Run, sir!" Lionel cried.

Marcus ignored him. He stepped forward, hands clenched, teeth bared in a snarl. This was exactly what he needed. A fight.

The footpads abandoned their stealth and rushed from the shadows.

Marcus threw a punch at the nearest man, connected solidly, and followed with a left hook that brought the footpad to the ground.

A second man aimed a sloppy blow at him. Marcus grabbed his attacker's wrist and twisted, tossing him over his hip. A perfect cross-buttock throw. *Pity Jackson didn't see that.*

"Sir!" Lionel cried, his voice high with panic. "Run!"

Marcus swung again, striking the third man in the mouth. Lips split beneath his knuckles. The satisfaction of drawing blood made him laugh, a harsh sound that echoed in the night.

The first footpad scrambled to his feet. Marcus sank his

fist into the man's belly. The footpad collapsed with a *whoosh* of gin-scented breath.

Out of the corner of his eye he saw the second footpad lurch upright. Lionel hit him over the head with the satchel.

Marcus ripped off his torn gloves and gulped a breath, gulped a laugh. He'd rarely felt so alive—the cold air in his throat, the sting of broken skin on his knuckles, the savage exhilaration in his blood.

He whirled to face the third footpad. The man ducked his punch and grabbed him in a bear hug that smelled of sour sweat and ale. They grappled for a moment, muscles straining. The footpad slammed his forehead against Marcus's.

The night dissolved into stars—then snapped back into focus: the moon, the scurrying clouds, the skeleton shapes of the trees. A knee jabbed into Marcus's stomach. "Cuckold Cosgrove," the footpad growled.

Marcus tore free of the man's grip, stumbling back, almost winded. *He knows who I am?*

The footpad struck at him with both fists.

Marcus brushed aside the first blow and caught the second on his brow, threw an uppercut that snapped the man's head back, grabbed the footpad and buried his knee in the man's groin.

The footpad doubled over with a choked cry. He collapsed when Marcus shoved him away. Two yards away, the first footpad was on hands and knees, retching.

Marcus gulped a breath of icy air. He tasted blood on his tongue, felt it trickle down his brow and cheek. His exhilaration hardened into anger. The footpads knew his name; this wasn't a random attack.

From behind came the crack of bone breaking and a cut-off cry of agony.

He spun around.

Lionel lay sprawled on the gravel path. The last footpad stood over him. Sheets of paper spilled from the satchel, scurrying across the ground, spinning in the wind like large white moths.

Marcus uttered a roar. He charged at the footpad, knocked him down. "You son of a whore!" He grabbed the man's hair and smashed his fist into the upturned face, battering him until he sagged senseless.

Marcus shoved the footpad aside. "Lionel?" He fell to his knees alongside his secretary. The anger snuffed out. In its place was a deep, sucking fear. "Are you hurt?" Blood trickled into his eyes. He blinked it back and shook his head, spraying droplets. "Lionel! Answer me!"

CHAPTER 2

October 13ᵗʰ, 1805
Westcote Hall, Essex

C harlotte Appleby laid down her needle and flexed her fingers. The handkerchief was almost finished: her uncle's initials intertwined, and beneath them a tiny red hand, the symbol of a baronet. *As if it helps Uncle Neville blow his nose better to know he's a baronet.* She snorted under her breath.

The back of her neck prickled, as if someone had moved noiselessly to stand behind her.

Charlotte turned her head sharply.

No one stood behind her. The corner of the parlor was empty.

Charlotte rubbed her nape, where the skin still prickled faintly. *A draft, that's all it was.* She flicked a glance at her aunt and cousin, seated beside the fireplace.

Lady Westcote thumbed through the *Lady's Monthly Museum*, barely glancing at the pages, her lips pursed. Anthea was bent over the dish of sugarplums, choosing the plumpest.

Charlotte rethreaded her needle and started on the border around her uncle's monogram.

Lady Westcote tossed the magazine aside. "Charity."

Charlotte lifted her head. "Yes, Aunt?"

"Fetch my shawl. The cashmere with the pink border."

Charlotte obediently laid down her sewing. She let herself out of the parlor and climbed the sweeping oak staircase. *Calm,* she told herself. *Calm.* But her resentment was sharp today—she almost tasted it on her tongue, as bitter as bile— and the tight knot of anger in her chest only seemed to grow larger with each step she took.

She knew why: Today was her birthday. Her twenty-fifth. *And instead of everything I dreamed of, I have life at Westcote Hall.*

Charlotte pushed her spectacles firmly up her nose. What she had was better than many others had—a roof over her head, food in her stomach. She was lucky.

Lady Westcote's maid, Litton, was laying out evening clothes in her aunt's dressing room: a gown of puce silk, a turban crowned with curling ostrich plumes, satin slippers. Beneath the cloying scent of Lady Westcote's perfume was the sour undertone of her perspiration.

"My aunt would like her cashmere shawl, Litton. The one with the pink border."

Litton nodded and turned to the clothes press.

For a moment they were both framed in the cheval mirror: Litton dressed in a gown of kerseymere that was in the latest fashion; herself in one of Anthea's castoffs, taken in at the waist and let down at the hem. Alongside the maid, she looked shabby, her wrists protruding from cuffs that were slightly too short.

I look more like a servant than Litton does.

"Here you are, Miss Charity."

Charlotte took the proffered shawl. "Thank you."

She let herself out of the dressing room. *I could run away and become a lady's maid.* At least she'd be paid for her drudgery. And no one would call her Charity.

Charlotte tried to imagine what it would be like. *Appleby, this petticoat is ripped. Darn it. Appleby, my hair needs to be curled again. Make sure you do a better job this time. Fetch my tooth powder, Appleby—and be quick about it!*

She pulled a face. No, Litton's job wasn't to be envied.

Charlotte went back downstairs, her hand gliding over the cool oak balustrade. As she stepped onto the half-landing, the hairs on the back of her neck stood upright.

She jerked a glance behind her. The staircase rose in empty, curving flights.

Charlotte rubbed her neck. *Idiot.* She walked briskly down the last half-flight, pushed her spectacles up her nose again, and opened the door to the parlor. "Your shawl, Aunt."

Lady Westcote took the shawl without a word of thanks.

Charlotte gritted her teeth. *I am grateful to my aunt and uncle for giving me a home,* she told herself. *Grateful.* She took her seat in the corner of the parlor and bent her head over Uncle Neville's handkerchief, trying to find a calm place in her mind.

"Only five months until I make my début." Anthea clapped her hands in delight. "Oh, I can't wait, Mama!"

Charlotte halted mid-stitch. She lifted her head and stared across the parlor at her aunt. *And what of my début? What of the promise you made my father on his deathbed?*

"I shall do better than Eliza," Anthea declared. "I shall catch a husband in my *first* Season."

"Your sister did extremely well." Lady Westcote arranged her shawl around her shoulders. "Tunbridge is a wealthy man. And well-connected."

Charlotte snorted silently. *And as stout as a pig that's been fattened for the Christmas spit.*

Anthea pouted. Her gaze slid to Charlotte. "Even if it does take me two Seasons, at least I shan't be an old maid."

Charlotte pretended the barb hadn't struck home. She curved her mouth into a smile—cheerful, unruffled.

Anthea tossed her ringlets and looked away.

Charlotte returned her attention to the handkerchief.

She tried to concentrate on her sewing, tried to make each stitch as small and even as possible, but her cousin's voice kept intruding. "For my coming-out ball, I want spider-gauze sewn all over with pearls, and a white satin gown underneath. And white satin dancing slippers tied with ribbons."

Resentful anger mounted in Charlotte's chest. It was a dangerous, reckless emotion. It made her want to throw down her sewing. It made her want to tell her aunt and cousin exactly what she thought of them. Made her want to storm out of the parlor and slam the door.

Made her want to risk being turned out of Westcote Hall.

Charlotte stabbed the needle into the handkerchief. *Gratitude.* She had a roof over her head. Clothes on her back. Food in her belly. Those were all things the Westcotes gave her. All things she was grateful for.

"Charity, pour me another cup of tea."

The pressure in her chest increased. *My name is Charlotte.* "Of course, Cousin."

Anthea curled a ringlet around one plump finger. "I shall catch myself a duke. You will all have to call me Your Grace."

Charlotte walked to the tea service. She picked up the teapot and poured. In her mind's eye, she saw herself throw the pot across the room, saw it shatter against the silk-covered wall, spraying tea and shards of porcelain.

"Your Grace," Anthea repeated, with a self-satisfied giggle.

Charlotte glanced at the door, wishing she was on the other side of it. A few hours of silence, of privacy—

If you want that, you know what you have to do.

Charlotte took a deep breath. She placed the teacup and saucer on the table alongside Anthea. "Your tea, Cousin," she said, and flicked the cup with a finger as she stepped back.

The cup fell over in its saucer with a delicate *clang.* The porcelain handle broke off. Tea flooded the saucer, spilling onto the tabletop, trickling to the floor.

"Look what you've done!" Anthea cried, pulling her skirts out of the way.

Lady Westcote surged to her feet with all the majesty of a walrus. "You clumsy creature!"

Charlotte turned to face her aunt. She felt marvelously calm. *Send me to my room for the rest of the day. Please, Aunt.*

"Broken!" Lady Westcote's face suffused with color. She advanced, one hand upraised. "One of my best Staffordshire teacups!"

The slap almost dislodged Charlotte's spectacles.

"Go to your room! I don't want to see you until tomorrow."

Thank you. Charlotte straightened her spectacles. Heat rushed to her cheek, but beneath the heat was a cool, serene calmness.

"And don't think you can ask one of the servants for food!" Lady Westcote cried shrilly. "You can starve until tomorrow morning! Do you hear me?"

"I do, Aunt." Charlotte curtsied and let herself out of the parlor.

She closed the door with a quiet *snick* and stood for a moment in the corridor. She felt light, as if she'd grown wings and was hovering a foot off the ground. *A whole evening to myself.* No aunt and uncle. No cousin.

Relief filled her lungs and spread across her face as a smile. *A whole evening alone.*

Her bedchamber was next to the schoolroom, a small room that had once been the governess's. Charlotte closed the door and let the silence sink into her skin. The rug was threadbare and the furniture had seen better days, but this room was hers. No one else came here.

She touched her cheek, feeling the heat, the stinging residue of pain. It had been worth breaking the teacup for this: silence and solitude.

Across the room, her reflection stared at her from the mirror. Brown hair, brown eyes, a face that was neither pretty nor plain.

Charlotte grimaced at herself. *Happy birthday*.

She curled up on the bed, hugging a blanket around her, enjoying the silence. Daylight drained from the sky. When the room was dark, Charlotte lit a candle and closed the shutters. The clock on the narrow mantelpiece told her it was dinnertime.

Hunger stirred in her belly. Charlotte ignored it.

She took the candle next door to the schoolroom. Here, she'd tutored the Westcote boys until their entry to Rugby. Here, she'd taught Eliza and Anthea until their seventeenth birthdays. No words had been spoken in the schoolroom for months, no fires lit in the grate. The air was inert. Cold had soaked into the floorboards, into the walls.

At the back of the schoolroom was the old pianoforte.

Charlotte pulled out the stool and sat, resting her fingers on the keys, feeling their smooth coolness.

She visualized the score, heard the music in her ears, and played the first notes. Quiet. Beautiful. The last of her resentment and anger evaporated. Joy flowered inside her like a rose unfurling its petals. The world receded. Westcote Hall was gone. Her aunt and uncle and cousin were gone.

The hairs stood up on the back of her neck.

Charlotte jerked around, lifting her hands from the keys. The schoolroom was empty except for shadows, and so was the doorway.

The echoes of music died away. She held her breath and heard only silence. No creaking floorboards, no furtive footsteps.

Stop this foolishness! Charlotte placed her fingers firmly on the piano keys and filled the room with sound. A jaunty, cheerful tune that begged to be danced to—

"Miss Charity?"

Charlotte jerked around on the stool. The piano strings vibrated with a discordant hum.

A housemaid stood in the doorway. "Mrs. Heslop said to give you this. Venison pie. And a newspaper that were in Sir's fireplace."

"Oh, Lizzie." Foolish tears rushed to her eyes. Charlotte blinked them back and stood. Her footsteps echoed hollowly on the floorboards. "Please thank Mrs. Heslop from me." The newspaper was charred at the edges, the linen-wrapped pie warm and fragrant.

Back in her bedroom, she slipped off her shoes, climbed up on the bed, and unfolded the newspaper. A warm glow of happiness spread through her. What a perfect evening: the precious solitude, the music, the kindness of the housekeeper.

Charlotte ate hungrily, read hungrily. A rich and varied world existed beyond the walls of Westcote Hall and the newspaper brought it vividly to life: the war with France, political debates and criminal trials, the doings of the Prince Regent and the *ton*, concerts and exhibitions and theatrical performances.

When she'd finished the pie, Charlotte gave a deep sigh of contentment. This was the best birthday she'd had since her father had died.

The thought was sobering. She frowned down at the columns of closely typeset print. Her eyes fastened on an advertisement.

Wanted by a Gentleman's Family in the county of Hertford-shire, a GOVERNESS competent to instruct two young girls in Music, Geography, and English. A thorough knowledge of the French language is required.

Charlotte reread the advertisement. She could do that.

Her gaze skipped down the page. *Wanted immediately, a single YOUNG MAN to act as a Gentleman's secretary. A strict Character required. Good wages will be given.*

She could do that, too. Hadn't she been her father's secretary until his death? And a secretary would earn more than a governess.

But she wasn't a man.

Charlotte pulled a face and read further.

A position exists for a JUNIOR SCHOOLMISTRESS well-qualified to teach English, French, and Latin grammatically. Applications to Mrs. Bolton, of Mrs. Bolton's Ladies' Boarding School, near Basingstoke. Testimonials of Character will be required.

Charlotte read the advertisement again. If she worked at a school, she'd have colleagues, other teachers she could become friends with.

Friends.

Charlotte raised her head and stared across the bedchamber, not seeing the stiff wooden chair in the corner. *I should like a friend.* Someone she could talk with, share confidences with, laugh with.

But who was to say that she'd find a friend at Mrs. Bolton's Boarding School?

And did she really want to be a junior schoolmistress?

It couldn't possibly be any worse than life at Westcote Hall and quite likely much better—at the very least, she'd be paid for her labor—and yet . . .

She recognized the uneasy, twisting sensation beneath her breastbone: fear.

The Westcotes were her only family. They might treat her little better than a servant, but they gave her a home, gave her safety and security. If she left, there'd be no coming back; her uncle had made that quite clear.

Charlotte frowned at the wooden chair in the corner. What was more important?

Family? Security?

Or independence?

If I leave, will I regret it? Or will I regret it more if I stay? Without foresight, there was no way of knowing—

The wooden chair was no longer empty. A woman sat there.

A scream choked in Charlotte's throat. She jerked backwards on the bed. The hairs on the back of her neck, on her scalp, stood upright.

The woman snapped her fingers. A fire flared alight in the fireplace, flames filling the narrow grate and roaring up the chimney. Four blazing beeswax candles appeared on the mantelpiece.

"That's better." The woman folded her pale hands on her lap. She was dressed in a gown that had been fashionable hundreds of years ago, blood-red velvet trimmed with gold. A high white lace ruff framed her throat and head. Her face was as pale as wax, her eyes as black as obsidian, not reflecting the candlelight, but swallowing it. "Charlotte Christina Albinia Appleby?"

Like to read the rest?
Unmasking Miss Appleby is available now.

$\mathcal{A}$CKNOWLEDGMENTS

A number of people helped to make this book what it is. Foremost among them is my sterling developmental editor, Laura Cifelli Stibich, who made these novellas immeasurably better. (Seriously, she did.)

I also owe many thanks to my hardworking copyeditor, Maria Fairchild, and eagle-eyed proofreader, Martin O'Hearn.

The cover and the series logo are the work of Kim Killion, of The Killion Group, while Jane Smith of JD Smith Design did the formatting. Thank you Kim and Jane!

And last—but definitely not least—my thanks go to my parents, without whose support this book would not have been published.

Emily Larkin grew up in a house full of books. Her mother was a librarian and her father a novelist, so perhaps it's not surprising that she became a writer.

Emily has studied a number of subjects, including geology and geophysics, canine behavior, and ancient Greek. Her varied career includes stints as a field assistant in Antarctica and a waitress on the Isle of Skye, as well as five vintages in New Zealand's wine industry.

She loves to travel and has lived in Sweden, backpacked in Europe and North America, and traveled overland in the Middle East, China, and North Africa.

She enjoys climbing hills, reading, and watching reruns of *Buffy the Vampire Slayer* and *Firefly*.

Emily writes historical romances as Emily Larkin and fantasy novels as Emily Gee. Her websites are www.emilylarkin.com and www.emilygee.com.

Never miss a new Emily Larkin book. Join her Readers' Group at www.emilylarkin.com/newsletter and receive free digital copies of *The Fey Quartet* and *Unmasking Miss Appleby*.

$\mathcal{O}$THER $\mathcal{W}$ORKS

THE BALEFUL GODMOTHER SERIES

Prequel
The Fey Quartet novella collection:
Maythorn's Wish
Hazel's Promise
Ivy's Choice
Larkspur's Quest

Original Series
Unmasking Miss Appleby
Resisting Miss Merryweather
Trusting Miss Trentham
Claiming Mister Kemp
Ruining Miss Wrotham
Discovering Miss Dalrymple

Garland Cousins
Primrose and the Dreadful Duke
Violet and the Bow Street Runner

Pryor Cousins
Octavius and the Perfect Governess

OTHER HISTORICAL ROMANCES

The Earl's Dilemma
My Lady Thief
Lady Isabella's Ogre
Lieutenant Mayhew's Catastrophes

The Midnight Quill Trio
The Countess's Groom
The Spinster's Secret
The Baronet's Bride

FANTASY NOVELS
(Written as Emily Gee)

Thief With No Shadow
The Laurentine Spy

The Cursed Kingdoms Trilogy
The Sentinel Mage
The Fire Prince
The Blood Curse